THE HARVEST CHILD

AND OTHER FANTASIES

BY STEVE RASNIC TEM

ACKNOWLEDGEMENTS

"Ancient Grass" originally appeared in After Hours #7 Summer 1990.

"The Artist and His Mother" originally appeared in Paradox #13, Spring 2009.

"The Brollachan" originally appeared in Nightmares Unhinged: Twenty Tales of Terror ed. Joshua Viola, Hex Publishers, 2015.

"The Carl Paradox" originally appeared in Asimov's Science Fiction Jan. 2014.

"Cornwoman" originally appeared in Dragon Magazine #145) May 1989.

"Daytimer" originally appeared in Horrors! 365 Scary Stories, eds. Stefan R. Dziemianowicz, Robert H. Weinberg, and Martin H. Greenberg, 1998.

"The Doors of Hypertext" originally appeared in Infinite Loop: Stories About the Future by the People Creating It ed. Larry Constantine, 1993.

"Dune Shack" originally appeared in New Frontiers, Volume II ed. Bill Pronzini and Martin H. Greenberg 1990.

"The Dying" originally appeared in Jabberwocky #2, Spring/Summer 1992.

"Dying on the Elephant Road" originally appeared in Beneath Ceaseless Skies #54 Oct. 2010.

"Eddie the Great" originally appeared in The Monkey's Other Paw ed. Luis Ortiz 2014.

"Embrace of Clay, Embrace of Straw" originally appeared in Crypt of Cthulhu #39, 1986.

"Filmmaker" originally appeared in Chrysalis 8 ed. Roy Torgeson 1980.

"Final Apprentice" originally appeared in Betcha Can't Read Just One ed. Alan Dean Foster 1993.

"Garbage" In Delirium 2 ed. John Everson 2006.

"Harvest Child" originally appeared in Elsewhere, Vol. III ed. Terri Windling and Mark Alan Arnold 1984.

"Hideout" originally appeared in Other Worlds 1 ed. Roy Torgeson 1979.

"In All Things Moderation" originally appeared in Fantasy Book #2, Dec. 1981.

"Janael" originally appeared in Pirate Writings #8, 1995.

"Lost Cherokee" originally appeared in Tales from the Great Turtle ed. Piers Anthony and Richard Gilliam, 1994.

"Markers" originally appeared in Cemetery Dance #2, June 1989.

"Morning Talk" originally appeared in Horrors, ed. Charles L. Grant, 1981.

"The Night Market" (with Melanie Tem) originally appeared in Expiration Date ed. Nancy Kilpatrick, 2015.

"The Orchard" originally appeared in Asimov's, v7 #8, August 1983

"Punishment" originally appeared in Night Visions 1, ed. Alan Ryan, 1984.

"Re: Vision" originally appeared in Swashbuckling Editor Stories ed. John Gregory Betancourt, 1993.

"Riverbanks" originally appeared in Grue Magazine #9, 1989.

"Robin in the Mists" originally appeared in The Fantastic Adventures of Robin Hood ed. Martin H. Greenberg, 1991.

"The Sound of Hawkwings Dissolving" originally appeared in Chrysalis 9 ed. Roy Torgeson, 1981.

"Tall Skies" originally appeared in High Fantastic: Colorado's Fantasy and Dark Fantasy ed. Steve Tem, 1995.

Sometimes a moment's mistake tells the whole story. In Abraham's case, it was love for a woman which sent him foolishly leaping in front of a panicked herd of elephants, waving his hands, shouting, trying to divert them from trampling his beloved, who'd already had the good sense to get herself to safety.

Abraham's own good sense, unfortunately, had always arrived late. His last thought, before the herd pounded him into gooey mortar for the stony trail, was simply, oh Lord, what have I done?

His next few thoughts were less focused, hampered by the fact that bits of his brain were widely scattered and confused by a vision of the tattered little man hovering over him with a small jar, one bent twig of a finger dripping ointment.

"Try not to wince overly much, would you?" the fellow admonished. "It makes it difficult to put things back together straight."

Abe recognized him—a ragged beggar who squatted beside the elephant road all day. Not a very successful beggar, since he never asked for anything, simply stared at the merchants and other travelers with large, red-haloed eyes. Never said thank you, either, when anyone threw him a coin. Was he taking advantage of Abe's unfortunate accident by robbing him? Abe tried to squirm away but felt, oddly, as if he had nothing to squirm. He felt his facial muscles shudder.

"No twitching, either, if you don't mind," the beggar said. "Or is having your chin under one ear a look that appeals to you?"

- From "Dying On The Elephant Road"

"Teddy Bear Winter" originally appeared in Magic Realism #4, Fall 1991.

"Ten Things I Know About the Wizard" originally appeared in Fantasy Book v.2, #2, May 1983.

"Time and the Exile" originally appeared in ConAdian Souvenir Book, ed. Shannon Reschke, 1994.

"Umbrellas" originally appeared in Nocturne #1, Autumn 1988.

"Wanderlust" originally appeared in Tales of the Wandering Jew ed. Brian Stableford, 1991.

"War on the Downside" originally appeared in Extro Science Fiction #3 (Ireland) July/August 1982

"Welcome to Rodeomart" originally appeared in Subtle Edens ed. Allen Ashley, 2008.

"The World through the Tree" originally appeared in Mythellany #4, 1984.

"Writing in the Dark" originally appeared in After Hours #11, Summer 1991.

TABLE OF CONTENTS

THE HARVEST CHILD

Two months ago I was doing volunteer work at a refugee camp in Somalia. I've done quite a bit of that—going where lives were so bleak, so devastated, no one but a handful could stand to witness it—since I retired from the army. Lieutenant colonel. World War II, Korea, Viet Nam. I suppose if I'd paid more attention to soldiering and less to sight-seeing disaster areas I'd have done much better than lieutenant colonel. But I stumbled across a harvest child in each of those places. The last one in Somalia.

I had just gotten off the phone with the United Nations people again. Trying to get food, seeds, anything we needed. We were getting practically nothing; the U.N. had really dropped the ball on that one. None of the refugees had received food rations in two days, and we had no idea when the next truck would arrive. The starving were lying in huts made of thornbush branches, animal skins, and rotten pieces of cloth. No blankets, and only two small hand-dug wells to provide water for 76,000 people. We soon discovered that the two wells were contaminated.

The mothers' breasts were no longer giving milk. The children's bellies were swollen, their eyes more vacant than the worst cases of shellshock I witnessed in my military years. So many unable even to cry, the encroaching starvation a slow, silent death.

The Somalis have an age-old tradition of caring for kinspeople; they will take any number of refugees in, despite the devastating cost to themselves. It was frustrating, watching the armies of starving continue to pour into land already virtually depleted of resources. I understood why the Somalis were doing it, perhaps more than most; my own people back in the Midwest would have done much the same. But that made it all the more painful for me.

There wouldn't be a harvest that year; I had thought about that a great deal the past few days. A terrible drought, almost no rain in nearly five years. Overgrazing, indiscriminate cutting of trees, intertribal war, wind and water erosion: it all aided the desert as it slowly took over more and more of the crop and grazing land. I had seen it happen before; the burning dust brought with it an indescribable chill.

I was walking toward a new group of arrivals, mostly old men and women, when she stepped out of the crowd: dark liquid eyes, glistening hair, mouth and cheeks that added up to the look which promised so much: green crops in the ground, flowing streams, corn, barley, wheat. A harvest child. She brought me back to the Kansas of my childhood—1934; I was nine years old. And just for a moment she brought back the dust storms that seemed a mile high, that swallowed the horizon and turned the sun rust-colored at noon, that made you afraid you'd be buried in your sleep. So you woke up every few hours from nightmares of suffocation, bothering your mother too many times with it. But one night when you awakened it had grown still outside, the wind gone off somewhere. Everyone else asleep. That was the night she came.

We'd spent most of the day indoors. In my daddy's house, the house my daddy and grandpa built with their own hands, when grandpa was still alive. Straightening nails and wiring up the rafters with bailing wire. A real roughshod affair; I can still remember the lopsided corners and the way the boards met off-angle in places, as if the wind had thrown them there and by some natural process they'd just grown together. I loved that house, even back then. It showed where my daddy's hands had been. My daddy who couldn't touch me, hold me, any of us really, or say more than an occasional kind word.

You couldn't even see to the edge of the front yard for the blinding dust. One of my uncles was due to come in that day but we really didn't expect him; we'd heard they were having to plow several feet of dust drift off the roads to clear them. We'd had to wear goggles over our eyes and handkerchiefs over our mouths and noses the past few days to walk outside at all. Even then the mucus in your nose dried out so bad it formed a rock-hard crust that burned your skin. When you could smell the dust it smelled burnt. "Hell," my daddy would say, and we all knew he meant that was where we were. It didn't seem much like we were in Kansas anymore.

That day had been especially bad, I remember. The wind howled like some big thing lost out there in the dust. Cornstalks hit the side of the house like bones. I'll never forget the way the corn had died: brown spreading from the tips down a dead vein in the center of each leaf, spreading 'til it bronzed the plant completely, the dry stalks leaning in the direction of the wind. When the winds started picking up the soil they took the corn with it.

The dust seemed more persistent in getting into the house this time. Mama was frantic. Usually you could keep most of it out by stuffing sheets and rags against the door frame and the windowsill. Even then a bit of it would slip in and gradually build up in the air, so that a fine layer covered all the furniture and you were always having to brush it off your clothes. Mama had to keep a cloth over the food. But this night the wind blew the rags out of the cracks and chinks and the dust just poured through. Mama ran around crying, trying to stuff the rags back in. Daddy made us put our handkerchiefs up over our faces, said it wasn't healthy to breathe that air.

Things calmed down some after supper. And Grandma told us another one of her stories before bed. Mama didn't approve of her tales, because Grandma believed things a good Christian woman just did not believe. She'd listen to anybody's tales and repeat half of 'em, Mama always said to my daddy. But Grandma was my daddy's mama, so Mama never could say too much. When Grandma was telling her stories my mama would just sit in her rocker and knit. And frown.

"Won't be a harvest this year, I'm afeared," Grandma was saying. "Guess it'll be a good time for the good Lord to give somebody a harvest child."

"What's a harvest child?" I asked my grandma. I didn't say

too much back then, which is why Grandma looked up at me in surprise.

"Why that's a gift, youngun, usually a girl. She'd be a sister for you boys." My brother Jack made a face and she laughed. "The Lord—or whatever does sech things—". She looked at my mama quickly. Mama just frowned some more and kept rocking. "He gives it to you, to make up for the lost harvest, and just maybe to help bring the harvest back to you someday, all things willing."

"Some gift," my daddy said. "Just givin' you 'nother mouth-to feed."

After we went to bed I thought about that a long time. I'd always wanted a sister, and I knew Jack did, too, although we were both too embarrassed to admit it. There had always seemed something missing in the house, something out of whack. I always figured that somehow a sister would put things right again. Not somebody to take care of, really, but a special friend. Somebody to talk to in a way you couldn't talk to your daddy or your brother or other male kin, even your mother, I guess. I just knew things would be better with a sister around.

When I woke up I stared all around the little house. I couldn't figure what had disturbed me. Everybody else was asleep. And so still—I suddenly realized the wind had stopped blowing. No more whistling or shaking. And the way the windows glowed, all silver. I could tell that the moon had come out from behind the giant dust clouds.

But then there was a tapping, and I nearly jumped out of bed. I listened hard. Maybe it had just been a tumbleweed blowing against the door. But there it was again, and I knew this time it had to be a knock.

I got up out of bed and padded to the front door, trying not to wake up anybody else. I turned the knob and pulled.

Her face and shoulders were dark, shadowed, as if they were covered with the brown dust. But her hair ... golden, like it was glowing on its own, moving on its own like the way the wheat heads seemed to sometimes even when there wasn't any wind. The color was like wheat heads, too, I realized, so gold and full and ripe, just before harvest time.

My grandma was suddenly there beside me, pulling the little girl in. That's what she was, I could see as she passed me so quietly. About eleven years old, same age as Jack.

Soon the whole household was up and surrounding her, wondering who she was and where she'd come from. But she couldn't seem to remember any of that. My mama took to her, and held her, but it was hard to tell if that was helping any. "Poor baby," my mama kept crooning. "Lost out in the storm."

My grandma stood back and looked at her. "Harvest child … " she whispered.

Mama looked up at her sharply and no one else said a word. Then we all gathered around the newcomer again, just looking at her. Daddy scratched his head, it seemed like the whole time.

After a while I caught sight of my grandma standing by the window, looking out. I went over to her. She was rubbing her hands, making them look raw.

"What's the matter, Grandma?" I said.

She looked down at me a little funny. Then she tried to smile, but not doing it too well. "A harvest child means many things, child. Most of 'em good." She gripped my shoulder. "But sometimes that means there's a lot more bad got to come first."

She didn't know her name, so we called her Amanda. That was Daddy's youngest sister who died of the croup when he was just a boy. Mama looked at him funny when he came up with the name; that was an unusual thing for him to do, taking that kind of interest. I guess it surprised us all.

There was a time at first, the first month I guess, when Amanda kept pretty much to herself, staying close to Mama and keeping out of the way of the rest of us. Not that she was afraid; more like she was shy. Except with my grandma. I do think she was a little afraid of my grandma. I'm not sure why, but she was even quieter than usual when Grandma was around, keeping behind Mama's skirts and staring at the old woman like a cautious little animal. Of course, that made things even worse between Mama and Grandma. Mama seemed sure that Grandma meant our new sister harm, although even she didn't know why. I never thought that about Grandma. It seemed to me she was just a little nervous about Amanda, as if she didn't know what was going to happen because of Amanda, and that scared her.

That changed a little. Amanda started bringing Grandma fresh-picked flowers, putting them in a vase by her bed, and making such a smile as I've never seen. Even Grandma, for all her nervousness around the child, had to laugh when she saw that smile. Funny thing was, none of us had seen blooming flowers under that dust for some time. We couldn't figure out where she was finding them.

After a while, though, Amanda started acting just like any other little girl her age, laughing and playing with dolls and chasing the hens and chattering away the whole time about all kinds of nonsense. It was hard to believe she hadn't always been with us. She even had fights with my brother Jack like most sisters and brothers do. Catcalling and crying and both of them running to Mama, who just shooed them out the door again.

I couldn't tell any difference at first between her and any other girl. Except that she was my friend.

First time I knew that was when she took the blame for something I'd done. Daddy used to take the things his boys did pretty seriously, with very little humor. He really expected us to be men. With times so hard he seemed to think that was necessary; there just wasn't enough easy time to indulge a childhood. He expected us to grow up fast. "Only way you boys are gonna survive is to be men jes' quick as you can," is fee way he used to say it, but not looking at us, That's how we knew something was bothering him; he'd always looked at us.

I'd been playing around the root cellar. I knew I wasn't supposed to be there, but I liked it so much down there—it was so dark, and cooler than anywhere else around. You could pretend it was a cave, or an Egyptian tomb. I daydreamed a lot down in that old cellar. It was harder to daydream out in the open air; everything was so flat, it used to seem that your daydreams and fancies had nothing to hold on to. The wind just picked them up and blew them away, left them crumpled on the ground, covered with a fine layer of dust.

I'd found a sack with a few potatoes in it. Dried out a little, but not too bad. The eyes were already long as little garden snakes;

I figured Mama had just forgotten about them. Or maybe that was just wishful thinking. I picked up one and stared at it. And thought I recognized a face. From some storybook or dream, maybe. Without thinking I pulled Grandpa's old pocketknife out of my pants and started carving into the potato, trying to uncover the face that was hiding there. Sharp, crooked nose and high cheekbones and slash of a mouth framed by long mouthlines. After a while the potato looked like some sort of witch or evil goddess, the eyes making long snakes for hair, wriggling in a disgusting way as I put in the finishing touches: cleft chin and wrinkled neck.

I stared at her. I vaguely remembered a woman like her in one of the school books, turning people to stone with just a look. Only with her gritty feel, the way the leftover peel made streaks in her face and hair. I figured she probably turned people into dust. Like the itinerant preacher who passed through occasionally used to say, "Dust unto dust." That was her. She could turn you, your brothers and your sisters, your whole world into dust with just one look. You had to be careful. Had to watch out. Or she'd turn on you.

That night my mama came into the house carrying this sack of potatoes. I wanted to run out; I didn't know what to do. She started to cry, pulling out the ruined potato. Daddy went over and grabbed it out of her hand, then turned and looked at me.

At the time I wasn't sure why everybody looked so upset over one potato. I guessed it was because we had so little left, even one potato meant more hardship. And then realizing they were upset over just one little potato made them even more upset. Because it told them just how bad off we were.

Amanda stepped up to Daddy and said, "I did it." She didn't even have to look at me. She knew. I listened to Daddy whipping her out past the barn that night with a feeling I'd never had before. Like I was almost devastated with guilt, but that there was something happy about the feeling, too. I never knew if she cried when he whipped her; I couldn't hear her and I couldn't ask Daddy. I was too embarrassed to ask her.

The next day Amanda came home from playing out in the dust with her arms full of potatoes. She wouldn't say where she got them, just that she'd found them in the dust. Daddy and Mama didn't know what to believe. They knew it couldn't have happened the way she told it, but they couldn't come up with a better explanation either. No one lived close enough to us for her to have stolen them. So they finally just took them, and Mama cooked them a few at a time, although I think it always bothered her the way we got them.

The next few years things were hard. Us kids knew, although Mama and Daddy would never say we didn't have any money, or that we didn't have enough food. We just didn't talk about it. So I guess in a way we were a little protected from it, and for the most part played and went to school the same as we always had.

Except some of our friends had to go away. We were lucky; we owned the land and house. A lot of the other families were tenant farmers, and the big land companies decided tenant farming didn't pay in a drought and started kicking people off the land they'd farmed for years, that they had kin buried in.

The land companies sent giant earth movers and tractors to knock the old houses down and plow up everything including the front yards. They planted cotton: green and dry. Daddy said it would ruin the land; the big land companies were just trying to get the most out of it before they sold it to somebody else.

So a lot of our friends had to leave, going to California and other places. That next school year there was just a handful of us left.

Amanda did well in school, although she was still pretty quiet. She still brought vegetables and other things home from playing, and one time a new shawl for Mama. Daddy and Mama had given up asking her about it a long time ago. And always bringing Grandma fresh-picked flowers, even when they weren't in season, even when there weren't any flowers to be had anywhere, the dust having killed them all. Amanda still brought them, giving them to Grandma with a smile.

Grandma asked where she got them, sometimes, shaking her head when Amanda said she couldn't remember.

Of course, Daddy didn't care to ask much of anything by that time. That's when he'd first started drinking. Sometimes he even dragged Jack along to a neighbor's place to drink. To have somebody to help carry him home, I guess. No matter what, he insisted on passing out and sleeping in his own bed, not at a saloon or somebody's place miles away. Mama and Grandma kept saying that was bad for Jack, that the boy would get to be just like him, but he didn't seem to listen.

I wasn't growing up to be like Daddy, or Jack, I realized. I used to be like Jack, I know, used to like all the same things: hunting and fishing and scaring the livestock every chance we had. We spent most of our time together. That changed pretty quickly. I started spending a lot of time with Amanda: talking to her, listening to her. Soon I spent all my time with her. Jack stayed with Daddy.

"You gotta be careful," she said to me one day. We'd been about a mile from the house, on a little rise, one of the few places around there that hadn't changed much the past few years; it was still green as ever.

"Careful of what?" I said. She talked ... abstractly, a great deal of the time. Like she was telling a riddle. I didn't like it all the time.

"Of your anger ..." She brushed grass and seeds off her dress.

"Anger? I ain't angry!" I felt anxious. "You know I most never lose my temper!"

"We all have anger," she said in a quiet voice. "Even me. You've seen lots of folk angry around here, haven't you?"

I nodded. There were a lot of bitter people. First they got pushed off their land, then for them to get to California and other places they had to sell most of what they owned. And there were always people around to take advantage, offering them far less than what their belongings were Worth, just because the people were desperate. I saw one man shoot his horse rather than sell it for far less than what it was worth. The two men had just been standing there with the horse in front of the house, arguing, when the poor farmer went into the house, came back with a shotgun, and stopping on the porch took aim and shot his own horse. I'd never seen anybody as mad as that other fellow, standing there looking down at the fine piece of horseflesh he'd intended to buy.

Mirrors and pictures and good pieces of furniture passed

down from grandparents to parents to children, valuable pieces brought over from the old country, cherished items once owned by dead relatives—I saw them stacked up in people's yards and burned, burned in anger because they couldn't bear to sell them for such shamefully low amounts. Kids' toys and mama's best linen, daddy's tools and grandpa's cedar chest. Anger striking the match. Smoldering. That was the scariest thing about it all: they were all so angry, but quiet about it. Lots of them never said a word. Just lit the match and stepped back, staring blank-eyed and pale.

They left their old houses to the wind and stray animals—birds and mice and skinny dogs and cats. Jack used to go out and break windows, tear down boards, wreck anything he could get his hands on. A lot of our school friends did the same. Jack more than anybody else, though. He'd just spend hours tearing up a place. It worried Mama and Grandma. I don't know how Daddy felt.

I felt strange about it. For some reason I thought Amanda understood what Jack was up to.

I did have the anger, deep down, but I knew Amanda was changing that. With her there, there just seemed to be less reason to be angry.

One night a year later Jack came home from town by himself. Pale and angry and trying not to cry. "Daddy's hole up down the saloon! They can't get him to leave!"

We all went down, even Grandma. All the men were standing in the street, quiet. No one said a word. They all stared at the saloon. A few young boys ran around the street bumping into people, but nobody really paid them any attention. I listened carefully. I could hear Daddy inside the saloon, screaming, busting things up. Amanda was sitting on an old log, her hands folded. She seemed to be waiting.

Nobody would go in. When Grandma tried, it took three men to stop her.

Suddenly, we all saw Amanda walking up the sidewalk toward the saloon. Mama began screaming. A couple of the men tried to catch her, but before they could reach the door she had walked in.

It was quiet for just a minute. Then I could hear my daddy yelling again. "Get away from me! Who asked you to come anyway?" Then I could hear things breaking up in there again. What if he hurt her? I'd never forgive him …

Then we heard him scream. "Get away from me, witch!"

And a shot. My mama began moaning to herself.

It seemed like a long time, but then Amanda walked out alone.

No one said anything. Except my grandma. I can still hear her whisper, so low it was almost as if she hadn't intended to say anything and a little breeze just came and picked her thoughts up out of her head and turned them into words. "Harvest child … " Those were the words; I do remember.

No one doubted Daddy'd killed himself. Lots of people said they'd seen it coming for a long time. My grandma never replied, except one time to say, "It was time. Time for the harvest," but she was tired, so nobody paid much attention.

Mama never would talk about it, so I don't know what she thought.

Things changed after that. Jack settled down some, enough that we stopped thinking he'd turn out like Daddy. He started doing better in school. And he fell in love with Amanda.

He had the right, I know; she wasn't really our sister. And I'd never thought about her romantically myself; she was my friend. Although I never saw her encourage him, she didn't seem to want to stop him, either. I couldn't blame him—she'd grown into a beautiful young woman, her hair even more golden than when she'd first come to us.

But I still felt it wasn't right. No good would come of it. And I knew Grandma felt the same way. When she looked at the two of them, it was with sadness.

There's something else, too, I realized at the time, although I couldn't quite think it out. My mind seemed to clamp shut when the idea was only halfway in focus. Jack was better without Daddy. Mama and me were, too. We all were. I still hate to think that, but it's true.

Things were getting better all over the Midwest by that time. It was 1940. The government had started a grass-seeding program back in '35 that was showing good results; a good deal of erosion cover had been replaced. Farmers had started using a three-year rotation of wheat and sorghum and a fallow year. There was increased contour plowing, terracing, and strip-cropping. You could see shelter belts of trees on the horizon now, planted to break the high winds. A lot of politicians were saying that the dust bowl years would never happen again.

And old neighbors were returning from California. They were coming home.

I'd noticed that Amanda had grown restless the last few months before school that year. She was seventeen; it'd be her last. But it wasn't the same kind of hurry-up-to-be-grownup I saw in Jack. It was as if she were waiting, and not too happy about what she was waiting for. And each time a storm came up she seemed anxious, sharp with the rest of the family for the first time I could remember. She'd spend long hours out on that little rise where she'd warned me about anger, just staring off into the distance. She looked sad, as if something were ending. I couldn't sleep most nights thinking about her, the way she was acting, and when I'd get up at night to use the bathroom I'd see her sitting out on the porch, looking toward the moon, watching, waiting.

Grandma seemed to be waiting, too. "Things are lookin' better," she'd say, talking about the way the land was now, and the old neighbors coming back, and all the things the government was doing for us. Then she'd stare off into the distance, just like Amanda, waiting.

Tornado season begins around March in Kansas. The old-timers say you can usually tell a few hours before one hits; the livestock seem restless, people's tempers flare, and the whole countryside seems to hold its breath.

That year the waiting seemed to drag on forever. I thought Jack and I were going to kill each other before school was out, always snapping at each other and quarreling over every little thing. Grandma had to separate us several times when we got into it at home. She was looking more and more worried herself; she and Mama weren't even speaking that spring.

Amanda wasn't paying too much attention to Jack anymore,

or me either for that matter. We'd both try to talk to her, but she usually wouldn't reply, just sit there staring at the dark fingers of cloud reaching down, raking the earth. Fake tornadoes, I used to call them. Those clouds looked a little like tornadoes to a youngster I suppose; they just didn't spin. I used to imagine they did that for protective camouflage, so that airplanes wouldn't fly into them and tear them apart. Self-preservation— back then I figured everything must value that.

Amanda had changed Jack all right. Despite our quarrels, I could tell he really cared about things. He had grown. He was sprouting new things just about all the time. Maybe that's why she didn't pay as much attention to him anymore, or to the rest of us; her work was done.

It was almost time for school to let out that day when the first twister hit. What strikes me the most now that I look back on it is how pretty it had seemed at that first sighting, like a giant gray feather off in the distance, one of those plumes The Three Musketeers might have worn in the book I'd read in school the year before. I said that to Jack and he frowned, poked me, and said it looked just like a big old tree in a heavy rain. One of the girls said it was like spigot water when dust got in the pipe, kind of muddy gray.

We all stood at the windows watching it jump over Thompson's barn and climb over the little rise separating the Thompson place from the school. We watched it coming closer and closer. Some of the kids were getting nervous. The teacher was from back east—our old teacher had stayed out in California with the rest of her family—and I don't think she had ever seen a tornado before. She stood there staring like the rest of us. Some of us recognized the danger, I guess, but we'd been seeing twisters all our lives; they were like old, friendly landmarks. You never really thought about one attacking you. That always happened to other folks.

Then I noticed Amanda.

I have never seen, before or since, such a look. She seemed to be straining upwards on her feet. A tenseness in her back; for a second I was afraid it was going to snap. But the odd thing about it, despite her painful appearance, I was convinced that she was almost thrilled with the approach of the tornado.

"There's another one!" Bobby Collins shouted, and I remember, clearly, the shrill panic in his voice.

Kids scrambled away from the windows and started for the stairs that led to the shelter beneath the school. The teacher shouted, urging them to safety, but they didn't have to be told. I think I may have been the only one who heard her.

"Another one! Three!" Jack yelled, and I thought my brother was going to cry.

Jack and I started down the stairs behind the others. Two of the tornadoes were almost at the school house. Then I remembered Amanda. "Jack!" I shouted, almost sobbing, and twisted back around, away from his hand.

Amanda had opened the door, and was walking slowly outside.

Jack must have turned around right after me, because he was shouldering past, then running toward the open door.

I'm not sure I'll ever know why I did it, if I was afraid Jack was too late and he'd just get himself killed going out there, or if I sensed Amanda was finally going home, her work completed, and we had no right to stop her. Sometimes I wonder, God forbid, if maybe I just wasn't a little scared of Amanda, and the way she had changed things in our lives, all of our lives. I do know it broke my heart, what I did. I leapt after Jack and grabbed him, held him away from the door, held him away from Amanda, then I knocked us both under the large oak table as the twister thundered past.

My brother finally forgave me. I think maybe after a few years he realized what Amanda was, and understood why I'd done what I'd done. He sent me a painting of a young girl harvesting wheat one year, right about the same time Amanda had disappeared. Her hair golden, a distant look in her eyes.

Everybody said she'd been killed, but no one ever found a body.

I searched all over the Somali refugee camp for the beautiful young black girl, that harvest child. But like my Amanda, I never saw her again. I figured there would be other chances, though. Besides, I now knew the bad times would eventually pass for these people, as they had for my own. It made the work a bit easier, the suffering a little more bearable to watch.

My grandma died in that storm. They found her in bed, looking out the window. They figured her old heart couldn't handle all the excitement.

But she was smiling. And there were newly picked flowers in a vase on her bedtable.

I think about Grandma a lot these days, now that I'm getting older, wondering what she saw, if it was anything like what I saw while I was pulling Jack away from the school house door. Out in the swirling dust, a young golden-haired girl lifting up her arms.

And three tornadoes bending down, surprisingly gently, to lift her.

When I'm older, Amanda, just a bit older. Bring me fresh-picked flowers. Come smile at me.

THE ARTIST AND HIS MOTHER

The young artist Pak never knew his father, and yet he knew his father's advice. His mother told him during idle moments—of which there always seemed far too many—when he was most likely to listen.

"Your father used to say that 'History is the dream of Change,'" she told him one day as they were gathering wood for the fire. The nights were cold in the Kaegonal Mountains, which was the winter name for the Kumgang, when it was solemn and old with ice. They never seemed to have enough wood to warm even a hut as small as theirs.

"I thought you said he believed that 'Change was the Nightmare of History,'" Pak replied.

"He said that also."

"Very well," he responded, once again suspecting that his father, and his mother, were both frauds. One thing he had learned over the years, however, was that when his mother repeated some bit of wisdom his father supposedly had imparted, that statement usually reflected her own obsessive concerns, and "change" had always been at the top of her list.

The major change in her own life occurred when she traveled from her small but busy village to this remote realm, the most beautiful in all of Korea. Hers had also been a journey from a pregnant young woman surrounded by neighbors who always knew better to a tired, single mother attempting to care for a young child prone to every sickness real or imagined. It could not have been an easy transformation. But then, "Transformation has never been easy," according to his father, as filtered through his mother's throaty sing-song.

"Even then I knew you would one day be an artist," his mother spoke proudly. "And as your father always said, 'An artist must live in a fluid landscape.'"

Far too fluid, I'm afraid, Pak thought bitterly, for even as he struggled to capture one adequately-rendered view of these mountains on his poor bits of scroll they suddenly changed, lines and textures blurred, hues blending and bleeding into some other color, the quality of light rapidly shifting, until all the world hid behind a new face and the mountains went by some other name. Kumgang became the Pongrae mountains in summer, birds drifting out of the mists and singing their way through clouds of green, then with the autumn the clouds caught fire, and scarlet and yellow rained down everywhere, and the locals called these mountains Pungak, then Kaegonal in winter, until the flowers were in bloom again, their heads exploding into fragrant clouds, and then it was the Diamond mountains as far as one could see, sparkling with color, spring in the Kumgang.

And what did his mother (and his father, obscured somewhere in the years and travels behind her, as if she were the puppet and he the hidden master) have to offer him as solace for his difficulties? *Transformation has never been easy.* For anyone unfortunate enough to be involved, apparently. Was it normal for people filled with so much wisdom to be so unwise?

His mother had always thought him a great artist, even before he took up the brush, even when he argued with her that he was not. Strangely, however, her foolish hope made him exert himself all the more, thinking that if he worked long enough at it he would finally prove her wrong, confirming his own suspicion that he was well-entrenched in mediocrity.

He took the raw inks she gave him and he added his own colors taken from roots and flowers, the small puddles of urine stolen from wandering tigers, the bowel movements collected from domesticated hares, the oils extracted from fruit and animal flesh. He spent long hours mixing and concentrating, matching these hues to the world he saw around him, attempting in fact to go further, to create colors from somewhere beyond this all-too-often disappointing world. But the colors he made from these found ingredients had no predictability, and often changed daily following application: fading, shifting, darkening, transforming.

"Change is good," his mother said, nodding approvingly as colors ran, as colors drifted and died or faded into stale perfume. "'The world is always changing,' is what your father would say."

"You might even say it's the dream of history," Pak replied, sneering.

His mother stared at him. "Sometimes I have no idea what you are talking about," she said.

Pak lost his temper but rather than descend into some disrespectful rant he went off to sleep among the trees, a dangerous thing, what with the tigers prowling about for the one who had stolen from them. But it had become his habit of late—his mother complained incessantly that she never saw him anymore.

It was not that he thought his art was completely without merit, he simply knew that he did not quite comprehend its worth, so how was he to make others understand? His mother was no help—he could not trust her.

And so it was that, despite the dangers involved, during the summer months, when the mountain was known as Pongrae, the artist Pak grew accustomed to sleeping away from the small hut he had shared with his mother all his life. He was now, after all, a young man, and deserving of his own place in the world. Some day he would build his own dwelling, with walls and roof like no other, but for now he knew his mother would feel gravely insulted by such a thing. Bad enough that he slept away and that she hardly saw him, but to replace the dwelling she had worked so hard to build would have been too much. Pak knew his mother well, although he did not understand her. Perhaps she was art. What was it his father used to say? "The best artists make of themselves a masterpiece." What a load of horse dung. The few artists Pak had heard stories about had been miserable failures as human beings, attempting to live in a world of normal people. Perhaps Pak would be unlucky enough to be everything his mother had hoped for.

So until he felt free to construct his own dwelling Pak had to be content with walls made out of pine and ginko, chestnut and the golden rain tree. His roof was the mountain mists, and birds flew through his open windows whenever they chose, with no objection from him.

He continued to paint, attempting to put any doubts as to the endurance of his materials out of his mind. And after a time he came to appreciate the transience and the unpredictability of the images he had labored over for so long. The world was always changing, indeed. A tree trunk carefully rendered would lose its freshness after a day or two, and in less than a week the bark would begin to peel and the leaves to fall. Pak had very little control over such changes, and eventually came to prize his lack of control. What good was an object frozen on paper in any case? It was simply a lie—nothing lasts forever, and nor should it. Pak began to lose interest in the careful and false rendering of objects. He soon realized that what he was really interested in was change, and so he began his quest to capture change itself.

Each day Pak would explore the woods looking for both objects and creatures on their way to being something else: pupae about to become Blue Admiral, or Painted Lady butterflies, rock fracturing into gravel, fawn developing into deer, fallen logs rotting into soil. He was constantly changing the formulae of his paints in an attempt to come up with the mixtures which would develop or deteriorate at a rate reminiscent of his models. Some particular browns might fade over time, but others, depending on the subject matter, should darken. Some animals changed their coloration according to the season—his depiction of them should do the same. Ailing hedgehogs should lose their spines. Old hares should gray, their hides should wither, and their flesh should dissolve.

Pak became convinced that if he could only find the right combinations of pigments and binders such effects as a painted caterpillar transforming unaided into a beautiful butterfly should be possible.

Perhaps his true ambition lay not in painting but in alchemy. At the very least his style had evolved into a mix of ancient apothecary, scholarship, painting, and calligraphy. Whatever his subject matter—whether it be a bird such as the Tiger Shrike or Willow Tit, a chestnut or nutmeg tree, a tiger lily, weasel, or raccoon dog—his task became not simply to render, like some cook or butcher, but to observe and chronicle, to write down and create the passage of time as embodied in these beautiful things.

Pak knew he must be on the right track for his mother had gradually grown speechless as far as his art was concerned. And consequently if his invisible father had any relevant advice it remained unvoiced.

None of these developments in his technique made Pak a great artist, of course. If anything, he suspected they signaled the opposite. Great technique does not guarantee great artistry. And if he were to ever impart his own humble morsels of wisdom to his own son, one might be something on the order of "Great art requires a great subject." The things he painted certainly interested him, and fostered a certain technical excitement, but none inspired within him a focused passion. He had not yet found his true subject. In that regard he felt like the eager young lover without a proper partner.

At the beginning of his third summer prowling the woods for subject matter the artist Pak encountered a silver fox. Perhaps "encountered" is an exaggeration, for at first he saw this fox only at some distance. He could see very few details in its figure at first, and although he had the unaccountable perception that it was a fox, he thought it actually might be a hare, or perhaps some grounded bird struggling to launch itself again, or even a small child, a girl perhaps, mistaking its luxurious tail for her untettered hair.

The next time he saw it, in fact, he was sure this was a young woman. He was at a closer distance, only a few tree-spans away, and the figure was much too large to be any fox he had ever seen, and yet from the way it moved, a swirling dance beneath the chestnut limbs, and its silvery gray and white color, he was sure it was the same creature he had seen before. But still, he could not imagine what she would be doing here. He had seen only the occasional wood cutter or hunter in all the years they had lived in this isolated portion of the mountains, and she appeared to be too young, too delicate, to live here without family.

Pak had only a few paints in his bag—concocted from recently found ingredients, no brushes, and no silk or paper to hold an image. But he found a good vantage point to sit and watch the young woman's dance, mesmerized by the invisible arcs she carved in the air with hand and movement and sweep of hair. Finally unable to sit still and watch without making some sort of representation of what he was seeing, Pak grabbed the bottom of his chogori (which he had always thought too long for mountain maneuvering anyway) and ripped away a large section which he spread on the ground before him. Then he found what stones and twigs he could that might make an interesting stroke, lathered each with pigment and spit, and began to paint, glancing up at the young woman for reference now and then, but soon forgetting the real woman entirely, so preoccupied he became with capturing the unreality of her dance on this ragged bit of his shirt.

Very soon, to his dismay, Pak discovered that his crude implements had led him awry, and what had appeared on his cloth was no woman, nor fox either, as far as he could tell. The body was ill-proportioned for anything human or animal, spine bending through impossible curves, eyes spreading outside the confines of skull, tail spreading and multiplying into a forest of swaying tails.

He looked up in time to see the woman's—or the fox's—figure disappear behind a thick trunk, only the great tail exposed, swishing the air. Its silver color had thinned unexpectedly, taking on a transparent appearance, reminiscent of some clear-fleshed fishes he had once seen, whose internal organs were easily detectable. This gave an unfocussed and blurry aspect to the tail, so that as it moved Pak imagined the fox had three tails, or five, or seven or nine. He had heard of foxes of many tails, but he had never believed this could be true, because what function could there be in multiple tails?

He looked back at his painting, and then picked up its edges, held it against the light. As the colors dried he could see the ghostly but definite imprint of dozens of tails, their outlines pressed into the fibers.

"You are a great artist," came the soft voice behind him.

Pak turned around. A young woman with dazzling silver and brilliant white hair gazed down at him. Her eyes were large and liquid, emphasizing the width of her head, and how it narrowed rapidly to her mouth and chin. She wrinkled her nose, as if not entirely pleased by his smell. Tentatively she leaned down and laid her hand inside his. It felt small, and bony, and he felt alarmed at how sharp her fingernails felt against his skin, particularly as they moved back and forth, up and down nervously, as if writing messages into his palm.

The following summer Pak and his new bride appeared outside the hut of Pak's mother. On their backs were strapped dozens of scrolls containing Pak's art. Some of these scrolls were silk, traded for paintings in some distant towns, and some were on hides taken from the small animals his bride would bring him at the end of a day. Some were also on scrolls of a special paper Pak's bride had taught him how to make. All contained paintings Pak had made of other parts of these mountains— twisted rocks resembling great crowds of people (as the painting changed in differing conditions of light and moisture, heat and cold, the people moved, and plays were performed); tall hillsides drizzled with yellow kenari blossoms, azaleas, purple bells, and China asters; distant coasts where the foothills had walked into the sea and drowned, whose waves crashed and foamed in slow motion as the paints depicting them continued their mysterious, alchemical journeys.

But the most important painting, as far as Pak was concerned, was the one he now held in his hand: a portrait of his mother, her flesh gradually blending into the texture of the silk scroll, features becoming fragile, angular, resembling something he was sure he had seen before but could not quite retrieve from the agitated kettle of his thoughts, her hair fraying and rotting, her eyes dark and hard and small like those of some small, trapped animal.

Pak had not laid eyes on his mother since he met his new

bride. He seriously regretted this, but what could he do about that now? "What genius can find the good in regret?" his father might have asked, if his father had ever said anything at all, which Pak had doubted for some time.

When his mother appeared in the opening of the hut Pak did not recognize her, she had changed so, but when he looked down at his painting he saw that these images were identical. The small animal eyes stared up at him, a barely contained fire suddenly alive in their centers. The mouth in his painting spat, and a faint mist of pinkish color spread across the lower part of the image. Her visage appeared sick, and angry. "My son the great artist, at last you have come back to me," the painting said to him. "But who is this woman?"

Pak hastily threw the painting to the ground and looked hopefully at his mother. Her lips appeared bloody, and a faint spray of blood had discolored her pale and narrow neck.

"She is ... my wife," he stammered. "Your daughter- in-law."

His mother walked slowly around his bride, sniffing. "What is her name?"

"I am. Orphaned," his bride replied. "You may call me what you wish." She appeared cautious, but not offended.

His mother stood close to her, peering up at her mouth. "I am sure. Do you drink tea?"

"Sometimes," his bride said, swaying.

"Then come inside. As Pak's father used to say, 'You never know someone until you drink tea with them!'"

Pak started to object to this foolish and fraudulent quotation, but his mother had already disappeared inside.

The three of them sat quietly on the mat, watching each other, waiting for the tea to cool. Pak found himself preoccupied with the look of the old place. He could not believe he and his mother had been able to live together in a place so small, and he wondered if she had somehow made the hut smaller while he was gone, to a size more suitable for a single resident. The walls were thinner, the colors paler it seemed, as if the hut were like one of his paintings, and so tied to the image of his mother that it failed in pace with her decline.

"Ready, drink!" his mother commanded, picking up her

own tea cup and pulling it to her lips, her eyes hovering above the rim like two suspended flies.

Pak took his own cup and drank greedily. It had been a very long time since he'd tasted his mother's good, sweet tea. He glanced over at his bride, who was proceeding more carefully. She had only gotten so far as lifting the cup before her slender and angular face.

"Drink, daughter-in-law," his mother growled softly. Pak looked over at her, startled, his stomach fluttering as he watched his mother's tongue reach out and lick the rim.

Pak turned to his bride, who at last began to drink, her longish, pale tongue dipping into the tea as if it were a finger testing temperature, then licking, flicking, lapping the warm liquid like a dog.

The sounds of his mother's own loud smacking and lapping and accompanying snarls snapped his attention back to her. She slurped the tea, bronze liquid splashing her face, splashing everywhere as with her bouncing dark eyes she watched his bride drinking her own tea even more loudly, matching his mother disgusting slurp for slurp. Pak felt his own tea lapping back up into his throat, a sour tide he could but barely contain.

"Enough!" his mother finally cried, standing and throwing her cup at her daughter-in-law, whose head ducked the hurtling object easily, pulling into her shoulders and to the side with smooth, animal-like grace. "She is no human girl!" his mother shouted, "but *kumiho*, the nine-tailed fox!"

Pak stood and wrapped his arms around his mother's flailing form, pulling her away from his bride. He tried not to hold her too tightly, because he could feel the fragility of her tiny bones, the crispness of her thin flesh, through the poor garment she wore. He turned to tell his bride to leave the hut until he could better control the situation, but all he saw was the trailing fur, the translucent delicacy of her multiple silver tails, as she escaped his childhood home.

Almost immediately his mother slumped into inactivity, as if sleep, or something more drastic, had overtaken her. Pak turned her around gently and examined her face. Her eyelids floated up off her milky eyes and her lips turned into the weakest of smiles. "Your father would have told you, if he could have," she whispered. "Never marry a fox. They are always trouble."

"Be still, Mother," Pak said, "or I will drop you." And he laid her down gently on the mat.

Pak's mother slept for hours, and while she slept Pak used that time to pick up around the dwelling (although other than a few broken pieces of cup there was very little to pick up—his mother appeared to have rid herself of most of her possessions) and to sweep (although the floor mats were worn so thin he discovered that for the most part he was sweeping ground), and to sort, and examine the paintings he had made since he had left this place.

At first he thought he should chase after his bride and apologize. He could not be sure what he had seen, and he had seen so very little. And wasn't it a husband's duty to stand beside his wife? He knew very little about *kumiho*, but he had heard that they were at least a thousand years old and that they ate human hearts and even stole their souls. Anyone who had seen his beautiful bride would know that she could not possibly be such a creature. Anyone, that is, except his mother, who could not be happy unless she controlled every aspect of his life. Even his grand adventure of painting, his "great" art—that had been what she wanted. It had nothing to do with him! He would never paint again—then she would see who was in control!

But after Pak studied all the paintings he had made since leaving here he found not one depicting his beautiful bride. It was impossible—she had been his great subject! But there were a great many paintings, almost too many to count, of a beautiful silver fox with tails uncountable, fading in and out of the grain of the paper, its eyes watching him, its teeth so sharp.

Pak sat for many days with his paintings spread all around, inside this place of his childhood, as his mother slept on. Sometimes her breathing was loud, and sometimes so shallow it almost wasn't there. And sometimes between her breaths the walls of this hut vanished, and the roof went away, and Pak sat alone with his paintings under the deep black and the shimmering stars.

"Son," she finally whispered. "Have you forgotten me?

Simply forget me and I will go away."

Pak crawled over and leaned over her shadow. All he could see were her milky eyes. "But I do not wish to forget you," he replied.

"Well," she said, and sighed. "If you insist."

"But I have a question or two, if I may."

The eyes, unanchored by a face, blinked. "But I am an old woman," she said. "I have forgotten so many answers."

"Only two questions, no more. That's all I ask."

The eyes blinked again. "If you insist."

"When we were drinking tea, my bride—she lapped her tea like an animal. But so did you."

"That is not a question. Put your thought into its proper form," she admonished.

"Mother, are you a fox?"

"No," she said, and yet her teeth and tongue came floating up out of shadow, decidedly bestial, suspiciously foxlike. "Not at the present time," she continued.

"Mother, please."

"I was a fox for a thousand years, perhaps more, it was so long ago. I was quite content as a fox and had no ambition to become a human being, and yet this is what occurred. Sometimes it happens that way—we cannot always control our destinies, my son. I did not want to be a human woman, but a human woman I became. I made the best of it. I arranged to have a child, and I raised a great artist. Do not *argue* with me! It is not for the artists to call themselves great—that is for other people to decide. Your father might have told you that, if he'd only been able."

"But mother, you were a fox, and yet you cast out my bride for that same condition?"

"Foxes are like people, my son. Everyone is different. I had no desire to be human. But the *kumiho*? It is a ruthless creature. It must eat a human heart to survive. It uses trickery to lure naïve young men such as you. It takes your heart, and then when it is done, it spits it out. Eventually, if it is clever enough, it becomes fully human. It consumes its husband until he is nothing. You are lucky to have escaped intact."

"Not so intact, mother. I may never love again."

The lips pursed, and then made a sad sound, almost a sob. "Then your heart is damaged. I am sorry, child. But still, you have your painting."

"I would ask about my father, now."

"You have had your two questions—that was our bargain."

"You have withheld so much. Do I not have the right?" The lips came together firmly, but after a few moments they softened. "Very well. What of your father?" "Did he really say all those things you've told me? Why did he leave us?"

"He *might* have said them, if he were any kind of father, any kind of man. But he always kept his mouth shut—he was stingy with his words, except when he wanted to berate me for some small error, and then there was no end to his words. He gave me all of his lust and none of his thoughts. And here I had given him this opportunity to father one of Korea's great artists! And on top of that, he slept with other women. He thought that if he did not speak, he could not give himself away. But I still had much of the fox still in me. I could smell these other women on him."

"So what did you do, Mother?"

"So many questions! As I said, I still had much of the fox still in me. So I ate his tongue!"

They continued in this way through the evening, Pak asking the questions he had always wanted answers for, his mother—or what was left of her—speaking as honestly as she was capable.

By morning she was gone, and her image had faded from all his many portraits of her.

Pak's travels took him beyond the mountains, and eventually to every part of Korea. He never thought of himself as a great artist, but he painted many pictures, including one of his mother as a fox in the afterlife, and one of the father he had never seen. He took these portraits with him wherever he went, even though his parents always argued when he put them together in his bag. But he still never regretted having painted his father a tongue. For "a tongue is but a poor flap of skin, but on its back it carries the world," as his father would advise him, again and again and again.

ANCIENT GRASS

Annie had a special relationship with the old people of the neighborhood.

If Annie had written a story about herself, that's the way she would have begun it. But those were her mother's thoughts, not hers. Several times when she'd gone off to visit the Clawsons, or the Smythes, or the Gordons, she'd overheard her mother say to some neighbor woman, "Annie has a special relationship with the old people of the neighborhood." Her mother would say it slowly, like it meant something special, and the neighbor woman—a different one each time—would nod with a serious look on her face. Annie guessed the statement must be true, otherwise her mother wouldn't have said it. Annie didn't think she knew herself very well; she didn't really believe that any kid could know themselves very well. She needed to have her mother tell her who she was and what she was like.

But Annie, all to herself, never thought about "special relationships." She thought a little about "old," but mostly it just confused her. Little by little the old people in the neighborhood were disappearing. Her mother and her mother's friends talked about death and nursing homes, but the old people weren't *their* friends, and the families of the old people lived in cities far away. So those times when Annie went to visit some older friend and the house was empty, or boarded up, her *mother* never could explain to her what had happened.

"Old people die, honey," she'd say. "I'm sorry, but it just happens." But it always happened so quickly, and she'd never seen them sick. Or sometimes Annie's mother would tell her that the family must have come and moved the old couple somewhere else, but not once had Annie ever seen a moving van, or even any family visiting, for that matter.

Most of the old people lived in ancient houses at one end of the street, where it curved into a small rise before dead-ending into the woods that spread out over the hills north of town. No one ever bought the houses of the old people after they'd moved out of them. Annie's mother said that most of them were in real bad shape. After a while the worst ones were torn down, leaving a big blank space between rows of tall trees, a few scattered piles of boards and bricks, weeds that came up over Annie's waist.

"Don't play in those old empty houses," her mother always told her. Annie never did. The old people had told her that much, that they were very dangerous, and Annie always believed what the old people said.

The Gordon house had several of those old empty houses around it, and weedy gaps, and places where the sidewalk was all broken up so that you had to walk in the street.

When Annie came to the screen door she put her face up against it. The screen was cool, and so old it felt soft against her skin. She could see Mrs. Gordon inside putting things into boxes.

Craack! was the sound the screen door made when Annie opened it, like ancient bones breaking.

"Well, Annie. This *is* a pleasant surprise!" Mrs. Gordon said. "You're just in time."

Annie looked around the kitchen. Boxes and crates were stacked everywhere. The cupboard doors were open, the shelves empty. She could see through the kitchen door into the Gordons' living room—all the furniture was gone. The emptiness of the house made Annie's stomach hurt. "You're *leaving?*"

Mrs. Gordon smiled. "I'm afraid it's time."

Mr. Gordon walked in with a tray. The huge cuckoo clock Annie had loved so much, that had hung in the brightly-papered living room, chiming each half-hour with a delicately-carved robin, lay in pieces on the tray. "I finally got it apart," he said to his wife. When he saw Annie he tried to hide the pieces; she could tell. "Oh, Annie. I'm sorry," he said. The robin lay on its side, its wooden eye staring at her. Annie turned and ran. The

loud slap of the screen door stopped the Gordons' calling out
for her, as if they'd been shot.

Annie didn't go home that night. She waited in one of the
weedy gaps near the Gordon house, waited until the sky was
black and the moon a silver coin, until the Gordons came out
with all their things, a box at a time. She followed them as they
walked slowly around the neighborhood, watching carefully
as they stooped down in the shadows, took something out of
the box, and buried it there. Sometimes they put things in trash
cans. Sometimes they hid them inside bushes or weed patches.
Annie began to think of all the old things she and her friends
had found over the years, playing in abandoned lots, burrowing
through weed patches, digging in the dirt. Once she had a funny
feeling, and stopped where Mr. Gordon had been digging—so
carefully as if he'd known she'd be watching. She brushed back
the dirt gently and there was the wooden robin, staring at her,
its throat full of black.

Finally when Annie didn't think she could walk any farther,
when a rose-colored glow had grown over the tops of the distant
hills like fuzz and she just had to lie down, the Gordons led
her back to their old house. They stood in front of it, watching
quietly, as if they were praying with their eyes open.

In the gray light Annie thought the edges of the house
were trembling. Then it seemed to get a little darker around the
house. Then the house began to fold, bending and creasing and
falling down inside itself, like a cardboard dollhouse she once
had, being put away in her closet for the night.

In a few minutes there were just the tall weeds and a pile of
old boards where the Gordon house had been. She thought of
the Gordon house being folded up and put away in some giant
closet somewhere, a closet big enough to hold the whole night,
and it made her smile. The Gordons stepped into the tall weeds
and stood a moment, then placed something at the center of the
old lot, then turned and left. Annie waited until they were a
block away before running over to the vacant lot.

In the thickest part of the weeds she found a tiny little house,
only a few inches square, like a dollhouse but more detailed,
more perfect. It was a modern-looking house, like the ones in

the new development several blocks away. She started to touch it, but the tiny windows suddenly began to glow, as if the house lights had all just been turned on. Annie backed away, and then ran after the Gordons.

They weren't hard to follow. They walked very slowly. Annie followed them through the woods, where they stopped and rested for a time, lying under a large oak tree with their eyes closed. Asleep, they looked like large gray foxes.

They slept for only a few minutes, though, and soon were up and moving out of the trees, into the hills beyond. Annie still followed, although the sun was almost up and she was very tired.

As the sun began its climb above the distant hills they at last turned and looked at her. Water filled where their eyes, mouths, and noses should have been, a quiet pool staring at her out of their bodies. Suddenly the water began pouring out of them, dark water with slivers of silver dancing inside. The old couple sat back on the ground, then lay down together.

By the time the morning had filled with light and heat they had become the ancient grass, stretching and sighing and moving with all the other grasses covering these low hills.

Annie turned and walked toward home, feeling the dark waters stirring inside her, beginning their long, painful voyage to the distant sea.

THE BROLLACHAN

Brenda didn't want Granny Adamina telling Lillie stories about the Brollachan. Lillie was a high-strung child, and too precocious for her own good, and Brenda didn't need one more thing to worry about in her increasingly complicated life. But Adamina didn't listen to anything but her own heart, and that old heart sometimes told her the most troublesome things.

"The Brollachan, he has nae shape," Adamina said in her raspy, Scots whisper, "until he needs one. Oh, except the bairns." She raised a finger like a bent oak twig. "Well, then he might hae webbed feet—who can say fur sure? But more common are the bogles, the wee dark clouds that float along the edges of the forest like smoke. Wee, but evil. If ye look closely enough, ye can see the two bright red eyes floatin inside, like burning coals."

When she was little Brenda would curl up on the rug at the fireplace and listen to the old woman's tales. Granny would laugh at this and call her kitty. "I hae another tale fur ye, Kitty," she'd say, and laugh at her little pun.

So many things her granny said were doubtful, but still had the power to fill Brenda with dread. "Ah, ye best stay close tae the hoose, lassie. Dinnae ye ken that the brollachan has an appetite fur the minds of the human bairn? Ye stay away from strangers—ye never know if they be hiding a brollachan inside! They see ye, and they be taken way that kitty mind of yours, they'll come steal it, leavin ye just an empty shell!"

Home had been a small farm in Virginia on the edge of an old-growth forest. They'd raised chickens, grown apples and berries. Brenda had loved it, as far as it went—it just didn't go far enough. She'd wanted the color and excitement of town, and to spend more time with kids her own age.

Granny Adamina came over from Scotland after Brenda's father died in a trucking accident. She barely remembered him— she'd been six at the time. She did remember Adamina's arrival, however: a large lady full of color and a funny way of talking, so different from her own mother, who would be distant and grim-faced all the rest of her days.

Brenda never really believed Adamina's stories, but her granny told them with such conviction they did give her pause. When she was younger she didn't mind staying close to home, just in case. At least it was beautiful there. And any time she saw a hint of a smoke cloud she would wonder, and search for the eyes inside. But what about the milky early morning fog that threaded its way through the ragged edges of the trees? Might that hide Brollachan too? And the way her mother was after her father died, the emptiness in her eyes—could a Brollachan have done that?

All that changed when they stopped homeschooling her, and sent her to the middle school in town, and little Brenda learned about boys. She was always a little scared of them, and soon learned that very few seemed to have her best interests in mind. And they might break your heart without a second thought. And the way they filled her mind and took it over sometimes, so that she could barely think a sentence without one of them nasty boys sneaking his face inside, could any Brollachan do worse than that?

"You don't have to believe everything Adamina says you know." Brenda could feel Lillie's eyes on her, but couldn't return her gaze. "I mean, you need to respect her, but some of her stories ..."

"She says you got pregnant with me because you didn't listen to her stories."

Brenda looked up, then, scowling. "She said that?"

"Not in those exact words, but yeah, that's what I think she said, pretty much." Lillie said it with a kind of half-smile. Was she enjoying this? Brenda might possibly have been this aggravating when she was a teenager, but if so she didn't remember.

"Adamina said lots of things to me growing up, most of it nonsense. I got pregnant with you because I was young and stupid, and Adamina never said anything that might have made me smarter, believe me. Still, I'm glad I did. I'm glad I have you." *Most of the time,* she thought, and made herself smile for her daughter. But Lillie gave her nothing in return. In fact she turned her back and returned to the sanctity of her bedroom. She didn't quite slam the door, but she'd learned the art of shutting it just hard enough to be infuriating.

Brenda sat on the couch, seething. The perverse power of teenagers was they knew you loved them but they could make you act like you couldn't stand them, which gave them permission to hate you, or at least act like they did. The end result was you were miserable either way. And they *knew* this, despite their pretense of innocence. Sometimes it seemed Lillie ate Brenda's misery for breakfast and long before dinner she was hungry for it again.

Brenda hated going to sleep angry with her child, and of course Lillie knew this, and used this knowledge to get what she wanted. And Brenda wasn't stupid—she recognized the manipulation even as it was happening, and allowed it. It had become one of their family rituals. So she wasn't surprised when an hour later Lillie came to her with that patented apologetic look pasted on her face. Lillie would make a terrible actress—she didn't even try for authenticity.

"Sorry, I guess I'm just in a grouchy mood today." Lillie gave her a quick, perfunctory hug.

"That's okay, Sweetheart. Guess I haven't been the happiest person today either." Which was a complete fabrication—Brenda had been fine before the argument.

"Can I go out with Caitlin and Ann? They want to go to a movie, or something."

"Do I know them?"

"Of course you do—they're my friends."

Brenda felt sure she'd never heard those names before. And Lillie didn't have many friends. "But it's a school night."

"I finished my homework *hours* ago. I almost never go out."

Which was true, worrisomely so. "Well, I suppose. But I

want to meet them. Don't just rush out until I've talked to them."

"Of course. Just don't embarrass me, okay?"

Seconds after Lillie left the room the grating sound of Adamina's voice issued from her bedroom. "Ye let the wean walk aw over ye. Jings! The gob on that wan! Ye cannae ken what goes on inside the lassie's haid. Dinnae be a bampot!"

"Adamina, I'm not raising her to be scared of everything like I was, afraid to go out, afraid to go anywhere by myself."

"But ye did, didnee ye? And leuk whit happened tae ye! Dinnae be sairy efter!"

Caitlin and Ann came up just as Brenda had requested, and Lillie even had them sit down so that Brenda could talk to them. It was an encouraging sign; she was unaccustomed to that sort of sociability from her daughter. And the girls were neatly dressed and very polite. By the time they left for the movie Brenda was feeling encouraged that Lilly had attracted such friends.

But she wasn't encouraged by the looks, or the manners, of the girls. Caitlin had long curly blonde hair which would have been beautiful if she'd just bothered to wash it. And her eyes were so caked with makeup that had been so sloppily applied it was hard to determine what the intention had been. Ann's, makeup was minimal—with her it was the clothing which was the problem. Her jeans were stained and faded, her top too tight and almost shredded around the hem.

Trying to get anything out of them was a futile exercise.

"Have you known my daughter long?" The two girls looked at each other vacuously.

"I guess ..." Ann finally offered. "As long as anybody. Sometimes it seems like, well, I've known her almost forever, you know? At least, I don't know, third grade maybe? Except I don't think we ever talked back then. I mean third-graders, they just never have too much interesting to say, do they?"

Caitlin didn't add much to the conversation beyond some giggles and sighs, except once she offered up, "friends forever! Yay!"

Brenda pulled Lillie aside. "Are those girls intoxicated on something?"

"No—they're, well they're silly, Mom. They're not too bright, and they're always worse when they're nervous. We'll take a taxi to the movie, and then I'll make sure they get home okay. They really shouldn't be out without someone to watch over them."

"So what was he like, my dad?"

"It's embarrassing—I've told you before. I didn't know him very well."

"Still, you must have had an impression. What about him attracted you?"

"He was quiet. I liked that. I guess he didn't feel like he had to talk all the time. He didn't feel like he had to fill every silence. I admired that."

"So he didn't talk much?"

"No, it wasn't like that exactly. He talked, but it was just so nice, the way he talked. It's corny, but it was like the words went right past my ears and straight into my heart. It wasn't like I heard his words, but that I felt them."

"But he left you."

"But he left me with you, so it wasn't like he really ever left at all."

"He burrowed deep inside you then."

Brenda stared at her. "I wouldn't exactly out it that way, but yes, it was something like that. It wasn't as if he were gone, but that he was hiding inside me."

"You know, I'd like it if somebody loved me like that." Before Brenda could answer Lillie left the room.

But I do, honey, I do love you like that, Brenda whispered to the empty room. It was true. Lillie was lodged inside her forever.

"It's Barbara Johnson, Caitlin's mom. We need to talk."

Brenda thought it might be an apology for how Caitlin had appeared that night, some revelation about troubles at home. But what the woman said was, "You need to keep Lillie away from my daughter."

"What? Excuse me?"

"My Caitlin hasn't been the same since she met your daughter. She's tired all the time, she can't focus, and most nights she can't even do her homework—her mind is somewhere else."

"I'm—I'm sorry to hear that. Perhaps it's some illness …"

"Her doctor can't find a thing wrong with her. He says it's something psychological. But she was fine until a few days ago, when she met that girl of yours."

"A few days? But I thought they were good friends?"

"Friends? Caitlin had never even seen Lillie before. They don't go to the same school. She says Lillie just latched on to her and Ann one day at the mall and they couldn't get rid of her after that—she'd just, she'd just latched on!"

"Now wait a minute—" But the woman had hung up.

"How long did you say you've known Ann and Caitlin?"

"I don't know, a while."

"How about just a few days?"

Lillie looked up at her. "Maybe. I don't think the time matters when you're friends. You don't count the hours. You don't count the days."

Brenda had seen the young man before, but she'd never been close enough to approach him. He was usually walking quite fast, as if he were afraid of what might be living in the woods, or perhaps he was returning from some job or other, and had promised to return to his family by a certain time. So surely someone like that was dependable, not wanting to worry the ones who loved him, and so wouldn't be a danger at all, especially if he was scared of the woods. He was just like her then, and not so experienced in the world, that he could still feel some fear when he was out and about. But still a bit braver than she, to be out so regularly, which was an attractive quality.

After seeing him from afar for weeks, she was surprised one late afternoon to have him step into the path beside her. She had no idea where he had come from, but his clothing was rough and dark, so maybe the shadows from the nearby trees had obscured him.

She made a small yelping sound, and he sighed. "Oh, don't say you're afraid of me. No one is ever afraid of me." His voice was soft and shy, so soft in fact she wondered if perhaps he didn't use it much.

"I just didn't see you, was all. I'm certainly not afraid of you." Which wasn't completely true, and she wondered why she was lying, unless it was because she was feeling extremely attracted to him, and she really didn't know anything about males at all, and she didn't want the truth to ruin things, as it so often does.

He tilted his head ever so slightly and smiled at her. It confused her, because all of his face didn't appear to move at the same speed. His eyes and his too-wide smile smeared through the late afternoon dimness, and the sunset gleamed across his gaze. Was this what love-at-first-sight felt like? She had no idea. She was suddenly giddy with fear.

"There's nothing to be afraid of," he murmured, "whatever the old folks say. I promise not to bite."

He may have kissed her then, she wasn't sure. She'd never been kissed before, and had no idea what it was supposed to feel like. She remembered that he whispered something into her lips, and the whisper traveled down her mouth and into her throat, and later when she woke up in the woods the whisper was inside her belly trying to speak to her, but she couldn't understand most of the words.

Adamina had looked at her oddly when she got home, claiming a stomach ache and a desperate need to lie in bed. Could Adamina see it in her face? Brenda had always imagined they could see it in your face afterwards. And when she examined herself in the mirror it seemed her complexion might be slightly darker than it had been before, as if some storm had gotten into her skin, and one eye was slightly bloodshot, and as she would later discover, always would be.

They all said she went wild after that. They couldn't control her in school. But she'd just been trying to shake herself back into normal again, into some semblance of happiness, to no avail.

Then when Lillie came, Adamina and her mother withdrew Brenda from school in shame.

Adamina never let her forget her mistake of course, and tormented her with singing, and teas made from a variety of foul herbs. Brenda was never sure of the purpose of it all— Adamina just said "fur ye betterment, d'ye no ken?" Of course Brenda didn't believe her, but tried it all anyway, desperate for a betterment that never came.

"I ken they be mad wae it."

Adamina had a strange idea of hospitality. "Gonny invite em in? It be the guid thing to do. But watch em canny fur their evilness."

In the weeks that followed Brenda acted as if everything was perfectly normal. She walked back and forth to school every day following the same path she always had, and when it veered close to the woods sometimes she'd close her eyes for a few seconds, or she'd stared at the shadows waiting for them to change shape, but she still went on. In fact she couldn't believe what she was doing. She was terrified she might meet that young man again, and yet it was all she ever wished for.

She didn't see him, but she saw the animals that came down to the path, that nuzzled her and asked for her hand: the dark gray deer with breath the color of wood smoke, the large fat rabbit who straddled the path and stared at her with gleaming red eyes, the owls that soared so close she could see smell the meat on their breath, who exploded into dust seconds after passing over.

"Dae ye mind how ye tried to droun yerself, not aince, not twice, but three times?"

"Why Adamina, I did not!"

"I kent ye widnae recall it, but it happened A trow!"

Brenda didn't argue the point further. Adamina might have been telling the truth—there was so much from that time she didn't remember, or tried not to remember.

Most of all she remembered believing there was a region inside, this space of shadowed boundaries, whose contents she could no longer call her own. A piece of her that wasn't her at all. It had been a terrible feeling, and no doubt she would have done anything to escape it.

All around her the black silhouettes of the broken trees, the red eyes of the animals, the sympathetic yearning from some space deep inside her.

THE CARL PARADOX

The fact that Carl did not recognize himself as the man at his front door was no surprise. In Carl's mind he closely resembled Raymond Massey as the young Abe Lincoln in that 1940 film classic *Abe Lincoln in Illinois*. Whereas a less charitable observer might have insisted he resembled more Mary Todd Lincoln in her oft-repeated fantasy *Robert E. Lee is at the Door Where's My Perfume*?

"Dad, what's *wrong*? You look terrible!" Carl said to himself at the front door.

The older Carl looked down at himself, or at least the self he had been thirty years previously, and replied, "You never were very quick on the uptake, were you Carl? That was always your biggest problem." He barged past his younger, less decisive self and entered his old living room. It was every bit as shabby as he remembered—a sagging gold couch with a stain roughly the shape and taste of Italy, multi-colored patch rug guaranteed to camouflage the worst of a twenty-year-old-something's bodily fluid spills, Kiss poster on the wall—Gene Simmons' tongue a fleshy pennant of Pepto-Bismol pink. It was far, far worse than he remembered. How did he ever get dates? Oh, that's right—he didn't.

He could feel the younger Carl breathing noisily behind him. It would be another five years before he would get that deviated septum fixed. "What's the matter, Dad? Mom kick you out again?"

That sounded about right. In another year she *would* kick the old man out, permanently that/this time, after catching him in bed with a cat, a curling iron, and ten pounds of butter. Carl and his dad had been quite close. He'd once asked for a puppy and his dad brought home a badger in a dog collar.

The older Carl turned around and embraced the younger Carl, pulling him close, eye-to-eye, and nose-to-nose. The younger Carl responded with "Hey, not unless you buy me dinner first!"

"Shhh, you idiot. Remember that time in the eighth grade, when you caught yourself looking at yourself from the mirror, so you spent most of the day locked up in your bathroom with your face against the mirror, peering from different angles, daring yourself to try that again?"

"Whoa!" The younger Carl broke away. "No one knows about that!"

"Remember that book you had to read senior year, H.G. Wells' *The Time Machine*? And how for the next week you had several imaginary romantic interludes involving Annie Oakley and a mule named *Whoa Pardner*?"

"Whoa! I mean—Gosh! How do you know this stuff?"

"It's *me*, or rather, I'm *you*, but in thirty years. *The Time Machine*, remember?"

"I read the comic book version."

"I know, I know you did. But it's the same basic story—guy travels through time."

"You built a time machine? *I* built a time machine? How cool is that!"

"Are you kidding me?" The older Carl wondered if traveling back in time might have shaved a few IQ points off the younger Carl. "*You* couldn't pass ninth grade math. It was your friend, *our* friend Hector. *He* invented a time machine."

"Hector? Mister uber-brow? He still can't keep his shoes tied."

"Doesn't need to. He invented the contour adaptable magnetic clasp around, well, ten years from now. He's become like Einstein, but with marginally better hair."

Older Carl became uncomfortably aware that younger Carl was staring at him. And he was pretty sure why. "But *Dude*," young Carl began. "What *happened* to you?"

"Watch it, kid. Remember when you started using that word? You were calling guys *Dud* for almost a year before someone took pity and corrected you."

"No disrespect, but you...we really let ourselves go."

Older Carl scanned the apartment, and then waved toward the dining room table stacked with beer bottles and pizza remains. "Look at that autopsy interruptus over there. We never learned to cook, not until we married Marianne, and as far as that went, what can I say? For her, lard was a condiment." Young Carl started grinning this loopy, I-just-had-my-frontal-lobe-removed grin. "No, wait—I know what you're thinking..."

"Marianne Higgins? She finally agreed to go out with me? She finally said *yes!*"

"No, no—this is *not* a good thing. She's going to ruin your life. That's why Hector let me come back. We're going to be *famous!* The first man to travel through time! He's a good friend to us, and he hates what she's done to me, to us, to pretty much every guy she ever came into contact with."

"Oh, but you're wrong about her. She's *great*, just this really wonderful person. You must know how much I love her—you know everything else! Are you telling me you've forgotten?"

"Not at all, not at all. You've got the backbone of lemon Jell-O around her. It's downright self-disgusting. I've seen parsley sprigs with more self-respect."

"You've just gotten old—you've forgotten what true love is like!"

"The love she had for us was like a washcloth. Soft and warm and comforting at first, but then after awhile it gets really cold and if you fall asleep with it on your chest you wake up with this frigid, uncomfortable, wrinkled square on your skin that lasts for hours and then you can't find that damn washcloth for weeks until you feel this crusty dry thing against your feet in the middle of the night and it freaks you out until you find this thing jammed into the foot of the bed under the covers all stiff and hard and smelly like a dead fish with your chest hair stuck to it. That's what life married to Marianne was like."

"Old Dude, that's just wrong on so many levels. Your story

doesn't make any sense anyway. I'm not dumb, you know—I watch *Doctor Who*. You *can't* be me! That would be like, a time paradox, right? Meeting and talking to your younger self. One of us should have, like, *exploded*, right? Didn't happen."

"Well ..." Older Carl started rubbing his face, a nervous habit that had begun years—he looked up—younger Carl was also rubbing his face. Older Carl stuffed his hands into his pockets. "I didn't really want to bring this up. And I hope you won't take this the wrong way. But the reason Hector was willing to send me back to today was that after he ran some figures and tested out some scenarios, well, he discovered that the severity of paradoxical consequences varied depending on the individual and that in certain select circumstances the chances of that consequence being of significance to the rest of the populace approached, well, zero."

"Come again?"

"Hector decided we, you/I, weren't important enough to change anything. *Whatever* we do, we're like, insignificant variables."

"Really?"

"I'm afraid so. The only difference, apparently, is the major dressing used on a roast beef club sandwich at a place called *Garalfalo's*."

"That's the sandwich shop down the street. I go there all the time."

Older Carl pondered this. "I remember that place—I just couldn't remember the name. Maybe after my visit you'll go there more often than you normally would have, maybe order different things."

"You mean my life is like, a condiment—my significance as a human being boils down to a selection of condiments. Not the bread, not the meat, not a choice of beverage—just the condiment being used?"

"You were always such a pessimist—that was another one of your big problems. Maybe if you'd been a little more optimistic about things you'd have held out for someone better than Marianne."

"Cut out all that crap about Marianne! I don't care if you're older, or even if you're me, you're cruisin' for a bruisin', Mister!"

Older Carl took a self-defensive stance. "Careful youngster, I know all your best—or at least your *one*—move. Ten years into your future *I'm* taking lessons."

There was a knock at the door. Older Carl stared at it, a creepy feeling rising from his stomach. He watched apprehensively as the younger Carl went to the door and opened it.

Carl Number 3 stood there, well-dressed in suit and tie. The other two Carls stared at him. No one spoke at first.

"He's older, like you," younger Carl finally said.

"The exact same age, I suspect," the older Carl replied, thinking that birthday gifts would be somewhat problematic this year.

"Actually, a few days older, but I've always taken good care of myself." Carl Number 3 entered the room. He held up a small remote control device. "You forgot something," he said.

The older Carl (beginning to think of himself as Carl Number 2 now) frantically searched his pockets. They were empty. "The return device—I'm sure I had it."

"No, you never did—you left it on Hector's work bench. You would have figured that out in a couple of hours. Pretty lame move, Carl."

The young Carl guffawed. "*Dude,* you're so *stupid*. How are you going to get back now?"

"He/I had to wait a little over thirty years, actually, so that we could pick it up off the bench where you," he pointed at the young Carl. "Left it."

"Whoa, Dude. I didn't—"

"You *will,*" Carl Number 3 said. "*He* probably wouldn't have made that mistake, if *you* hadn't been so irresponsible most of your life."

"Wait, just wait a minute," Carl Number 2, the former Older Carl, said. "So *you're* me, in about thirty years?"

"That's right, just a little, well, a *great deal* better dressed."

"But you've hardly aged."

"It's the thing about time travel. You don't start aging again until you reach the age you were when you first traveled back.

We only know that because you forgot the return remote. If you'd/I'd gone back the way we were originally supposed to, we'd never have known this."

"Wait wait wait!" Carl Number 2 cried. "So you and I are the *same version* of Carl? So how can we be here at the same time?"

"Well, unfortunately, it's a factor of our personal insignificance. The universe doesn't seem to care we're both here at the same time."

"Whoa, that sucks, Dudes," the younger Carl said.

"Shut up!" Number 2 and Number 3 said to him simultaneously.

But Carl Number 2 still wasn't satisfied with the explanation. "But why did you come back? I was already here—you didn't *need* to."

"I had to come back to counteract your message." He turned to the younger Carl. "Don't listen to him, Carl. You need to marry Marianne."

"What? After all she did to him, to me, to us?" "I kept my distance, observing," Carl Number 2 replied.

"So we don't get to be buds?" the young Carl interjected.

The other two Carls ignored him. "I could see the young, immature mistakes young Carl was making. Marianne wasn't a bad person; she just needed an older, more mature man. We're together now."

"You bastard!" Carl Number 1 shouted, running toward Carl Number 3. Carl Number 2 stepped between them and struggled to keep the young Carl (forever after to be known as Carl Number 1) from attacking Carl Number 3.

"You had your chance," Carl Number 3 stated smugly.

"Come on guys, shake," Carl Number 2 declared. "After all, we're all Carls here."

Carl Number 1 approached Carl Number 3 shyly. "Sorry," he said. "All Carls together, right?" Suddenly he reached out and yanked the return remote from Carl Number 3's hand. "See ya!" He disappeared.

The remaining two Carls stared at each other, stunned. Carl Number 3 ran out into the hall, ran back in again and shut the door. "No sign. He actually went ahead in our place."

"So what's *that* going to do?" Carl Number 2 asked.

"No idea." Carl Number 3 shook his head. "He could do a ton of damage down the timeline. You *know* how he is."

At that moment there was a crash against the door, and then two struggling forms burst in: the younger, red-faced Carl Number 1, and a much older, white-haired Carl clutching young Carl's arm in one hand and the return remote in the other.

"Let go!" Carl Number 1 screamed. "Give that back—it's *mine!*"

"Then behave yourself," Old Man Carl said, his voice strained and hoarse. "And I'll be holding on to the return remote for now. You're just a kid."

"What about Marianne?" Carl Number 3 said. "Is she okay?"

"Don't talk to me about that witch!" Old Man Carl shook a thin, tortured-looking fist. "Woman ruined my life. She's been cheating on us with Hector the whole time!"

Three Carls burst from the bathroom, shoving each other, all of them covered with shaving cream. Four more Carls walked in from the kitchen, laden with beers and food which they distributed to any Carl who wanted some. Carl Number 1's whining protests were ignored.

A line of Carls appeared at the shattered front door. Carl Number 2 asked them to please wait in the hallway. There were some arguments over seniority, but eventually they all complied.

After a half hour or so things settled into a kind of uneasy silence. Carl Number 1 lay slumped against one wall of the living room, drunk and dejected. The old couch bowed at the middle from all the Carls silently sitting there. There were Carls standing, leaning against walls, and Carls sitting on the floor, examining their fingernails.

Carl Number 2 looked at Carl Number 3 and pointed at young Carl Number 1 lying on the floor. "Reminds me of some of the parties he used to throw. Him, him, and him, sitting on that couch, wondering why no one else came."

When the moment arrived, they all looked up, and at each other, not really understanding what was about to happen, but sensing with some relief that there are limits to insignificance, and that enough insignificance can become surprisingly significant in a very short time.

The apartment building disappeared in a cloud of smoke and debris. Some said the resulting sinkhole went down for miles. Others said its depth was beyond even that.

Within a few hours a late model convertible stopped and parked well behind the police line. A beautiful young woman and her perhaps twin/perhaps older sister got out for a better look. Some later said the young woman was breathtaking, but the older one—well, they just couldn't keep their eyes off her. A few less charitable observers were overheard to say the older one had obviously had a lot of work done.

"What do you think happened?" Marianne asked in a whisper.

"Oh, I don't know," the older and more experienced Marianne replied. "But I'd say there was obviously way too much Carl. Believe me, I'm an expert."

Then they climbed back into the car and left, each holding firmly to one half of a small remote. Hector would be expecting them, and neither intended to be left behind.

EDDIE THE GREAT

The clerk at the dietary supplements store wore a tight yellow T-shirt, "Power Supplied," emblazoned in a large red, lightning-bolt font across the chest. The young fellow had an abundance of muscles, but something seemed odd about their configuration, as if he had been crudely sculpted by a child well-versed in comic books but with very little knowledge of human anatomy.

Eddie examined the huge keg in his hands, also labeled with the store brand. His own muscles trembled under the weight of it. "So this powder, it gives you the nutrients you can't get even with proper eating?"

"It's because of the way the environment has impacted our food supply." The clerk spoke eagerly, and a little too wide-eyed. "Even when you farm organically, the water, the air, even the soil, it's all been poisoned, and for so many generations we don't even recognize it as poison anymore. Don't get me started on what a joke the current EPA standards are."

Eddie had no intention to. "And this will help me build a great body?"

"A great body, a great mind, superior eyesight, and phenomenal emotional health as well. It's all yours—you just have to make a start, and stay with the program."

"How long?"

"With the proper exercise program and the right attitude I don't see why a gentleman of your age couldn't have miraculous results in two years, three tops."

"I'm only forty," Eddie said tersely.

"Oh, a great time to start!" The lad said, smiling, though his face looked scarlet with embarrassment.

Eddie looked the young man in the eye and asked, "What if I said that your two, three years was too long?"

"Well, Mister—"

"Call me Eddie. I want everybody to call me Eddie."

The fellow looked doubtful, and Eddie realized he was probably even younger than he appeared. "Well, it's just that good health takes time. It's like Mr. Boyer, my boss, says, 'it took you all your life to get out of shape—you can't undo that damage overnight.'"

"Very true, very true," Eddie grinned as if his question had been some kind of test. "But I've also heard that your Mr. Boyer has done a great deal of research in the area, and that he might have some special, um, formulations available? Some special product line available to customers with sufficient funds? I just wanted you to know, Mickey …"

The boy's face had reddened. "Sir, my name isn't …"

"… isn't Mickey, I know, I know, no offense. It's just that I am a very busy man, young whatever-your-name-is, and money really is no object. After all, good health is a priceless commodity—as I'm sure your Mr. Boyer would agree."

"Um …" The clerk was clearly out of speech. "I'll ask." Red-faced, he walked away without saying another word.

The smart phone in Eddie's pants pocket was thrumming. If it was so smart, why didn't it know he was busy? He thrust his hand in, caught it, and brought it to his ear. "Yeah?"

"Eddie, your work called. Your boss says you haven't been into the office all day!" He could hear his kids in the background, screaming. They made his teeth hurt, but at least they had good, healthy lungs.

"Emily, I've got it covered. Don't answer any more calls. Turn the damn phone off!"

"I can't do that—Mom might call. Why aren't you at work? We've got *bills*, Eddie!"

He put the cell phone almost entirely into his mouth, barely holding on to it by the edges of one end. "That's *my* job," he said, or tried to say. With the phone in his mouth it came out like a growl. He ended the call.

A much older, much better built man replaced the young clerk at the counter. He simply stared at Eddie, his lips set into a narrow unyielding line splitting the middle of his massive jaw. There were no other customers—no doubt he could have handled the problem Eddie presented any way he wanted to. He watched while Eddie counted a large quantity of cash onto the counter, and then studied Eddie's face for a discomfiting period of time. Finally he went into the backroom, returning with a case of unlabeled blue bottles and a typewritten sheet of instructions.

Eddie had never thought of himself as one of the geniuses, the ones who took instant grasp of any intellectual problem, immediately placing their own individual spin on it, even contributing some creative twist that increased the store of human knowledge. He was both in awe and frankly frightened of such people, and consequently disappointed and relieved not to be among them.

But you didn't have to be a genius in order for people to remember you. The formula for achieving fame was much more complicated, and harder to divine. And certainly the famous were possessed of a kind of divinity. Eddie did not pretend to understand the machinery of that divinity, but he had faith it could be learned, and that anything, including chance, could be manipulated toward that end.

Insisting that everyone call him "Eddie" had some obvious risks, the foremost being that some might not take him seriously. "Eddie" was the name of a kid, or a comedian. Eddie Cochran, Eddie Van Halen, Eddie Murphy, Eddie Munster. But he counted on its non-threatening quality, and its potential as a singular identifier. The world had had its Napoleon, its Einstein, and its Madonna. He intended to deliver its Eddie.

Eddie opened one of the blue bottles and drank it on his way to acting class. It had an underlying citrus tang and a vinegary aftertaste. Nothing you'd want to be addicted to, but he thought he could tolerate it as long as it brought results.

The cell phone in his pocket was buzzing again. Eddie jerked it out, saw that it was Emily, started to throw the phone out of the car, and instead tossed it into the back seat.

In acting class Eddie's Henry V sounded more like Henry Kissinger, but a career in acting was not in his sights. What he wanted was simply to sound more sincere, to have people convinced that he really believed the things he said. It made them pay attention to you when you spoke, even when the actual content of your speech was plainly nonsensical.

He was thirsty after class as he often was—sincerity always seemed to dry out his mouth. He emptied the contents of another blue bottle down his throat but it didn't help any—it just created more gas. In the initial meeting with his new PR consultant he let her do most of the talking. She was a dark, curly-haired woman of some intensity, who seemed a bit off her stride when dealing with him. "It really doesn't matter what you do—business, politics, entertainment—I'll do a great job for you. But it would really, help," she said, looking a little hesitant, "if I knew more about *what* you do."

"I work for an insurance company," he stated, through the beginnings of chest pain.

"Insurance," she repeated doubtfully.

"Yes, but that's not what I need you to publicize. I mean, who would want to publicize *that*," said through gritted teeth. "I need you for what comes *after*, for the things I'm *going* to do." He squeezed his eyes shut on the pain. Was he having a heart attack? Not now, not when he was on his way at last.

"Well, advanced preparation, that *can* help, especially if it's an involved campaign. So, exactly what do you have planned? Say—are you alright?" She put her hand on his arm, which made his skin burn so he brushed it away.

"Fine," he said, the discomfort making him growl. "Sorry, a little gas, that's all." He saw her frown, chose to ignore it. "My plan—is being planned right now, you know? I'll let you know when the plan is ready. But surely there are things you can do in preparation, right? I mean, I imagine the preliminaries are pretty much the same, whatever the job?"

"Well, we can take some photographs—I'll send you to my guy. And we can do some basic design work, typography, letterhead, that sort of thing.

"Great, great," he said, cutting her off and rising to his feet. "I'll call you," and then he left the room, ran down the stairs and out the door, quickly finding a cool brick wall to lean against, take comfort from.

It wasn't until he got into his car and stretched to roll the window down that he realized his chest had expanded somewhat, his arms bigger, tighter inside the thin cotton sleeves. He grinned deliciously, feeling all John Wayne, John the Baptist, John Belushi.

His cell phone hummed from the back seat. It was important to have a family. Successful men had families. But families didn't understand the dreams, or the pressures, of an ambitious man. Sometimes they just weren't worth the trouble.

By the time he stopped at Tomorrow Digital Design he was feeling tremendous, expansive. He approved the new website design, gave the little fellow with the unfortunate glasses the new PR contact information, and gave him the go ahead to move forward with the social media plan, all details to be filled in later, of course. When he himself learned those details. He put his hand on the receptionist's lower back as he was leaving, and she did not stiffen. He rolled the top down on the new convertible for the ride home. Emily did not understand why he needed such an expensive automobile, but someday he would explain the plan to her, and with such powers of communication she would agree completely.

She was fixing dinner when he arrived, their boys in the backyard playing together like little animals—they'd come to the table later scratched and bleeding, but happy, eyes shiny with excitement. Eddie and his brother had been the same way. Insufferable.

He nibbled on her neck. She squirmed away. "Your work called all day," she said, not looking at him. "You never went in at all, did you?"

Eddie sighed, and when Emily wasn't looking stuck two fingers into the steaming pot of mashed potatoes, jammed them into his mouth still steaming. His eyes watered, but he made no sound. "So ..." he said, drawing it out. "What did you tell them?"

"I told them you were too sick to get out of bed, too sick even to get on the phone. What else was I supposed to tell them?"

"It'll be okay." He sucked on his burnt fingers. "I work hard for them—there's no one else in the department with my experience level. They can afford for me to miss a Friday every now and then. I'm not their only employee that does that."

"I know you've got ambition, Eddie. And that you're doing work way below your potential. But we need that paycheck. Your side expenses alone—"

"—are an essential investment," he continued for her. "Not just for me, but for what I can eventually get for all of us."

"We don't need—"

"It's not about need. It's about deserve. I've been working on the plan every weekend; you know that, just figuring out the possibilities. Most people have about twenty years to become something, something other than what they started out as, and most people start out as nothing much at all—somebody's near-invisible kid, somebody's anonymous schoolmate, poor relation, or maybe that casual acquaintance whose name you can never remember. Not much at all. Less than nothing. That's not going to be me, and working in insurance isn't going to get me where I need to be."

"People have different ideas about success." As she began talking he noticed how very birdlike she was, had always been, with her narrow jaw, and pointy lips like a little curved beak, and with her hair swept back like that, she was just this perfect little bird, hardly even a mouthful, you'd barely even taste anything even if you ate her whole. "You can be a successful husband," she said, with that cute little beak. "You can be a successful father. That's what's really important."

He kept his hands deliberately away from her. A bird's bones were hollow, and extremely fragile. "And I don't want to minimize that, not in the least, but people say things like that, forgive me dear, when they just have no faith a man can be more than that. I'll be a great father, I *am* a great father, but I'm going to be lots more than that. I started late—most of the real success stories—the Bill Gateses, the Bill Haleys, Bill Clinton, Bill Bradley, Bill Blake, Bill Maher—they started young and kept working. I have to be exceptional, starting as late as I am. But you'll see, dear," he said, almost sneering, his mouth feeling strange, not quite his own, his teeth, his tongue not quite fitting, "you won't believe your eyes, all the things that you'll see."

He began his Saturday with the contents of two more blue bottles, followed by two hours of vigorous exercise, doubling and tripling his normal number of reps at each routine. Then at the end he could have worked that stationary bike all day, but he didn't have the time. He drank another blue bottle down and headed to his office in the basement, where he'd spent most of every Saturday for years, locked away, planning, figuring, invisible and oblivious to the rest of the world.

Plans and diagrams and dreams. Eddie obsessed over them, making them both occupation and preoccupation. Once he went through his office door (thick, barred, double-locked, the most secure door in the house) he was surrounded by the tools necessary to envision, develop, and achieve them—everything someone like him needed to become someone else. One wall was jammed with books on business, wealth-building, creative expression, how-to's and how-not-to's, and guides for everything from taxidermy to makeup to Astromechanics. On another wall he had created charts outlining the education and career development of Stephen Hawking, Toni Morrison, George Washington, Muammar Muhammad al-Gaddafi, James Baldwin, James Mason, James Thurber, King James, Etta James, and countless others. Another wall held tools both electronic and mechanical, antique and recent, musical and silent, complicated to construct and handmade simple. There was a mirror to practice body language and expression, a video camera for self-observation, an artist's easel and a sculptor's wheel. Down here he had attempted to become a writer, a painter, an inventor, a ventriloquist, a musician, a magician and a mime. Nothing had quite clicked as yet; nothing had set off that complex chain reaction through which a star was born. But lack of complete success did not trouble him—as far as he knew he was training for something no one had even invented or imagined yet.

Every Saturday he locked himself inside this room, not even returning upstairs for meals, having brought a small supply of sandwiches and bottled water down with him. For the rest of the family this became "Dad's Invisible Day," and the children weren't allowed to speak to him, to break his concentration in any way, even if he ventured upstairs seeking additional supplies, food, or the bathroom. Emily had enforced the rule with the children early on, though a bit hesitantly at first, and then as the years passed the practice became part of the fabric of their family life, never questioned and rarely even commented upon.

Today, however, today there was a great deal of agitation during Eddie's time in the basement. There had been agitation before—you could not focus such ambition, such yearning, and such energy into one small space without there being some agitation, anxiety, a nervous display of high emotion. But today it seemed worse than it ever had been, resulting in bouts of aggressive pacing, and due to the cramped quarters a kind of winding occurred, a winding up, a coiling, a building up of incredible energy impatient for release.

As if attempting to quench a fire Eddie had taken to consuming more of the blue-bottled fluid, and although it continued to promise a certain satiation, that state was never quite reached, remaining always just of reach of teeth, tongue, and desire. In fact his teeth and tongue continued to feel ill-fitting, increasingly alien in his mouth, and when he went to the mirror, opening his mouth so impossibly wide that he imagined his entire head must be hinged around it, and that if he wasn't careful the back of his head might collide viciously with his spine, he saw that his teeth had expanded, become both more numerous and twice as wide as they had been, and his tongue as wide and as loose as a pennant down the cavern of his throat. Something also had happened to Eddie's hearing. His ears rang, as if over-stimulated, as if full. It was difficult to pick out an individual sound that annoyed him—the entirety, the soup of sound had become excruciating. But over time the individual threads of annoyance separated out, and he discovered that the sound of his watch's internal electronics was more than he could bear, and took it off, and crushed it under his heel. And then there was that tinny clamor, that munchkin squeal of quarreling monkeys, and god knows where their mother was, who'd promised, who'd *promised*, they wouldn't disturb him.

He was through his office door and up the basement stairs and rushing into the back yard before he'd even realized what he was about to do, his thoughts consumed by a painful white heat. He stretched out his hands—amazed at the reach of them, the length and thickness of his fingers, like sausages, like tree limbs, the incredible breadth of his palms—and knocked his little boys out of their perches on the jungle gym. They tumbled giggling, believing this was all a joke, that Daddy was playing monster again, snapping and growling, but Eddie knew it wasn't play, and that the growls, the inarticulate snaps his jowls and lips were making, were involuntary, and not pretense at all.

"Daddeee!" He stopped, looking down at Liz, his Elizabeth, his youngest, as she cowered on the ground at his feet, consumed by his dark shadow, which appeared so impossibly swollen, so immense and ill-proportioned.

He dropped down slowly, collapsing into himself, sprawling loosely on the ground beside his shuddering child. "Oh, Liz," he said. "Liz, Liz, Lizzie," he repeated, thinking about how small she was, and how appallingly mortal. "You'll live forever, my Lizzie," he lied. "Like all the great legends. Liz Taylor, Elizabeth I, Elizabeth Bishop, Liz, Elizabeth Browning, Liz Lizzie Borden, Liz, look at me now, don't you cry. I mean it."

Eddie left work early Monday morning to get to an appointment downtown at the offices of Unlimited Potential. They never called what they did hypnotism. Instead they used phrases like "subconscious query" and "cognitive therapeutic sleep." Not that he cared, as long as the job got done, and he arrived at who he needed to be. Everyone had the right of renaming, he supposed.

He finished off his last blue bottle downstairs in the parking lot before going in. He tried not to panic. But what if he couldn't get a new supply? And what if he ran out again? It wasn't right that he might be denied his journey for lack of a few bottles of the right lubricant.

"When last we left off you were talking about your goals."

When Eddie had first met the counselor her youth had put him off—she looked barely out of college. But she proved to be a quick study. Besides, the world belonged now to people her age—who better to help him conquer it?

"I didn't use the word goals. That's a defeatist term, in my opinion. If you call them goals you leave open the possibility, by definition, that you might not achieve them. These are *requirements*, have-to's. Failure is not an option."

"But let us just suppose, for argument's sake, that you did not achieve them—what would you do then?"

"No, no argument about it." He grinned broadly at her, but it wasn't sincere. "Can't happen. If you leave that door to self-doubt open, even just a crack, you're done for."

"I see. So why are these requirements so important to you?"

He felt a violent rush of impatience. He couldn't understand why she insisted on droning on like this—why couldn't she get on to the hypnosis, or the therapeutic sleep, or whatever they wanted to call it? That's why he'd been coming here. That last drink from the blue bottle had fatigued him—he could barely hold his eyes open. All that stimulus—eventually you had to pay the price. "Look," he said, grinding his teeth, which were so large now it felt like he had a mouth full of marbles. "*Look.* I'm forty years old now. Next month I'll be forty-one. Do you think they give you much time to make a name for yourself in this world?" He answered for her. "They do not. And some would say, *some*, that I'm already well past my prime. I would do *anything* to become who I'm supposed to be. *Anything.* I'm a *shy* person, I always have been. But not where this is concerned. Where this is concerned I would scream from the rooftops, eat live chickens like one of those geeks in the old sideshows. Do you think that embarrasses me? That does not. At the end of the day you're just as dead, whatever you've done to get there."

"Eddie? Eddie, are you all right?"

"Well, of course I'm all right! I'm still alive—how much righter could I be?"

"Your chest ... your arm."

He looked down at himself. Part of his chest, the portion roughly over his heart, had swollen to three, four times its normal size. The swelling had spread to his left arm, his bicep ballooning, his best sports jacket and the shirt underneath, beginning to split from the pressure. He looked directly at her and grinned his patented Eddie grin. "I've been working out, you know? That's self-actualization in action, baby!"

"Should I call someone?" She looked so uncomfortable, so awkward sitting there in her women's pin-striped business attire. It was to laugh. Maybe she wanted to kiss him, maybe she really wanted to lay one on him—maybe that was why she was so uncomfortable.

"No, no it's okay, sweetheart. Never you mind. You have to understand, most people, they want to be someone else, they would just *love* to be someone else, but the problem is most people are toadies—they're followers. They're too damned scared to go out and *seek* what they want to be. Instead they *hide* inside themselves. They cower. They hide when they should be seeking, get it? Hide and seek, it's humanity's game, and most of us are losing that game, big time." He said that last bit rather calmly, he thought, but at the end of it he reached over and broke the corner off the counselor's heavy oak desk. He hadn't really intended to—he supposed he just didn't know his own strength. He grinned at her charmingly and showed her the piece.

He called Emily and told her he'd be working late. "Eddie, the mortgage check? It bounced! Do you know anything about that?"

"I haven't the time to talk about that now, Emily. I don't know—there must have been insufficient funds."

"But *why* wasn't there enough in there to cover it?"

"I don't know, expenses, I guess. Don't worry about it—it'll be taken care of."

"What have you been spending *our money* on, Eddie?"

"I told you! Expenses! It costs a lot of money to succeed in this world! But it's an *investment*, can't you understand that much? It'll be *okay*. Once my plan rolls out we'll be *drowning* in money—we'll get a much bigger house. *Don't worry*." He hung up.

Eddie drove to a truck rental company a mile or so from

Power Supplied, renting one he thought would probably be big enough for what he had in mind. If not, he'd just make two trips. He pulled up in the alley behind the store and started beating on the steel door in the back wall. He beat as hard as he could for a very long time, and it didn't hurt his hand at all. In fact his hand made a rather satisfying dent in the metal.

Finally the owner, looking fresh and splendid in his bright yellow and red tee, came and opened the door. Eddie pushed his way inside, Mister Muscles unable to stop him.

The oh-so-reluctant proprietor didn't want to sell the stuff to him, but Eddie had a big sack full of money from their now-depleted bank account, and he was very insistent. The fellow even helped young Mickey the clerk load the truck, before leaving with a somewhat disgusted look on his face.

Before Eddie drove off the clerk passed his receipt through the window, his hand trembling. "Good deal," Eddie said. "Who knows, maybe getting to the new me will be a tax-deductible journey?" He tossed his paperwork on the seat beside him and flashed the young man his best, his hungriest, his toothiest Eddie grin.

The clerk stepped back. "Mister," he said. "I really shouldn't say anything, but this supplement, it's really … nothing special. I mean it's healthy enough—it's loaded with vitamins and sea weed extract and protein additives, and all kinds of enzymes."

"Sounds like a *power supplier* sure enough!" Eddie declared, his extreme grin beginning to hurt his face, but he figured no pain no gain in any case so no problem there.

"But there are a lot of products out there with pretty much the same stuff in them, only cheaper. Mister Boyer, he's no crook, but a lot of what you're paying for, it's the blue bottles—he orders them special."

"Well, I do like *bluuuu*," Eddie crooned.

The clerk shook his head. "But it's just a *supplement*, a vitamin, juice, and enzyme cocktail. Boyer, he oversells it, makes it seem all mysterious and forbidden, that's why he keeps it under the counter, or in the back room. But there's nothing magic about it."

"Kid, let me tell you something. Remember how you told me that you needed the right attitude?"

"And exercise—I also said exercise."

"Yeah yeah. But the attitude part? Kid, I've got that in *spades*. And this." He held up his arm, which pulsed visibly, pumping so much blood into his hand the hand had gone purple. The kid stumbled back. And Eddie drove off in a cloud of smoke, enveloped in the happy sound of rattling bottles.

He got back to the house late—the kids were probably already in bed, but the light was still on in his and Emily's bedroom. Emily liked to read at night, and Eddie approved—anything that might improve her—it might help her appreciate his own quest. If she only better understood the sacrifices he'd made for this family, and still continued to make, she might be a bit more supportive.

It took him a while to unload the truck. Good thing that he'd been working out. Even better thing that he'd been drinking all that pretty liquid blue. That kid back at the store was obviously envious, probably worked there all this time thinking his boss would let him in on the secret, and now Eddie comes in, lays down the cash, and takes it all away. He didn't blame the kid, but Eddie had himself to think about. And his family. Besides, Eddie was obviously genetically predisposed to benefit the most from whatever formula had been used in this blue brew. Some people were just born with physical and chemical advantages. Maybe that wasn't fair, but it really couldn't be helped—such was the way of the world. When Eddie fully became, he knew he'd encounter a lot of envy, a lot of sabotage. He was going to have to become extra vigilant.

But Emily wasn't reading. He caught her red-handed, packing a suitcase.

"What's this?"

She twisted her tiny bird head around, startled, pecking at the air the way startled birds will. "Your boss called. They've fired you. He was nice enough, but he said you've missed just too many days."

"Huh!" He put his hands on his hips dramatically. "How about *that*! That bastard!"

"Ed, how *could* you?"

"Hey—" He waved his forefinger at her. He wasn't positive, but he thought that finger was a lot longer than it used to be. "I *told* you—it's *Eddie* now."

"I always trusted you—Eddie. I must have been a *fool!*"

"No, no, we're all fools, little bird, until we decide to do something about our lives. Until we stop being prey, or road kill, and climb into that driver's seat, and become old-fashioned predators again, meat-eaters."

"Ed—Eddie, you need help." She turned her back on him, continuing to pack as if he weren't even there. He gingerly put out his hand, cautious of his new strength, and gently cupped her shoulder with it. And still the little bird shrugged herself away from him, as if his touch meant nothing to her.

"Listen to me!" He spun her around, and although he felt some pain in a distant part of his brain from the shocked look on her face he didn't let it deter him. He sat her down forcefully on the edge of the bed, making her bounce a little, which made him squeeze her arms just a little tighter because he was afraid she might fall off the bed and hurt herself. Her face went pale and she closed her eyes. Now afraid she was going to pass out, he shook her. Her head bounced around to a frightening degree.

"Listen, just listen," he ordered softly, and knelt on the floor in front of her. He was obviously much taller than he used to be, and she was obviously much smaller. She looked dazed, little bird caught in some steel-jawed trap. "I just want this family to be the most it can be."

He relaxed his hands somewhat, and instead tried to hold her still with his eyes, which he understood now to be enormous, luminous, and unforgettable.

"It started with me, but I can help you, too. Then later we can extend the benefits to the kids, make them so superior none of their classmates will be able to even touch them.

"Surely there's someone you've always wanted to be? Emily Blunt, Emily Dickinson, Emily Bronte, maybe Emily Post? We can make that happen. Did you know there are exercises, supplements, advanced techniques now, that can make you someone else? Reach your potential? I can *help* you, and the kids. I really can."

But she was crying. Not loudly. The tears were simply leaking out of her, like ice, sweating. "I don't want to be someone else," she said, her little bird body trembling all over.

"Well, *fine!*" He leapt to his feet. He'd inadvertently dragged her to her feet as well. He let go and she collapsed on the bed like a frail old person. "That's just *great*. Wait right there—we're going to have a family meeting right *now.*"

Eddie locked the bedroom door behind him, pounded down the stairs to the boys' bedroom, scooped them up one under each arm and strode across the hall to Liz's. He shifted one of the boys to his shoulder—he wasn't sure which one—but the kid was half giggling, half asleep. Eddie pulled Liz, who still hadn't stirred, close to his chest, and headed back upstairs.

With his family arranged on the bed in front of him—Liz still asleep, one of the boys rubbing the sleep out of his eyes, the other staring at Eddie wide-eyed while clutching his mom, who still looked out of it, like some sort of crazed deranged person—Eddie began to pace back and forth.

"I've got a plan for this family." He wanted to look serious about it, but unable to keep the grin out of his face, "not just some idle thoughts, but a carefully-thought-out, scientifically reasonable plan. It may be too late for your mother—sometimes as we get older we get too set in our ways—but you kids, you can reap the most benefit out of this plan. I promise you, you just listen to me and follow this plan and someday you'll have everything you ever wanted out of life. One of the boys said, "Toys?"

Eddie threw back his head, dropped open his mouth, and brayed so long and loud it made his head hurt. Then he looked down at the boy, who looked surprised or scared—it was hard to tell which.

"Oh I *promise* you," Eddie declared, "there will be *lots* of toys!" He started pacing again. "Now, most people, *most people,*" he said, looking at Emily, "they live their lives waiting for things to happen. Good or bad it doesn't matter—they have no control over it. They spend their time daydreaming about what they might have been, and then they die, with all those dreams, that potential, wasted.

"Now, I'm not pointing any fingers, kids. After all, most of the human race is like that. And I don't want to see you kids pointing any fingers, either. You have to be respectful. You have to feel sorry for people like that.

"But I want better for my family. I don't want the members of *my* family to die unknown, like they were nothing more than dumb cattle. I want each of you to become famous, celebrities—the people all those other anonymous people spend all their days reading about, envying. Do you know what celebrities are in this world, boys and girls? They're divine. They're gods—people read about them the way some people read the bible."

Emily had been lying on the bed through all this, her face toward the ceiling. Eddie had thought her passed out, sleeping, or maybe even dead. But now she spoke up, still not showing him the respect of looking at him while she was talking, but at least she was talking. "Okay, okay, Eddie. So where's this plan? At least we should find out what we're in for."

He wasn't expecting this. "Well, sure, I guess it's about time. I just have to put it together into some kind of format the rest of you can digest. Print it out, or something."

"Come on, Eddie, quit stalling. We all want to see your glorious plan."

She didn't *really* want to see the plan. She was just trying to get his goat. Well, consider it got. "Come on, then!" he cried, sweeping his arms in melodramatic enthusiasm. "I'll take you down to the office, show you around! I'm not going to need it anymore, anyway. From now on we share, and this entire house will be *our office!*"

The kids cried because he was herding them so hard on the steps and they couldn't keep up. Emily looked wide awake now, alarmingly alert, as if she had been sneaking sips from one of his blue bottles. She'd better not be. If he ever found out she had, he'd be obliged to deal with her harshly.

They piled into his office, and suddenly this cozy space in which he had spent some of the most important time in his life seemed unbearably cramped, with all of them packed in there, as if he couldn't possibly find room for them all in his plan, in his life, and quite possibly at least one of them would have to go.

His skin prickled as he saw his children touching his things, laying their grubby hands on the charts and diagrams and schemes posted on his walls. Elizabeth picked up one of the old dusty books from a pile of them on the floor and he really thought he might scream.

"Neat, Dad," one of them said, although he couldn't remember the name, or recognize the face. In his anxiety he grabbed one of the blue bottles piled haphazardly across his desk, snapped the cap open on his teeth, and chugged it.

"Is it in your 'puter?" Lizzie said, and he made himself smile.

"Yeah ... yeah." He sat down at the keyboard, sweeping stacks of papers and books off his desk onto the floor with a swing of his pulsing, warping, agonizing arm. His fingers were obviously much bigger than they had been the day before, which made typing difficult, but not impossible. After a few attempts he managed to get his user name and password in, and then he saw the folders—Plan 1, Plan 2, Plan for Next Year, Backup Plan, and so forth, and began opening them one at a time, peeking at the individual files randomly, and then with furious thoroughness, as file after file appeared to be blank, or full of gibberish, or consisted of apparently random words and images copied from various internet sites, the only coherence a relatively consistent color palette of reds and purples and patterns stimulating to a primitive and bestial eye.

"Who! Who!" He couldn't quite find the words, even as the sheer volume of the sounds he was making grew louder.

"Ed! Calm down!" Emily had her hands on his shoulders. What did she want? Her fingertips were scalding!

"Eddie! It's Eddie, you bitch! Who's been down here? Who's been in my computer, erasing me? Erasing every bit of me!"

"Ed—Eddie, no one! No one's been in here!"

"Lie to me! You all would lie to me!" He felt himself rising, his head expanding, his shoulders, his muscles, all rising into perfection, into bliss. "I will show you! Show you!" he bellowed, did Eddie, Eddie the shark, Eddie the sixth, Eddie the great, the great Eddie Hyde, as Emily struck him from behind, and struck him again, yet again, and he could almost admire her spirit, almost rejoice in her transformation, as his mind went as brilliant, and white, and blank as his plans.

ROBIN IN THE MISTS

Knowing that his band virtually fed on elaborate tales of adventure, Robin was always eager to enthrall his good stout yeomen with the details of any encounter of action or mystery. Save one. This particular tale, begun one night after his men had drunk themselves into a deep sleep, he locked forever inside, until and including that day when with Little John's aid he would let fly his final shaft.

The greenwood had been a blackwood that night, still and colder than at any time Robin could remember; so cold he wondered if even the prodigious amount of drink could keep the ice out of the bones of his sleeping men as they lay asleep under a giant oak's boughs. Unable to sleep, he crept softly from body to body, laying animal skins over the death-like figures, moving among them like a wolf or a badger. He halted at the end of the circle, below the edge of the great tree's reach, and stared down at the mottled mass of beasts his band had suddenly become, snapping and growling in the cold grip of dreams.

"I feel a dream myself," he said softly to the icy dark. Wondering, Robin looked back across the masses of fur, looking for his own sleeping head, but could not find it in the cold damp mist which now filled the spaces beneath the trees.

Neither could he find in any of this vision the forest he knew so well. No sanctuary here, no familiar wood where the flowers bloomed forever and the birds always sang. No plenitude of bright spirits. No abundance of game. Here the rains were stark and chilling, turning to snow beneath his tired gaze. Here the forest was endless, unknowable, and abundant only with winter.

Though it should have seemed impossible, Robin suddenly knew that this winter had developed harsh beyond all bearing for the outlaws. The ice which now filled the wood had begun to grow razor-sharp in his belly weeks ago. The images of Little John and Friar Tuck suddenly floated up out of the white vapors, laughing and drinking—the flames of their spirits bright in these dark woods. Robin was filled with sadness at this vision, for their images felt too much a memory now, too soon to be lost, too near ghosts of themselves. And yet still they caroused with the others in his misty dream; good fellows all, bellies full of game and throats full of song to ease the too-quick passage of their meals. They had always depended on him for the best game to be foraged from the great wood, but this cold season he had failed them miserably. Their images began to fade, as if finally acknowledging their starvation.

A change in light, as if the misted moon had suddenly grown expansive, made Robin shift his gaze to the nearby hill. A great white hart had appeared upon the crest of this clearing, and Robin could sense the hot, angry blood of it coursing as it pranced back and forth below the huge yellow moon. His long bow was in his hand, and his feet were moving him toward the hart's bold dance.

Be still was the message he sent, not to the hart but to his own blood, which he sensed flowing wild and overly full in his veins, as if ready to break the bounds laid upon it by his flesh. With this fullness of blood came a rising anger and impatience such as he had not experienced since his youth. He prayed such reckless anger would not spoil his shot. In such a harsh season, the hart's meat was life itself for his band.

"You shall die for my taste of you ..." he whispered into the goose feathers as he let fly the bolt toward the deer's great heart.

There was a stillness and a slowing of the world, as always occurred when Robin took aim and released a bolt. He stared into the shadowed gaze of the deer, prayed his arrow on its way, and watched as the mists wrapped the deer until only its head, then only its dark gaze was visible. Snow suddenly filled the mist, and the moonlight turned it into a cloud of stars.

Then the hart was gone, and Robin's fingers stung from the cold.

A male deer can be a swift thing surely, but Robin had never before encountered the likes of this. He knew he could not have missed, for he had felt that self which travels in dreams fly with the arrow and pierce the chest of the deer. But when he ran to the crest of the hill, there was no sign of his deer. He stepped slowly around the clearing, unleashing his eyes and ears to explore the gray edges and black hearts of the surrounding trees and the regions between. But there was no motion of escape as far as his poor senses might detect. He would have gone back to camp, thinking the beast's escape was deserved, if he had not been so worried over the health of his companions.

Robin sensed a change in the forest's light once again, and turned his head to see a trail of white mist rising out of a ground dead with leaves and damp black branches. There, beyond a row of slanted trees, the white hart solidified out of the milky fog, its head turning to return his gaze as if in mockery. The deer's chest rose, and Robin could see his arrow wedged there before it appeared to float back out of the creature's fair hide and burst into flames, becoming a gray line of ash which broke in two then tumbled slowly to the ground.

He should have turned back then, he knew, returned to sleep with his companions where his body even now lay; for surely he was a mere nightmare of himself, and the true Robin lay dozing in his white mist of drink. But he did not, for dreaming or no, his men still lay on cold ground with empty bellies.

Robin had no hope of outrunning this magical creature, certainly, but could hope to outwit it with his near-animal knowledge of the trails. He forced himself through thickets of harsh brush where there were no trails, his eyes open for the mist, his heart full of rage for the deer, his tongue eager for the taste of its blood. Since a youth, Robin had taken what he wanted and given away what he had wanted. Long had the greenwood and all its creatures been his to order and dispose. He had been the stern father and the champion son, the yeoman's god and the Sheriffs devil. His blood ran fast with a forest's worst savagery, and hot with a man's strongest feeling.

Robin followed the deer into another clearing, this one broad and flat and layered with a carpet of black leaves now silvered over with ice. The moon hung fully exposed here, reflecting off the icy leaves so that a resemblance to a wide lake was created. Robin hesitated, watching as the deer leapt through its own halo of brilliant white mist, through layers of shadow, and into the dark air above the silvered leaves. It floated there a moment, its head bold and upright; then it began to fall, its front legs straightening, pushing forward, as it descended to the carpet of reflecting leaves, then through them, passing through the vague barrier of ground, its legs disappearing, its long belly, its broad chest, its proud head. Thus the hart vanished completely, leaving the delicate iced surface unruffled, only a soft smoke settling out of the night above it like sediment in a tankard of ale.

Robin was sorely tempted to follow the hart out onto this mockery of water, a temptation which disturbed him deeply. For standing at the edge of the silvered skim of leaves, he was able to gaze lengthily into its depths, and saw his good dead yeomen killing their enemies, and the friends of their enemies as well, in ways more like butchery than the combat of noble men—severing limbs from torsos and freeing heads from the jealous tethers of their necks—and there was he, too, as a younger, wilder bowman, with his long shafts making sieves of the bodies of those who opposed him.

Robin tore himself away from these unpleasant visions in time to see the deer rising up once more out of this fanciful pond, shaking itself off and spraying the clearing with a disturbance of leaves both shiny and black. He might have lost his quarry then, if the hart had not waited at the far edge of the clearing while Robin made his way around its bank. But once within arrow-shot, the beast leapt and was gone further into the twisted dark trunks of the other side.

As the deer led Robin deeper into these great woods of night, he found himself puzzling over the awkward strangeness of his surroundings. For Robin knew the greenwood better than he knew any man, and yet here were stretches and rises and twisted clearings and odd groupings of timber which were completely unfamiliar to him. The weather here was far harsher than before, despite the increased height and thickness of these tree trunks he would have thought capable of blocking the worst of storms. Flying ice pierced his cloak and leggings, leaving him bleeding. Black damp spread from sodden ground through flesh into bone. Cold winds stripped him of protection and wrapped him in garments of their own ill fashioning.

Yet all this hardship of travel only made the need for a taste of the pale flanks of the hart—glimpsed rarely, but still glimpsed—all the more desperate.

When the hart once again paused some distance away, as if cautious of Robin's losing sight of it completely, Robin returned this gesture with similar caution. He paused as well, standing with bow at the ready. After a moment's stillness, the hart turned and came further in Robin's direction. Robin permitted his bow to drift up before him. As the deer crept into Robin's range, an arrow found its way onto the nock, although Robin had no recollection of putting it there.

The deer stood its ground, waiting. Robin breathed out slowly, and the arrow went with his breath and warmed the cold chest of the hart with its piercing affection.

Robin held his breath, waiting for the hart to vanish. Instead it appeared to grow taller with the agony of the arrow at its center. Its head lengthened, its horn rising into a tall helmet framing startling silver and red eyes. A long white beard poured out of the base of this helmet, wrapping the body and its dark robes and trawling the ground for secrets like a thing alive. A narrow pink mouth glowed for a moment at the center of the helmet, and then appeared to turn upside down as it began to speak.

"You hunt well, fair Robin. But hunters do not always seek what it is they find."

"I hunt meat for my band. I would beg that you forgo the riddles, however. If it were philosophy I need, then I can always find it in some good ale."

"You have come a long way, Robin. As have I, to show you these things."

"This is not your home, noble hart? It seemed a likely spot for someone so … changeable."

"No. This is *your* home."

"Mine? I live in the greenwood, with my loyal men."

"You live *here*, as have you always. In the cold and in the angry dark."

Robin shifted uneasily, stroking the goose fletching across his arrows. "This is madness," he said. "A dream. Too much drink. Too much song. The greenwood was never so dark, so empty of fair game."

"It is your greenwood all of songs and mornings which is the dream. The fantasy of an outcast, a tale told by a hot-headed outlaw."

"What is your tale, then, fair hart? Or shall I say magician? Or wizard? I have heard from the knights of one such as you ..."

"My name is unimportant. It is what I have seen, what I shall see."

"Your tale, then?"

"This morning I came upon the grave of a man recently buried. From the depths of this grave I heard a distant squealing, like that of a pig. Fearing that the poor man had been buried alive—there is so much ignorance hereabouts, I am always aware of such possibilities—I used my staff to uproot the burial. I found the man's corpse, and was curious to find that the dead man had quite devoured his own clothing."

"Curious?"

"Aye, wouldn't you be?"

"Oh, that and more. But curiosity seems an unusually mild response, is what I meant."

"I fear little excites me anymore, fair Robin."

"And yet everything excites me, magician."

"Aye and too much it would seem. First, there were the King's foresters when you were a mere youth. Fifteen of them, I believe. When one welched on a wager concerning a shooting contest, you, I believe the song goes ...

took up his noble good bow,
And all his broad arrows all amain;
And Robin being pleas'd, began for to smile,
As he went over the plain.
And smiling so gaily, you proceeded to shoot all fifteen."

"That is not how I remember it, magician. This story about the buried corpse, what does it mean? I do poorly at riddles."

"And what does your story of the fifteen foresters mean, Robin? Or when your good men Little John and Much the Miller's son cut off the head of the monk's page so he might not witness to the Sheriff? Or when you yourself cut off the head of Guy of Gisborne, planted it on your bow's end, then took up the knife and mutilated his face so that no man born of woman might know whose it was? What does that story of Robin Hood, outlaw among men, mean?"

"There is no justice, magician. You tell too many tales." Saying this, Robin took up the bow again and began to shoot at the figure before him, filling the cold air with his shafts, anxious that this lying magician make no escape.

"Here, Robin," the magician said from the top of a great tree. "Perhaps stones would be more effective. I will wait here until you gather some."

"Keep that promise and I will join you soon." Robin crouched and began searching the ground for the sharpest stones, clawing like a desperate animal in order to pry them from the frozen ground. "While I search, what other lies might you have to tell?"

"Oh, there are many events about the land you may have failed to notice while in your greenwood of eternal summer. There have been several severe winters of late, and a flood or two, the usual sheep and cattle plagues. Many of the smaller towns are in ruins, the land having taken over them once again. Tall grass grows in a surprising number of streets. The markets are closed and the crops do poorly."

Robin stood with a particularly vicious stone held firmly in his palm. He watched the tree for movement, and then tossed the stone into its dark center. "So what do the poor people eat?" he shouted.

"You missed," the voice in the tree replied. "But I congratulate you; you were quite close. The poor have eaten fairly well, actually. I know they would appreciate your concern, and your charity. Currently they consume cats, dogs, dove droppings, and their own children."

"You tell a good story, magician," Robin said as he tossed another stone into the darkness. He was answered by a satisfying thump. A shadow fell from the tree and lay still. Robin strode over cautiously, his hand on the knife hanging from his belt, the knife he had once used on the face of Guy of Gisborne.

He turned the body over. The magician stared up at him with a face half-man and half-deer, his thin lips virtually hidden by a long snout of pale, soft nose. "You throw a good stone, Robin," the narrow mouth whispered.

"But your story of the corpse in its grave and how man had eaten his own shroud. What does it mean? I bested you—now reveal the riddle."

"There is no riddle to it, fair Robin," the voice replied, although the magician's lips were no longer moving. "Look to your own body."

Robin gazed down at his hands where they held the magician's robe. Great boils had suddenly appeared in the flesh about his knuckles. Robin let go of the robe and stepped back. He felt a sudden discomfort beneath his arms and threw off his own cloak, pulling his shirt away from his hot, sticky chest. A large knob of softness had filled his armpit, and he could feel another the size of an egg growing in his groin. Now minute and numerous black spots spread in all directions across his skin, like an infection taken from the magician's dark, night air. He turned back to the still form, but the magician was gone.

"Stop this!" Robin pleaded with the night. "I did only what I must!"

"What you felt you must ..." the night said back. "That much, certainly, is true."

"How do I stop this dream?" he shouted, covering his face with blackened, sore-ridden hands.

"To stop this dream," the fading voice in the night replied, "you merely create another. Dream of an endless summer in the forest, fair Robin, where flowers bloom forever and the birds are always singing. Where ale and beer flow like water in a brook, and outlawed men are always fair, and always just."

CORNWOMAN

Cornwoman crouched behind the skeletal stone outcropping, ignoring behind her the trembling form of Bird, her former childhood companion, and squinted up through the mountain mist. Like most of the Human Beings, neither had been on the mountain before. Cornwoman had thought on it, had thought there might be valuable knowledge to be gotten here, but had still never made the attempt. She imagined she saw Night hiding there, in the space between the tall black pines, partially hidden by the narrow fingers of white—only a mist so thick and white could hide Night. For many of the Human Beings did not believe Night lived on the mountain, traveling down the rocky face narrowly like a snake, then expanding suddenly like a bat as it came into contact with the warm sky above the valley where the village lay, until it had covered the entire visible world with shadow. What appeared to be Night between the pines moved. One edge of it glistened. Behind her Bird gasped, and despite herself Cornwoman felt bile coming into her throat. Raven's head peered out of the mist, and for a moment she thought perhaps he had seen them. His black feathers were greasy with blood, and bits of entrails still clung to his beak and claws. Fully upright he was enormous, taller than three average-sized Human Beings.

Then as suddenly, Raven had disappeared into the mist again.

"Where was the child? I didn't see the child!" Bird whispered behind her, his voice still hoarse with fear.

Cornwoman silenced him by gripping his wrist roughly. She squeezed, restraining herself so that he would not whimper. He was really still a child, she reminded herself. She shouldn't have brought him along, even if he might help negotiating some of the cliffs. Of course, no one else would have gone with her. Only foolish Bird, in his awe and respect for her.

She slipped down to the base of the stones and, thinking of Lizard, let herself flow up the mountain in the stones' narrow shadow. Bird followed with much less skill but well enough that Cornwoman found herself excusing him his recklessness.

The tall trees stirred ahead as Raven—darker than shadow, darker than Night—moved through them. Ravenmocker. Deathkeeper. And somewhere with him, the lovely child, stolen prematurely from her sleep. It was as much her fault as Bird's that Raven had abducted the child. The child's parents had died in a strange way; they had turned on one another in a delirium and practically torn each other apart. The villagers had wanted to kill the child, thinking the family tainted, but Cornwoman had intervened, and of course no one stopped her.

But she had been careless of her responsibility, too pre-occupied with her meditations, her attempts to join with a pure animal past before the Human Beings had gone their separate path, to consider whether Bird was really capable of watching after a child. He'd turned his back briefly, in fact, to talk with some of the young village women. When he turned back the girl was gone, and a dark shadow, darker than anything he had ever seen before—it actually seemed to soak up the light Bird had said—was drifting swiftly across Cornwoman's hut.

She'd felt the cold chill pass, even while in her meditations. She found herself gasping into wakefulness, and then staggered out of the hut already knowing that Raven had taken the child and had a good start.

She'd felt his sharp beak against her cheek, his eye cool upon her. There was no mistaking him.

Cornwoman straightened and began ascending that rocky slope rapidly, the young man trailing behind her. She saw no need for caution now, for surely Raven knew they were following him. It was a measure of his arrogance that he did not lose them, as she knew he was quite capable. Like many of the old Animal People, he was prideful.

The mountain grew colder as they ascended, for not only Night and Raven but many other of the old Animal People lived here, ghosts of themselves—it was late for them. Cornwoman had sensed before that the old Animal People seemed to like the cold over the summers. And the mountain was a cold place. It was as if they linked those summers with an earlier time, when all animals were made large and they were alone in the world, playing or competing for dominion. This was a less active time; few saw them. Most animals now were smaller and lesser creatures than the Human Beings.

A stony ridge appeared to shudder in front of them. Cornwoman stopped and quieted Bird. Her eyes felt hard with seeing this ridge. Then it moved again, the gray stone expanding upwards, the rock ribs breathing out, unmistakable this time.

Cornwoman had started whispering his name when the Uk'ten' raised his gray stone head and began flowing toward them down the mountainside.

"Stone … moving like a stream …" Bird whispered hoarsely.

As Uk'ten' grew closer his features became more distinct, his legs growing feet with clawed toes, heavy-lidded eyes and scales dissolving out of his rocky face and side.

"Quickly! His touch is deadly!" Cornwoman raced diagonally across the path of the Uk'ten', Bird straining to keep up with her as she leapt into a shallow ravine.

Bird leaned against the ravine wall, staring at Cornwoman with an animal fear in his features. It disgusted her to see this, and she turned away.

"Wait!" Bird cried. "You have the magic. Stop this dream!"

"Fool!" she spat. "We grew up together. You know me. I have no magic!"

"But you brought the corn to the Human Beings! You do what others cannot!"

"The knowledge is not magic, nor does it come easy. I worked for it!"

"Stop this dream!" he cried, and Cornwoman saw the beginnings of madness in his eyes. And more than anything, more than Uk'ten' or Raven, madness frightened her.

She looked over the edge of the ravine. The Uk'ten' stood a

few feet away, waiting for them. Its great orange tail lashed the ground, its twelve-horned head beat furiously at the trees. And whatever it touched sizzled, smoked, and burned.

She reached into her pouch and began to pull out black feathers, greases.

"Yes, magic!" Bird cried.

"Disguise," she said calmly. She looked up at him with a sad face. "We grew up together. I would have thought ..." She stopped when he held out his hand. The object was a flimsy knife of bone, crudely and badly made, much too thin to have any strength. "Put your toy *away*," she said, and began placing the things from her pouch out on the ground.

Cornwoman slipped out of the ravine like an early morning shadow rising with the fog. She knew how she must look to Bird, to Uk'ten', and it gave her satisfaction: her black feathers gleamed, her darkly painted body absorbing the light, killing the day. Bird would be amazed; he would never have recognized her. She seemed to walk with a different presence in her footsteps, the lift of her head. Her body appeared to have expanded, the dark makeup having given her the weight of Night, of the death-sleep itself. Of Raven.

The Uk'ten' stirred but slightly, waving his great head ponderously about. Cornwoman stepped dangerously close to his large, dull eyes, her tread heavy, sounding with more weight than her lithe frame could possibly have borne. The feathers fixed about her head made it appear as if swollen with darkness, with secrets imponderably ancient, great curtains of black between the bird songs of Raven.

Bird would almost be able to see the great orange beak of Raven, Cornwoman thought, speckled with blood and entrails. And the eyes, staring at him, staring at the Uk'ten', taking the entire world into that timeless gaze.

Uk'ten' remained still, as if waiting for some sign from her. She was aware of Bird's terror as she strode even closer, her great masked head seeming small against the Uk'ten's gray flank. She tilted the headmask slightly, then seemed to stare at the Uk'ten' from the short distance. Then the Uk'ten' turned and crept up the side of the mountain, slumping to rest in its original place, where it again became as if part of the mountainside.

Bird started to run toward Cornwoman but stopped, her Raven visage frightening him. For she stood like Raven, breathed like him, even turned her head to stare silently at Bird as Raven would have done.

"You will never learn, my friend," she whispered sadly. "It is only magic because you do not understand. It is something which may always be between us, I fear," she said, then began pulling Raven from her body and putting him away in her pouch. She helped Bird to his feet. "Raven does not believe we will succeed in following him. Like many of the old ones he is arrogant, and that will be his downfall."

They made their way up the remaining ridges with relatively little difficulty, their hardships limited to the physical strains imposed by the formidable climb itself. In some places they had to cross deep chasms or wedge their way upward within deep cracks in the monstrous stones. There were many things Bird had to learn in making the climb, but he learned quickly, and Cornwoman felt herself softening again toward her childhood friend.

They passed Night on its journey down the mountain. It was dark, although not as dark as they had imagined, but very cold so near its home, and Bird shivered violently in its wake.

When they reached the top of the mountain they discovered that Night's departure had left a twilight of gray there, as if the soot of a badly burning campfire had filled the air, making their images fade and dim to the eye. They moved cautiously, pale shadows, to the rocks above a small amphitheater of stones. They heard thundering footsteps below, the snap of many enormous beaks, and the flap and clatter of great wings.

The two crept closer to the stones. Bird began to straighten, to look over one of the boulders, but Cornwoman pulled him back down. She pushed him to the side of one of the large stones and they peered around its base.

Great shadows within the amphitheater appeared to circle slowly, occasionally growing long wings which swept the sky above the dancing forms. After a time, Cornwoman could make out traces of an orange beak, a shining eye, and, in the midst of the darkly feathered bulks, the sleeping girl child.

"Are all these Raven?" Bird asked behind her. "There are so many; is this, too, part of his powers?"

"He sometimes has the Crows help him," Cornwoman said. "There are so many of the tribe of Human Beings in the world now, he cannot manage the deaths of all. That, too, will lead to his downfall, I think. His time is swiftly passing." She gestured toward the group of dark figures. "See there; he shows himself."

The great orange beak of Raven had risen out of the dark pool of feathers, followed by his large, dull eye. Bird gasped. Cornwoman started to caution him once again about his carelessness, but had to admit Bird's surprise was understandable. Despite herself, she too had been startled. Raven looked far more frightening than she could remember, even in her dream visions of him. As the dark purple-black feathers of the great Crows spun rapidly beneath him, faster and faster, his giant head seemed to grow larger, soon rising far above the spinning feathers, his dull eye alight with fire.

"He sees us! He must!" Bird exclaimed beside her.

"No ... I do not think so. He is blind to all when he dances his death ecstasy."

"Do we get the child now? Perhaps it is too late ... if he dances?"

"The child is safe for a time, I think," Cornwoman replied. "They are not ready yet to take her. Do not lose your courage now, friend."

Below them the Crows had stopped spinning and were slowly spreading out to either side of Raven. He stalked ponderously now the line of great preening birds, his huge neck bending side to side, beak flashing as he opened and closed it with a sharp clacking sound. Although the Crows were several hands taller than any Human Being, Raven was far taller than they.

"Look, the child.... . How can she still sleep?" Bird pointed toward the small girl sleeping peacefully on several large leaves near the middle of the grouping.

"No ordinary sleep, friend, but the beginning of a sleep without dream. We will need to move quickly."

The footing about the rim of the summit was loose, so they had to move with care. Below them the Crows were agitated, busily making ready their departure for the land of the dead. Fortunately, the clamor of these great old ones obscured any sound the pair might make as they maneuvered to a point closer in.

Cornwoman crept up beside a broad stone pillar and looked around its base. The Crows, and the child, were mere heartbeats away.

Several of the Crows had brought a basket and kicked it beside the sleeping girl with their large claws.

"That is to be the vessel for the little one's last journey," Cornwoman replied.

"We must do something!"

"Hold ..." she said. The Crows picked up the child in their beaks, surprisingly gently, and laid her in the basket. Then they turned and began flapping their wings with a loud crying, lifting themselves up and down and turning black and purple heads from side to side in a kind of dance. "Now!" she whispered, and began racing toward the Crows' basket. She could feel Bird at her heels.

Cornwoman slipped into the basket and just as quickly was handing the girl child out to Bird. "Go!" she shouted.

"But you ..."

"They would notice the loss of weight. Go!"

Bird looked at her solemnly, then thrust his flimsy bone weapon into her hand. "Here! You may need this!" he whispered harshly and, Cornwoman thought, with pride. Satisfied that Bird had turned and was following her orders, Cornwoman closed the lid.

After a few moments, Cornwoman felt the basket begin to move, first tilting up on one side and then the other, until with a wrench it was airborne. She looked beneath her and between the strands of reed could see an endless field of downy black. The Crows were carrying the basket on their overlapping wingtips.

And above her she could see the deeper black of Raven's own feathers, watching.

The basket rocked on its flying support until she was

sickened, and sickened further by the stench of the Crows' wings. She cracked the lid slightly and looked ahead of her. The sky was hazy; they were high above the mountain. Yet the mists here seemed part of their own mountain, a mountain of mists high in the air. The land of the dead. Suddenly a great dull eye drifted past and Cornwoman eased the lid shut. Through the reeds she could see Raven's large form drifting back and forth a small distance from the basket, his great eye staring, beak clacking slowly. *He knows,* she thought to herself.

Suddenly she was tumbling. The lid flew off the basket, and yet she knew instinctively to hold on to the basket itself, keeping herself inside with great difficulty.

She tumbled madly for what seemed hours, as if she were tumbling within one of her dreams, Crow cries surrounding her like a cloud. The Crows apparently did not understand Raven's action, had not as yet seen her, and were instinctively fighting him, keeping him away from the tumbling basket. Sometimes a Crow would slip under the basket to stop her rapid fall, and although they failed in these attempts, her headlong descent was slowed.

Periodically, Raven's enormous dull eye would come and almost fill the opening of the basket, and she would kick out angrily, risking her leg when his beak was open. But the Crows soon had him away again, as she prepared for his next attack.

The mountainside came up swiftly, and it was only a last swing of the Crows, bumping the underside of the basket roughly, which prevented her being smashed into the rocks. But still she had tumbled out and seen the Crows eyeing her, now realizing their mistake. They flew off in a band, leaving Raven descending toward her in slow, easy spirals.

He glided to a spot a small distance away. His great dull eye seemed to swivel in his head independently before it fixed on her. Raven began to walk forward.

Even as she moved to escape, Raven slashed down with his beak, splintering the rock and making the mountain thunder. She tumbled over several fallen tree trunks, allowing their upright branches to give her some small protection from his wings, now flapping, their hard edges swinging dangerously close. The branches snapped one after the other under the weight of his wings, and Corn-woman was quickly forced to run again, starting back up the mountain slope.

Raven lifted a small distance into the air and flapped slowly, inexorably after her.

She dashed between two boulders as he swung low above her, his gigantic claws catching her hair. She ripped away from him and squeezed between the walls of rock, only vaguely aware of the painful and bloody rending of hair from scalp.

Then Cornwoman turned and faced Raven. An image from her dreams came back to her: facing the dark, slashing out at it with a gleaming weapon of purest white. The confrontation was inevitable then. There seemed no point in running in any case. The child was safe, and she found it distasteful to be ripped apart from behind.

She turned with a stick and jabbed it upwards between the two boulders. It caught Raven in the soft padding near one claw and he screeched, tilting his outstretched wings crazily.

He tumbled forward on the slope and lay still. Cornwoman ran from between the rocks, howling, the stick clutched in both hands raised above her head.

Foolish girl! she thought, even as Raven turned and snapped his beak around the stick, crunching it into several pieces. In her impatience—and fear, she admitted—she'd acted like some young hunter.

Raven's wings pushed back against the earth violently, quickly righting him. He screeched, and the closeness of his garbage-filled mouth sickened her. But she ran, her legs aching with the effort.

She was upon the narrow crevice before she saw it; it had already thrown her off balance. Cursing in an effort to wrest some advantage from the blunder, she twisted her body and fell almost backward into the crack. She immediately pushed herself as deeply as possible into the crack, scraping shoulders and thighs painfully in the process. Raven's open beak suddenly filled the opening, his comparatively small tongue twirling into a blur as he screeched a high-pitched victory call. Cornwoman shuddered.

The beak, the dull eye, a massive claw inserted into the crack; Raven tried viciously to get at his victim. Cornwoman was scratched but remained safe within.

She felt foolish. She had behaved with no more expertise than her foolish friend Bird.

Cornwoman found herself reaching for his silly, thin bone knife. Gleaming white. Raven's cold, dull eye was above the crack.

She thrust upward with the bone into the soft eye. Cornwoman had to push Raven's body away from the crack to extricate herself. The body was heavy, and she struggled with it for some time. When she looked down at the old one's bloated form, the white bone knife still jutting from his ruined eye, she thought he seemed much smaller than before.

Bird's silly little knife, she thought. But sharp enough to destroy Raven.

"Arrogant One ..." she whispered. "See where it has gotten you? Soon there will be no more of your kind to bother the weak Human Beings. You will be small, and they will hunt you. ..."

It was a long trek back to her village, and Cornwoman thought she should begin it soon. But there was much to be learned from Raven's feathers, Raven's eye, and the juices from Raven's body.

She pulled the bone knife out of his eye and began dismembering this dream.

DUNE SHACK

IN GOD'S MAD WINDS

It was 1885, the year after the death of his wife and daughter, that Neal McCutcheon put all the remaining money from his years as a buffalo hunter into a wagon and team of horses and moved out of Denver all the way south to the Sangre de Cristo Mountains and the San Luis Valley. He had been told that here the wind blew all the time, and now well into his fortieth year of living, that was exactly what he wanted.

A MAN CAN LOSE HIS LIFE

Neal McCutcheon arrived in the valley in early winter, and he knew most people would think he was crazy for having undertaken such a journey at that time of year. And he couldn't really argue with that; in fact, he figured craziness had a great deal to do with it. He'd spent most of that year since his family died drinking his way through the Denver saloons, sleeping out on the sun-holding stones of Larimer Street, and talking himself into frenzy with whatever old-timer he could find. He'd never figured himself for a towny before, but after the smallpox took Elizabeth and Sarah—but not before it left them scarred and pocked as bad as any red sandstone cliff he'd ever seen—striking it rich with a mine up in Fairplay seemed damned pointless, and he had no place else to go.

The San Luis Valley stretched fifty miles between the two great mountain ranges of the Sangre de Cristos and the San Juans, the sky above it so big and empty that Neal felt skittish about trying to cross underneath it. It was as if God had left out something. And once God started forgetting things, anything could happen—Neal could get halfway across and the wagon, team, everything, might just lose track of the ground, go floating up to where there was nothing but the almighty wind blowing, and he and everything he owned be scattered from China to the moon and back. Just the thought made him drunk. He drove the team down into the valley, reeling on his seat.

Snow hadn't had much luck sticking here. As far as he could see, the ground was banded in white, browns, and gray-greens. Under the wheels of the wagon, the frozen ground cracked and snapped like glass. Now and then the wind picked up, stinging him with tiny pieces of the mountains blown against his face and hands from distances farther than he could imagine. He pushed his collar up as far as it would go. Brownie, up front, kept snorting the frozen dust back out of steaming nostrils. He tried to keep her turned so her head wasn't so straight-on into the wind. Briefly he considered giving her the robe covering his shoulders, the last he had from all those years in the trade, but then that really would be crazy. As it was, the skin was falling apart into clumps and streamers.

He'd figured on setting up a place on one of the lower ridges. Maybe raise a little cattle, some horses, shoot whatever bighorn he could find. Civilization. He used to love civilization, in small doses.

He remembered afternoons in Abilene just back from a hunt, skinned buffalo meat delivered to the railroad in piles twenty feet high, getting paid, and then forgetting all about the damn buffalo until the next hunting trip. First he'd get a good scrubbing (though the smell never seemed to completely go away—he smelled buffalo death even in his sleep), then to the barber's, and then to the dry-goods for a new suit that wouldn't last him longer than the weekend, if he spent his time right. He never looked for fights, though they usually came his way. He was looking for fun, and back then he wasn't used to the drinking.

He'd eat oysters and ice cream first, and between drinks he might shake the wooden sidewalks walking up and down the street, nodding his head and looking at the ladies. That was back before the wife and daughter. After they came, he just spent most of his time drinking, trying to wash the buffalo death down, swallow it just for once, so maybe he wouldn't have to see it or smell it all the time. But he never did manage to get quite that drunk. He had to save some money out at the end because the family had to eat, and no matter how bad he got, at least he was always able to remember that one thing. He was a sorry excuse for a husband throughout their marriage, but at least he never let them starve.

So instead, just a few years later he takes them up to some godforsaken mining camp and lets the smallpox eat them till there's nothing left. Like the coyotes and buzzards gnawing away at the buffalo carcasses after he'd taken what he wanted. Lord knows he took plenty from Elizabeth, Sarah too. And they loved him too much, or maybe they were just too stupid, to stop him. Some of God's creatures were just too stupid to live. They let the smart ones devour them. And Neal McCutcheon, God help him, had always been a smart one.

Back then they could use the buffalo for anything: their hide for robes, their horns for spoons, their bones for fertilizer, and their hooves for glue. If the Good Lord hadn't wanted them killed, he shouldn't have made them so damn useful. Hear that, Elizabeth? Why'd you have to be so damn useful? Why'd you have to be so damn willing?

A cloud of dust blew up and covered the wagon. Neal bent his head, could feel the wagon turn slightly, the horses drifting to one side, whinnying their fear. Then he could hear the thunder, then feel it in his seat, in his skull, as if thousands of hooves had pounded by the wagon and pushed it aside. But he couldn't look up into the blowing grit, could only pull his head as far back into the collar and the tattered robe as it would go, and clutch the reins.

As the wind began to die down, debris falling into the back of his collar, he glanced up just enough to see the multitude of brown backs disappearing into the sandstorm.

"God save and protect us!" he shouted, and Brownie started to rear. "Did you see?" he asked the panicked horse, but there was no reply. And no herd. He strained his ears; there was no trace of the great thunder sound.

The sand slowly fell around him. Like a light Denver snow, he thought. And no cleaner. The wind gusted suddenly, and blew away what remained like smoke.

Off in the distance, a light-colored spread of humps and peaks pushed up against the mountains; Neal thought of ten thousand buffalo corpses stitched into one great mound. Large enough to cover a small city. Gold and cream and tan and gray, with streaks of white snow, piled up against the silver-gray Sangre De Cristos. He'd heard stories about these mounds, but he'd always thought of them as just some drunken old-timer's tale. Great sand dunes, like in the stories of Egypt his mother had read to him as a child.

AS THE SANDS OF MEMORY ACCUMULATE LIKE BONE

Along one side of the dunes was a stand of ponderosa pines, passed over so many times by the dunes and wind they'd been sandblasted into branchless, ragged, ghost trees, black and gray upright silhouettes against the darkening blue sky. Neal found solid ground a few yards away and tied his team there. The trees came down easily. In two days' time he had a fairly tight shack built on this edge of the dunes. Sand made its way through the cracks to the inside—no way to stop that completely—but it didn't seem enough to be bothersome.

Those first few nights he dreamed of blowing sand, revealing and concealing, cutting and lulling to sleep. During the mornings he watched the wind push the sand into long, perfect waves, peaking here and there, making circles, piling up and leveling off. The sand traced the shape of the wind. And the wind was full with memory.

One morning the sand brought back the memory of Neal's first trip out on the hunts. He hadn't been a hunter then. A fellow by the name of Jamison had hired him on to help skin the "King Beast" and pile the meat on the wagon for the railroad. When he first got out there, he'd thought the hills were moving, that some kind of earthquake was shifting all the land from horizon to horizon. Great brown waves piled one against the other like some great muddy sea, or like the swells of a stained desert caught in the turmoil of the greatest wind that ever was. Then he'd seen the great dumb heads. And dumb they were. Jamison picked them off one at a time; the rest of the herd didn't even budge. It was as if they wanted to be shot. Just stood there. Just like it was Jamison's job to shoot them and Neal's job to skin them, it was their job to get shot and skinned with as little complaint as possible. They went down quick, one at a time, like giants falling in some fairy tale. Hell, they were huge! Ten and twelve foot long, a tall man coming up to their shoulders. But such hideous ignorance! Their death seemed preordained, as well as Neal's part in it. And there was nothing he could have done to change it.

Month by month great masses of them vanished, leaving nothing but fairy rings and wallows and wasted parts of them for the buzzards.

By the time Neal decided that he was going to be the big brave hunter and got his own Sharp's "Big Fifty" rifle, most of the buffalo trade was in hides. Then he could pay his own skinners to turn the corpses over, slit them neck to tail and peel off their kingly hides. The meat was usually left on the ground to rot. That bothered him some, but he didn't know what else to do. Some nights he dreamed of all those skinned corpses getting up for a last demented drive, shaking the ground with their thunder until the dirt flew up and covered them, replacing their missing skin with landscape, so that after a while it was the whole countryside climbing out of its grave and galloping toward some distant ocean, leaving behind a great abyss for all the hunters and skinners and the ones that traded with them to fall into, an abyss that surely didn't stop until it reached Hell itself.

After the buffalo were gone, there were the bones. Mile after mile of them, like endless snow. By that time he had the family, and they had to eat. So the big hunter swallowed his pride and he and the family took their wagon—the gray boards still stinking of buffalo death after all those years—and went out on the prairie to collect bones. Eight dollars a ton at the peak. Somewhere back East they were made into fertilizer. After a few months, every major railway center had huge stacks of buffalo bones piled by the tracks awaiting shipment. Thousands upon thousands of bones drifted by Neal's shack. Some mornings, if he was patient, he could count each one. They drifted by singly, in pairs, in groups, no two exactly alike. He could be a rich man. But there was no railway nearby. Some mornings it would snow, and the wind would pick up the sand, and the bones would tumble, and there would be no difference between sky and ground and bones. There would just be all these pieces of the world, all these pieces of a life, picked up by the wind and blown across the flat, endless valley.

One morning in the sand outside his door he found tracks of deer and coyote. Another morning it was bighorn. Another morning some kind of rodent. Indian rice grass and pioneering sunflowers established brief colonies, and then disappeared. Sand and sun blasted his cabin until it was as black as char, a shadow moving with the dunes.

Wild horses drifted by, dancing on webbed feet. He saw them only at odd moments of the day, but he had no doubt that they were there. A creek meandered through the dunes, creating occasional pockets of quicksand. He wondered how many web-footed horses, or lost pioneers, had spent their final moments in the embrace of those wet sands.

Brownie, and every other horse he owned, became bone, then sand, then memory blowing against his cabin walls, blasting them into darkness.

TO BURY HIM IN HIS OWN SHADOW

On one morning of rare stillness in the dunes, Neal found his reflection in the creek that wound slowly through the sands. His hide was pale and hung loosely from his frame. Won't bring top dollar, he mused. Besides, the market's glutted. But he knew that that outer layer of skin had an importance—it held his appearance. It was all the world had to remember him by now that Elizabeth and Sarah were just a memory and his memory alone. What lay beneath—muscle and organs and bones—were his own secrets, and inaccessible to anyone besides himself. Might as well feed that part to the buzzards, the coyotes, the flies.

The wind of memory shaped the sand into Elizabeth, then into Sarah, who cried out once—the long, modulating cry of a wind that's traveled too far—before falling into a drift of fragments again. Neal pulled out his old Sharp's Fifty and shot it off into every pillar and mound of sand, trying to kill his wife, his daughter, the buffalo, again.

But God cranked up the wind once more, and when it hit Neal, it hit him with all the force of a mad god's voice. His skin grew raw when he touched it. He fell to his knees beneath the force of a cleansing guilt. When the weight of memory finally pushed him over into his shadow, he kept his eyes wide open, content to spend his last moments staring through miles of blowing snow and drifting sand.

In God's mad winds, a man can lose his life as the sands of memory accumulate like bone to bury him in his own shadow.

THE DYING

When Ellen was six years old her mother made her bright dresses of red and blue velvet with lace around the collars and cuffs. "Party dresses," her mother called them, but there couldn't be real parties, because their farm was miles ±rom the next, from any other children. But her mother would bake her special cakes, and sit with her and her dolls, the tiny plastic dish set on the grease-stained card table, for hours at a time.

When Ellen was nine her mother taught her how to ride a bike. Her father avoided the lessons, whether it was because he thought them improper for a girl, or because he wanted her to stay forever young, forever his baby, she never knew. Her mother would hold her by the shoulders, give her a little push, then run awkwardly alongside her, holding up her yellow calf-length dress. Ellen steered carefully, worried that she might run her mother down, might grind her mother into nothing.

When Ellen was fifteen she was terrified of nuclear war. She dreamed of bombs and fire and everyone she loved consumed by a blinding white heat. Nothing left but desert and black glass. Her mother read her the same fairytales she'd read to her at six, ot fairy kingdoms thousands of years old, of princesses who would sleep a death sleep forever, until awakened by the kiss of a handsome stranger.

When Ellen was twenty her father died. She had never asked him why he didn't want her riding a bike. She could not remember where he had been during the parties, where he'd been when she dreamed of holocaust, or what he thought of war. Suddenly it was as if he'd never existed, as if Ellen and her mother had grown up alone.

After his death her mother cleaned house and prepared for company. Not once did she speak her husband's name.

When Ellen was thirty her mother was suddenly old. They had not had a mutual conversation in years. Her mother spoke her husband's name constantly, ritualistically, a chant.

Her mother was no longer there for her. It was as if she had died. And to Ellen's shame, she seemed incapable of giving her mother what she needed. She could not be there for her. It was like watching an old, faded movie of their life together, the actresses badly cast.

"Only two left now." Mary Alice's voice was harsh with congestion. Ellen might have commented that she seemed to be coming down with something, but she stopped herself.

Ellen turned to face her. Mary Alice leaned against the jamb of the door. She was blonde, and large, but her starched whites still seemed much too big for her. Ellen tried to remember if they had always fit so loosely. Mary Alice stared past her shoulder. It made Ellen uncomfortable; she wondered, briefly, if someone had walked into the room behind her. But there was no door behind her.

"I don't know about you, Ellen, but I think I'll be leaving for good after my shift tonight. There's no reason to stay on here."

Ellen didn't say anything. She glanced at the clock hanging from the corridor ceiling.

"The administrator ought to be here, takin' care of things. She thinks calling' in once a day means she's doing' all she can. She can't stand watching' 'em either," Mary Alice said, rubbing her eyes. "Those two'll probably be gone by morning anyway. I want to be home with my kids, Ellen. You should be home with somebody, too."

"There isn't anyone there."

There was a long pause. "There won't be anybody in this nursing home either after a few more hours. Go on home, Ellen."

"Mrs. Meadows needs me. And … Jennie's just a little girl."

"They're *dyin'*. honey. Should be going real soon now. Nothing we can do. And I can't take it … watchin' the way they go."

"I don't plan to look in on them this evening," Ellen said,

"not unless they call first. I'll be okay."

Ellen looked out the window. No one was out in the streets tonight; there weren't even any cars. "Go home to your kids, Mary Alice. Hold them real close, don't let them slip through your fingers. I'll be all right."

Mary Alice didn't say anything for a while. Ellen listened carefully for the sounds of her breathing, waiting for the exhalations to stop, to disappear.

"You look beat," Mary Alice finally said. "Why don't you just go home and rest? And don't come in tomorrow—I'll stay 'til morning. It's not worth it, honey. I've seen how it gets to you."

Ellen turned around.

"I heard you talking to your mama again," Mary Alice whispered.

"I ... I suppose I dozed off. I think I dreamed about her."

"You better rest, Ellen."

"I will ... I will. I'll just make rounds, and then I'll go."

The nursing home's corridors were empty; all the equipment, the cleaning carts, the wheelchairs, had been stored away. Most of the rooms had been stripped of linen, curtains, and all furnishings except the beds. The rest of the staff didn't come in anymore; there was no need. They'd laid people off once census was down to half, and as the home continued to empty people quit voluntarily. They stayed at home questioning their sanity, she suspected. Yet Ellen still insisted on making complete rounds, even through the empty wings of the home. As if she expected the patients to reappear in their beds as suddenly as they had left them, gazing around in bewilderment. Ellen had her own ways of dealing with disorder, of grieving.

She had sneaked Martin Reynolds his *Playboy* magazine the second Monday of every month. The old man would blow her a chaste kiss in gratitude. On Fridays she always helped Liz Danport cut pictures out of *Life* and *Redbook*. She never knew why the old lady wanted to do that; most of them ended up in a cardboard box under her bed.

The hardest thing about working here—at least the hardest thing before the way of death changed so drastically—had been the interchangeability of the residents. Someone would die or be moved out, and someone very similar in age and manner would take the place. There were mornings she'd come into work and find an empty bed and the body taken to the morgue during the night. Sometimes she'd be assigned the packing up, the stuffing of garbage bags with clothes for the poor, the dumping of old cosmetics into the trash, the gathering of odds and ends into boxes for redistribution to others.

But now there was something worse than an ordinary death. The morgue was no longer needed. It started with the weak, the elderly infirm, the sick children, all those so hard to care for. Something that took them away every morning at first, but soon there were several going each day. Soon they couldn't re-fill all the deserted beds. Now there were two residents, two beds.

"Miss. Miss ..." The voice was dry and hoarse, like her mother's voice before the end. Ellen had completed her circuit of the building; she could have gone home. "I ... something's happening!" Mrs. Meadows' room was across the hall. Ellen went to the door.

The old woman's face was brown, brittle-looking. Like an old letter.

"Please. The candle ... light the candle."

Ellen went to the bedtable and lit the candle, placing it as close to the pillow as she dared. The old woman's eyes darted frantically for a moment, and then fixed on the flame.

Sometimes the dying thought a candle delayed the moment of their departure. It was supposed to give them something to concentrate on, and that stopped the disappearance, or even reversed it temporarily. Ellen herself had never seen it work for long.

"Where am I going?" the old woman asked.

Ellen leaned closer. "I don't understand what you mean."

"I'm not gonna be buried. You can't tell me I'm gonna be buried."

Ellen lowered her eyes. "No, ma'am."

"Won't be nothing left *to* bury!"

"No, ma'am. Try not to upset yourself so. Watch the candle, see how pretty it is."

"So where does it take us? Is it just this old raggedy body it takes? Oh Lord, does my *mind* stay here?"

"Oh, no, ma'am. I'm sure it doesn't," Ellen said, not sure at all. The possibility that something would survive here should have been reassuring, but it wasn't. "Please. Just watch the candle." Ellen could hear the begging in her own voice. Foolishly she found herself wishing there were a doctor around. She and Mrs. Meadows could both handle the dying part; it was the vanishing that so terrified.

She held the woman's hand for hours. Sometimes she'd hear Mary Alice coming to the doorway, but neither acknowledged the other. Ellen watched Mrs. Meadows' face intently, looking for the slightest change, the smallest shift in coloration.

It had begun about a year ago. Once the sick or infirm became ill, their sickness invariably became worse, and they died very quickly. No one ever improved. They were all used up.

And when they died, they faded out of existence. No open caskets. No bodies to bury. Just gone.

"It's the Lord's punishment!" her mama used to cry, before her own time came. "People don't appreciate each other! They don't take care of the old, the sick!" Ellen had wanted to shake her mama, make her say it, make her say that she was to blame. But she couldn't bear to touch those tensed, scrawny shoulders, smell that sour breath so full of death. She couldn't bear even holding her mama for comfort, to hug her and cry. "It's the earth itself, judging us!" her mama would say in her last days. *In preparation for the final times when the dead shall walk the earth,* she'd heard a preacher on the radio say. "Earth ain't got no more room in its bowels for all the dead!"

No one seemed to have any better ideas.

Something had happened to grief as well. Grieving used to help you accept loss, to solidify memory into a memorial, make the past stay real and concrete. But how could you grieve properly when the body vanished before your eyes?

Ellen had been denied a good grieving for her mother.

Ellen tried to stay awake; this time she wanted to be there when it happened. But she was so tired. She blinked, and then was startled by the flicker of light. The old woman was pushing herself up from the bed, moaning softly.

"Mama." Ellen stirred in the chair. She turned toward the dim face. From the side it looked like her mother, but that couldn't be.

At first the parchment face became clearer, but then it appeared to darken and brown. Ellen gasped. Through the thin skin she could see the candle flame flickering on the table beside the old woman's head.

"Mrs. Meadows! The flame ... concentrate!"

The moan broadened into a harsh cry. The eyes widened, the whites now blending with the sheets behind her, the sheets showing through her transparent hair, her transparent brain.

Ellen reached out but could not bring herself to touch her. She could see the bed through the impossibly wide mouth, the bed showing more and more resolution through the blurring flesh.

And suddenly Ellen was looking at the bed, nothing more. Mrs. Meadows was gone.

"Mama ... I ..." She felt tears on her cheeks. She stared at the bed. It felt as if Mrs. Meadows had never existed, or that she had, indeed, receded into nothingness. Ellen almost expected to find all the woman's clothing gone when she began packing her possessions.

She should have held her, hugged her. She should have made herself hold the woman to this world.

It was as if part of Ellen's own life had never occurred, the part spent with Mrs. Meadows. The memories were still there, but focused more vaguely. Without the physical reality of the person, the memories seemed far less real. The past seemed far less real. Death by death, Ellen's past was being eaten away. All used up. And if everyone you ever knew died, maybe your own life had never occurred.

The candle flame sputtered and died, but Ellen was dimly aware of the room lightening. She looked toward the window; it was morning. She had stayed up with Mrs. Meadows the entire night. More than she had done for her own mother those final hours.

She glanced at the bureau. It was full of flowers; people—strangers, most of them—were sending a great number of flowers to hospitals and nursing homes these days. But she couldn't make out individual blossoms in the room's dim light. Just a misty cloud of color.

"Get out of here, Ellen. Go on home." For a moment it sounded like her mother, telling her to join those already gone. She looked up. It was Mary Alice.

"Mary Alice ... I'm sorry. It'll be time for me to come back on soon. There's still Jennie Taylor."

"Don't worry about it. I'll have Jim bring the kids here today. There's nobody for them to bother, really. Get some sleep."

But Ellen was afraid to sleep. No open caskets. No bodies to bury.

It was cold when she went out to her car, the streets almost empty. A lot of people stayed home now, as if they thought it made them safer. She wondered how many of them brooded the way she did, and how many tried to keep it at their backs like Mary Alice.

Her car rocked in the wind. The dead streaming past, she thought. She stopped at a stoplight and a shadow crept across the intersection. She shivered and pulled out before the light changed.

The dead like small animals. The dead were intent on their sudden disappearance from the earth, haunted by it. With every bump and lurch of the car she imagined she had just run over another one, the lost thoughts of the dead scattering beneath her wheels, faintly echoing through the dark streets.

"You're hurting me!" A whine had crept into her mother's commanding voice.

"I'm sorry, Mama. It's just hard to change the sheets when you refuse to get out of bed!" Ellen wrestled with one of the corners of the fitted bottom sheet while her mother leaned against her. "I'm doing my best."

"I'm just a poor, defenseless old woman and look how my own daughter treats me! I'm dying, you know that."

"I know!" Ellen said with fury, instantly sorry for it. And sorry too because she could not bring herself to tell her mother how much the dying hurt her, frightened her, making her need her mother more than ever before. Her mother turned her face into the pillow at the first mention of death.

After a long struggle Ellen would get the bed made. "Could I have some orange juice, please?" her mother would ask her formally.

And quietly, Ellen would reply, "Of course."

Her mother had been an invalid several years, long before the new way of dying had begun. As the youngest unmarried daughter, Ellen had been expected to care for her at home. But she had refused; she had seen what such arrangements did to families. She was afraid of what it might do to their relationship. She still loved her mother; she held on to the memories of what her mother had been. So as a sort of compromise her oldest sister had put their mother in the nursing home where Ellen worked.

"You spend all your time here," Mary Alice was always saying. But who else could she trust to take care of Mama?

"The pan is cold." Mama had whispered harshly. But Ellen pretended not to hear her. She learned to be distracted when she brought the bedpan, took Mama's temperature, gave her a bath.

The dead rocked the car, and Ellen tried not to scream.

It was as if an entire generation's slide into death had quickened to a terrible speed.

A relationship lasting nearly thirty years, yet Ellen could feel the memories beginning to fade. She remembered a little less each day; a little less seemed real. She couldn't even be sure of the times in the past she thought her mother had said she'd loved her.

Her mother had been among the first to vanish. Irrationally, Ellen wondered if it might have been her fault. Hadn't her mother even told her as much?

"You *wanted* this to happen," she said from her deathbed, the image of the candle flame beginning to peek through her aged skin. "You wanted all the sick and the old to just vanish so you didn't have to think about us anymore."

"Mama!" Ellen drove through the smoke-gray form in the middle of the street.

Her house, at the end of a dimly-lit street and surrounded

by trees, seemed quiet and peaceful. The shadows appeared to peel away from the house as she pulled into the driveway. She got out and looked at the sky: dark clouds drifted back toward town.

She noticed the disarray when she opened her front door and entered the living room. The house hadn't been cleaned in weeks, but she hadn't realized it had gotten this bad. Photograph albums lay on the floor, spines broken, loose pictures fallen out. She had been trying to figure out where and when they had been taken. She could hardly recognize her mother in those pictures.

The house smelled of standing dish water and garbage, of sad decay. She'd been too busy, preoccupied. She had done nothing for weeks except go to work at the nursing home. Eat a little. Sleep a little. Dream. Someone had to take care of things at the nursing home now that most of the staff had abandoned it. Someone had to police the streets, pick up the garbage, run the city, and carry on with living. They couldn't all huddle at home, holding each other, waiting to die. She had done nothing, really. She might sicken herself. But she could not bear to think that, so afraid was she now of dying.

Dozens of books, wedged open at various pages—but all toward the beginning—were scattered around the house. A trail led from her bedroom to the kitchen, a path cleared by kicking all the magazines and newspapers and garbage out of the way. The constant pacing.

She sat on the couch and turned on the news. First was a story about a boy finding his lost dog. Then a national story concerning economic indicators. A piece on welfare cheats. Then a story on the epidemic of absenteeism in public service agencies and businesses across the city. A related story on agoraphobia. Then a story on the disappearances. There had been one every night for two weeks. The media obviously knew something was up; they just didn't know what. Ellen wondered if it was just people like her—people in the hospitals and nursing homes— who sensed what was really going on. But in a few months, maybe less, they all *had* to know. They couldn't keep their heads in the sand forever.

"A psychologist at Wayne University, Dr. Marvin Deckler, has proposed the theory that the disappearances can be explained as a variety of 'mass hysteria,'" the news anchor with the mock-serious expression said. "Deckler says that victims of this condition may have hallucinated the presence of loved ones who have already died. When the hallucination wears off, these people disappear. Deckler states that this may be the most widespread such hysteria on record. In a related story, Jim Burns takes us to Atlanta, where scientists at the National Center for Disease Control are testing air and food samples from around the country in order to determine a possible cause for these hallucinations ..."

The news story seemed silly and intrusive, like one of the televised news program "explanations" in *Night of the Living Dead* or in the sequel Ellen never could remember the name of. Any rational explanation was bound to sound like that, an exercise in the surreal. Unconscious satire. They were all trying so hard not to see it.

It was the same every night. A new theory to explain the unexplainable, to take the guilt away. They really don't know what's happening. Ellen thought. They're denying the evidence of their own eyes. They think it's some kind of disease, for Christ's sake.

The phone rang.

She eyed it warily. It rang again. But she would not answer. She didn't think she'd ever be answering another phone.

It happens; it has always happened, she told herself. People die and they have always died and will continue to die.

But not like this.

You had to learn to accept it.

Not like this. Not like this.

She liked to imagine herself disappearing. It was something she thought she could do.

Her mother got up from her favorite chair and went into the kitchen to fix breakfast.

"It's okay, Mama. I don't need any."

The woman smiled at her but continued toward the kitchen.

"I can fix it myself."

Her mother kept walking into the kitchen.

"You're all in my head!"

The shadow fell apart and drifted back under the chair.

"I miss you, Mama," Ellen said, and held herself.

She did not like eating alone, so increasingly of late she snacked on small items from the refrigerator. She sat with her tea and a piece of bread, sometimes a wedge of cheese, and stared out the window at the dark street. She spent much of her time examining the shadows, trying to determine if there was anything peculiar about any of them. She would make up her mind one way and then another—the strange became ordinary and the ordinary became strange.

"Ellen, I need another pillow." Her chair well back so as not to block her mother's view, Ellen had stared stubbornly at the television. Now, she knew, it would be impossible for her to eat, because her mother was angry. "Ellen!"

"I'm your daughter, not your slave," she had said, and left the room.

By the time she came back her mama was gone.

She looked everywhere. Acted crazy. Even knowing what had happened, that the dying had occurred, she had still asked all the nurses. She'd even looked under the bed, barely resisting the impulse to call out Mama.

As if her mother had never existed. As if her mama had never loved her. Ellen wondered how she was going to grieve.

She did not know what had been on her mother's face when she died.

Ellen sobbed aloud, and waited for the shadow to walk out of the darkness of her bedroom, and head toward the kitchen. She spent the day lounging on the couch, stirring occasionally from a fitful sleep to study the failing light, to trace shadows as they traveled from day into night, life into death.

Just before sunset she drove out to the nursing home. She was feeling guilty about letting Mary Alice stay there all day, but knew she couldn't have managed another shift without some rest. She wondered what kinds of games Mary Alice's kids must have played in the empty corridors, going into darkened rooms and never coming out again.

Mary Alice was in the parking lot, waiting by her car. Jim nodded to Ellen from the driver's side; the kids were in the back seat.

"Jennie's still there," Mary Alice said. "Poor little thing. I was nervous about letting the kids play with her, but I couldn't help myself. She's real weak, Ellen. I don't think you'll be here long tonight."

Ellen touched her hand. "Everything else okay?"

Mary Alice looked down at her feet. "I don't think there's any point in my coming back here." She looked at Ellen, smiling vaguely. "You either, after Jennie in there dies. I'm gonna be home with the family. My parents are staying with us now. Guess we'll all just stay real close 'til this thing is over with."

"Did you see the news tonight?"

"Yep. Maybe they're right, but it doesn't look that way to me. We can't *all* be crazy. I think people just have a hard time acceptin' a thing like this. It just doesn't make any sense. Maybe it'll just stop of its own accord, before things go too far. That's the way I want to look at it. You try to look at it that way, too, Ellen."

"I'll try, Mary Alice." Jim looked impatient. Mary Alice hugged her and hurried around the side of the car. Jim left the parking lot with a screeching of tires, sideswiping several garbage cans as the car bounced down the driveway. "Hurry home," Ellen said to no one.

Ellen walked the corridors of the nursing home, entering each room, examining walls, ceiling, floors, as if searching was part of her job. She didn't know what she was searching for. She saved Jennie's room for last.

Daughter …

She had imagined the plaintive call, some stray memory of the nursing home when it had been full of residents …

"Daughter."

Again. Ellen opened the door.

Jennie Taylor, eight years old, lay on the bed, her image wavering, overlapping, and becoming transparent in spots. She looked up at Ellen.

"I want my mama," the little girl sobbed in a faraway voice. But Jennie's own mother and father had been dead a long time. Jennie had been ill for years.

"I'm not ..." Ellen began, but the little girl stopped her with an outstretched arm, the hands and fingers looking like clear plastic, or a glass doll's limb. "I can't." Ellen backed away. Jennie faded noticeably.

"Mama. Please."

Please honey. stay with me. Don't look away.

"Please hold my hand, Mama."

I need you. Ellen. Please listen.

"Keep me here a while longer, Mama."

Hold my hand ...

"Hold my hand, please, Mama." Ellen sat down on the edge of the bed and grasped the little girl's hand, and thought of learning to ride a bike, of her mother holding on for dear life as the bike picked up speed. "People don't really disappear, do they, Mama?"

"It's all in our heads, I think," Ellen said. "There's a disease some of us have—it makes us think things that aren't true." But Ellen didn't believe that. Didn't believe that at all. "If you really don't want someone to go away, they don't. You can keep them with you."

"Will you keep me with you, Mama?"

"Oh, yes, Jennie. Yes. I'll even tell you stories, about fairy kingdoms a thousand years old, and princesses who'd have slept forever if a handsome stranger hadn't kissed them."

Ellen watched in fascination as her own fingers became translucent, then transparent in spots. She watched it spread up her arm. She imagined some pieces of herself, her memories, her childhood, flowing into the little girl's body. Ellen's hands, fingers tensed and hooked, stretched out to the girl's face, as if she intended to trawl that hidden place where the dead had vanished.

She could see her mother's face within Jennie's features, her skin beginning to brown. Ellen watched as her mother and Jennie receded into the gray shadows of the bed. She tried to imagine the place they were going to, but her imagination failed her.

She blinked and the world seemed to disappear, blinked again and it was back. She felt her hair lifting from her scalp. She looked up: the roof was gone, the walls fallen away. The building had been all used up. She lifted her arms to embrace the sky before it could leave her, but the sky began to melt. The trees flowed upward, the buildings swirled. The world became parchment, then milky glass, then nothing. All used up.

When someone dies, part of your life goes away. As if it never happened. Ellen's thoughts drifted apart.

And then her thoughts went away.

EMBRACE OF CLAY
EMBRACE OF STRAW

Lannie prowled the small back-street shop for something of Philip.

A color, a picture, a sign, a symbol, a texture, even a particular nuance of incense (the shop also carried scents to match your sign), a brass bell of the right note, a shape, a weapon—anything that might help her focus all her energies on him, concentrate all the power in her senses if only for a brief time in the service of his harm, his destruction, his complete disintegration. She smiled softly; it surprised her she could still get so worked up over him, so intensely angry.

She'd been in the shop several times, but that had been before her initiation. She hadn't known quite how to react to the place even then; it had been a lark, someplace to go for unusual gifts and cards, and to act spooky in public. But there had been all these strange people hanging around; it made her nervous. Now it was still a source of some amusement, even the name above the door, ZELDA'S OCCULT CASTLE, sounding like some children's magic shop. But you could buy things here that could be useful; you could make contacts that might turn even the proprietor pale. Lannie was sure the lady didn't quite know who or what she was dealing with; she wasn't aware of all the possible connections.

Lannie suddenly realized she was walking about the shop much as she had that long time ago; with a look of intentness, keeping to herself, being silent, and holding herself delicately somehow, elegantly, as if she'd really known what she was doing, as if she had the "knowledge." Back then she'd wondered how many people in the shop had assumed she was some sort of independent sorceress, out working freelance.

A fat woman in a loose pink pant-suit appeared through the beaded curtains at the back of the store. Zelda herself, surveying her customers. Lannie was acutely aware of the way Zelda had targeted her, and knew she would soon be accosting her much like any overly-helpful saleswoman in a downtown department store.

Zelda walked directly towards Lannie. A small gray-haired poodle burst through the curtains, scurrying to keep up.

"Your first time in Zelda's, my dear?" The fat woman pursed her lips and gazed up at Lannie's hairline.

Lannie pressed her lips together, unaccountably annoyed that the woman didn't remember her. Then she smiled, and thought. Black … knowing what that would do to the "energy" around her for anyone even half-way sensitive to it.

Zelda shifted awkwardly on her feet, her eyes suddenly looking nervous, agitated. She pulled back a moment, looking at Lannie with a puzzled expression. "I … please feel free to call me … if you need assistance …" Then she backed up a step more, turned, and walked too quickly for grace to the back of the store.

Lannie sighed with unthinking satisfaction. What she'd actually done had been only a slight thing, a visualization exercise really, something that would have changed the quality of her presence for others only momentarily, but a certain sense of power did go with the exercise and she had to admit it thrilled her, excited her much more than sex or anything else ever had.

Then, suddenly, she was appalled. She used the talent so easily, so automatically, and that facility could just as easily be used to hurt people as to deceive them. After all she'd been through the need had remained constant, something that would always be a part of her. It made her feel ugly. It made her hate herself.

She continued her inventory of the shop's goods with a bit more amusement than before, noting that Zelda had expanded her stock of candles, art objects, and the kind of ornate boxes and containers she had seen available in some of the trendier gift shops. Although she had to admit Zelda's prices were much more reasonable.

The shop's specialty was incense. Lannie remembered her first time here, and the smell of baking cookies in one of the lids. Then peppermint, cherry, raw venison, cat's breath, bone, roasting bird.

But still, Zelda's seemed much more the tacky knick-knack shop than ever before. Unicorn prints were jammed next to astrological posters, dragon mobiles and owl photographs on the walls. The paperweights were all scurrying crabs, lounging unicorns, flying dragons, overweight toads. You could get any style box or phial you might desire in Zelda's: stained glass, soapstone, decorated brass, inlaid wood, marble, or all manner of small animal statues with spaces hollowed out and "secret" doors affixed—all ostensibly for the purpose of storing important powders or pills. The countless burners were of a similar style, with the addition of a vent for the smoke. The statuary was pseudo-Egyptian, Sumerian, or African. There were cheap rings and necklaces of every style. And flashy popular exposes of the various magic arts were displayed alongside scholarly and sincere works on the shelves along the back wall.

An old black man had entered and was making his way to a counter along the left side. He studied a wrinkled piece of paper in his hand mouthing words silently. Zelda slipped behind the counter and waited for him impatiently.

"Yes ... how are you?"

The man looked up at her and stared a moment. He handed over the list.

"Love potion ... I think, well, except for these last two. You'll have to go to a drugstore for those."

The man nodded his head slowly, and suddenly grinned.

Zelda seemed vaguely uncomfortable as she went into the back room for the required substances, the black man grinning fixedly, staring at her retreating form.

There had been a time when Lannie thought that perhaps Philip had used something of a love potion on her. In her more lucid moments it was difficult to explain the attraction otherwise.

But it took much more talent than most dabblers imagined to make such a potion really work; power had attracted her to Philip, nothing else. And unfortunately, she had to admit to herself that power was probably the only thing that would ever attract her. Close relationships were more frightening than truly satisfying to her.

And Philip had opened her up to the powers, the talents within herself, and made her see things about herself she never should have known.

She'd met Philip in this very shop. Zelda would die if she knew what kind of real talent had been there. Her gaze had been drawn to him immediately: the dark, deep-set eyes, curly raven hair, and a dark three-piece suit which seemed much too old-fashioned for someone his age. And then … she'd lost a few moments of time; something had occurred she'd never been able to remember, and then he had been beside her, holding her hand and looking into her eyes.

"You knew I'd introduce myself," he'd said.

"Yes."

"You know that we're soon to become lovers."

She'd looked at him then, her concentration broken, and almost laughed at the audacity of the man, but still, why she would never completely understand, she'd said, "Yes."

The lovemaking had been good with him, better than with anyone else, even though she could never get very close, even though—as she had to admit many times later—she hadn't really wanted to get close, to him or anyone. It just wasn't in her. She guessed Philip had shown her that too. Sex had always been difficult for her; she was cold to her lovers and eventually they reacted in kind. She'd hated to be touched.

But there had been something dynamic between them, something powerful.

Zelda returned to the counter bearing several tubes full of multicolored liquids, and two small bags of powder. Lannie recognized some of the ingredients; they were for an old Voodoo love philter. The man might have gotten the ingredients from one of the cheaply-printed pamphlets Zelda had imported from the Caribbean. The potion wouldn't get the man's dream woman into the sack, but it had been known to retard epilepsy.

"You have talent," he'd told her one night.

"You're not so bad yourself," she'd giggled and punched him playfully in the ribs.

"No ..." he'd said sternly, and she'd stopped laughing. He appeared deadly serious. "Look into my mind and tell me what you see."

Her initial thought was of the ridiculousness of his request, but something inside her consented, and she'd looked, and looked in a way she knew was different somehow, as if a switch had suddenly been thrown inside her head, a light glowing to life ...

... and what she saw! Philip dancing naked, then throwing himself at other nude men and women in a manner that was both hostile and sexual. Then the orgy ... and Philip drinking blood, feeling its warmth trickling down her throat ...

She'd screamed and Philip had slapped her several times, coldly, efficiently, with just enough force to get her to listen to him. Then he'd held her tightly by the shoulders and made her look at him as he told her about himself, about what he wanted her to do, about what she would soon become.

His talk had pulled so many things together, how she always seemed to know beforehand when certain people were going to call her or drop by, how when anyone ever lost anything they'd come to her because she had such good luck at finding things, how some animals were extremely drawn to her, and others extremely frightened, how she'd known the exact moment her father had died and the phone call a half-hour later had confirmed it. Little things by themselves, but they'd added up to a part of herself hitherto unknown to her, now opening up and demanding attention. All she needed was a little tutoring, and Philip was going to volunteer.

Lannie watched the black man leave, whistling a tune merrily. A young man in a denim jacket passed him at the door and approached Zelda just a bit too casually.

"Good day," he said, in an obviously affected tone. Lannie winced. Another Mickey Mouse pretending to be a wizard. He wore an ostentatious ring inscribed with alchemical symbols.

Zelda had them on sale now. "I'd like some information."

"Certainly!" Zelda exclaimed. Such clientele always brought out her enthusiasm. "What can I do for you?"

"I've a problem … with relatives, you see. We don't get along. I want to bring us closer, but in the gentlest, most loving way you understand."

Zelda began to babble. Lannie knew she was a great believer in positive energies, Wiccan, white magic, fertility worship, that sort of thing. Well, at least the young man couldn't get too much over his head in that area.

Lannie turned and saw the two men in gray watching the exchange taking place at the counter. A shudder ripped through her like a physical presence. They dropped by periodically hoping to find someone unhappy with his or her progress in the mysteries. Then they'd offer so much more, in exchange for some small pledge of loyalty and assistance. Just as Philip had done.

The walk back to her small house was a long and cold one. Lannie smiled grimly, thinking of broomsticks and astral-projection. Maybe someone had these tricks in their repertoire, but not her. Her large weight loss over the last few months didn't help, either. She pulled her coat tighter around the neck.

She'd done a lot for Philip, but what had angered her most was the realization she'd wanted to do those things just the same. She'd certainly had no pangs of conscience. The first time they'd butchered a cat she'd thought she'd be upset, maybe even throw up. But she hadn't. She'd felt nothing, simply found the entire procedure mildly interesting.

And when they'd murdered the girl, sharing her blood from several stone cups, all she had thought about was what that act would *bring* her, the power that she would have. Philip had opened up that realm in her also, developed her latent talent for coldness, thoughtlessness, a bestial rationality.

She'd always heard that "working black" resulted in a backlash; the power turned against you threefold. But that never seemed to have happened to Philip, or any of his friends. She wondered if perhaps it were merely another of the many myths promoted to keep people from playing around with the dangerous aspects of the talents. There seemed nothing, however, to really stop the power once it had gotten hold of you. All the old wives' tales in the world weren't about to stop Philip.

At home she gathered all her props around her, the items which would allow her to focus all her energies on Philip, herself, herself and Philip. How the love-making had gradually changed, how his skin had turned to clay for her, his hair straw between her fingers. It soon became like embracing a corpse, yet still she continued.

A small brass bell ringing out his particular note, another bell matching her tone, and the two together; an off-key chorus, an argument, a self-destructive dialog. She lit one incense burner for herself, another for Philip, and breathed the intermingled scents in deeply, down, down into her lungs until she was nauseous. Then she switched on the two lights: red for her and green for him. Her eyes burned but still were drawn to the colors.

Soon she was staring without blinking, her eyes watering, but still she was unable to turn away. She held her arms up into the colored light, examining them in wonder, at their unfamiliarity. How much weight had she lost so far? Twenty pounds? Forty? She could see the bones; she caressed them in fascination. With a sharp intake of breath she imagined the smells in the room had gone sour. She smelled corruption, rotting flesh. She saw herself rolling around, wrapped in soiled bed sheets, funeral shrouds. Her bedroom was covered with spider webs, the walls smeared with grime and the filth from her own body.

There were snakes, lizards, and vermin in her bed. No one would ever love her … she would never love anyone …

Her mouth popped open as if by itself and she began to cry. Her stomach roiled with pain, as if knives were ripping down into the soft tissues, probing. But she was empty, she knew she was empty.

Suddenly filled with self-loathing, seeing the young girl's pale white neck, pulled back, then the thin red line widening across the skin. Lannie began coughing, dry heaving, trying to vomit the self-loathing out. Hatred for Philip and herself welled up inside her brought along by the lights, the smells, the tastes, and the unbidden images of herself and Philip rolling around on his bed. She felt full, fattened with the sense impressions of the two of them. She felt ready to burst.

Lannie staggered to her feet and stumbled through the back door into the garden. She fell to her knees in a wet spot in the dirt, began clawing and digging with her bare hands. She came up with the small clay doll which had been buried there, the clay discoloring from the dampness, the extremities just beginning to crumble.

"Philip ..." she hissed. Image-magic, sympathetic magic. It was the simplest, crudest thing she knew. A magic for amateurs, familiar to almost everyone. It worked on the theory that there was a secret sympathy between things that resemble each other, or have been in contact. What happened to one affected the other.

But she discovered through Philip that you had to have the talent to really make it work, and the image talent had always been there for her. She remembered when she was in high school and had thrown her boyfriend's picture against the wall. For a second she had actually hated him. He hadn't died in the car crash that day, but both legs were broken, and he'd always have that scar across his nose, a scar that matched the crack in the glass almost exactly. At the time she'd just thought it a horrible coincidence.

She'd used an old recipe to make the doll: clay broken down to the fineness of meal, sifted through a sieve, mixed with water, and kneaded to just the right consistency. She'd had to try half a dozen times before coming up with just the right texture. Then she'd stuck it into the fire, roasting it on one side and then the other until it was hardened and a little shrunken by the heat.

Her talent, with the right amount of focusing, had done the rest.

Lannie smiled, even with the pains wracking her stomach. Philip had taken to bed three weeks ago. She knew he'd never be getting out of it. A little water poured into the ground each day hastened the process of the decay, although sometimes she'd skip a couple of days just as he'd think he was getting better.

Then with some sadness she returned the clay figure to its

burial plot, and picked up the straw doll.

Clay and straw. Straw and clay.

She stroked the straw doll tenderly, like the little girl she could not remember ever being, playing with her toy. She admired the craft. The arms were perfect, the thin strands twisted to make the arms looking more and more like the veins and bones she could now see so close to the surface of her akin.

She was no better than Philip. Perhaps that was the most important thing he had taught her.

"Straw and clay. Clay and straw."

She put the straw doll down on top of the clay one and arranged them into a kind of obscene embrace, covered them over with dirt and dumped a full bucket of water into the soil.

Which would be the first to rot? Funny how she'd never considered that angle before.

GARBAGE

Sam loved Hannah and Hannah loved Sam. That was all any-one needed to know. Leave it to younger people to ask *why*. Kids who didn't yet know what they wanted and middle-aged *why*ners. Sam had loved Hannah for so long he couldn't remember why. Long ago he had forgotten anything he really liked about Hannah. In fact, he wasn't sure if there *was* anything he really liked about Hannah. She complained about everything. But then, so did he.

"It smells like garbage in here!" she called out from the big chair in the living room.

"How would you know? Your nose stopped working fifteen years ago," he mumbled to himself.

"What was that?"

"I said it's the roses I bought you last week!" He called. He struggled getting the icing on the cake—it seemed a little greasy, kept sliding off. "Remember, fifteen of them? I said it was an early birthday present? Remember?" Of course she didn't—her brain was like old oatmeal these days.

There had been no roses.

But could he be sure of that?

"Early?" She sounded suspicious. He hurried with her birthday cake. Of course he'd forgotten candles—no surprise there. His own brain was like cottage cheese, just beginning to turn but turning just the same.

Sometimes when he was cleaning his ears, digging at the deep places, he'd hear a pop and he was sure he'd broken through—he could feel stray bits of song and old conversation slipping out, along with a few names, always a few names in the leakage. One of these days he would forget Hannah's name, and Sam's—for just a moment he almost forgot *he* was Sam—and then where would they be? Out on the scrap heap. But every time he popped through the ear like that the smell was worse, his thoughts going bad.

He looked around, caught sight of the Menorah by the window, grabbed it and stuck it into the middle of the slimy cake. They used to be Jewish; he couldn't remember if they still were. He had only one match so he just lit the candles on the ends. Not enough candles if she was counting—he didn't know if she still counted. She was eighty now, or ninety, a hundred and a hundred more, what did it matter?

"I don't remember any roses!" Hannah shouted.

"Happy Birthday to you!" He sang, rushing into the living room so fast he knocked a six-foot pile of TV Guides over onto the cat, which did not move. Once again Sam had forgotten to take it out to the trash while Hannah had slept—she wouldn't let him touch it while she was in the room because she said Sam had never loved her cat. True, of course, but Sam could still smell a little, and that cat certainly smelled a lot. "Happy Birthday to you! Happy Birthday Hannah Alexandria Rubenstein! Happy Birthday to you!" He plopped the cake down into Hannah's lap so hard the Menorah shifted, exposing a layer of rancid yellow butter. Hannah looked at it suspiciously. Of course she wouldn't have eaten it anyway. He couldn't remember the last time he'd seen her take a bite. Was it because she didn't trust her bowels? He didn't trust his bowels either but he still tried to eat a little something every day. A little fish. A piece of rye bread. One of those stale French Vanilla Crème cookies from the cigar box under the bed. That's what had killed the cat, actually. The ragged little pussy stole one of Sam's French Vanilla Creams and choked to death on it. Sam had been there, in fact, his hands wrapped around its scrawny little neck.

"Make a wish!" he exclaimed, forcing his smile to stretch around to the sides of his head. "But don't tell me what it is or it won't come true!"

"I wish I were dead!" She sputtered, spitting all over the cake and that Jewish thing whose name Sam had suddenly lost.

An hour later Sam had gotten Hannah all cleaned up and onto the couch where she slept and he watched, an old black beret which might have been his or might have been hers a long time ago pulled down so tightly over his head it looked like some kind of formal bathing cap. He'd never seen a formal bathing cap but people dressed up for all sorts of things. He'd taped a few colorful pieces of yarn to it to look more festive.

Hannah snored and drooled a substance that might have been petroleum jelly. Sam thought he'd have to hide the jar again if he could remember where it was. He went rummaging through the sideboard and found a lacy napkin, brought it over and wiped her face as gently as he could. His hands shook with the effort of being gentle. "There there, my sweet, my alabaster dream," he whispered. Oh, he could tell the young people a thing or three about love, if he could think his way through to the end of the sentence.

He'd finally rid the house of the cat. He didn't think he could make it all the way to the garbage cans out back, so he'd tossed it over the fence into the neighbors' yard. They were Baptists who played the bingo so they probably would notice nothing wrong. The cat had sailed gracefully, bent as it was into a kind of stiff L, like a boomerang, a beautiful thing to see, but it had not come back. A good thing.

Sam hated it when Hannah spoke of dying. He himself did not speak of it. What more was there to say when it was all around you? In people's eyes, the light dying beneath an increasingly milky haze, the eyeballs like fruit going bad. In people's voices, their words growing increasingly garbled in the ruins of their mouths. In people's hands, palsied, cracked, and bleeding. Whenever he went out he saw people like moldy bread, people like putrefying fish, people like graying meat awash in souring blood. Sometimes Hannah's failing health seemed a blessing—it kept him inside, away from all that moving garbage.

Strange it was that his love for Hannah was what first made him aware of such things, the watching and the waiting for any dangerous change, the focused attention on the details of her cascading failures. She wouldn't last the summer, that last doctor said, the young one, and the one with the sweet breath. Sam did not trust anybody with sweet breath. Such people looked as if they'd just had a perfume enema. That was no way to be in the world.

Not that he himself lagged in self-deception. For most of his life he had avoided death, had absented himself from all funerals, including those of his own parents. He had tried to treat all illness as if it were just a change in makeup.

Hannah had changed that. Hannah was dying, too slowly as far as she was concerned, and far more rapidly than he could bear.

"What are you doing out there!" she screamed from inside, awake and in pain. "You have a woman out there, don't you?"

Earlier in their marriage there had been opportunities, although he had never taken them. But he still felt somewhat embarrassed about those opportunities. "If you're looking for trouble you'll surely find it!" He wasn't sure if those were his thoughts or her shouting. She knew how to shout wise, that old woman.

Sam hobbled back inside, around piles of mildewed egg cartons and those white foam trays that hold frozen meats. He looked to see if Hannah was still on the couch. She wasn't. She'd gotten up and destroyed everything in her path, like one of those Japanese movie monsters that set people on fire by belching on them. He knew the feeling. Digestion had not been his friend in years.

Hannah was his friend. Hannah and no one else.

He could feel heavy movement in some other part of the house, but his sense of direction was poor. Through the dining room he followed the vague displacement of debris— the collection of bundled soup can wrappers tumbled over and scattered, the greasy sardine cans emptied of their dried mouse and baby bird specimens—and trotted into the living room in search of her. Boxes full of rusted small engine parts. Dolls missing their eyes. Clocks with their insides pulled out by ferocious hands. Bottles and cans and envelopes full of coffee grounds. He had once thought of mailing the grounds to one of the poorer third-world countries in an act of generosity that could not help but beef up his obituary. He'd discarded the idea when he realized they couldn't afford that much postage.

She could not get far in all this lost memory. Not unless she traveled incognito. He had no idea what kind, but he knew the dying always traveled in disguise. It saved embarrassing questions.

A Teddy bear, one of Hannah's babies, sat up on the back of an overstuffed chair. Someone had cut a hole in its balding fur belly and filled it in with dripping liver and a white carnation.

It struck him how much worse the house looked when you were trying to find something, seeking a lost object within a constellation of lost objects. Most days all the trash that filled their six rooms did not bother him: how could you throw anything away when you could no longer remember what was important enough to keep? Most of the world did not come with expiration dates, and in any case what was rot to those who could not quite smell or taste it? And with the exception of Hannah and him, what did not work today might certainly work tomorrow.

All of which might justify, he supposed, the three dozen or so radios in various states of disassembly that littered the floor, their corpses delved into by creatures hungry for sound.

Or the collection of drinking glasses from around the world. Holding dust—and what was dust but garbage ground so finely it became essence—that had traveled no less far.

Or the stacks of unread mailings from some of the country's finest mail order firms.

Or the rinds and crumbs from favorite meals. The soggy newspapers pressed by playful hands into faces, the used razors undisposed, the ruptured cushions full of rustling insects, the rusted bits of metal memorializing some traumatic unfastening, the stained cups full of ancient eyeglasses, the balls of greasy string, the collections of cut-out letters like a kit for kidnappers, the wooden blocks with indecipherable lettering, the enormous nests of hair, the animated wires, the endless, broken down shabbiness of the day-to-day.

Cherished or thrown, digested or left to smell, packaged or scattered, shed or glued or polished or grimed: it was all garbage with a shelf-life no longer than frail human memory.

"I'm hungry!" Hannah called out from somewhere ahead of him, accompanied by movement sounding like the tearing down of walls. He started to call back when soft bits tumbled out of his mouth to disappear into the general porridge of floor before he could identify them. Perhaps he had been eating, but he could not remember eating. And in any case he seemed to have lost the difference between garbage and food.

He could hear her pawing at doors, stumbling through passageways ahead of him. He found threads of shredded flesh on the doorjambs, clinging to the knobs like drying strips of pasta.

"Honey, I think you best settle down," he said, but his voice had a certain unfamiliarity, like a singer's voice he had never heard before. It was the strangest thing, because he had always believed that the voice that sounded inside your head when you spoke would always remain the same, even when those around you said it had aged past all recognizing.

Old gears gathered fearfully in the corners. They belonged in the garage, of course—he'd have to berate them later. Hannah had blocked the kitchen door with the battered trashcan. He apprehended it too late and stumbled, garbage scattering in panic over his shoes and across his path. There were things in the garbage that made no sense to him—neckties and dog collars and half a murdered chicken. He closed his eyes and pressed on.

He caught up with her in the kitchen. She was dancing as he had never seen her, a slow waltz with brooms and butcher knives. She'd managed to slice a great chunk off her left arm, and then mended the place with butcher paper and freezer tape. The black marker scrawl of letters A and G and B and E and F trailed off the edges of the paper, an attempt at labeling gone awry. "I love the sadness of the music," she cried, love in her eyes. Sam had to agree, but could not bring himself to reply.

Before he could stop her she had jerked open the cabinets, showering the floor with months of their discards: rotted vegetable flesh and blackened meats, a sculpture of spotted breads and green-skinned cheeses, the movement of worm and fly, the rich composty accumulation leaving him faint with impressive detail. He couldn't exactly remember putting the garbage in the cabinets, but he knew he had, thought Hannah had as well, the cans by the alley being so far away, and besides he knew he would miss it once he threw it away, since every passing month had become just another opportunity for missing things.

"Don't cry, my darling," Hannah whispered into his ear. He hadn't seen her approach.

"I wasn't weeping, honey," he replied through a screen of tears. She held his hands and led him into dancing—what was she thinking? She knew he'd always been a terrible dancer—and yet his feet did move, although so heavily, stomping and stomping the garbage into a rich brown wine.

"I'll never throw you away, *never,*" he spoke fiercely into her hair. He kept running his fingers through the thinness of it, unable to stop himself even when it fell away in waves.

"I *am so sour,*" she cried, rubbing her loose head against him in distress.

"Sweet smells are for fools," he said as strongly as he could, although he did not know if he truly believed this or not.

With a shout she stumbled backwards. His attempt to hold her upright only made matters worse: one of her arms split off at the shoulder, a leg bent wrongly and foul-smelling blood escaped her nose. Pain made her eyes fly open, her lips pulled forward as if trying to catch departing food. Her face began to discolor. Her face began to rust. His hands slipped trying to hold on to the moist grayness of her, and she was falling, calling *Sam* in a soft and passionate moan as she landed and was swept under by a tidal wave of the discarded.

Sam fell to his knees in the moist filth and frantically pushed the garbage aside. A thick brew of juices and spoilings slimed his hands and he thought he'd choke on the odor. But he uncovered bare red linoleum without uncovering her, and another hour's searching brought him nothing but stinking fingers and cramped knees.

There were things to be done, phone calls to be made and official types to be contacted. Sam didn't have the heart for any of this, and besides he had no idea what to say. He was a crazy old man. And like Hannah, he was slowly becoming garbage.

By the time midnight had come and gone and he had done nothing, he was pretty sure there was nothing he was likely to do. He sat on the living room couch and listened to the sounds of his own body, imagined he could hear fluids arriving, fluids going away, the breakdown of cells, the scattering of cellular integrity.

Movement began within the trash piled high in one corner, traveled along one wall, then across the rug in the center of the room, if there still was a rug in the center of the room. He had not seen it in months.

For a moment Sam wondered if it might be the cat, then realized he'd finally gotten rid of the cat. But perhaps it was yet another cat, some neighbor's cat who'd decided to move in with Sam now that Hannah was gone. The thought was unbearable and Sam began to cry. "It's all just … *garbage!*" He wailed. "You live in garbage and garbage is all that you become!"

At his feet the trash parted. Eyes of withered orange slices and the dark lips of cat turd. But something in the expression was still enormously inviting, although he'd never been able to figure out why. Something that made him want to lie down with her and sleep embraced by the long reach of memory and lives irrevocably entwined.

Those young kids, he thought, *they'd never understand.* He lay down in the garbage, rolled in the trash, and was swept away by the falling apart. For Sam loved Hannah. Hannah loved Sam. Hannah loved Sam. Sam loved Hannah.

HIDEOUT

Pennsylvania, Florida, Colorado, California. Bobby, with the help of his three friends, always made his secret hideouts the same way.

The green tunnel made a ninety degree turn left, then right, before opening up into the central chamber hidden in the densest part of the growth. Bobby's small hands had apparently pushed weeds aside and down and packed the earth firmly to form a solid floor. Longer stems had been twisted overhead to make a tight ceiling.

His name was McMahon. He was a tall man, and he had to crouch as he left the tunnel to enter the chamber. Only thirty-two years old, but so aware of his muscles protesting the exertion. For some reason this part of the tunnel was always the narrowest. McMahon had forgotten why. He stood and began brushing weed chaff and stickers from his tweed pants. He looked around the chamber. The broken cover of leaves and branches overhead lit irregular patches of ground. The objects in the darkest areas were hard to see.

A small patch of gray and yellow moved off to his left. It was Bobby. For once McMahon had come in time.

"Hello, Bobby," he murmured.

The little boy rose on his knees and looked up at McMahon. His face was in shadow. He returned to his hidden play without a word.

"Don't you think you should go back? Can't stay out here forever."

Bobby stood and walked over to McMahon, stopping a few feet away. He gazed large-eyed at the man, his mouth an expressionless line. "I'm never going back."

McMahon could see that Bobby's right cheek was bruised. Three lines of blood trickled down from a cut open over the cheekbone.

"I'm sorry, Bobby."

"So why are *you* sorry?" Bobby walked back into the shadows and sat down. He was doing something with his hands in the dirt.

McMahon grabbed a fold of cloth about each of his knees and pulled, at the same time crouching. He picked up a stick and began doodling absentmindedly in the dust.

"Oh, I think I know how you're feeling, Bobby. Your dad's hurt you, and ... it seems nobody cares about you, that you're all alone ... everything stacked against you." It seemed weak. After all this time thinking about it, he really didn't know what to say. He followed the stick with his eyes as he made a deep cross in the dirt. "I care, Bobby."

The little boy turned and scowled. "Why are you always following me?"

McMahon tensed his shoulders and stared at the ground. "Who's following whom?" One of his ex-wives had said that once.

"Will you stop it?"

"I was just trying to help." McMahon had stared at his feet.

She turned and snapped at him. "You just want to feel *noble*. That's why you pick such losers."

She thought he was a hypocrite. He thought she was emotionally handicapped. Maybe they were both right.

There was a dull clink of metal behind McMahon, followed by another. The sound was unmistakable.

The crippled girl had come out of the tunnel into the chamber behind him and was making her way around his crouched form awkwardly, sliding her braces along the ground and twisting herself between the crutches as if McMahon were something to be avoided at all costs. She plopped painfully down onto the ground beside Bobby. She had on the same dark blue dress with white trim McMahon remembered. Her yellow hair curled around her head like an aura.

Bobby and the girl began talking to each other quietly, entangling their hands, giggling.

"It'll be a big house, with plenty of woods around it. No one will ever bother us there."

McMahon wasn't sure whether he had actually heard that, or imagined it. "Bobby?" They were piling twigs at their feet. "Bobby, I want to talk to you." Bobby laughed and grabbed her hands, pulling. "Dammit, Bobby!" They both turned, and it seemed to McMahon the girl's eyes were pink, pupils and all. "Just because I'm an adult now you think I'm the enemy! You always were stubborn." McMahon sat down and crossed his legs. "You know, Bobby," he gestured toward the girl, "Cripples aren't always going to be fun to be around."

Bobby clenched his teeth, cheeks puffed. He turned his head abruptly in the opposite direction, and became quite still.

McMahon knew he was blowing it; he might never have another chance. He sighed audibly. "Bobby. I'm on *your* side. I wasn't talking about her legs. It's her other handicaps you have to protect yourself from." McMahon shook his head. "You're going to be meeting a lot of women like her in the future."

Bobby stood and held his hands down to the crippled girl. McMahon imagined dancing with her, his arms full of her, her pretty blue dress flapping in the wind. McMahon remembered dreaming this scene so many times. Her fragility entrusted to him alone.

The girl stood and Bobby guided her off to the side. They were giggling together again. McMahon crawled over to where they had been playing, snagging and tearing his pants in the process.

It was a miniature landscape of dried mud and twigs. A tall, spire-like structure rearing up from the center. Triangular windows. Alien landscapes. Bobby always had a home there. McMahon remembered imagining the house, on another planet, the friends there would be, yearning so hard for it, it always became real for him.

He watched the short alien crawl out of the underbrush and try to wrap an arm around his leg, then pushed it away in sudden disgust. He stole a frightened look at Bobby, then back to the little alien. The alien's eyes seemed to grow larger, its blue skin sickly, turning grayish on the sides of its enormous belly. It tried to squirm over to McMahon, squeaking hideously.

"Damn you, get away from me!" He slid backward a foot or so.

The alien seemed to be choking on something. McMahon was feeling nauseous. "No, Bobby!"

The alien was crying, trying to hold its enormous belly with spindly, webbed hands. It rolled back and forth in the dust.

"Bobby, stop it!"

Bobby and the crippled girl watched the alien silently.

The alien's torso was convulsing violently, its legs thrashing, making shallow furrows in the ground. McMahon was whispering to himself, almost a whisper. "The food and atmosphere had never been right for the little alien."

The alien was making gurgling sounds.

"It could never fit the pattern of this world."

A yellow tongue-like strip flashed in and out of the alien's mouth.

"And soon it died."

The little alien's thrashings ceased. No one moved. Thick yellow foam suddenly poured from the alien's mouth and made a large pool next to the body.

Bobby walked over and picked up the alien, stuffing it under his arm like a teddy bear. He reached up into the crook of a thin sapling and wedged the body there. Those large eyes were still open, staring down at the sapling's exposed roots.

McMahon's face was covered with sweat, his thin black hair plastered to his forehead. He watched his feet and said nothing.

After a while McMahon stood and cleared his throat. He brushed off his pants, pretending nothing had happened. Having just entered Bobby's hideout it was important to say the right thing; he had been looking for Bobby for twenty-five years.

"I know … you can take me to school with you Bobby, introduce me to your friends. I've… I've been married, Bobby, a few times, and I see a lot of women now, all the time in fact. We can show your friends some of them too. They never figured you'd ever have a girlfriend, did they? I know, you didn't think so either. And we can treat them to something; I have plenty of money now. What will they think of that, huh? To see how I've turned out. Women like me now, Bobby. Lots of women. They really do."

But Bobby wasn't listening. He was humming, playing gently with the crippled girl's hair.

"Bobby, listen to me!"

Bobby hummed more loudly to himself, as if he were trying to block McMahon completely from his mind. Bobby could be infuriating that way.

"Bobby... Bobby, I swear you *want* to be hurt!" Bobby hummed still louder, rocking his head side to side in time.

"You *let* people walk all over you!"

Bobby was talking to the crippled girl now, but so loudly, so obviously for McMahon's benefit, "I don't need *any* old men."

"Bobby!"

McMahon suddenly realized he had both fists raised over Bobby's head. Staring at his straining forearms in disbelief, he buried his face in his hands, and crumpled to the ground.

Had he always been so irritating? It was beginning to make more sense—how women could be both attracted, and repelled by a little boy like this. He suddenly realized how much *power* Bobby possessed. He had complete control over his small world. A control which would limit his life, McMahon knew how that would be, but which also allowed him to create fantasy solutions, tragi-comic companions when things got rough.

Arnold the Anteater dropped out of the highest branches into the middle of the chamber floor. He performed a somersault, almost losing his pink derby. His yellow bow tie glowed in the dim light. He staggered side to side from the weight of his enormous brown shoes. He stood still and lifted his long snout arrogantly, brushing the dust off his double-breasted blue suit with two, four-fingered, white-gloved hands.

Bobby and the girl were laughing and cheering.

Arnold crouched and jumped, landing right in front of McMahon, the large brown shoes slapping dust up into his face. Arnold examined McMahon's sad face, and then put a thumb in each ear, wagging out a snaky, pale pink tongue.

McMahon kept his face expressionless.

Arnold paced back and forth, his brow furrowed in concentration, his shoes making a slapping sound. At the apex of a turn he tripped himself and fell forward, his snout sticking pick-like into the ground.

Bobby laughed out loud; McMahon still said nothing. He had seen it so many times before.

Arnold grabbed his snout with both hands and pulled. No luck; it was as firmly wedged as ever. He planted a shoe on each side of his snout for leverage. His arms, legs, and back showed visible strain from the effort, his large rear quivering in the air.

The snout gave way. Arnold flew backwards through the air, knocking himself out on a tree branch. Visible stars encircled his head.

Bobby rolled on the ground laughing.

McMahon stood and walked over to the anteater's unconscious form.

The ex-wives never cared much for his fantasies. "You're so strange sometimes! Like a perverted little kid, dreaming about deformed babies, catatonics, and awful tortures.

"It's just, imagination…"

McMahon bent and prodded the snout. No reaction. Arnold was quite a character, one of the liveliest cartoon characters McMahon had ever seen. But this cartoon had never made it to the screen; Bobby had merely imagined it into being, a long time ago.

Bobby was looking at McMahon. So steadily, so quietly it gave McMahon an involuntary shiver. Arnold the Anteater got up off the ground. McMahon didn't say a word, just nodded slowly, when the anteater drew out a large knife and began cutting a hole in itself. At first there was nothing, then a trickle, then a gush of blood. The anteater began to howl, but still cutting, and watching Bobby's face anxiously.

"Bobby, cartoon characters don't bleed!" *The little martyr,* McMahon thought.

The blood disappeared. Arnold bent over backwards and pushed his head out through the hole in his stomach, wagging his tongue. "Wug-awuga!"

"I *know* they don't," Bobby said.

Arnold untwisted himself, clapped, then jumped back up into the trees. Exactly where, McMahon couldn't see.

Bobby folded his arms across his small chest.

"You're not going to let me help you, are you?" McMahon said. Bobby remained silent. "Bobby... you have to face your parents ... someday." Still no reply. "You have to be strong and... and be up front with them, with everybody. Say what you feel. Don't wall in your feelings. If they stay inside they'll *kill* you. I *know*! I know... Bobby." It was obvious to McMahon now; it wasn't going to do any good. Bobby was just a child. "You know... you won't be a child forever. You... *shouldn't* be a child forever."

Bobby's face was bleeding, first from the spot over his cheekbone, then from a gash in his forehead, his nose, a nick in his chin. The blood ran without clotting, soaking his clothes, matting the long edges of his black hair. He stood statue-like, his blue eyes penetrating.

McMahon felt his own face for the healed-over childhood scars. He could still feel the ones on his chin and nose, the ones that had taken the most stitches. He was sweating profusely now, and the sweat suddenly felt like blood.

"Bobby, *please!*" McMahon was sobbing.

But Bobby had gone back to his play with the crippled girl. The blood had disappeared. Bobby was holding a long stick, making doodles in the dusty ground.

The way out of the tunnel seemed more difficult than when McMahon went in. New growth seemed to have begun pushing its way into the opening of the green tunnel.

Robert McMahon, aged thirty-two, stumbled through the weeds and down the embankment to his car. The years drifted away from him, a replay of women, lost friends, connections too tenuous to hold because he had remained so insulated, so self-protected. He couldn't stop it. Even finding Bobby, he couldn't stop it.

When he got into the car he began carefully mopping the sweat off his face with a clean handkerchief, daubing the corners of his blue eyes to remove the grit.

A hundred yards down the hill from the hideout, construction crews were plowing over several acres for the new shopping complex. McMahon had been exploring the back road the day before for a good lunch spot when he had discovered the hideout.

It always seemed to happen that way. He'd leave a project looking for some solitude, and he'd stumble onto one of Bobby's secret places.

One of the foremen walked over to his car when McMahon pulled up to the office trailer.

"Should have that northern section plowed up by this afternoon, Mr. McMahon. Nothing up there, is there?"

McMahon gazed off in the direction of the hideout. "No... nothing at all."

"Fine." The burly foreman crossed his arms and took in the entire sweep of the site. "I wouldn't mind being part owner of a project like this, Mr. McMahon. No sir. You're going to be a mighty rich man."

"I suppose..." he said, wondering what, if anything, Bobby would think of that.

DAYTIMER

8 AM Talk to the lady in the park, even if she tries to run from me again. Emily and our daughter had the picnic by the statue of Jackson. Twenty years ago, but the lady would remember. A beautiful woman, my wife, and our beautiful child. Anyone would remember them, even after twenty years. Jackson still has his sword raised, as if intent on killing someone. Things never change, even after twenty years. Even after twenty years, I wait for them to come to me.

9 AM Walk the sidewalk along the park's outer edge. This was the way they would have come. So many trees along the way, creating shadow. Our daughter Jean, so afraid of the shadows. Shadows change, even as you watch. Shadows change everything. I cannot remember my daughter's face.

10 AM Check the sewer that runs under the park. Here it is large enough for a man, or two. Grates open to the sewer all along the sidewalks. Something might have fallen, might have rolled and slipped through the grate. Clues might still be found, even after twenty years.

11 AM Call Jean's friends. Again. Even though they are terrified when I call. Young women now, saw in a paper on a park bench that one of them was married last week. Didn't trust the look of her new husband in the picture. Twenty years ago, he would have been older than Jean. Almost a teenager. Teenage boys will do anything. They haven't learned how to stop themselves.

Noon. Stand at the center of the park. Listen for the dogs. Dogs were barking that day twenty years ago. Many times I hear the dogs barking. Large packs of them sweep down from the north, taking what food they can from garbage cans. Sometimes they attack old people, snatch babies in their jaws, find secret places for doing their secret animal things which no human has ever witnessed.

1 PM Seek out each child in the park. Look carefully at their faces. She might not have aged. Certainly in my mind she has not aged. Find out if any of the middle-aged women answer to the name Emily.

2 PM Crawl under a bush somewhere in the park and nap. Dream twenty years' worth of memories. Ask them where they've gone, why they haven't called, if I deserved them, if I deserved this and what I can do. Tell them I will do anything.

3 PM Pull the insects out of my hair. Comb the dirt and leaves from my beard. Lying under the bush I would scare anyone, especially in these ragged pants, this coat with the pockets missing. But who needs pockets anymore? I used to keep candy for my baby there, keys to the house. Each day I would jangle the keys, make faces, and give her the candy. She would laugh like music. My wife would kiss me, whisper in my ear. *You sweet man. You dear, sweet man.*

4 PM Check the park benches for the dead. Check under the bushes where the dead sleep, dreaming of their families. Ask the trees where they've gone. Make inquiries of the wind. Sometimes it *will* answer, if asked politely. Ask the couples passing by if they know my name.

5 PM Dance with the wind in thanks for its cooperation. Throw up my arms, let my mouth open and sing. Fall to the ground and roll through a hundred feet of flowers. Let the animals stare at me in wonder.

6 PM Watch the police shut down the park. A curfew, due to increased crime over the years. Watch them pull their coats tighter, gaze around nervously. Watch them stare at me, their slightly puzzled expressions, then watch them leave.

7 PM Examine this loose calendar page, blown by the wind, torn from someone's appointment book. I used to have one just like it, back when I had no clear understanding of the relative importance of things. It's completely blank, optimistically awaiting its appointments.

8 PM Try again to leave the park. Fail. Remember the panicked look on my wife's and daughter's faces when they looked down at me, and I was in so much pain. Remember. The terrible weight on my chest. And all I could worry about was how I had ruined our picnic together. We'd spent so little time together. I'd been so busy.

9 PM Remember.

THE ORCHARD

Something is wrong in the orchard.
Everything moves so quickly. Too quickly. The lunch hour over, Yancyville Park is an orchard once again, the clerks rushing from their spots beneath the trees, the technicians getting up from their sunny naps in the grass to return to work in the communications terrace, the gardeners trotting out to their orchard jobs, all knowing that the big day approaches, all trying to get ready, catch up, evolve. Trying to be ready and completely willing when the colony moves out into the distant cold stars.

I, too, am trying to be ready, trying to be willing. It is difficult for me to adapt to such speeds.

But now something is terribly wrong in the orchard. Something doesn't fit. I can feel it. I've spent a great deal of time in this place; I've always felt relaxed here—the only place in this colony where I've ever felt at peace. Yet now, for some reason, I'm overcome with dread each time I enter the orchard. I grow anxious; my palms sweat. If I wasn't so committed to performing my job, to doing my share in this endeavor, I know I would drop my tools and run, never to return to the orchard. I am afraid I may be about to lose my sanctuary.

Perhaps some intruder, some alien presence? Perhaps a straggler, someone late for his shift? Wasn't that a rustling in one of the peach trees? A sudden movement, there? No, just a bicycle. I scan the distant horizon where it curves upward in the colony. It wouldn't have been the distant movement there I felt, or on the residential terraces climbing part way up the right wall. I gaze out at the small apartment areas down center, ringed by crop-gardens and statuary. No movement there.

I'm usually one of the first to arrive after my other job, but I've been having some problems with one of the new satellite components. I'd work the orchard fulltime if I could—at least I felt that way until recently—but the labor shortages have always left that a dream; the bureaucratic difficulties with Earth slowed the influx of new colonists to a trickle this past year, and soon new colonists will be impossible anyway.

There …. there! Along Wilson's Wall, a small creature climbing down …what is it?

It's only one of Hatchett's mutated squirrels. He keeps a few down in this part of Yancyville, more I'm told in the other communities. He's been trying to adapt a few to zero gravity out near the hub; I'm told their acrobatics are truly impressive … should make it out there sometime. He's been saying these squirrels, and the birds and lizards he's brought along, are already showing some adaptation in the offspring.

But still… something's wrong here. I know. I always seem to know when things are wrong.

It's getting busy now, and my anxiety lifts a bit. I must get to my work. A bright red … blue … behind that stand of corn. But they're gliders in the distance after all, circling the central elevator tower shining in its ceramic and aluminum decorations. I look for the near edge of the Yancy window—I always do that when I feel agitated—and beyond that, seeking a strange comfort from one of the larger asteroids hanging out in the darkness and stars. That view always stops me; the asteroid pulls my gaze down to the orchard beneath it, this orphaned vegetation from Earth. I close my eyes and imagine the orchard on a planet's surface, the colony vanished, and this asteroid some moon, or, better, sun, providing an alien illumination and source of life for these plants and animals in their new, adopted world. It is a hopeful image, and it consoles me. I try to hold on to it as long as I can.

It makes me giddy; I wonder if I've been here too long. Or perhaps, not long enough, But the desperate rushing about—I can't be the only one who feels unprepared. I can't be the only one who isn't… ready. I do want to go; I'm sure this recent nervousness, this sudden reluctance is only a temporary thing. And the nightmares ... should pass.

Again, anxiety washes over me like a light, cold rain. This isn't the first time I've felt this in the orchard. I am often anxious. The counselor tells me such feelings are to be expected in this environment. The colony has generated a number of new neuroses, the best known being the Solipsism Syndrome—new colonists sometimes evidence a great deal of tension because it seems everything is under their control up here, too much under their control. That was one reason I've gotten jobs like the orchard work in the first place—my counselor put in a special recommendation. The plants grow; you can't always predict how. It is comforting.

Yet something is still wrong here. Something doesn't fit. Not exactly a presence, I think now. But something is terribly wrong.

I find I want to attend to my plants immediately, feed-and trim them, care for them, prepare them for the long journey. I've said often that the plants up here are changing; Hatchett understands, but not everyone believes me. It's always been that way: people who speak the uncomfortable truth are never believed. We must watch the changes carefully; perhaps not all of them will be desirable. I grow afraid sometimes when I think of all the possible changes. In plants, in people. It seems to me I have been saying the same warnings over and over again.

But that the plants and animals can change gives me some faith that people can live in the colonies. People, too, can change for the better. Perhaps I myself can outgrow my fears and reluctance.

Everything changes here; I wonder how different we'll be by arrival time. The animals and humans here detached from their ancestry, and these plants, likewise detached from their Mother Earth. What work has to be done, before any of us can feel at home again?

The miniature trees are my own responsibility. I ponder their slight changes closely. I couldn't tell as much from a larger tree. Repotting, shaping, arranging the diverse species in order to achieve harmony, avoiding competition, antagonism. I've learned my lessons from the Japanese flower arrangers.

But something is wrong here; something in the orchard does not fit. I sometimes feel I can almost grasp it; I sense that it is something I know, yet do not know. It eludes me. I continue to work on a dwarf cypress, trying to ignore the strangeness I feel. I'm suddenly angered by my own paranoia. My part of the orchard provides the only privacy I've had, the only peace I've needed. And when the area is scheduled as the orchard no one may trespass against my solitude. There's so much to do here and even though I know this process cannot be rushed the general excitement has had me quickening the pace with trembling hands.

And now, to feel this … strangeness about. It's intolerable!

I've been twisting the trunk of the cypress with a brace and wires to imitate the wind-swept look. Now today I carefully wire one branch out and down to imitate a natural droop—all to duplicate in miniature the old tree in a photograph I have hanging on my bedroom wall. It stood on my family's farm for generations before the pollution finally killed it. At one time I believed I might never have a home like the home of my childhood. But in the colonies, anything might be possible. I could recreate my family's farm somewhere beyond the solar system. I could have my old home place back.

If only I'm brave enough, if my imagination's strong enough.

Weather changes here are slight and dull, but sufficient to be of some interest to my plants. The artificial changes in illumination can be deceiving; I can see shadows that weren't there moments before. But still, something seems amiss; something is wrong in the orchard.

I'm suddenly afraid for my position here, as if this presence might change things. Perhaps they wouldn't let me go with them? I've tried other things during my stay; most of us have. Perhaps we're all misfits, we who garden. At first I worked in the children's nurseries, and then I moved to the stock-breeding chambers. Just five years ago I supervised one of the fish ponds in the agricultural section. It's the unexpected, unplanned-for quality of these activities I find necessary. "A controllable range of unpredictability," my counselor says. You don't know how a life will turn out; there will always be surprises.

Something must grow.

I worry sometimes about saboteurs, rival factions. Is that what's bothering me now? One issue facing the Agronomy Association is whether our limited land space justifies the expenditure of time and energy on so-called purely decorative plantings. For that reason, many of our gardeners use crop or fruit trees in their art. Carter and Gould take care of the dwarf apple and peach. Ballard plants corn stalks in house planters, tomatoes in window boxes, and a mixture of parsley, broccoli, and chard into irregular nooks and crannies. Each weekend you see colonists combing the landscape, peering into the unlikeliest corners for Ballard's semi-hidden little treasures. The regular crop-supplies out of the agrozones are higher quality, but Ballard's are highly prized because of their novelty.

Wilson uses his wall for espalier gardening and if it were up to him the orchard would be a labyrinth of walls and trellises suitable for his two-dimensional effects. His fruit trees grow flat against the wall (allowing even ripening), and are trained into such shapes as palms, T's, U's, candelabra. Currently he's doing T's and U's, the wall greenly inscribed TUTUTUT.

There are some in the colony who would cut funding completely to all but foodstuffs. Could they be the source of my agitation? But I can see all the other gardeners, the crop-growers: Ballard, Carter, Gould, Wilson. They seem innocent enough. What's got into me?

The people rush about; it must almost be time for the evening shifts. So soon—I've been paying so little attention. It's hard to leave. Soon the orchard will become a park again for the evening strollers, the lovers out becoming acquainted, whispering one to another. At least there's consolation there, to give up my beautiful orchard for that.

There ... there it is again, an uneasiness, an uneasiness rippling through the park with the slight artificial breeze. A young couple is walking ahead of me, by some bushes. Is the problem there? They look around nervously, with vague expressions of uneasiness. Perhaps a terrorist, planning to rip our delicate bubble of air?

That seems ridiculous, yet why do I feel such unease?

In just a few weeks they'll be turning the rockets on. The colony will be moving, always moving, out into the black with stars. But so many of the lovers stroll unconcernedly, as if they don't know what is ahead of them.

The two lovers look around again. Nervous. Agitated. Somehow I know the trouble has something to do with those two young people. Something is wrong in the orchard. Something doesn't fit, and I think I am coming closer to finding it.

I cross the open grass, quickly. I step carefully, silently behind the lovers. The agitant, the wrongness here, feels just out of grasp.

The lovers are so unaware of the changes which have already occurred to them, the changes in mental perspective and perception which will one day translate into actual, physical changes. They are young; they don't know. They are a very different breed from myself.

As one who changes so awkwardly, so painfully—I should know.

Our bodies are living memories of all the changes. The colony is fast becoming one more link in a chain leading the colonists into their final selves. It sculpts them slowly, more slowly even than my plants are sculpted, but this adventure transforms them just the same.

So fast, so rapid the movement—I'm afraid if I blink I'll miss it. The wrongness, the strangeness will elude me; I'll be standing here alone with empty arms.

Something is terribly wrong in the orchard. Something does not fit. And when the lovers turn suddenly, I almost collapse in fright, their eyes wild, their faces angry. What are you doing! he shouts, and I am speechless to answer, though it is only my sudden presence which bothers them; I have been doing nothing wrong.

They leave me alone—for I am the intruder, the strangeness, the wrongness here—to cry by myself under the trees in the orchard. They are the adapted plantings, the ones who will survive this dark and lengthy voyage. I do not belong; I do not fit. It is so hard for me to change, hard to make friends, hard to leave what I have known.

The lovers stroll, the park lights dazzle like stars within the small trees, so brilliant they hurt my eyes when I look up out of Yancyville window and see, what is it, this orchard seeming to rise into the dark, dragging me, the wrongness, along.

THE DOORS OF HYPERTEXT

His brother told Cole to just type on the keyboard whatever he was thinking about, anything at all, as long as it had something to do with his life and who he was. But *everything* had something to do with his life, so he just typed and typed, sometimes for hours at a time, everything that came into his head.

Cole typed crudely at first, hunting letters and pecking them out—he'd never taken typing in school and had no experience with computers whatsoever. But the persistence, the relentlessness of his entries improved his skills rapidly, so that after a few months his fingers danced across the keys, caressing, slapping, and taking no prisoners.

At first he hadn't fully understood why his brother had put him to this task. He'd figured that a large part of it had been just a sense of responsibility: Cole had had emotional problems of one kind or other since his teen years, which had rendered him chronically unemployable. Jim, on the other hand, had worked his way through graduate school, seeing everything he touched turn to money, and now he owned a major software firm specializing in databases, in particular "hypertext."

Cole hadn't heard from his brother in several years when he got this call from him asking—no, begging him, practically—to come over to his company for a chat. Cole hadn't left his small apartment in weeks—he'd started having this feeling again that people were having secret thoughts about him, that somehow they knew more about his life than he did, and that there were pages and pages full of text about him and his life that he'd never known about, but someday he was going to pick up the newspaper and every word in the newspaper would be about him, even the captions and the dialog in the comic strip section.

But he hadn't had any sort of family in years. And the need in him for family was even greater than his fear of other people.

The day Cole first arrived at his brother's software company a huge party was going on, spread out over the entire suite of offices. Cole was in a panic, facing a wall of people he was convinced would crush him if they were to permit him into their midst at all. He'd turned to leave when he was grabbed from behind and whirled around. He was hyperventilating and his vision grew foggy, but he recognized his brother, looking young as ever.

"Cole, you old rascal!" Much to his dismay his brother was pounding him on the back. Cole didn't think anyone had ever done that to him before—he didn't quite know how to take it. But it was worse when Jim wrapped him in a bear hug. Cole liked it, but he was also embarrassed by the gesture. He could hardly breathe. He thought he was going to faint.

"Jim … Jim." It was all he could say. He thought he was going to cry. He didn't think he could live if he cried in front of all those people. He wanted to find a door and leave, or at least hide behind it.

His brother apparently could see what Cole was going through, and took him by the arm, introduced him to people, filling in the gaps with small talk when it became obvious Cole had nothing to say. He could only respond with nervous jerks of the head. Cole assumed he was making a spectacle of himself, was no doubt embarrassing all of Jim's employees, but he really couldn't bring himself to look at any of them long enough to tell.

It had been like this for years. He simply could not believe he was like other people; he wouldn't know where to begin to find any sort of commonality. Other people were doors he could not open.

After the party Jim said he had a job for Cole. He said it might even make him feel good about himself again. Cole wondered if it was in fact Jim who wanted to feel good about his little brother again.

After nearly a year Cole at least had some idea of what hypertext was: a knowledge system, text interconnected by a network of nodes, links, and cross-references. Certain words became "doors": open them up and they'd tell you their secrets. You'd find definitions and explanations, but more significantly, more "doors." Sometimes you'd open door after door and it would be as if you were in this endless dream house of ideas, a big old ramshackle palace of a place with ancient and modern sections blending surrealistically together because of all the remodeling that had been done, so that you were completely lost, you couldn't get out, and much of the time you didn't even want to get out.

Some of those doors might lead to pictures, although not initially in the convoluted hypertext of Cole's life. Jim told him he should get a substantial number of the words down first, but after the first year Jim showed him the expensive scanner, which Cole would use to create doors with pictures: photographs from his past, drawings, images clipped from magazines, books, and catalogs. Sometimes the juxtapositions of all these images would drive Cole into a frenzy of work as the associations triggered secrets and memories long buried and forgotten.

Occasionally Jim would attempt to explain why he was paying him to record his life in this fashion, but for the most part Cole wasn't particularly interested in the "whys." He had become obsessed with the shifting interconnectedness of "what is,"

Jim was always trying to explain how theirs was a new sort of hypertext system, an intelligent, expert system which linked Cole's recollections with a vast reservoir of general, factual references. This system could determine where new doors should be in this growing mountain of remembrance and association, and make the decision to create these doors without any input from a human operator, such as Cole himself.

"Maybe it'll give you some focus, Cole. Help you connect. Successful lives have a hierarchy-—they're not random affairs at all!" Jim would wave his hands about in the air like a minister when he explained things, gesturing toward heaven. "You just need to know where the doors are. Your *life* might be the ultimate test for the software! Just think of that! You can make a real contribution, and figure out what's gone wrong with your life at the same time!"

Cole just nodded and looked at the books and magazines and notes he surrounded himself with. Of late he'd become impatient with Jim's explanations—they kept him away from the keyboard and his own research into his convoluted mind. "Whatever you say, big brother." With his nose in a book he waved his hand over his head, as if conducting some counter musical theme. "I owe you a great deal for all of this. I'm glad I can repay some of it." And then he would run to the scanner to add some vague image or impression to the network.

Doors within doors within doors. After a year Cole grew tired of filling them, of opening and closing them all the time. Besides, he seemed to have nothing new to enter.

Except his name. He initiated a query, a beginning point from which the network of his life might unravel. QUERY. He typed in his name. COLE BLACKMORE. Press ENTER. Working...

Words and phrases, associations and doorways to more associations began filling his screen.

His mother had always smelled of apples. Genus *Mains* of the Rose family. Rose was his mother's name. Fruit is a firm, fleshy structure taken from the receptacle of the flower. Firm, sweet, flesh, Sweet apples. Delicious. Washington Delicious. Jonathan. Cort-land. Gravenstein. Kissing his mother on the pale flowers of her mouth as she lay in her coffin. She used to say when she was pregnant with him she couldn't get enough of them. The apples. Apple pie and apple brown betty.

Betty Grable—that's who she looked like. He hadn't realized that until the actress's picture came up on the monitor. He'd had posters of Betty Grable, and he used to watch her movies on the Late Late Show all the time—he thought she was just about the most gorgeous woman who'd ever lived. But he'd never made the connection before. His mother. His mother and Betty Grable. Biting the apple that feeds you. The sweet taste, the hard caress.

This was just too much. A little frightened, he sat back and looked at the screen. It was as if the program were reading his mind. Doors within doors within doors, but did he really want all those doors opened?

"What do you mean you're quitting? You can't quit now! We're *close*, Cole, *damn* close. Why do you think you've been entering all that stuff the last couple of years? Just writing your damn memoirs? We're poised for a breakthrough in intelligent software and you're going to *quit*? You're going to stab your own brother in the back? Quitting like you've done everywhere else? Afraid to look anyone in the face? Quitting *me*?"

"Jimmy..."

"My name is Jim."

"Jim, I'm sorry. Really I am. It's just that it's making me so anxious. I'm reading along on something I put in there and then it jumps me someplace else and insists that these things are related somehow and I know it's telling me the truth, but I just don't know if I can handle that much truth in my life right now. It just keeps opening door after door and I don't want to see what it's coming up with behind those doors but I can't help but look."

Jim became quiet and leaned forward, and Cole knew his brother was getting ready to be calm and purposeful, like one of the doctors at the hospital. "The program doesn't *insist* anything, Cole. It doesn't tell a *truth*. It's just a piece of software. An idea processor, if you will. In that way it can *teach* you things, but it will teach you things based only on what you entered originally. There's really nothing here to be afraid of."

Despite himself, Cole reluctantly agreed that he was probably overreacting. He would continue to help with his brother's project. He owed him that much. Later that afternoon he shut himself in with his terminal. Jim arranged to have meals sent in to him, even though Cole hadn't asked him to.

He started typing. QUERY: THINGS THAT WENT WRONG.

His dad's old Chrysler. The back window catch. His mother's vacuum cleaner. The built-in dishwasher: fixed a dozen times and never once right. The Chrysler again. The plumbing, again and again. The light switch in his bedroom that almost electrocuted him after a shower when he was sixteen. The lawnmower. The Chrysler again. Several TVs, none of them lasting more than five or six years and his dad blaming him for turning the channels too often, too quickly. Four toasters. Six coffee pots. His dad's old Chrysler again. A broiler oven that hadn't worked since the first day they got it...

Cole halted the listing. He considered a moment, and then started typing again. QUERY: MOMENTS IN MY LIFE WHEN A MISTAKE WAS MADE THAT WOULD DAMAGE ME PSYCHOLOGICALLY.

His dad's old Chrysler. At first he thought he'd worded the query incorrectly and that he was going to get the same output as before, but then he started receiving some different text.

Chrysler, Walter Percy. Originally a machinist. Worked his way up, resourceful, clever like Cole's father, who had accumulated a small fortune through hard work. Except Jim had always called it stubbornness. Meanness. He'd tried to manage the lives of everyone who came into contact with him, Jim said. Walter Percy Chrysler became manager for the American Locomotive Company, switched to automobiles, president of Buick in 1916. In 1922 joined Maxwell, which in 1925 became the Chrysler Corporation.

A photograph of his dad's Chrysler flashed on the screen. Like some kind of ancient cat, grill rusty but still grinning. Cole used to think it would devour him one day. Carnivore. Flesh-eaters. *Car-nivora.* Dogs, cats, weasels. His father had loved that car, and there had been no question, not even any discussion, about the fact that his father had loved the car more than he'd loved his own family. Films from Driver's Ed class, images thrown up on his monitor screen of bodies burned black, the tender pink inside, heads through windshields streaming blood. *Death on the Highway.* Then his father's old Chrysler up on the screen, the twisted metal wreck of ancient cat, the way the grill teeth had been smashed in, and in the window...

Cole blanked the screen, unable to proceed. He turned and looked at the door, ready to get up and leave, then found he could not. He turned back to the keyboard and keyed the sequence back to the image of his father's Chrysler. It made him feel suddenly personally powerful, as if he'd been able to turn back the clock at his command, the car straightening out its bends, reassembling itself, his life reassembling itself.

QUERY: PARTS?

It should have been a safe sequence, a way to kill time while he readied himself for his father's death again.

Internal combustion engine. Gasoline. Spark ignition. Anger. Fury. Rage.

He stopped the sequence and backed up a bit. Liquid-cooled, four-stroke cycle. The words appeared like the unveiling of a poem. Overhead valve, carbureted, reciprocating type. Four-stroke cycle.

Stroke. Caress. Embrace. The way his mother held him at his father's funeral. A picture of them together flashes up on the screen: the way she holds her arms around him, the way she inclines her head.

Head gasket. Manifold. Reciprocating engines. Mix gasoline with air. Spark ignition. Oil and water don't mix. His father's voice retrieved, crackling on the computer speaker as if from some long distance, as if from beyond the grave. His father used to say that all the time. It described the relationship with Mother. It described Jim and Cole's relationship. Always so different. Always on the verge of combustion, just a little more gasoline needed in the mix.

Pistons. Crankshaft. Converts the reciprocating motion of the pistons into rotary motion. Anger converted into hate. Smoldering passion into a drive for action.

Front-mounted engine used to drive the rear wheels. Steering system. Steering arms, wheel supports. Brake system, master cylinder, brake lines. Pressure of the fluid forces the brake shoes to press against the drums. Drum, drum, beating as Jim throws another fit. Driving off in their father's car. The list of repairs that had to be made on the screen. Quarter panel, fender, transmission. His father's rage taken in drum blows to Jim's face and chest. Jim clutching at his face, clutching at his father's arm to make him stop.

Clutch. A device for connecting and disengaging the engine. Clutch and hold and pull away. A listing of the times he could recall his father holding him, holding Jim, holding their mother. Clutch and connect, engage and then disengage. His mother clutching at him, weeping hysterically, and Cole doesn't know what to do. He's only sixteen. She wants him to drive her somewhere but he can't drive. He'd always felt uncomfortable in automobiles, vulnerable. Only Jim and his father can drive.

Drive shaft. Connects the transmission with the differential. So many differences in their family. An arrangement of gears that allows the wheels to rotate at different rates when the car is turning. Different strokes for different folks. Jim was always saying that. His voice comes over the computer speaker, saying that again, a perfect simulation of the young Jim's voice. But Jim actually hadn't been so different from their father. The same calculating abilities, only Jim had used them to become a rich man. Cole had been like their mother. Jim like their father. The drive, the powerful drive of those two. The ruthlessness.

A list of Jim's assets flashed up on the screen. He hadn't realized the system had access to those financial records. And he hadn't realized his brother was so wealthy. But there were vulnerabilities, he noticed, serious vulnerabilities, such as the vast amount invested in this particular hypertext project.

A slip joint and a universal joint in the drive shaft. These allowed the drive shaft to change its length and direction as the car wheels moved up and down. Up and down. A close-up view. Vulnerabilities there. Oil and water. Gasoline and a spark. A memory typed in a year ago without even thinking, now flashed up at the center of the screen:

I remember the night before the accident. Jim had been in the garage late, working on our father's car. The next morning, I asked him what he'd been doing, and he smiled and said he was going to surprise the old man for Father's Day, with a much smoother running car. Then I remembered it *was* Father's Day and I'd completely forgotten it, and how mad my father was going to be. But Jim had thought of everything, Jim was going to be the hero. But surely there were certain risks involved in what he had done, certain vulnerabilities.

Up and down. The picture of his father's wrecked car appeared on the screen again. The twisted grinning grill and broken windows. And where a window should have been, his father's head propped up, grinning, grinning a bright red grin.

Now there was a picture of the twisted, grinning Chrysler grill.

Now there was a picture of Jim taken a few years after the accident, just as he was starting his own software company. His door was open: Cole could see him at last for who he really was. Jim had always been so clever with machines. The twisted grin on his face. Carnivorous Chrysler grin. He'd had complete control over the money after their mother committed suicide and Cole was ruled incompetent and sent to the state hospital. Cole's mother hanging there, the broken rod, the crushed fender, slip joint, the shaft changing its length. All Cole could think to do was slam as many doors shut as he could, and hide in the dark. Cole had been unable to help her—she'd desired too much from him. Too many doors. Doors within doors within doors.

Cole's own picture flashed onto the monitor screen. It was the picture taken of him when he first entered the hospital. Dark eyes, a confused look on his face. It looked as if he never slept, and so was forced to view his bad dreams while he was awake.

Cole stared for some time at that image of himself on the monitor. He imagined he must look very much like it at the moment. He must look very much the image of the classic madman.

His brother had killed their father, designed it like an efficient piece of software. He'd killed their father and that had destroyed their mother, which in turn had almost destroyed Cole. He could feel all the doors in his head trying to slam shut, as if the rooms behind them could contain no more.

But he couldn't let them close now. Cole couldn't go back to that way of life.

He went to one of the filing cabinets against the wall and pulled out a file of pictures and newspaper clippings concerning his brother. One at a time he scanned the images of his brother into the computer's memory. He overlaid these images, musing vaguely that by this method he would somehow discover how many faces his brother really had. He began entering words across his brother's face, words like *traitor,* and *bastard,* and *scum.* His brother, who had once been so perfect, so dependable, so honorable. He pounded on the keyboard, doors of text, houses of text filling the screen until the terminal started beeping at him, squealing at him to stop, screaming...

"Hey, bro? Don't beat it to death!" Cole twisted in his chair to see Jim striding confidently into the room, every inch the high-level executive. "Working hard? Or hardly working?" His brother's grin twisted and gleamed. Cole longed to see it crash. His brother leaned over the monitor and nodded at the garbage there as if it were the most interesting thing he had ever seen. "So, how goes the battle? What's this stuff, anyway?"

Cole thought to tell him, *Why, it's your deceit, brother,* but he did not.

But what good would it do? And how could he prove to others what he knew? The hypertext connections were too fluid, practically unrepeatable, a product of the moment. There was no way he could establish an acceptable chain of evidence,

Besides he didn't feel bad about his father being dead. He hadn't felt bad about it even at the time.

His brother Jim would probably just laugh at him, or get Cole into the hospital again. His brother Jim was laughing now. "Abstract art? Is that what you're doing? Is that *my* face under all that garbage?"

To his own surprise Cole started laughing along with his brother. Maybe he would learn some deceit of his own. He thought of slamming the door in his brother's face, and never opening it again. But he'd done enough of that. He'd become a hermit thanks to what his brother had done. He'd kept all those doors closed; he'd been alone, a friend to no one. But if he could keep the doors open now, maybe he would find the secrets of someone else's heart, besides his brother's. The good secrets. Perhaps even the good secrets of his own heart.

"Well, won't bother you again. You're turning into a real workaholic, little brother, and I *like* that." Jim headed for the door.

Maybe if he kept the doors open, he'd find out enough about his brother to make him pay someday. Make him pay long past the point at which it began to hurt.

Cole sat down at the keyboard again. He typed QUERY. COLE BLACKMORE. Then he inserted a processing command:

MAKE EXTENDED USE OF EARLIER LINKS AS POSSIBLE.

He watched his picture grow until he was seeing the individual dots. Then one individual dot grew in size until it filled the screen.

There followed a stream of data taken from his health records, genetic tests, ancestral data, religious beliefs, his psychologist's files on him, his school essays, his thoughts on all subjects imaginable, entered during his years at this keyboard, the expert component of the system making doors and choosing doors at lightning speed, creating link after link after link, and the whole time Cole didn't have to touch the keyboard at all, couldn't have even if he'd wanted to.

Doors within doors within doors. Behind one of those doors would be Jim's punishment. Behind another would be the passage which would lead Cole back to his own life, and to the secret hearts of the rest of humanity, from whom he had been so long estranged.

IN ALL THINGS MODERATION

Rebecca could feel the network around her, pulsing just beyond the tree tops, sending its reverberations through the short wheat about her bare calves. She could hear it singing to let with that little-used part of her mind, faintly distorted by the sound of the wind ruffling the trees.

That part of her mind was singing to her, and she soon found herself swaying to its tune, humming spontaneously. The rhythm caught her body in its grip, taking her arms and throwing them up over her head, sending her feet suddenly out of control. Her feet danced the wheat down, dancing on their own …

The small group of women gathered in Goody Putnam's house was tense, nervous over the gravity of its deliberations. Goody Putnam herself found it difficult to meet the other women eye-to-eye. She gazed through the leaded panes of the narrow windows, hoping perhaps to find an answer there, then searched the exposed roof rafters, counting the cobwebs. She should have cleaned better before the meeting. What would they all think of her?

"Looking for spirits there to help you, Goody?" Abigail Smith asked with a laugh. "Or the Devil?" She slapped her thigh.

"Quiet, Abigail!" Sarah Matthews cried. "There be serious deliberations to be made here by us all. Cannot blame Goody for being so agitated. You act as if it were sport!"

"What's to decide?" Abigail leaned forward from her hard chair and laid her elbows on the small table. "While we talk, the rest of the village be getting ready to go to the meeting house to hear accusations against our Rebecca!"

"She be far too willful!" Goody Putnam cried out suddenly, rocking back and forth. "She lacks control!"

Several other women nodded silently, watching the older woman out of the corners of their eyes. For all her talents, Goody Putnam had not lately been well. Sometimes her erratic behavior embarrassed them all.

Rebecca danced herself into a frenzy, her feet pounding the wheat flat, her eyes raw and burning. She was blinded by the dazzling power contained within the web of the network. Her mouth was dry as dust, her throat raw with a continuous scream silent to all save herself.

Suddenly, she stopped all movement and raised her head at an odd angle, stretching her neck, her eyes wide as if she were looking for something in the distance. She could feel the network building in strength about her, focused by her dance.

She knew the others would frown on what she was doing. She'd used far more than her share of the network's power already this week. But she couldn't help it; when the power filled her she gave no thought to the possible consequences. It did too much for her. It filled her head and her loins with a brilliant white light.

Besides, the women were too cautious. They always seemed to have something to worry about, whether that be the superstitious reaction of the other villagers or the way their skill in manipulating the network was waning with age.

She thought perhaps they were jealous of her.

"I tell ye, it's your doing our Rebecca's in such a strait, with all the villagers suspecting her," Priscilla cried, standing up from her bench despite the entreaties from the women sitting beside her. She looked directly at Abigail Smith, so angry she was shaking. "My daughter was nearby when you told that Reynolds woman how you'd heard tell that Rebecca had been seen dancing naked with the Devil in the glade."

At that, a number of women in the room burst into laughter.

"That's a good one, Abigail!" Hannah cried, trying to hold

back the tears of laughter. "Sounds just like the superstitious folk. I expect you told her Rebecca'd been spoiling milk and engaged in the making of deformities as well?"

"It be a lie!" Abigail shouted. "I ne'er said the thing."

Several of the women began shouting all at once, leaping to their feet, some of the angriest even taking a few steps toward an adversary. Goody Putnam rocked in her corner, crying softly to herself, calling down a spell of peace which would not come.

"That be enough!" Sarah cried. The women halted almost instantly. Sarah was the most talented among them, and often served as a leader in matters of such import. They returned to their seats with eyes downcast. "You ought to be ashamed, Abigail Smith, spreading such tales and encouraging the villagers' superstitions."

Abigail stared at her feet, saying nothing.

"The spreadin' of such tales be a serious matter in and of itself, Abigail," Sarah murmured.

Abigail Smith looked up, the fear evident in her wide eyes and tightly drawn lips.

Rebecca drew the network into herself with a sudden inhalation of all her senses. Quickly she pinpointed her mind on a vast grid within her imagination, allowing all her attention to focus on that point, allowing herself to be both grid and point. Then she filled that point with a dazzling white light which radiated outward until it had filled the entire grid. She watched the point closely within her mind, and sighed joyfully when the vague, shimmering outlines of a flower began to form there. The entire grid quickly filled with the ghostly, coruscating flowers, and she was compelled to cry aloud.

When she opened her eyes, the wheat had been replaced by a field of bright yellow, blue, and red flowers with enormous petals. She danced among the flowers, picking them and tossing them into the air, letting their exotic fragrances fill her.

Who could resist such beauty? How could her sisters think she could ever limit her use of this? The network was meant to be used!

Abigail Smith had regained her confidence and spoke to the group with conviction tinged with bitterness. "Rebecca is deserving of all troubles coming her way. She's violated the code. I been to my assigned section of the woods to practice the arts twice this week, and there be no power in the air, nothing for my use at all! Rebecca had drained off the network from my part; she'd used far more than her rightful share o' the grid!"

A number of the women mumbled agreement.

"She took off my rightful share of the network a week ago Tuesday," Priscilla said.

"And mine two rounds past," Hannah added.

"There be deeds need doing in the woods for us all," Abigail cried, "but we cannot get our fair share of the power when the woman uses up the air, then flaunts her disobedience of our rules right afore our eyes!"

Goody Putnam began to wail aloud, her voice rising and falling rhythmically. Her bench began to rise with her on it, tilting until it had almost spilled her out. The broom in the corner next to her began a slow dance.

Sarah Matthews closed her eyes sadly. After a moment, the broom stopped dancing, the bench floated to rest, and Goody Putnam's cries became muffled as if under an invisible cloak.

Rebecca lay among the flowers, drawing even more power out of the grid. She laughed half-guiltily. It was obvious to her now that part of the joy of using the power was merely evading some of the rules her sisters had attempted to impose upon her. How could anyone regulate the grid? Such a joy should be free for the use of anyone with the talent.

She let the excess power from the network drain into the flowers, making their colors and sizes change every few seconds. Periodically, she would stop and survey the new arrangement. Then, dissatisfied, she would let the flowers transform further. Occasionally, she would add a few small animals—squirrels and such—to enjoy the flowers with her.

"It be a bad habit she has," Priscilla was saying, "and it can come to no good purpose either for us or her. The woman will not control her use o' it. I see nary a way to stop her with mere talk."

"She'll end up a black one," Hannah agreed. "Listen on it. Once she enjoys the power that much, next she'll be using it in other causes."

"But our Goody almost came to such blackness," Sarah said, looking over at the confused old woman. "Yet she was able to stop herself in time."

"But Goody and Rebecca be two different spirits, Sarah," Abigail replied. "Rebecca be more headstrong than were Goody. The blackness seems likely. That … or she'll end up like Goody be now, havin' used the power so much it's made her feeble-minded, used up an' half-mad. Surely it be one or t'other. And if it be the blackness, who be there to stop her? Her use o' the network makes her stronger each day!" There was an uneasy silence in the group. It was thought ill-mannered to discuss poor Goody's plight.

Suddenly, Goody was standing, her hair awry, waving Sarah's cloaking spell out of the way with frantic hands and screeching at the top of her lungs. "I be like her! Like Rebecca! It be too much, the power! Stop her! Stop her now!"

Rebecca allowed the grid power to envelop her. Her mind turned white-hot and blazing with light. She felt the light curling under her like a wave, then the wave lifting….

She rose ten feet over the field of flowers.

Sarah Matthews watched as the other women calmed Goody, lulling her to sleep with their words and gestures. Sarah frowned, and then called the meeting to order once again. "Enough," she said. "It appears the charges against our Rebecca be well-substantiated. She has, despite repeated admonition, used far more than her allotted share of the network on numerous occasions this past year, leaving little power for the practice of the rest of us."

"I was making a lovely day for the Widow Parsons." Hannah called out from the back of the room, "and run out of power only half done."

"We've all had a treasured project spoilt!" Abigail Smith shouted.

Sarah silenced them with a raised hand. "We have also found her wasteful in her use of the grid, and there be some here who see the possibility of our Rebecca turning to blacker deeds."

"Tis a danger, to be sure!" Priscilla cried out.

"So what do we do about the thing? We cannot use the magic on her else it be turned against us." Sarah searched the women's faces. All were silent with their own thoughts.

Rebecca floated out over the treetops, the sun warm on her body. The sisters frowned on flying, but who was to see?

"So call the vote," Sarah said solemnly.

"All for revealing ..." Abigail Smith called.

With but few hesitations, all eyes turned to face Sarah Matthews.

"So be it," Sarah said. "The villagers already suspect her. Our only act need be one of omission, I think. I declare we must remove the cloud which protects the sisterhood until such time as Rebecca be discovered. Then let the curiosity and suspicion of the villagers themselves decide her fate." She turned to a large woman sitting near the window. "How does it appear down at the meeting house, Mercy?"

The large woman stood up, closed her eyes, and seemed to sway ever so slightly. After a few moments, she said, "They suspect her a bit, but they waver, Sarah."

Sarah sighed. "Then let the cloud be removed!"

At that, the other women in the room stood. They, too, closed their eyes and swayed like saplings in a mild wind. Soon, several of the villagers would remember things Rebecca had been seen doing in the past—things which they had been unable to recall before now—kettles dancing, doors opening by themselves, heavy stones flying up out of the ground ....

Goody Putnam began to cry, imagining the heat, the burning she herself had barely escaped a few years before. Only a last failing of the will of the villagers had stopped her from turning black.

Rebecca floated down onto feet as light as feathers. She felt giddy and began to laugh. She turned around, knowing but not caring that she'd exhausted the accessible power of the network for a good month. None of the others of the sisterhood would be using it soon. The thought pleased her. She thought of running all the way home.

But then she saw the two village men at the edge of the field, and she knew instantly that their watching eyes for once were clear.

She shivered. She could already feel the heat. With the last vestiges of the grid's power, she could see into the future. She could witness her own body burning.

JANAEL

Janael ran through the low-lying, shin-gnawing brush, the grim sister fast on her heels. Once or twice she glanced back to gauge the progress of the dark-robed old woman, and each time was spurred on by fear raised to a higher power. The woman's black garments flapped closer, closer, beating the brambles down like a great western bat.

Janael thought she could hear the old woman screaming, but then realized it was the storm in her own thoughts. She sought desperately the gray outlines of the next town—the man who'd sold her the grain in her bag had promised her she could reach the next civilized place before nightfall. Then he had looked bemused; for someone so strong and capable, Janael was afraid of the dark.

The low trees and bushes were losing their distinctness. "The Lael Hills are soaking up the light," her mother would have said. Again Janael peered over one shoulder—the right one, the perfect one—and watched as the dark woman winged her way across the rough ground. Janael looked hard to find the woman's feet, but could not discover them within the floating black folds. The grim sister dragged the darkness with her.

If Janael did not reach a building before dark she knew the nightmares would be far worse than the dream of this one old woman. Why this particular nightmare she could not begin to guess.

Child …

Janael tried to ignore her.

Child, please stop …

Janael opened her mouth wide, hoping that would make hearing difficult.

Child, I am not your nightmare!

Janael was tired anyway; it made it easier for her to slow. *No tricks!* she thought, and then started chanting it silently to herself.

Janael had always imagined that she herself would evolve into a grim sister someday, so maybe that was the source of the dream. But a coincidence was certainly possible. She had noticed the woman following her for some miles, since the last village. Her nightmares usually did not operate in that way.

Sometimes Janael would not have minded becoming a grim sister. For grim sisters did not dream.

Child, slow down! You are ill!

Janael slid her hands down the rough-hewn staff, establishing a grip on the lower third. Again she stole a glance back at the old woman. The late afternoon shadows of tree and bush, rock and fence, tore from their gray moorings and flapped alongside the racing figure, until after a time much of the landscape lost its roots and slipped into the woman's wake. Janael felt the illness sweep into her face, where she held it even though her skin grew hot and her lungs sore from unnatural restraint.

Enough!

Janael agreed. She swung her body around low, the thick staff following. Black wings enveloped her. The grim sister's startled eyes flew toward the sun.

"You might have killed me!" The old woman's voice sounded childish, petulant.

Janael looked up. The woman hovered over her like a carrion bird, the nose sharp and the eyes wet with longing.

"You *are* real," Janael said. "No dream. Your speech *smells*."

The old woman chuckled low in her throat. "Spoken truly like a storyteller. No, no dream. And the sour breath comes from too much bad meat and not enough fruits and grain." She grinned sloppily, exposing yellowed, worn teeth.

"The *child* of storytellers, old woman. And how did you know?"

"I prefer being called Malg, child, my birth name. An ugly

name, I admit, but better than being labeled with my affliction. A disease makes a poor name, and grim sistering is a *disease,* believe that if nothing else. The lack of dreaming wears us out and makes us ill. And I knew you by your clothes, child or not. I have not seen those robes for many a year. Your mother's?"

Janael sat up and brushed the dust off the three dark blue panels that hung from her shoulders. She felt suddenly self-conscious of her clothing, now that it had been mentioned. She had not heard anyone speak of storytelling for some time. "I'm not sure," she replied. "My mother and father dressed the same, and they were of similar build. When they disappeared they left three of their outfits behind. This is the last one. It was too large for me at first, but I grew into it."

Malg seemed to be about to inquire further, but then the multitude of lines trapping her narrow lips reformed themselves, and she held her peace. Malg helped Janael to her feet, and then produced the staff from behind the voluminous black folds of her dress. She handed it to her so easily, as if it were a delicate branch she'd dropped. Janael's arm trembled as she took it. The frail-looking old woman was amazingly strong.

Malg grasped Janael's hand as if to steady her. "I do not know what it is. Perhaps when we do not dream there is all this strength that is left over. But a high price to pay for the loss of dreaming."

"I would pay such a price," Janael said solemnly, "if it meant not to dream. If it meant I could know what is real again, that the shadows would not change as I watched them."

"You are ill, child. Believe me. And courage does not come easily with such illness. But we are *all* ill in this world, not just you, and not just the grim sisters."

"Everything changes so quickly …"

"Yes, child. The rules are changing in this world. Magic dies and the age of mechanicals sweeps over us all. *That* is why there is so much illness, and so much dreaming gone bad, and gone out of our heads to populate the landscape. I think the dreams simply do not know their place anymore. Sometimes we cannot travel the smallest path without stumbling over the dreaming. Whether hideous or laughable, the dreams all get in our way.

You are not the only one so afflicted, Janael."

Janael started to walk away, searching the horizon line for some hint of a dwelling. "Why do things have to change?"

Malg was soon beside her, matching her stride for stride. *The old woman can fly!* Janael mused, then immediately banished the thought before the inevitable images came with it and the woman *indeed* began to fly.

"Things always change," Malg said. "The old minds die, lose their grip. As magic changes, the mind changes. Toys grow in the mind, first as playful thoughts, and then one day they leave the confines of the skull to walk among us. Our old world cannot hold in the face of that. This change is greater only because there are greater minds that are dying. There has been a war, I suspect. Someone wanted too much. Now the heavens come crashing down to earth, dragging our dreams kicking and screaming with them. The toys are loose in the playground, playing by themselves. The world will never be the same, child. The mysteries have shifted their focus. Now people are being valued for what they have, not for what they can do. Wise minds are in short supply, and I sincerely doubt we will see many of their kind aweing and entertaining us with their trickery. And there are no more traveling storytellers, perhaps save one." Janael felt the old woman's claw-like fingers at her shoulder. "Do you have your parents' talent, child?"

Janael faltered, suddenly unsure where to step. "I do not know."

"I hope you do, even a bit of it. It may save you from the madness yet, sweet sister. It may save you from becoming the likes of me."

A city finally did appear on the horizon, although it was not the kind to steal the breath away. The walls were in serious need of attention and built of an ugly yellow stone that resembled mottled clay. People were keeping busy, however—a team of workers had the old paving stones torn up, replacing them, and other workers busied themselves tearing down several old structures flanking the gate. The discarded wood and clay stank of age and waste. Malg had become steadily more protective—to an irritating degree—during their long trek across the plain to this, the city of Noren. Even now she nudged people out of the path, away from Janael. She wouldn't let even a close brush-by pass without a withering glance. Occasionally she would steal a nervous glance at Janael, and then continue her monologue about all the changes evident in the world.

"I knew this place once," she said, and made a broad gesture with one great and black, wing-like sleeve. "It is among the oldest cities in this region. It had no streets for the longest time, just flattened earth, and pathways around where the animals and drunkards slept. Wise men and wiser women lived here, not the most powerful and certainly not the wisest, but wise enough, I think. They played games with one another, tricks and jokes, and made toys for the children, toys which appeared to have a life of their own. They say that sometimes you can find some of those toys still, toys living in the Noren woods, as if they too were animals, and perhaps they are just that now, gone feral from neglect."

Two men fell out of an opening in a house being demolished. Malg stepped over one without even glancing down, despite his moans. "When I was a child I knew some of those living here. Among the last of the wise, I imagine."

"There does not appear to be a surplus of wisdom here now," Janael said, as more brawlers spilled into the streets from taverns and meeting halls. "In fact I see no wisdom at all." Two men stood in front of Janael and the grim sister, engaged in a punching contest: first one man beat the other man several times across the top of the nose, and then the other man struck back, punching his eyes repeatedly.

Malg stepped up to the two men and threw her cloak over their heads. The tall shapes under the cloth collapsed almost immediately, and Malg drew back her cloak to reveal the two forms sleeping on the paving stones. "Cursed them with the dreamless sleep, I did, but did them a favor, I think, considering what dreams they'd have."

Suddenly a giant baby appeared, blocking their passage. Janael gasped, but she could not claim any great surprise.

"One of yours, I take it?" Malg asked, stepping up to the

great infant. She reached up and felt the huge, chubby cheeks one at a time. "Cute one, this. Guilt inspired? You think you do not do enough for the little ones?"

"It's hungry," Janael said softly. "I can feel it. We have to feed it somehow."

"How do you feed such a thing? It fills the passage!" Malg stepped back. The baby was expanding.

"I have no idea," Janael said with tears rolling down her face. "But it suffers from a terrible hunger—I can feel it in my head!"

Malg sighed. "You *are* an ill one! Then give it a cow and let's be on our way."

The cow appeared almost instantly: night black with broad, irregular patches of snow. It gazed up at the giant baby, and then looked back at Malg and Janael dumbly.

"Sorry, poor cow," Malg said, as the giant baby—gurgling deeply—snatched up the cow and jammed it into its rubbery mouth—chew chew chew and the cow was gone.

And then, its hunger satisfied, the giant baby was gone and the passageway was clear.

The two walked silently for some distance through chaotic lanes apparently reserved for sleepwalkers, drunkards, fetishists, and other victims of the illness, until Malg spoke again. "So where would you be heading, daughter of storytellers?"

"Wherever my feet determine to take me," she replied wearily. "I gave up on the idea of destinations some time ago. And certainly I would not risk imagining a place to be. For what I imagine comes true, and as you have seen I am not always in control of my imaginings."

"Then permit me to be your feet. You could do no worse. And perhaps I've a cure in mind-to keep your storymakings inside your head where they belong, if you have the courage."

Janael looked at her wide-eyed, more awake than she'd been in months. "Truly? What would it be? How …"

"I said 'perhaps'. This illness affects each one differently. And I never attempted a cure on a storyteller before."

"I am not convinced I have that talent of my parents. Perhaps madness is all it is."

"Then madness we will call it. Makes little difference to me."

"Where will your feet take us?"

"The Noren Woods. Beyond. But first we will need provisions for such a journey."

The large, open ruin might have been a tavern at one time, even a hall. Now it was a collection of broken pillars bridged by canvas and multicolored rags, with all manner of food, clothing, crafts, and supplies spread out across the cracked stones beneath. Malg dragged Janael from station to station according to some obviously preconceived yet incomprehensible plan. Along the way she argued with the vendors fiercely yet briefly, querying them for specifics, projections, recommendations, then gathering up purchases in a different-colored cloth bag before proceeding to the next stop.

It was while hurrying from one merchant to the next that Maug ran into, literally, another grim sister, knocking her flat to the ground and stepping up onto her midsection before noticing, gasping, and stopping.

Janael thought the one on the ground might very well be dead. Her eyes were shut tight beneath huge, bluish lids. Her lips were a pale wrinkled scar.

"Daid!" Malg cried, stepping off the grim sister, who Janael could now see was male.

Daid pushed open his lids. "Malg," he said, his tongue a dried-looking white thing. Then he began to shake. "You are … a dream?"

"No, Daid. No!" Malg cried.

But Daid continued to shake, and spoke of the dreams he could not have. Until his face became brittle. And the brittle became broken. And his features flew away like dry leaves caught up in a whirlwind.

Malg sat quietly staring into the shadow Daid had left behind. "Those who cannot dream," she whispered, "cannot live." Then she stood up and went on to the next merchant in her undisclosed itinerary as If nothing had occurred.

"The Noren Woods are full of all manner of things mechanical," Malg explained as they stood on the edge of the forest. "These are toys escaped from their wise makers, as I explained before. Harmless enough in the hands of their makers, I suppose, they have since had generations of progeny, and cannibalized one another for new and startling likenesses. Here it is where the dreaming first died, I think, in the souls of all the grim sisters. And here it is, I believe, where your storymaking first became a disease. Your parents may very well have passed through here, back when Noren was the city hungriest for storytellers, and all plots eventually wound their way there."

Janael gazed out over a horizon of trees and metal. She warded off an anxious recollection of her mother leaning over her bed, mouth opening for a song or sleep-enhancing tale, and the metal thing in her mother's mouth suddenly spinning and whirring, exploding into color and noise.

The trees of Noren Woods were as tall and thick as had been told in the legends. But interjected among those trees were objects which glittered and spun, rose and fell as if their regularity had been ordered and constructed. Many of these objects had edges which were sharp and unpleasant to the eye.

"Do not hesitate, my child," Malg said behind her. "The dark and my dreamless sleep will be bowing virtually together tonight I think. A ballet I could not miss even if I wanted to."

Once Inside the Woods Malg insisted that Janael lead the way. "Your feet have more knowledge here," Malg said. And indeed that appeared to be the case. Janael's feet found pathways her eyes could not see. She led Malg around bits of metal which appeared harmless (but, terrifyingly, were not), through ranks of machinery which looked deadly (but, thankfully, were not). She felt as If she were navigating her way through the dark heart of one of her own stories, but one which, for the first time in ages, she seemed to have some control over.

There is no magic,
we ate it for thinking.

The voice was a harsh one, but Janael still recognized this as a piece of song.

We ate the magic
and drank all dreaming.
We wind up tall

we wind up small
By the time we're finished
you people will be done ...

Janael followed the song until she and Malg had reached a small clearing. There a metal serpent with long eyelashes and breasts of shining silver, yellow dripping fangs and a long red moustache, sang and spat poison at them.

"Tell that abominable toy a story!" Malg cried out behind her.

"But if I tell it poorly, or if I lose control of the tale ..."

"Speak to it, child!" The serpent leaned down to within a few feet of them, its eyelashes flapping with sleepy seduction.

We ate the magic
We ate the dreams
We ate the girl child
and the tales she told ...

"A man ate a serpent for breakfast," she began.

"Ooooh," the mechanical male and female serpent replied, pulling back.

"It wasn't a very tasty serpent. In fact the man thought it was a bit snaky, but he ate it all anyway. He found it filling enough."

"Oooooh," the mechanical serpent replied, and backed up a little more.

"But when the man went to bed that night he had several strange dreams. He dreamed that instead of eating the serpent, it was the serpent that had eaten him."

"Ah!" the mechanical serpent exclaimed, and leaned closer again.

"Then he dreamed that he built a mechanical serpent to replace the one he had eaten. But this serpent did nothing but sing all day and refused to eat the rats and vermin which soon completely overran the countryside, making it necessary for the people to live in high towers so that the children could not play outdoors anymore."

"Hmmm," the mechanical serpent said, swaying back and forth at a great height.

"And then he dreamed that the serpent he had eaten was not only a true serpent, but the last true serpent in the world, and now there was nothing more to dream about."

The mechanical serpent swayed back and forth, dreaming its mechanical dreams. Janael and Malg slipped past quietly, hoping not to disturb it.

Janael told more of her stories out loud to Malg as they maneuvered through the wood of trees and metal toys. There was the tale of the Siamese witches and what happened to their four lovers. The story of the three turtles and what they did one evening after dinner. There was the legend of a Sinbad who was not a sailor. The narrative of Janael and the grim sister called Malg who went in search of 1) a cure for Janael's faulty storytelling, and 2) the restoration of dreaming.

"But haven't I told my stories well?" Janael suddenly exclaimed. "And no grim dreams have left my head and come to chase my sanity away! Am I not cured?"

"Only in these woods, and only in this darkness, dream child," Malg replied and gestured at the night falling swiftly around them. "If you were to take the stories away with you, into the light of day, once again they would follow you around and terrify you. To confine them to your head and your performances you must first feel the pain delivered up by one of the old dwellers of the dreamtime."

"But I've no story for that," Janael said with dismay.

"Then follow as I plot it," Malg replied, sweeping her dark clothes around her as she turned and headed into the darkest part of the woods.

For some time they passed through a region where the forest floor was covered with immense, hairy vines. In some places these vines were so thick passage was almost impossible. Janael was ready to take out her dagger and begin hacking when Malg cried, "Stop. We are here."

Janael looked around her. This was the darkest part of the forest they had been in. "But there is nothing here."

"Oh, here there is plenty. Look inside your story, little one."

So Janael closed her eyes and looked inside the story which had been putting itself together since they entered this part of the woods, though she hadn't realized it. There she saw Malg eaten by an immense spider.

An immense, hairy spider. Janael opened her eyes at once, certain that her dreaming had gone bad again and to confirm this there was Malg halfway into the giant spider's dark mouth, its long hairy legs writhing along the ground and in the trees.

"Malg!" she screamed, racing forward. "I would not have told such a horrible story!"

"But little one. *My* story is inevitable. The darkness falling. My dreamless sleep. This spider of too many legs would rather tear me apart and eat me, but all you require is a poisoned bite to cure you! Courage, child!" And then the giant spider ate Malg, and turned its enormous red eyes on Janael.

Janael stood her ground, shaking, trying to imagine her way out of this. Nothing happened. "I would not *imagine* such a story!" she said to the spider defiantly as it began its approach. "I would not!" she said again as the long hairy legs whispered around her. She leapt then, right In front of the spider's mouth. So startled the spider was by her movement that it bit her without thinking. Then Janael was running away from the giant spider before it could eat her, its poison in her veins.

Janael is an old woman now, or so she tells the story. Her grandchildren do not always believe she is old at all. These days the toys have come out of the woods and fill the city streets with their noise and color. Magic has gone away, except in dreams. And storytellers like Janael travel the deep woods looking for their tales and tell them without fear that their dreams will come alive and chase them, the poison of the oldest spider in the world in their veins reminding them of from where their stories first came.

FILMMAKER

I stand in the doorway of the old home place with a new Bell & Howell, Super 8, Zoom Lens. It's dark back in the empty rooms, so I've brought along a couple of flood lamps. Walls settle. There's the sound of film being replaced in a camera. Other sounds move in and out of range: low voices, laughter, and glassware against wooden tabletops.

Sounds freeze within the objects of the room. I follow my own footsteps through the house, tracking myself for a film plan. A few shots here and there, several short sequences, but most of the footage unwinds only inside my brain.

I want to do a film about objects, preferably old objects, the ones associated with my childhood here. I don't want to comment on them, symbolize them, or change them in any way. I just want to see them, and film them as objectively as possible. They should define the collector.

I have to duck to get through the door. The entrance hall curves back toward the left. I set up a lamp in the hall, playing white light down its length.

The floor is covered with scraps of paper, books, small objects: a silver Appaloosa mare, a gold candlestick, a shiny black locomotive, four red jacks, an unused frosted light bulb, wooden checkerboard, three enameled clothespins, tiny cut-glass canister, five yellow cats eyes, a steely, a milky, a dried dogwood branch with two blossoms, an amber bottle containing a green pill, an orange wooden top, my mother's white lace handkerchief embroidered with orchids, an Armour's Baking Soda can with two Buffalo nickels stuck to the bottom, a Circus Boy hand puppet, a small compass, a blue ball, a rubber snake, and two bright yellow paper cups. I focus on each object cautiously, individually, zooming in for close-ups., try out different angles, lighting schemes. I use up two rolls of film and begin another. Light bends off the different surfaces, and then flows back into its source at the lamps.

Silver triangles grow larger inside the curved metal ridges simulating hair. They become small again as the camera pulls back, the ridges becoming a mane, then a horse head with wild eyes, then growing a body and becoming a complete horse again. Oval thumb prints delineated by green tarnish spot the flank.

A golden teardrop grows in the darkness. Sparks radiate from the center as I shift the spot lamps. The teardrop elongates and gains a flat base as it comes into more light. As the gold stretches slowly, the top of the candlestick spouts shouting lips.

Three enameled clothespins drop slowly into a tiny cut-glass canister filled with five yellow cats' eyes, appearing, disappearing from the transparent glass filled with winking light. The cat's eyes revolve slowly in the bottom of the container, on an endless pathway.

The top of an orange wooden top. The camera shifts to the bottom, the side. The side. The top. The side. The bottom.

Whiteness is bordered by a deep black frame. The whiteness wrinkles, winks. Orchids grow out from the farthest corners.

An oval of blue light. The oval grows as the camera zooms in. The oval grows. The oval becomes a very large ball, the light from the spots revealing three-dimensional curvature. The top of the blue ball. Then the lower half. The left half. The lower half. The right half, cut off by the frame of the picture. Rapid cuts: the top, the top, the top.

Rapid cuts: the candlestick. My nose. The mare. My cheek. The ball. My left eye. A lace handkerchief. My face. The black inside the closet. My face. The spotlight, making red burn circles in the air.

I study the objects over and over, knowing that these things I choose to remember somehow trap me. My fear of them holds my attention.

Some things appear to be missing, or out of place, but I can't decide what they are. I wish they would re-order themselves when I'm not looking. I move the flood over and slide the second in beside it, move the first across the hall; the objects are caught in the cross-beam. No dust. Not on any of the objects after twenty years. Not even a trace. The Appaloosa is still shiny, the candlestick glows, the canister still sparkles, the dogwood seems freshly cut.

I remember the day we left, the eviction, the furniture and clothing piled outside. When the men boarded up the house I ran around the side and peeked through a crack: our little things unpacked, neglected, scattered everywhere. The moving had raised a cloud of dust, and there had been an eighth inch of gray over everything. Now they are all clean, shiny, and beautifully separate under the light. I don't understand. My future has bent, and sent me back to this point, caught me in a time loop. The candlestick a thin golden nose,cat's eyes rolling in my head. The horse's thin, old, wise father's face. Can I live the way I've filmed them?

A black-and-white mouse runs from behind one of the lamps out into the two overlapping, oblong spots. The pet I had as a child scurries under my feet. An offspring? He stands on his hind feet, scratching his cheeks with his forepaws. Close-up: thin nails scratch a pink bag of flesh. He scurries into a large room, no, a large open closet at the end of the hallway. I follow.

I hope to find a mouse nest here. Shredded paper containing squirming, pale pink, eyeless little bodies. The mouse, as an object, should lead to related objects of its own making. Progeny. I close the closet door two-thirds the way on us. The mouse stands in the corner; I line up the camera on the three converging angles.

No nest. I'm disappointed. But the closet floor is covered with shredded paper. No—cut paper. Perfect one-inch squares of clean, crisp paper. The squares contain letters, sections of multidotted pictures, and splotches of cartoon color.

I know the man is my father. The face is old, but there's a scar, wide and sickle-shaped, running down the left side of his neck. He coughs hoarsely then staggers forward. We hug mechanically, our heads upright, each not trusting the other enough to put his head on the other's shoulder.

My father leans against the wall beneath the flood. He picks up the objects in the hall slowly, carefully, and carries them into the next room. He then comes back for the flood, and slides it into the room behind him.

I hold the camera steadily, about shoulder height, and truck slowly to the doorway. I pan left and right across the room until I reach my father.

My father sits on the floor in the room, playing with the toys. He takes polish and cloth from the sack and shines each carefully. A black locomotive stack looms in the foreground, with a lip of silver. Zoom in on a red strip circling a tin can. Zoom in on two fingers rubbing a column of gold, over and over. Brown wrinkled fingers knead a blue rubber ball. I close in on cracking skin. Brown skin dries into a hundred dry rivers.

He takes a fresh dogwood branch from the sack and replaces the old one. A stack of newspapers and a pair of scissors lie beside him, and expand rapidly as I zoom in, filling the frame.

I try to find the proper frame in my past, and plan the movie from there …

My older brother sits on the floor with his children, two boys aged five months and four years respectively. My brother is tall, blonde, bearded, and green-eyed. He wears a heavy white turtleneck sweater. The boys play with their toys. I close in on the teeth of a silver mare flashing against skin. Suddenly my brother begins to scream at his children, waving his arms in the air. He leaps up and over the green-blanketed bed, spilling the checker set onto the silver-colored rug. On top of the mahogany bureau a heavy-framed picture leans against the white porcelain lamp. A lady, black hair in a bun, yellow ribbon, lies in a bed surrounded by orchids. He throws the picture at the children. His pink lips stretch back in a painful snarl. His shocked eyes fill the frame. Close-up on three white teeth, filled with light. Curious, I close in further, but he moves, and the picture blurs. One child is cut and bruised, crying, the other knocked unconscious. Their faces join in a fog. The blue ball bounces. The unconscious baby secretes green blood from his left ear. My brother crawls over the bed in slow motion and bends over the children. Close-up of the green smear. Why the green? I don't know why I remember it this way. CUT.

I try to edit myself from the sequence and see it another way. Strike the child from the picture, but which one? Or the brother? I don't know which one I am. I feel a connection with all the characters and can imagine myself inside each one's head. I cry, clutch my toys, leap off the bed with tensed muscles. My long black hair falls between my pale breasts.

I hold myself and hold them inside myself. The dogwood branch blooms abruptly, filling the room with blossoms as the child screams. The tail of the mare swishes back and forth, casting silver and white light back into the lens of the camera. The thin pink tongue of the horse hangs loose and exhausted.

I take another look at the final sequence of the film, the shots with Jenny filmed over the last few days. The earlier film of the murder should lead logically into this final episode. The final episode should frame the language of objects developed throughout the film, frame the action, and give the earlier sequences their significance. But where are the connections?

The objects refuse to stay still: they withhold their secrets. I find it difficult to hold them in focus without the feelings washing over me, carrying the objects away into dream. The blue ball explodes, and fills the room with blue-filtered light.

Slow dissolve into Jenny's face, three days ago:

In my film Jenny scowls into the camera; blonde bangs are plastered to her forehead. A wet moustache glistens on her upper lip. She doesn't like being filmed and snarls soundlessly into the lens. She backs up against the kitchen sink, whirls around and begins aggressively scrubbing a heavy black iron skillet. A tear rolls down her right cheek and catches in the corner of her mouth. Straight lines move up and down her pink lips in the close-up. I approach her and try to touch her, but she moves away from my hand. I zoom in on the hand, as it turns on its side on the endless white porcelain.

In my workroom a storyboard covers one wall, sketches of the film tacked neatly to the gray surface. The camera lingers on each sketch, these details from various murders: several babies, a boy in charcoal, a blackened object with a flanged base, two black lips, two black-haired women with crushed skulls and bleeding noses. Giant, circular cats' eyes.

Close in on sections of the sketches: gray curved streaks cover a white expanse. Red watercolor strokes form triangular dabs on blue paper.

A list of weapons lies on my desk; the camera zooms in on the reckless scrawl: candlestick, mare, gun, knife, weeping, broken hands.

In another close-up dark ink grows slowly in rivers over pink, over spatulate fingers as the camera pulls back, over my hands rifling the pages of my film notebook. Jenny turns away from me in bed; my hand strikes the back of her head. Her eyes turn and leap to fill the frame, struck with fear. A mouth moves in slow motion in a tight shot. Jenny screams at me.

But wait. Looking once again at the film, I see that her silent eyes and slow-moving mouth don't say these things. Perhaps I've let my interpretations mislead me. I must stick with the image, the bare object without speech. Gold solidifies in a film close-up, bathed under pink light. The still shot resembles the walls of my stomach, the emptiness filled with the gold of the candlestick. I can live the way I film it; I know it. I can make my own pain and emptiness a beautiful thing. Jenny screams silently at me, moving her arms violently up and down, a hysterical figure in a silent motion picture.

In the last shots of the film Jenny's eyes are dark with makeup. Her cheeks and forehead white out. In a distorted close-up the teeth of the horse nip her lips red. The horse's dark shadow obscures the backlighting. I slap Jenny and cringe backwards, curling fingertips into my palms. I reach for her, zooming in to two fingers touching and pressing into pink expansiveness. Jenny turns away from the camera and me, pressing her stomach against the sink.

The frame loses focus. It will need further clarification, a more perceptive editing. The final sequence loops back into itself, and becomes a beginning.

A man pulls up in a yellow sports car outside the house. The telephoto lens captures his stiff image through the window on the far side of the room. My brother sits on the floor, playing with his two children. The boys play with their toys.

I zoom once again through the window and focus on the man getting out of the car. Close in: pale fingers caress a silver handle. He opens the door to the accompaniment of the children's laughter. When he bumps his head on the roof of the car they squeal in delight. He walks closer to the house and examines the dogwood tree out front. His hand touches the blossoms; the fingers are covered with yellow pollen. He breaks the branch, smiling, for my mother. He has a red Vandyke beard. My father, when he was younger? Flash through a montage of my ancestors: grandfathers, great-grandfathers, all in beards. In a tight close-up, red hair moves wraith-like.

My father opens the door into the room. He begins screaming at my brother. One of the children clutches the locomotive against his left cheek. Black-shiny, metal circles move in and out of focus accompanied by laughter. My father crosses to the bureau, picks up the picture of a lady surrounded by orchids, and throws it at my brother. My brother ducks and the picture strikes the children. In a greatly magnified shot, wood grain blurs and dissolves to the accompaniment of short train whistle blasts. One child is gashed about the cheeks; blood and bruises make him unrecognizable. The other lies dead, his forehead crushed in. Green blood secretes from the left ear. Why green?

Enraged, my father attacks my brother. My brother pulls a knife, and plants it in the left side of my father's neck, below the ear. My brother screams in pain. CUT.

EVENTS (for possible inclusion in the film):

One. In my freshman year of college a girl breaks a date with me, and goes out with another guy. I don't even remember her name. I got more upset than I could understand. Drunk, hysterical. I cried all night, wanting to slash my throat. I felt as if I were falling down a well with no bottom, spinning, with nothing beneath me.

Two. I met Joanne at the insurance office where we both worked. She liked me because I talked about "serious things."

Then I started recounting dreams, visions, and images from my past. I couldn't really help it; they were with me all the time—scenes, faces leaping out of the objects around me. I made her cry all the time. So she left.

Three. When I dated Jenny, I didn't tell her anything. But then, nights, after we were married—I couldn't sleep. She was never, never attracted to me, but I was tender with her, so she married me. I remember this image from a dream: my body exploding, ripped apart, flesh hanging like cast-off clothing on the frame of the dream. There was nothing inside. Close-up on dogwood roots soaked in pinkness. At great magnification skin rips, and red rivers begin growing out into the picture frame. In the dream my body is torn apart by birds; a distant landscape of bare rock and cactus shows beneath the wounds. I work on my film. Jenny cries.

Reorder the three events. Is there any progression from one to three? From three to one? Could two replace either? How do these three events relate to the central multi-versioned murder sequence of the film? A causal relationship? Replace the well in event one with the murder, the faces in the objects of event two with the murder. Replace the destroyed body of event three with the murder. What would happen to the three events if the murder were completely edited out of the film? Would there be significant changes? Would Jenny's face dissolve into blackness? Would the silver mare become quiet and subdued, and fall asleep standing up? The events might be criticized as bordering on the bathetic; how would I answer that? Does the preceding/ concurrent murder make them less so? Can the behavior exemplified in the three events be altered? How so, if the murder remains in the film? Can I improve my life through careful editing of my film? Can I improve my life by merely making the film carefully, realistically?

The man in the red Vandyke beard runs full speed toward me as I lean against the doorframe filming his breakneck approach. He scatters enamel clothespins, marbles, and a medicine bottle lying on the floor, to the far borders of the frame. Objects bounce off his feet. Zoom in on cats eyes as they expand and explode into shattered glass, a waterfall of shards. Other objects spin so rapidly I can't determine their true form. The two children play with a blue ball in the background. They are separate from the man, and not involved in the action. He doesn't even notice them as he runs past. My older brother is asleep on the bed. Then he is half-awake, bewildered, and filming the ceiling from a hand-held Bell & Howell. A giant blue ball of a fist bounces around the room in slow motion, trying to smash me. The man screams into my camera, threatening me with a candlestick in his left hand. I get a tight close-up on an angry red scar running down the left side of his neck. Close in: a wide scarlet ribbon on a pink field. The scar seems to glow in the dim light as the muscles in his neck move spastically.

"Leave her alone!" He screams. Screams. Motive? CUT.

MY VIOLENCE (for possible inclusion in the film):

One. Dreams: a disembodied claw enters my chest beneath the breast bone, ripping a thick red line down to my navel. My chest opens: empty. Frantic, hysterical, screaming in agony, I try to fill it with knives, forks, bullets, objects in my room, the surrounding debris. But I will not be filled.

In a darkened cave I thrust my left forearm upward into the air as a call to order. I take out a long-bladed knife, and begin carving off strips of flesh. In a few minutes white bone appears through the red tissue.

Two. Jenny and I sit in the darkened projection room. Blurred ghost shapes flash across the wall. The film gains focus; shapes become more distinct. Sequences with napalmed children in Vietnam are intercut with segments from Auschwitz and Belsen. Film of an oriental execution. A car accident. Independent of me, the segments repeat themselves, varying the order, varying their length. Faces interchange or are lost from the film entirely. Bodies all look the same: naked, clothed, dead, living, or in shreds. In the darkness of the projection booth I think of other possible orders, new paths for meaning. Jenny sobs next to me.

Three. I sort through sketches in my workroom. Sequences fragment and make no logical sense anymore. Thoughts are confused and scattered. Cause and effect dissolves. Motives edit themselves. The film persists in tearing at important points in the action; it persists in breaking down into individual frames. I throw my right hand through the window next to my desk. Glass fragments. Ribbons of blood web my hand. Grinning cats' eyes fill my mouth. Gold blazes in a far-off corner of my right eye.

Four. Jenny watches me as I edit film. Her face is drawn; the lines around her eyes deepen and flow into the two knothole-like spaces. I know she senses my pain, has been exposed to my nightmare images. She wants to do something, but realizes no one can really help me. I admit to myself I want her to feel guilty about me. I hope it will force her into giving me what I need. I slap her gold eyes.

What do these incidents of violence have in common? How can I account for their air of passivity? How do they change once the murder sequence is edited from the film? Why do I inflict these images and sequences on my loved ones? Are they melodramatic? Can my life be melodramatic if my attitudes aren't? How can I get over the fears expressed in these incidents? Change my expectations? Change my future?

My father of gray, of black, of white, of red hair sits on the floor in the room, playing with the children. He hands each of the boys a toy: a silver Appaloosa for the four-year-old, an orange wooden top for the baby. Its top, bottom, its side. A man in a red Vandyke beard enters the room carrying a picture of a lady surrounded by orchids. My father leaps up angrily, and attacks the man with a gold candlestick. Close-up on the tensed hands: lines crossing fingers. The light shifts and the fingers darken. The bearded man throws the picture across the bed and it kills my younger brother. Dark blue blood seeps from his ear. The other child is cut about the head and neck. My father pulls a knife and stabs the man in the chest. My camera records the soft red explosion. CUT.

THE TRUTH OF OBJECTS:

When I was a child I used to bury a different toy in the backyard each week. Later I'd dig them up, and discover them as if surprised. I keep many souvenirs of my past in my workroom, stumble on them now and then am shocked with what they remind me of. Lovers, a day at the fair, someone's illness or suicide. Quartz stone, a plastic yellow flower, a rubber armadillo, a green yarn bookmark in the shape of a worm, two Mickey Mouse cups. Golden things. Objects can trap you; they stop you in time when you examine them, and ponder their significance.

The two children play by themselves on the floor of the bedroom. One holds a silver Appaloosa horse. My younger brother holds an orange wooden top. The scent of orchids fills the room. I focus on a mirror in one corner of the room. Bright yellow flashes fill the blackness. A young man stares out at me from behind a camera, the gray shadow of a light beard on his chin and cheeks. A swinging shade on the window casts winged shapes against the wall. A man in a red Vandyke beard runs out of an adjoining room, chased by my father with a knife. I zoom into the open doorway: a black-haired woman pulls bed clothes up around her. Her mouth is open, hair awry. My father slips and the knife runs up into my little brother's throat. My father doesn't stop. The other child screams and is thrown against the wall when the bearded man leaps on my father. The child is knocked unconscious; he leaves a brown smear on the wall. My father hacks at the man, puts a gash down the left side of his throat. The bearded man gets the knife away, and stabs my father once, twice in the side. The wound spreads, and becomes an unnatural burgundy red gouged out of his side. Becomes a spot, brighter than anything around it, glowing, like a rose petal, folded concave. The man with the red beard screams. CUT.

How does the action of the film relate to my life?
    Name six women who felt sorry for me, and their feelings evolved into guilt. Name six men who felt threatened by me, who could not understand my anger. Consider the people as objects. Am I any of them? Does it help?

My brother and I play with the toys our father has given us.

I with my silver Appaloosa mare, my little brother with his orange wooden top. We hear shouts in the next room. We begin crying, afraid someone is going to hurt us because we've been bad. A woman screams. A man with a red Vandyke beard runs out of the room, chased by my father with a knife. I zoom into the bedroom: furniture is scattered. Toppled, broken; a black-haired woman in the bed pulls a sheet up around her. Her hair is awry, face red, mouth twisted. An open window on one side, green curtains blowing toward the bed. My father slips and when he gets off the floor he stands shaking over my little brother's body, the knife buried to the handle in my brother's stomach. The bearded man tries to leap on my father and his shoe catches me under the jaw, opening a gash. The bearded man pulls the knife out of my brother's body and puts a wound under my father's left ear. The blood explodes softly from the gash. My father gets the knife away and struggles on top of the bearded man. The knife flashes, steel and burgundy; my father hacks and hacks and hacks. He opens raw hamburger in the man's side, unnaturally red, brighter than all around it, glowing like a concave rose petal in the man's side. My father screams and screams and screams. CUT.

MOTIVES:

Jealousy. Lust. Playfulness. Incest.

Fear.

Hatred. Revenge.

Loneliness.

Love. Terror.

(Choose any of the above. Make them interchangeable. Does it help?)

Question: In view of the three Events, and the final version of the murder scene, is the sequence with Jenny really necessary or inevitable?

I pack the camera away in its carrying case and move back into the entrance hall. I finish polishing the toys, putting another thin coat of lacquer on the checkerboard, washing the marbles in pink, liquid soap, exchanging the old light bulb for a new one, polishing the gold candlesticks.

I take up the stack of newspapers and begin cutting along

the pencil lines I had marked previously. Soon I have perfect one-inch squares. Under the floods the scissors and my right hand make sharp, distinct shadows on the newsprint. Wing-shapes flutter like dying hawks. The high intensity lamps begin to burn the back of my neck, and sting like a left-handed slap on the right side of my face.

I pull the pink lace handkerchief embroidered with orchids from my back pocket and wipe my face with it. It hangs over my fist like a miniature chair cover.

The angry red scar on my neck begins to itch beneath my beard, burns, and seems to engorge and grow with every rub from the handkerchief. I throw the handkerchief into the corner behind the lamp and begin dismantling the floods.

I stop.

I run the sequence with Jenny over and over again. A golden column, dogwood tree, blue ball shrink and expand in the small room with the camera's lens changes. Jenny seems to fade more with each rerun. A blank space in the negative forms where her sad eyes, slow-moving mouth, and nervous hands used to be. I make my decision and edit her out of the film:

In the final shots I go to the kitchen sink for a drink of water. Close-up of my wandering eyes. Cats' eyes roll out of a mouse hole, one yellow and one blue. The black skillet turns in the spot lights. Gray smiles flash in the metal. The skillet is clean and unused. Trucking the camera through the hall into my workroom, close-ups focus on orange and red flowers sprouting from pots on the windowsill. The petals move in slow-motion. Close in on my black hair: it becomes large strands of coarse fiber, then a dark blur. The wind moves oak branches against a deep blue backdrop outside my window. My mouth moves slowly. I move away from the camera until my whole body can be seen. I dance a jig and make silly faces into the lens. I scowl. I am familiar to everything I see. Close-up on the enormous whites of my eyes, the corners of my pupils. Expanding whiteness.

I become a stranger to my own childhood.

I stop.

LOST CHEROKEE

Oct. 3, 1839: The old man crouched down before the fire with his grandchildren—the elder boy of ten summers and the small girl who had jumped down but six years before—the grandfather's clothing worn, fraying, too thin for the cold as the wagons swung north and away from Cherokee land, his brown turban stained, his eyes filled with the sadness of four family members dead, these children's parents collapsed on the trail, only two of the fifteen lost at each stopover on the Removal, and two others slain by the Unecas, the whites, when they refused to give up their small mines, their nice houses, the well-tended gardens.

"This is what the old men told me when I was a boy." His grandchildren drew closer, as this was always his way to begin a tale.

"In the beginning the animals and the land were not friends of the human being. The human being was new, some say created by Coyote, some say by Rabbit, and new things are not always embraced. The human beings lived on a high rise cleared out of the great wood, and they never left there. You see, they were afraid of the great wood where the animals lived. It was dark there, and the ways of the animals were not the ways of the human being.

"Then the animals were not as they are today, you see. The animals were bigger, stronger, and more perfect. They spoke the same language as the human being and lived in villages arranged much as our own Cherokee villages. They had chiefs and clans and councils. Frog was council leader. Rabbit was messenger and led the dances.

"These animals are now gone. Some time ago, so long ago the human beings have forgotten, the animals left this world and flew up to the seven heavens, where they live in Galunlati this very day. These animals we know today then came to earth to be the imitators of these great ones. But these great ones once lived, believe this.

"Long ago, those who would someday become the Cherokee lived among the other human beings in this bare spot on the mountain. One day, one of these early Cherokees woke up, as from a dream, and knew what it was he must do, that he must leave this place and travel into the wood, that he must make friends of the animals. He also knew the sadness of being alone after this dream; the dream gave him this. And he knew that only the animals could doctor this new pain. He did not understand, then, what he would find: demons, ghosts, and little people, as well as the great animals.

"No one, of course, remembers his name. This was before the time of names. I call him Tsalagi, the ancient name for the Cherokee, which means 'cave people' or 'mountain people.' For this man stood for us all, you see, like our other old heroes such as Oconoslota, Doublehead, John Watts, or Chief Junaluska, who saved that devil Jackson during the Creek wars. The Cherokee have always had someone to stand/or them when it was needed. This is Tsalagi's story, my grandchildren."

When Tsalagi woke up that morning a cloud bank seemed but a few feet above his head. He rolled over and gazed at the land about him: he was on the ground outside the bark huts, and the only one of his people awake. He could not understand this, as the sun had already risen, and besides, he had slept in the hut with his family the night before, not outside, exposed to the darkness. He crawled to his knees, climbed to his feet, and found himself ducking as if to avoid bumping his head into that cloud bank. But the cloud bank now seemed farther overhead, circling, and as Tsalagi moved, the cloud moved with him.

He entered the hut of his father and looked around. Everyone was asleep, but such a strange sleep. Their bodies looked stiff, uncomfortable, their breathing so shallow that at first he feared they might be dead. His brothers lay like a pile of young warriors killed in battle with Raven, but Raven had not bothered them since before even his lather's time. His sisters and mother lay huddled together. His father slept alone, by the door where Tsalagi had crouched and entered. This startled Tsalagi; his father should have been alarmed, up and ready for battle. But he continued to sleep.

He bent over his father and gently pushed at the old man's chest. Then harder. Finally, forgetting himself, he slapped his father, and then stumbled backwards in fright. His father continued to sleep the sleep of the dead. But his flesh was warm, his eyelids fluttered.

Tsalagi went to every hut in the village. Everywhere it was the same. He examined the sky for signs from Yowa and the Elder Fires Above. Nothing. He examined Sun, the creator, but nothing seemed out of place.

Then he saw the cloud again, circling rapidly directly over his head. Was this the sign? He suddenly felt adrift, dizzy, and then found himself with a clear head again, looking deeply into the great wood. And he knew what he must do.

He returned to the family hut for a pouch of food—nuts, roots, berries—then hefted the spear he knew his father intended to give him when Tsalagi became a man. He slipped into his skirt of overlapping bark and feathers. He also took the hollow reed and a few wood-and-feather darts in case the smaller animals allowed him to eat them. He knew his father could always make another, and he did not know if there would be reeds where he was going.

When he emerged the cloud was still overhead, but very soon began to fly rapidly in the direction of the clearing's edge and the border of the great wood. Tsalagi barely kept up. He stopped momentarily at the clearing's boundary, where the human beings had blackened a narrow circle around the village with the flame the Thunder Beings had given them. It was not known what the Thunder Beings meant by this gift— some thought flame still another thing sent to trick the human beings, or a new toy the Thunder Beings wanted to try out on the village first—so since its first discovery in the tree, flame was used only for magic, or for bathing the meat before eating.

Tsalagi looked at the black band before his feet, and then searched the sky again for the cloud. It seemed to have stopped just over the edge of the wood, waiting for him. Tsalagi took one cautious step over the boundary; then, when nothing happened to him, he ran straight for the wall of trees as fast as he could.

The cloud was circling madly.

He had never felt so close to things. Branches poked him in the back and ribs and he whirled with his spear ready, and then stumbled backwards over fallen logs. He looked about in wonder. The green and blue leaves moved in the slight breeze like countless waving hands.

Tsalagi felt other thoughts brushing up against his own, other voices that always seemed to fall apart into rustlings and drippings and swishings when he tried to make out the words. Sun seemed to have disappeared, and the heart of the wood seemed much like the times when Moon had just come out of hiding. But now and then he gazed hard at the branches overhead, and he could still catch some glimpse of white mist. Knowing that the white cloud was still there somehow reassured him.

The ground beneath him seemed to be rising, which bothered him, as he'd always imagined the ground hidden by the wood to be as flat as the village clearing. He had visions of a great monster stirring out of the fallen leaves and moss, much like the ones he had seen inside his head during the dark time. Great wings knocking him off the world. He shivered and crept up the rise, expecting to flee at any moment from a gigantic upraised claw or beak. He watched his feet, seeing himself stepping into an enormous, watery eye.

He discovered that the farther he traveled from the village the hungrier he became. For some reason he had lost his ability to go without food for long periods. He had good luck with the blowgun, telling the small flock of birds that he must take one of the group, but no more than was needed, and for good purpose. The birds quieted almost instantly, and seemed to rest until he had chosen one of their number. The second day he killed a small lizard with his bare hands, and imagined taking the power of this strange creature within himself. All the next day he felt fleeter of foot, and better able to control his thirst.

As he went farther and farther into the great wood, Tsalagi discovered that not all of the forest was the same, as he had once thought. The trees were of many kinds, the flowers countless. In some places great, twisting vines draped the trees. In others the bases of the trees were surrounded by thick undergrowth and he had to go around, the swiftness of the little cloud overhead not allowing him the time it would take to chop and tear his way through. He thought many times of his family, but they felt as distant as a dream to him now.

One day the cloud stopped him at a wide place in the stream. Tsalagi tried to go on, but the small cloud was persistent, lowering and circling over a small area. He looked into the stream at this point and discovered some whitish objects on the bottom. Examining these, he found he could pry them open at a seam. The gummy flesh inside tasted good.

Suddenly, Tsalagi bolted upright, a feeling like a knife suddenly crossing his secret thoughts. The edge of this knife seemed to trail off into the most shadowed part of the wood behind him. He turned and stared there, unmoving. He barely touched his blowgun, then felt foolish with such a small weapon against such a big darkness, and grasped the end of his spear. He could now see there was movement in the dark, but his eyes were not good enough to see what beast caused this.

Then two yellow eyes, a great orange beak, glistened back in the wood, and that surrounded by blackness deeper than any of the shadows. Judging from their placement, Tsalagi knew the animal to be two men in height. He was sure this was one of the great animals, the first he had ever seen. He thought it must be Raven, or one of Raven's brothers.

Raven seemed to be traveling in a large circle around Tsalagi, but made no sound, even when crossing the stream. Tsalagi did not know how this could be, but this was one of the great animals, he thought; they could do anything. Every few moments Raven would turn his enormous head and look directly at Tsalagi, straight into his eyes, and Tsalagi would tremble all over.

Raven's movements were so slow, ponderous, and deliberate that Tsalagi didn't quite know what to make of them. He thought Raven must be acting out some sort of plan, dancing some kind of pattern, but he did not know what it could be. And the slowness of Raven's movements made it impossible for Tsalagi to determine whether the giant creature's circle was narrowing.

At last Raven stopped and stared at Tsalagi for a long time. Unblinking. In the dim light Tsalagi could see the sleek outlines of the enormous head, the way the feathers tufted in back and extended over each yellow eye. Then Raven closed his eyes and covered his beak with midnight wings, and vanished back into the shadows.

Sometime later Tsalagi heard a woman scream, and sounds of a great struggle a little distance away, where the trees had grown closer together and more tangled. He saw that the cloud had now sped up, the falling sun seeming to turn its outer edges the color of milk with some blood mixed in. Then it stopped over this place, the woman screamed again, and Tsalagi raced forward, snapping branches out of the way, bruising himself against hidden trunks, pulled and clutched at by thin vines and briars. When he reached the thickest part of the entanglement he thrust himself between two large trunks and squeezed himself through. He proceeded like this toward the source of the screams, going as fast as he could, scratching his face, tearing skin and scraping the feathers from his skirt, and all this time not sure why he was doing this. Raven would be there to crush his skull and suck out his thoughts, he was sure.

The woman was no longer screaming when Tsalagi reached the small open place. She appeared relaxed, leaning back and gazing at him. Smooth dark skin, narrow face, white teeth. She wore a white cloth wrapped around her waist. Her breasts were large and full.

It was the woman's barest movement, the way she wrinkled her nose and widened her eyes slightly, that led to Tsalagi's quick movement to the left.

A black hand swung down beside him, striking a large stone near his feet. Sparks flew, a burning smell in the air.

Tsalagi whirled and crouched with his spear thrust forward. He looked around anxiously: the woman, tangled trees, vines, branches, undergrowth, and stones. Nothing else? Then his eyes were drawn to the shadows between two large trunks about six strides in front of him. A darker shape within the gray. He stared in confusion as a dark head thrust itself forward.

"Flint?" he said in wonder.

The figure stepped completely out from the trees and stood motionless, legs apart. His skin seemed as dull as unpolished stone, except for an occasional shine where the muscles made hollows or rises in the flesh. Dark as the dark time. At first Tsalagi thought the man was naked, the shadowed flesh hiding his member, but then decided he was wearing a small skirt that was somehow joined to his body almost seamlessly. The same black color, and that moved as he moved. Tsalagi could distinguish nothing about the man's face, the roughness of it reminding him of broken stone, until under what might have been the man's eyebrow ridge two new shiny places suddenly appeared.

Tsalagi stiffened. "Flint," he said again, with more conviction. Flint was staring at him.

The village grandfathers talked about Flint all the time. Tsalagi remembered several stories from childhood. Flint the Terrible, they liked to call him, a very wicked man. He liked to eat people, especially babies and very young children. His father used to warn him that he shouldn't stray too far from the hut or Flint might get him. There were stories that when parents tried to save their children from Flint, he just ate them up too. No one was safe from Flint.

Flint knocked Tsalagi sprawling over fallen logs and stones. Tsalagi moaned and clutched his back. Flint laughed a hollow laugh like rocks rattling inside a gourd. Like an old man, Tsalagi thought.

Flint ran up to Tsalagi, thrusting one massive foot toward his chest; Tsalagi rolled and scrambled for a higher perch. Flint roared behind him and beat at the rocks. The air smelled as if it were burning.

Tsalagi crouched on the first branch of a large tree, just out of Flint's reach. Flint swung one sharp-edged hand against the wood. Chips flew.

Tsalagi could see now that Flint did look much like an old man in some ways, in some ways as old as the village's oldest grandfathers. Great seams ran down Flint's chest and tangled together on his stomach. His neck had a wide crack in it. What might have been hair seemed the same as the rest of Flint, and looked like small broken stones on top of his head. Flint tilted his head up to Tsalagi, and the two shiny places were there again. Tsalagi shivered and leaped to the next tree just as Flint hacked the trunk rapidly in two.

Then the rattling laughter again, and a voice like stones grinding together: I'll *take you, too. I'll eat the woman first, and I'll finish off with you.*

Flint lowered his head and charged the tree. Tsalagi jumped just as the tree flew to pieces and small fires burst out all around his feet.

Tsalagi found his spear on the ground and turned. Flint charged again, but with his head up. Tsalagi threw the spear. The point shattered and the staff fell beneath Flint's thundering feet.

The rough valleys etched into Flint's stomach were clearly detailed for Tsalagi before he tumbled out of Flint's way. Flint stopped short, turned, and stood looking for the small human being.

Tsalagi had Flint's cracked stomach vaguely in mind when he saw the large trunk resting within a sling of vines just above eye level, but later he would not be able to claim any organized or intricate strategy. He was exhausted and frightened; he also thought the vines might carry him to safety. He was too panicked to notice the precariousness of the tangle of tree trunk, branches, and vines overhead. He simply ran madly, leaped, and clung to a vine.

Tsalagi bellowed as it seemed the entire forest was crashing around him. Vines whipped his back; branches tore at his face and arms as they tumbled past. The vine he clung to bobbed and twisted, spinning him around like a spider at the end of a strand.

But as the vine twisted him toward Flint, he saw the trunk falling and striking the unmoving Flint directly in that tangle of stomach seams.

Flint roared, and then burst, and hot flint flew all over the wood.

The woman's foot was injured, so Tsalagi had to carry her. She was heavier than he would have thought, and he soon began to wonder whether he must leave her behind. The cloud was overhead again, and seemed to insist that they travel faster. And she was ungrateful; why should he help her?

But again he was impressed by her beauty. Narrow face, white teeth. Raven's eyes, shining. She pushed up against him, and his stomach began to tighten.

Then he looked down at her again, her long face growing longer, her teeth long and sharp, bright light in her eyes ... she began to laugh, high-pitched and shrill, the way an animal might laugh.

The old grandfather laughed uproariously and slapped both his knees. The children broke their intense, wrinkled gaze and giggled, winked at each other, and stared dreamily into the fire.

"So that's how Tsalagi destroyed Flint. That's what some of the old people who lived long ago said about it. Now some say Tseg'sgin, the human trickster, killed Flint, and others say Rabbit killed him, but I think it was probably Tsalagi."

The little boy turned and asked, "But, grandfather, what about the woman? What was happening to her?"

"Ah ..." the grandfather sighed with satisfaction. "That was no beautiful woman, children. That was just Coyote, up to his old tricks again.

"Coyote isn't always a coyote, and you can't always describe him. Some call him the Great-Hare, the Crow, even Raven. Our own name for him is Tsistu. And some say he's Old Man, Trickster, Imitator, First Born, Changing Person, Creator.

"*Coyote doesn't know about good and bad; he just does what he needs to do. But you know, you can't know the land, you can't live*

*with it and be part of it, unless you know Coyote. Coyote helped the
Cherokee befriends to the land and the animals..."*

Tsalagi stood wordlessly as the woman's outline began to blur,
and then overlap with that of someone else's. For a moment
he thought he saw his own father's face in the cloud of bodily
and facial features the woman had become, but then her body
started to fade out completely. Her eyes grew brighter as the
rest of her disappeared, until finally they hung suspended by
themselves in midair, all that was left of her. The two dark orbs
fell to earth with a plop. Tsalagi approached the eyes uneasily,
glancing from side to side for any signs of her. He looked up
and could not see the cloud, and was instantly filled with panic.
Even though he didn't know the cloud's purpose, it had made
him feel safe in this mysterious home of the animals.

The wood had grown darker, the shadows back behind the
trunks moving forward and closer to Tsalagi. He stopped to
look at the eyes. They looked like two pieces of dark stone. He
picked them up and rolled them around in his palm.

Suddenly each eye uncurled from within and stood up on
eight tiny legs. Two spiders began walking up his arm. Tsalagi
yelped and slung his arms to the side to get rid of them.

The cackling seemed to come from every corner of the
wood. Tsalagi watched the two eyes scurrying up a tree trunk.

The laughter continued in a voice half-human and half-
animal. A bird swooped low and tormented him with this
same laughter. A small squirrel crossed his foot, looked up, and
opened up with this same laughter. He jerked his head from
side to side, frantic, but could see her nowhere. He wasn't even
sure what to look for: the woman, or something else.

An old man walked out of the shadows, adorned in a bark-
and-fur skirt and a long bulky cape of feathers. His face was
painted in whites and reds, with swirls of bright blue on each
cheek. He seemed emaciated but vigorous as he strode directly
toward Tsalagi. Then he winked, threw up his cape as if it were
a pair of wings. He gestured toward the sky, and thousands of
tiny bright dots appeared on the blackness.

He turned and stared at Tsalagi. "Well?"

Tsalagi stared at the old man, then at the small dots of light, then at the old man again. He could think of nothing to say.

The old man spat, turned to the sky, and waved his hands again. The tiny points of light began to swirl, then rearranged themselves in great agitation. The old man looked back at Tsalagi. "What do you say now?"

"I don't understand … what are they?" Tsalagi answered.

"Stars!" the old man bellowed. "I was mixing them up! How did you human beings ever get to be so stupid? I wish I'd never made you."

Tsalagi gasped. The old man grinned.

"Yes … it's true, young human. If not for me, you wouldn't be standing here so ignorant, nor having all those strange anxious dreams." The old man drew up his knees and was suddenly sitting in midair. "It was a long, long time ago, but still long after I'd created the earth." The old man eyed the boy sharply. "Yes, I did that, too. See, there was nothing around but water, me, and all these ducks. Just ducks, no other animals. So I told the ducks that it wasn't good to be alone like that. The grebe dived to the bottom of the water and brought some mud up. So I started in the east, and as I traveled I spread the mud around and made the earth—I made it large so there would be plenty of room. Once we had the earth, there would be things who wanted to be there. We heard a wolf howling, so I knew he would be there. Then came the coyote, and the stones. A star came down and became a tobacco plant. A lot of other things happened; I started the whole thing,"

Tsalagi sat before the old man in awe. "You did it all?"

"Everything. Didn't take me that long, either."

"And you made the human beings?"

The old man broke out of his trance and looked down at Tsalagi. "I don't need you to remind me that I haven't finished that particular story, young boy." Tsalagi began to smile, but the old man raised his hand. "So far you human beings have been a great disappointment to me."

Tsalagi noticed something wrong with the old man's head.

It appeared to be flat on top. He couldn't remember it being flat before, and then it suddenly seemed even flatter. And wider. And wider. The old man's head was stretching out on both sides, narrowing, and then his neck pulled up into this narrowing, then his arms, his chest, his belly, his legs, all drawing up and widening out into a thin line. Bumps began to grow out along the length of this line. These became larger until Tsalagi realized he was gazing at a distant horizon of mountains. He looked around him: the trees were all gone, the plants, the streams, the rocks. Nothing but an expanse of empty, flat land, extending in all directions.

Moments later a large gray shape was approaching Tsalagi from the horizon line, too rapidly. Tsalagi could not understand the swiftness of the movement, and his head began to pound. Long hair, gray and brown, in front. Narrow head and long teeth. A four-legged animal, as tall as two human beings at its shoulders.

Learn the patience of the spider, the leap of the panther …

Tsalagi heard this in his head. "Who are you?"

The voice laughed within his head a time, and then Tsalagi realized he was now hearing it aloud, but the animal's lips weren't moving. *Some call me Coyote,* the voice said.

Coyote's lips began to move. "Or Old Man Coyote. But I prefer for you to call me Coyote."

Coyote winked at Tsalagi with one great eye, and then his body seemed to rearrange itself. Coyote appeared thinner now, his legs larger, and he stood as human beings stood. His stiff front legs slowly began to bend and became as flexible as a human being's arms and hands.

An enormous forest tree suddenly burst full-grown from the land before Coyote.

Coyote plucked out his eyes and threw them up into the air above the tree. "This is how I see long distances," he said. Then the eyes returned to his paws when he commanded. "Now you try."

Coyote handed Tsalagi his eyes, and Tsalagi threw them into the top branches of the tree. But they would not come down when he called them. Coyote called, too, but still they would not return.

"I never should have made you!" Coyote screamed, jumping up and down. He pleaded with his eyes to come down, but they remained where they were.

The sun rose quickly in the sky; in but a short time Tsalagi was able to watch it rise to a spot overhead.

The eyes of Coyote began to swell and attract flies beneath the hot sun. Coyote cursed them.

"The day is fading and I still have much I must teach you," Coyote said to Tsalagi. Then Coyote felt the earth, made a hole with his foot, reached in, and pulled out a struggling little mouse. He plucked out one of the mouse's eyes and fitted it into an empty socket. But the mouse escaped before he could grab the other one.

Coyote pawed at the ground until he had dug up a huge mound of earth. The dirt made a face, then a body, and soon a buffalo stood before them. This time Coyote asked permission, and the buffalo gave him one of his eyes. "The buffalo helps me in my troubles," Coyote explained to Tsalagi. Tsalagi knew he'd never seen such an animal as the buffalo, but for some reason he seemed to know all about him.

Coyote could see again, but he couldn't walk straight. The buffalo eye hung outside the socket, it was so big. The mouse eye rolled around inside and often fell back from the hole so he couldn't see out of that one.

After much practice, Coyote tilted his head and walked that way to keep the small eye from rolling out. Afterwards, Tsalagi always saw Coyote with his head tilted. "Follow me ... and your first lesson is to beware of overconfidence in magic of any kind," Coyote said.

"Stay awake while I'm talking to you!" the voice shouted in Tsalagi's ear. He opened his eyes to the small white cloud and towering trees overhead.

"It's time you faced facts!" the voice cried again, and Tsalagi rolled over and searched for his tormentor. But all he could see was green and blue leaves, dark bark, stones.

"You've a job to do, a quest! Yes, a quest it is!" the voice shouted again, and Tsalagi finally saw the speaker: a filthy black cockroach lying in front of his feet. Tsalagi pulled back in disgust. The cockroach had an enormous, red-painted mouth.

"Coyote?" Tsalagi whispered.

"What does the forest say?" The sound of Coyote's chuckling coming from the cockroach distressed Tsalagi.

"I… I don't know."

"The trouble with you human beings is you never listen. I told you my name once before. But there's no time for that."

The old man stood up and waved to the cloud overhead. It began to lower.

But Tsalagi was still staring at the old man. He wore Raven's head over his own. He looked down at the obviously troubled boy. "You must learn to make a friend of Raven, too."

Tsalagi stared at the back of Raven's head, the old man's narrow shoulders, as white mist swirled around them both. The head turned and the dark woman smiled at him with needle-sharp teeth.

"Let us go," she said.

The cloud rose up above the trees, bearing the woman and Tsalagi toward the sun. "Yes, this is mine too," she said without turning, answering a question Tsalagi had been thinking.

Tsalagi was remembering several things he *may* have done with Coyote during their time together, but they could have been dreamed, or Coyote might have just told him about them, he'd never be sure: picking berries from the bottom of a stream; watching as Coyote made one dark and twisting wind after another and sent them marching across the flat land; eating snakes; taking himself apart piece by piece and throwing the pieces through a small hole in a hollow tree; and images of other events he couldn't even begin to put together.

The giant cockroach spoke up. "This is but one possible future, Tsalagi; there are many. The choice is yours."

The high mountain clearing with his village had replaced the sun before them. The cockroach stepped out of the cloud and walked toward the hut of Tsalagi's family. It turned at the halfway point, a tall handsome man with dark, dark eyes, Raven's feathers draped over his shoulders. His voice was somber, "I've but one more tale to narrate for you, young boy."

Coyote entered the family's hut, and it was as if Tsalagi could see through walls.

Coyote told one of Tsalagi's sisters that he was very fond of her and, spreading the Raven's wings over his chest and calmly rearranging his skirt, told the father that he would kill her if she refused to become his wife. Tsalagi's father became enraged and shouted, "You're no good! She won't have you!"

Tsalagi watched as days passed before his eyes. His sister grew ill; he watched her waste away until she was on her deathbed. His father brought in everyone in the village who thought they might have a cure, offering everything he had in exchange, but she only grew worse. They could do nothing. She died.

Tsalagi cried as they wrapped her in blankets and laid her on a raised platform outside the village. An old woman in a black hood came into the clearing and stood beside the platform. When everyone was gone she threw back the hood and Tsalagi recognized her as an older version of the dark beautiful woman. He gritted his teeth. "Coyote!" he cried.

Coyote laughed his old woman's laugh and then called up to the platform, "Get up! Get up!" The body moved on the platform! Tsalagi clenched his fist; perhaps Coyote wasn't so bad after all, just a trickster, a joker.

Then Coyote took Tsalagi's sister to a pool in the sky. There he sang a power song and bathed the body. The girl sat up in the water and Coyote touched her eyes and fixed them so they would open, washed away the smell of death from her body, and put a sweet smell into her breath again.

"I am your husband," Coyote told her. If you ever leave me, you will die again." Tsalagi watched in anger.

It was not long afterwards that Tsalagi's father discovered the desecrated grave site and followed his daughter's trail to the pool in the sky (although Tsalagi knew it wasn't really in the sky—Tsalagi knew this was just Coyote's way of showing him). His father shouted at Coyote. Coyote said nothing.

Tsalagi's father grabbed his daughter, saying, "We are leaving. This one is no good."

"But if I go back he says I will die again," she said.

"This one is always lying," spat the father, and took his daughter away.

Again Tsalagi watched nervously as his sister lay in bed. She would not eat; she went to sleep right away. The next morning she made no sound, and Tsalagi's mother discovered that she was dead once again.

Tsalagi moaned as his father returned to the pool in the sky where Coyote had been watching. Would Coyote kill his father too? But then, Coyote had died many times and been revived by the bluebirds; perhaps he would do the same for his sister. Of course, it must just be Coyote, up to his old tricks again.

"Please come and doctor my daughter," Tsalagi's father said to Coyote. "If you do this you may have her as your wife."

"But I'm no good, remember? After this, medicine men can doctor the sick, but no one will be able to help the dead." Then Coyote laughed his strangest laugh, a laugh like screaming birds. He shrank into a small dark bird and flew away, still laughing.

"I never make promises," the old man told Tsalagi, "but if you do a thing for me, perhaps I will reconsider and bring your sister back to life."

Tsalagi frowned and looked at his hands. For a moment they looked like Coyote's paws and he was afraid, but then they appeared as hands again. "But, Coyote, why do you pull these tricks to make us do things? Why not just ask us?"

"You human beings will only respond to tricks, that's your shortcoming. You do not understand the animal ways."

They were back in the forest again, in a part darker and stranger than any other place Tsalagi had been. Odd sounds broke his thoughts. His body did not feel good.

"All right, Coyote. What do I do?"

"I have a dragon for you, called Uk'ten', that you must kill. But first you will need another weapon."

"I have a spear with a point from Flint. And a blowgun." Coyote snorted. "Uk'ten' would break those in two. You need Snake. I'll take you where you can find him."

"Why am I to kill this Uk'ten', Coyote?"

"Everyone is frightened by Uk'ten'. You need to make friends with me, with the Thunder Beings who hate Uk'ten'. You human beings need animal friends if you ever want to leave the village and live in the great wood."

Coyote showed Tsalagi how to burn a log until it was almost hollow, then to scrape away the burning parts. This made a vessel that Coyote called a canoe, for traveling the stream—which had now grown much larger—through the wood. The stream would take him to Snake and Uk'ten'. A little of the cloud went with Tsalagi, floating on the water around the edges of his canoe. The rest stayed behind with Coyote, swirling around him until he was completely covered up. The last time Tsalagi looked back before heading down the stream, both had disappeared.

"What did this Uk'ten' look like, grandfather?" The children were agitated, staring into the fire wide-eyed.

"A dragon, children, is many things which never belonged together, suddenly all inside one animal. The darkest of all the dark animals. In all its parts, the forest is as much a part of it as it is part of the forest.

"The old grandfathers had different stories about how Uk'ten' looked, but I believe he was like this: head of a great raven, chest of a buffalo, hips of a giant cockroach, legs of a hare, eyes of a spider, tail of old possum."

The children giggled.

"Don't laugh, children," the grandfather warned. "Uk'ten' was a bad animal, terrible. All the animals, even the great ones, were afraid of him. No one knew what to do, until Coyote thought maybe this new animal, the human being, might kill him since Uk'ten did not know or understand the human being. But it was a dangerous quest for Tsalagi."

The grandfather set tied back to continue his tale of Tsalagi, trying to ignore the wails of those mourning their dead in the other wagons. What could be the future for these children? He hoped they would not hear the wails for at least the short time of this tale.

The place where Coyote had told him he would discover Snake was easy to find. Not long after he had left Coyote, Tsalagi recognizedthe landmark he was to seek: a huge stump at the bend of the river. He used the long pole he'd cut to steer over to the bank, and pulled his canoe up on shore only a small distance from the stump. As instructed, he climbed up and stood over the many holes at the top. Then he chanted the charm Coyote had taught him:

"Red Lightning! *Ha!* You will be holding my soul in your clenched hand.

"*Ha!* As high as the Red Treetops—*Ha!*—my soul will be alive and moving over there.

"*Ha!* It will be glimmering here below.

"*Ha!* My body will become the size of a hair, the size of my shadow!"

And the next instant a long black snake leaped out of one of the holes and was writhing in Tsalagi's left hand. Tsalagi yelled and struggled with the snake which seemed confused, darting head and tail in opposite directions as if it were trying to stretch itself, making short, tight arcs with the length of its body.

Tsalagi heard Coyote laugh, and the snake suddenly went rigid in his hand, then a sheen crept over the hardened body.

A snapping turtle had appeared on the edge of the stump. It bobbed its head up and down, and then said, "Don't just stand there, sharpen it on the top of my shell."

"Sharpen it?" Tsalagi looked at the curious black implement.

"Yes, stupid; it's a weapon."

"Weapon?"

"Sharpen it! Uk'ten' will be here any time; I sent a message to Thunder to lead him here. Snake is a kind of long knife, very hard. It's your only chance against the dragon."

Tsalagi held the long object against the rough surface of Coyote-turtle's back and rubbed it back and forth. The snake had straightened out enough so that it did resemble a long knife, but with a small bend here and there. The rocklike snake head made a good grip.

"Find his underside, some soft place there," Coyote-turtle said, even as he was changing himself into a rainbow-hued fish and flapped back into the stream.

Tsalagi turned, Snake in hand, as a large cloud of mist was settling into the forest floor. Before the mist had drifted away, he could hear the snarls and tearing sounds of a fierce battle.

A large, dark shape, something like a human being's shadow blown all out of proportion, stumbled back out of the mist, followed by the dragon Uk'ten', swinging its great-beaked head from side to side and lashing out with its segmented tail. The dark figure roared: Thunder, as Tsalagi had learned. Then the figure suddenly vanished, leaving the air spotted with small fires that quickly died out.

Uk'ten' seemed to stare at Tsalagi with his enormous spider-eyes, and began advancing slowly toward the trembling boy. Tsalagi raised Snake to ward off the attack.

But the long knife suddenly began writhing in Tsalagi's hands. He clutched the squirming head and snapping jaws tightly, maneuvering his body in a rough circle as Snake attempted to slap his face and shoulders with the tail. Finally Snake pulled free and escaped Tsalagi's grip.

Beware of over confidence in magic of any kind... Tsalagi hadn't even considered acting without the sword, and at first ran around the clearing while Uk'ten' chased him. He grabbed at a stick and turned just as the dragon had him backed against a large stone, and used the stick to keep the snapping, drooling, venomous jaws away from his face.

Uk'ten' curled his tail from overhead and brought it down against the stone, but Tsalagi had already leaped aside.

Once behind the dragon, Tsalagi reached for a large stone to throw at the raven's head, but once the stone moved, Tsalagi realized it was part of the dragon's foot. He turned and ran for shelter. *Things aren't as they seem sometimes...*

Uk'ten' roared and twisted around in the undergrowth, crushing plants flat and uprooting small bushes. Enraged, he swung his tail in a blind maneuver, apparently attempting to find the young boy's body, and the great segmented tail crashed through a small tree trunk. *Learn to be resourceful...*

Tsalagi searched the brush frantically for a stone, a limb, anything he might throw. Without thinking, he found the turtle, picked it up, and threw it at the surprised Uk'ten'.

The turtle shouted, startled, with Coyote's voice as it bounced off the dragon's scaled hide. Uk'ten' swung to find the creature, but Coyote had already turned himself into shadow.

"Observe what happens if you touch his tail, boy. I suggest you avoid it," Coyote's voice whispered in Tsalagi's ear. Coyote materialized behind the dragon, grabbed the tail rather comically, and his arm immediately fell off. Then the rest of his flesh dissolved, leaving a pile of bones behind the dragon.

The dead sometimes are reborn ...

But then Coyote was beside him, saying, "See how poisonous an Uk'ten' is? See what happens?" before he disappeared once again.

Tsalagi ran to pick up the spear inside his canoe, when he tripped over the turtle which had again materialized. Needles of pain worried his back, and his head seemed to have become a cloud. *Remember to watch your step...* Uk'ten' turned and rushed behind Tsalagi. As Tsalagi fell, the dragon tumbled over him, stood upright, and did not see the frightened Tsalagi cowering underneath. Then Tsalagi pulled out his flint knife and began slashing at Uk'ten's soft underbelly.

Uk'ten' bellowed and twisted around even as Tsalagi rolled out and leaped into the brush. There he landed on Snake, who was now stiff and weapon like again. With renewed confidence the boy stood up and motioned arrogantly at the dragon. After all, Coyote wanted the Uk'ten' slain; he would not betray him now, surely.

The dragon stood and stared at the boy, its head bobbing up and down. Its great legs pounded the forest floor in impatience.

So Tsalagi made the first move, with the long knife Snake feeling rigid and reassuring in his hand. He watched the scales carefully. They made fine armor, he thought. How would he get through? He took a cautious side step to the canoe, the dragon watching him carefully, and retrieved his spear with the other hand. He continued his approach, both weapons raised and ready.

Uk'ten' roared and thundered forward. Tsalagi pushed the great head off with the spear and began hacking at the cracks between some of the scales with Snake. The strange clang the two surfaces made upon meeting bothered him, but soon he could see a thin line of pale liquid seeping between the seams. He hacked and levered with the crooked blade, until finally great rivulets of the pale liquid began to flow.

Uk'ten' whipped his tail around and Tsalagi had to throw himself to the ground to avoid it. He could taste the poison as it passed.

Tsalagi shoved the spear deep into the dragon's neck. The dragon swung its body around and several of its scales ripped into his side. He doubled over with the pain, surprised he hadn't died instantly. Perhaps the poison wasn't the same in every part of the dragon's body.

Uk'ten' attempted to move its great bulk around in order to get a good place to swipe Tsalagi with its poisonous tail. But instead it ran afoul of the shoreline and Tsalagi's canoe. It made one false step into the canoe, and then flipped over on its back at the water's edge. Tsalagi ran and positioned himself by the white and tender belly. He looked down at the great Uk'ten', listening to its labored breathing, and slowly raised Snake overhead for a thrust.

You must learn to make friends of Raven, too … Tsalagi gazed into the forest: the great dark head, the yellow beak, the all-encompassing midnight wings …

… and thrust down with all his strength. It took a long time for the great Uk'ten' to die.

Tsalagi did not see Coyote again that day, nor did he stay around to gloat and fill himself with pride. He climbed back into the canoe to head upriver, already planning the difficult if not impossible journey back to his home village.

He had seen something in Raven's eyes he did not like. He had seen himself, and had shamefully enjoyed that sense of recognition.

You must learn to make friends of Raven, too ...

And much to his pain, Tsalagi had. He had made a friend of Raven the killer, who enjoys what he destroys.

"But, grandfather, that can't be the end of the story!" the children wailed. "Did Tsalagi have any more adventures? Did he ever see Coyote again? What about his sister? Did Coyote bring her back to life as he'd promised?" They watched the fire anxiously; the old man could tell they'd stayed up too long. They were restless.

"Tsalagi had many more adventures, most of which I will tell you in the future, many of them with that devil Coyote. And remember what Coyote said about promises. No, he did not revive Tsalagi's sister. Those who are dead will always remain so, after Coyote made his decision that time.

"Never believe anything Coyote says. He is complicated, hard to figure. He is an opposite to himself. This, I think, was his big lesson for Tsalagi."

The children fell asleep, and the grandfather sat by the fire and waited for the sleep to overtake him as well. He loved the old stories about Cherokee heroes; he was glad the children did, too. Somewhere, someone was crying. He'd seen them carrying the bodies out of the wagons even as he finished his story. Three more dead. The Ravenmockers were busy this night.

He felt greatly tired, but said a prayer they wouldn't come for him this week, not until he'd finished his tales.

MARKERS

Willy was familiar with this place; he had been here many times in his dreams, like this, after dark. So many times, in fact, that the markers, the stones, felt like part of his own body. Part of his backbone, pressing so hard against his thin, fatless skin that he was afraid they were going to burst through at any second. The stones ground together in his stomach until he was sick. The stones clacked together in his brain until he thought his head might split.

ABIGAIL, LOYAL WIFE OF JOHN

"Willy!"

Willy could not believe his mother was dead. He had seen her lying there; all still, stiller than sleep, still the way a doll or a statue was still. And they all told him his mother was dead. His father and grandmother had told him. Softly at first, but then his father had gotten louder and louder and finally started crying when Willy kept saying "no."

They had the same conversation before and after the funeral. Willy and his dad and Grandmother and the doctor and the minister, all of them sitting in the living room so sad and serious it made Willy nervous, and when Willy got real nervous he started to laugh, and when he started laughing after the funeral they looked at him funny and pulled him into the living room for another talk.

"We buried your mother today, William," Grandmother had said, but Willy just kept saying no no no and finally ran out of the house. To here. Where it was almost night.

"Willy! Willy, please!" There were several of them out there looking for him, calling him, but he stayed quiet, hiding behind the headstones.

His mother *couldn't* be dead. She was the one who had given him the name "Willy." His dad called him Bill and his grandmother always said "William," do this and that. But finally everybody but Grandmother started calling him Willy because his mother gave him that name. They *still* called him Willy so his mother couldn't be dead. If his mother was dead, then he didn't even *have* a name anymore.

"Willy! It's getting dark! You have to come in!"

But Willy knew that now, of all times, he didn't *have* to do anything.

OUR MOTHER, IN ETERNAL REPOSE

Willy didn't believe they ever *really* buried anyone. That was just a lie. The adults kept all the bodies hidden away someplace, probably in a giant building far away, where the kids couldn't see them or talk to them. Where the mothers were hidden away so that they couldn't read you bedtime stories anymore, and where the fathers couldn't give you rides on their shoulders.

But if his mother really *were* here then maybe she could tell him what the truth was. And maybe she could get all the others who stayed here now to tell him things, too. Right now Willy felt closer to these stones than to any living relative, especially his father. His father didn't pay attention, didn't even talk to Willy much, until his mother was gone. Disappeared. Kidnapped by robbers. But he would never believe … dead.

The lie on the stone said "Abigail." His mother's name was Abby. Willy had never heard anybody call his mother Abigail. It was just another adult lie.

HERE LIES THE BODY OF SIMON APPLEGATE

This headstone was old. Dark and mossy and cracked, it was probably just about the oldest headstone in the cemetery. Willy wondered if the man's body was still there. And if the body was still there, and then maybe it could speak to him, tell him about itself, and how things had been when that body was up out of the ground, walking around. Maybe it would even know where they'd hidden his mother away. All the headstones looked like secrets; some of them were just older, longer-kept secrets than the others.

Willy put his head against the ground below the headstone.

He wondered where Simon Applegate's chest must be, if maybe right below the earth, right below Willy's ear, was Simon Applegate's stone heart. He wondered about Simon Applegate's lips, if they looked like earthworms, and if the whispers that might come out of those lips would be soiled, full of earth.

He tried to imagine his mother's lips as earthworms, but he couldn't do it. His mother's lips were soft and warm, and nibbled at his cheek when she kissed him.

DEPOSITED BENEATH THIS STONE THE MORTAL PART OF MATTHEW BANKIER

When his hamster had died, his mother had held his shoulders while Willy flushed the body down the commode. He had cried a little, and he had cried even more when he knew he *liked* watching the hamster's body swirling round and around the twisting tunnel of water. It was like his hamster was on a carnival ride. It was like an adventure. Like dying was an adventure. But then his hamster disappeared. Just like his mother, when they'd closed the lid.

His mother always pinched the blossoms off the flowers so that they would grow better. He hated that. He wondered where all the colors went. Every winter he would wonder if all the colors were just waiting under the snow. If the ground hadn't been frozen, maybe he could free them. Once or twice he'd tried, but he never could get the shovel into the hard dirt.

He wondered if his mother was waiting for him under the ground, needing him to go get his father's old shovel and help her escape.

UNIVERSALLY LAMENTED

After a few hours it seemed like the stones were getting used to Willy. There weren't any other people around now, so maybe the stones felt it was safe to talk. To whisper. To have the low, mumbled conversations all headstones must have after all the guests from the funeral have left.

Willy kept listening for his mother's voice, and although he heard many soft, women's voices, many mothers even, calling their children in for supper, or singing them to sleep, he did not hear his mother's voice.

IN MEMORY OF MARY

My sweet child.

The stone had flowers carved on it. He could tell they were supposed to be beautiful flowers, but they were all colorless and cold. His mother said she loved *all* flowers, but maybe even she could not love flowers like these.

My baby …

Willy would have been this woman's—Mary's—baby, if he could, be so liked the sound of her voice, but he had a mother, so he was very very sorry, but he could not stay. He had to go to the next stone, and then the next, to every headstone in the cemetery if he had to, until he found one that could tell him something about where his mother had gone.

Baby …

HENRY FELLOWES, LATE OF WILLIAMSTOWN

A man was riding on a horse in the old, yellow-stained picture. Willy didn't like photographs on headstones—they felt like a mean joke. He could smell a strong smell of tobacco, just like Great Grandfather had had before he, too, had disappeared. After-shave. Eucalyptus cough drops. Willy liked the mixture of smells, but the man in the photograph wouldn't tell him anything, no matter how much he asked, so Willy went on.

THIS WINGED SKULL

The illustration on the stone gave Willy a creepy feeling. A lot of the older headstones had a carving like that. He wasn't sure what it was supposed to mean. Like a picture of what your head feels like when you're sick, or a little dizzy, your head floating around, and your eyes too large, and too empty, for the room you're in. You can't trust what you see when you're feeling sick like that. And it's like you're all head. With no body at all.

Maybe it was a picture of what your head looked like after you were dead.

His mother always took real good care of him when he was sick. She'd bathe him and hold him and whisper little secrets— secrets just for the two of them—that made him feel better.

Without his mother around to take care of him, maybe his head would grow wings, too, and fly off somewhere. Maybe without his mother around to take care of him, Willy would die.

MOMENTO MORI

A few of the stones had strange words on them. Like a special code, a key to all the secrets. A special code to make the headstone open up like a door and let you inside. Willy spent a long time standing on those graves, staring at those strange words, hoping maybe someone would whisper the meaning of the message to him, so he could break the code and find out where they had hidden his mother. But no one ever told him a thing,

BRAVE FREDERICK, WHO DIED IN DEFENSE OF HIS CHILDREN

Frederick's kids should have stayed out of trouble. Kids were always getting into trouble. Willy wondered if Frederick's kids ever felt it had been their fault.

BENEATH THIS STONE ANGEL

But it wasn't a very friendly looking angel. The stone eyes were huge, the nose bulbous, the mouth a deeply carved frown that would be there forever. But it sang songs a little like his mother's. It had a voice a little like his mother's, a little like all the other buried voices in the cemetery. Several of the stones had pictures of this angel, or the angel's sisters. (Could an angel be male? For some reason he could not understand, Willy didn't think so.) So he began to wonder if maybe this was the guardian angel of his mother's cemetery.

He wondered how much this angel was like the real angels of heaven. His grandmother always talked about the angels in heaven. She'd even said that that was where Willy's mother was now, that she was "with the angels in Heaven." *She's with the angels now ... don't worry yourself; let the angels take care of her. ...* His grandmother wanted him to feel better, but he just couldn't feel better right now.

If anything, he thought true angels must be far bigger than the ones on these headstones. They must be ten, twelve feet tall, with wings like a huge bat's, enormous eyes, and long teeth, one or two feet long, dripping poison. They *had* to be like that, so that the dead people would do whatever they said.

ADDING LUSTRE TO AN AMIABLE CHARACTER, BY SUSTAINING HER LAST ILLNESS WITH CHRISTIAN RESIGNATION

Willy soon got tired of going from stone to stone, looking for his mother, or at least information concerning where his mother might be hiding. There must have been hundreds of stones in the cemetery, maybe even thousands, and once the cemetery filled up he thought maybe they just brought in more dirt and planted more stones on top of the old ones. Who knew how many stones there were here under all those layers, how many dead people? Maybe millions. He'd never find his mother among so many.

He started ignoring some of the stones, paying closer attention to others, running to them at random, following the voices inside the graves, listening especially to the saddest ones, and the ones who were so angry even their dead whispers made the ground shake.

Sometimes he ran so hard he had to stop and rest, lying on a cool grave, his head leaning on the stone.

MOURNFUL PARENTS HERE I LIE AS YOU ARE NOW SO ONCE WAS I AS I AM NOW SO YOU MUST BE

He stared sadly into the little boy's eyes. The gray little boy was dressed in old-fashioned clothes, and sang old-fashioned songs to himself. Willy thought maybe the songs were to keep him from feeling so lonely. He thought maybe the songs gave the little boy a way of crying, without really seeming to cry, and he'd never had a friend his own age die. He knew that children died—it was on the news and in the movies; he just hadn't known of any personally.

He looked around, but couldn't find the graves of the little boy's parents. They couldn't still be alive—the grave was quite old. Maybe they had moved away after the boy died, so that they wouldn't remember so much. Willy didn't think that could have worked. Memories were like graveyards: the stones were everywhere. You couldn't take a step without tripping over a headstone, old or new.

The boy's songs rose and fell like the ocean. They got down into Willy's ears and throat. They got down as far as his belly and then they made him feel bad. He ran away from the gray, singing boy, but couldn't keep himself from being sick in the tall weeds that surrounded part of the cemetery. He wiped his mouth on his sleeve and started running again, afraid of this dark corner of the cemetery.

IN MEMORY OF THE WIDOW SARAH COTTON

Willy ran and ran, and accidentally fell into the pale woman's arms. He didn't scream, and that surprised him. He'd become used to them, he guessed. But finally he had to squirm his way out of her embrace; her fingers pulled at him, pinching his skin, and that did scare him a little. He was terribly sorry, but he had to find his own mother. When he finally broke away the woman disappeared with a great sob, but her sweet smell stayed behind, and clung to his clothes much as her fingers had.

MY GLASS IS RUN

He stumbled again and again over hidden parts of stones. He could see a little of light on the horizon, and once day came he knew his father and grandmother would probably find him. He grew sick with panic. He fell face first into the dirt, and got up with a mouth full of grave.

IN REMEMBRANCE OF PHILIP YATES, WHO WAS KILLED BY LIGHTNING

Willy had known this man. He'd been about the age of Willy's grandmother, and he used to work on the flower gardens in the park. Willy used to stop and watch him on his way home from school, and once Mr. Yates had given Willy some flowers to take home to his mother, just because Willy had asked.

The story about Mr. Yates getting struck by lightning had been on the front page of the town paper. It had made his mother real sad. It would have made Willy real sad, too, and it did, some, but at the time he really didn't understand what it was all about. At the time he didn't understand why they just didn't dig Mr. Yates up and take him to the hospital and fix him. Why they just didn't put a machine inside him that would make him work again.

Now he knew. When his mother disappeared, for some reason he knew things didn't work that way.

Mrs. Yates stopped going outside anymore. His mother told Willy there were too many memories for her—she couldn't get away from them. Mr. Yates' daughter, who had been in college, came back to take care of Mrs. Yates. You almost never saw her either. Willy's dad had said that the two of them might as well move out to the cemetery and live there. His mom had told his dad to hush up. Willy's grandmother had said that some people spend half their lives in graveyards. That sounded like something true to Willy, but he wasn't really sure what it meant.

Willy stared at Mr. Yates' grave, and wondered what it would be like to see that stone in your mind all the time. The longer he looked at the stone, the more it resembled Mr. Yates' wide, white face, looking at Willy as he handed him the flowers that day. Willy imagined what it would be like to have your head full of all these stones, a graveyard full of stones that looked like people's faces, maybe that even looked like people's whole lives. Willy knew.

He turned his head and walked away slowly. He didn't want to hurt Mr. Yates' feelings any, but Willy could feel him staring at him.

IN THE COLD BED OF DEATH FREE FROM TROUBLE AND PAIN

His mother had always hated sleeping. There was just too much to do in a day, she said; she didn't have time for sleeping. Willy could do the sleeping for the both of them, she said. It wasn't fair she had to sleep now, no matter what his grandmother said.

DEATH IS A DEBT TO NATURE DUE WHICH I HAVE PAID AND SO MUST YOU

His father told him that life wasn't fair. It didn't seem to Willy that death was very fair either.

"Mom!" It was late and there weren't any adults around—no one wanted to live next to the cemetery, he guessed. So he didn't think anyone would hear him.

They answered. One at a time and then whole groups of them, sounding like the choir at Grandmother's church. They were alone, the voices told him. They wanted him to spend some time with them. But he knew that none of the voices, coming out of the ground, coming out of the stones, coming out of the leaves blowing down from the trees and catching on the black iron fence, was his mother's.

DEAR CHILDREN REMEMBER THAT YOUR MOTHER LIES HERE

Where? He wondered if those children at least knew where their mother was, or if they had been lied to, too. He wanted to meet them and ask them when was the last time they had seen their mother, talked with her, and held her hand.

Now and then, passing by a stone, Willy felt a light touch on his arm, his leg. A touch like a twig catching on his clothes, or a leaf pressed against his bare skin by the wind. They wanted to hold him here. They wanted to get inside his head and live there forever.

More than ever Willy wanted to run away from the stones, but he had to find his mother first. He found himself running again, faster and faster, looking at every stone for just a second, trying to find his mother's face in the stone, then running away before the others, the ones not his mother, could touch him. He'd already forgotten where the grave was where they'd lied and said they'd buried his mother.

THERE IS REST IN HEAVEN

Willy couldn't run any farther. All his breath had run out of him. His chest hurt, like he was breathing pain in and out of his body, not air.

He felt like giving up, and lying down among all these whispering stones, these dreams and memories, but he was afraid of how it would feel when the shadows touched him. So he kept running, the stones growing fuzzier as he ran, seeming to twist and float away.

IN CONSEQUENCE OF INCURABLE ULCEROUS SORES UNDER WHICH HE PAINFULLY LINGERED IN GREAT AGONY

"At least she didn't suffer," Mrs. Reynolds across the street had said. "We can console ourselves with that."

The pale shapes of the dead twisted and distorted beside him, trying to grab onto to him with their deformed fingers and hands. But they couldn't run on their warped and broken legs. They stumbled and fell and rotted on the ground, their cries filling rapidly with dirt.

People's lives get messy, a voice inside him said. *But you can't let the mess get you. You'll die that way. Willy.* His mother was always telling him things like that, but now he couldn't listen. All those things she had said didn't matter in the end. Her magic words didn't work. His mother was still gone.

Willy suddenly realized that his mother was hiding inside his own head, somewhere under the hardening bones of his skull. He could hear her now, singing him to sleep.

MY WIFE

A finger at the center of the stone pointed upward. It was a terrible lie. The finger could have pointed in any direction.

Inside his head, he could see his mother's smile, stretching so widely it began to give him a headache, the corners of her mouth pushing so hard against the inside of his head, leaving no room for his own thoughts or feelings.

But he had his mother now. He began running toward the front gate of the cemetery.

LITTLE ALICE

The little girl with the empty face tried to grab him as he ran toward the gate of the cemetery. He tried to get away, but her arms were very long for her size, and she finally got him, holding on to his wrists so tightly Willy imagined that was the way handcuffs must feel.

She whispered into his ear that she was going to kiss him. Willy turned his face to her then. Sharp, curved teeth suddenly sprouted all around the edges of her empty, oval face, her face becoming a huge mouth ready to eat his head.

Willy's mouth flew open, stretching wider the louder he screamed, so that suddenly he was afraid *he* might swallow *her* instead.

He felt his head stretching, his hair pulling, and suddenly his mother was coming out of his scalp, growing out of his hair, dragging herself up and out of him as she cried *What's wrong, Willy? Did you have a nightmare again, honey?* Like all those other nights so long ago when she had gotten up to hold him when he'd cried out in the night.

O! RELENTLESS DEATH

Before he knew it was happening Willy was past the gate, and staring back at his mother, who was unable to leave. And as much as he wanted to, he could not bring himself to walk back inside.

Grandmother had told him several times the past few days, "This is very important: we cannot let ourselves forget that she is dead." But it was even worse, wasn't it, for the dead to forget—maybe just for a moment—that they were dead?

Willy wandered home a little after dawn, thinking about what he should tell his father about where he had been all night. Maybe he should tell his father he'd found his mother. Maybe he should tell his father he'd found a cemetery inside his head.

TALL SKIES

Leadville: The Old Man's Story. 1960

Foolish old man, Mrs. Guerra thought. He had been sitting out in his backyard for days. Mrs. Guerra had the crumbling brick house north of him. At one time the old Indian would have been at her door offering to shore things up again at the first sign of crumbling brick, but not anymore. He always used to say that he was one of "the blue sky people," and now that's where his mind was most of the time. She guessed he just got too old. Maybe her house had done it—seemed like he'd always been there fixing it, and Lord knows it had made her old just watching it falling apart, and that old man doing his best to stop the decay. It had been a miner's shack originally, and not meant to be anything more, but in Colorado things had a way of becoming something much more than they were ever intended to be,

The old man hadn't seemed to mind too much. All that fixing, all that changing. Like he expected things to age and crumble and get shored up again until some day it all fell apart on you and became just another Colorado ruin. Just like him. Just like her.

Maybe the old man went in at night, but Mrs. Guerra never saw that. Maybe he slept, but she never saw that either. But dreaming, she knew he'd been dreaming. Seemed to her he'd been sitting out there dreaming day and night. But he was Indian, so maybe she just didn't understand.

She supposed the neighborhood children were missing his stories, as much as she missed his help and his company.

They used to gather around every afternoon in that backyard and he'd tell them about the old times, the long ago times, back when Colorado was Paradise.

Once upon a time, farther back than you or the oldest grandfather can remember, the Great Spirit Manitou gave Colorado to the Indians for a Paradise ...

The old man watched as a green feather floated out of the sky and landed at his feet. He did not move to pick it up; he wasn't even sure he could move. He was stone, and in the way of stone he would not move or speak. But he would watch.

From his backyard overlooking the mountain town of Leadville he watched as clouds dropped out of the high peaks and drifted through the town, making it impossible for all but the old man to see. Here and there the clouds would solidify, turn to stone, and it would be as if the stone had always been there. He knew no one else would notice any difference. Only the old man would see. Sometimes animals would turn to stone. Sometimes people. And sometimes the stones themselves would become animals or people. This is the way it was in Colorado, home of the red rock. And only the old man would see.

But strange as it may seem, the Indians grew tired of Paradise. Because Paradise is uneventful. Criticism began, and the troublesome urge to improve things. The Indians wanted to change everything. They thought the Great God Manitou was stupid! Finally they decided that Paradise was too far gone, and they would have to travel west through the Portal of the Sun and into the land of the gods.

He used to tell the children that things were not always as they are now. Once his people were hunters of buffalo, and lived inside the skins of those they had killed. Once his people lived in great castles in the tall skies. Here were Toltecs, Aztecs, Anasazi. Here Coronado walked within fifty years of Columbus's landing. Here the lands and the skies change even as you watch, until in amazement your eyes turn to stone even as his tongue had turned to stone. No more stories would be told. The stories would live inside his body and his dreams until one day he would die from their numbers.

So they gathered bundles of earth, rock, and maize and

went to the Sun, attempting to reach it while it was open wide and golden, before it disappeared into the Western Sea. They commanded the seas and rivers to release their waters upon the disappointing land and utterly destroy it!

The old man gazed south toward Pike's Peak, knowing it was there even though he could not see it. As a boy he had lived at its foot, climbed its back, whispered into its Cave of the Winds. Years later he had searched there for his kidnapped children, his lost son, his lost daughter, finally to wander among the frozen red giants of the Garden of the Gods where he found among them the small frozen shapes of his children, and their faces turned to stone.

Their faces remained stone in his memory.

Now these original people could not rid themselves of their discontent, even on the road to Heaven! They struggled for position; they trampled the squaws and children under foot, even as the rising waters licked their feet!

While still a young man of twenty-five winters, he had left the lands of the southern Utes and had journeyed to the "Cloud City," Leadville, to work at the Carbonate Mine. His brothers called it the white man's hell, but when he walked into town that January of 1896 it was like a return to the Colorado Paradise of Ute legend. For they had created an ice palace in Leadville, a Crystal Palace, three hundred twenty feet across and four hundred fifty feet deep, a castle of ice, the highest in the world.

He had gladly paid his fifty cents admission, even though it was all he had. He had marveled at its wonders: its great rooms and statues of ice, its indoor skating rink and high towers. And when a mild winter closed the ice palace after ten weeks he felt no sadness, for this was Colorado, and Colorado was a dream of the Great Manitou, and in dreams everything must change.

Finally Manitou had enough, and his voice thundered out of the tall skies, "Enough! Drop these burdens of Earth, Foolish Ones!"

In terror they dropped their bundles containing all that was glorious of the world below. And don't you know, my children, it made a vast heap to the very threshold of the portal where the Great Manitou stood.

And don't you know, my children, that today the white men call that stairway to heaven by the name Pike's Peak.

The old man had told that story many times, and now would tell it no more, even though it transformed and multiplied in his head like a story told in the clouds, and sometimes the weight of it gave him headaches, and sometimes the smells and colors of it made him sick long into the night, until he thought he would die unless he got the story out of himself and out into the world where it could stretch and grow and infect other people with its truth, its color, its madness.

The old man struggled to move from his chair but could not. He could not lift a finger, could not shift a foot. Up in the tall skies he could hear Quetzalcohuatl, Green Feather, laughing at him. Finally in anger the old man opened his mouth and could feel his stone face breaking, his stone tongue splintering, as he released his changing story into the world. He could see it filling the sky as it spread and traveled across Colorado.

The Great Plains: The Old Ones' Story, 5,000 B.C.

They believed that the land would give them what they needed. They had many beliefs, but this was the most important: the belief they breathed and ate and slept and died with—the land would give them what they needed. However flat or brown the land might be as they journeyed from place to place, one day it would open for them, and share with them its flesh.

They sat quietly in holes, spear and skinning knife close by, dogs piled together beside them. And waited. Soon the thunder began, and they always looked up into the tall skies, even though they knew the thunder did not come from there. When they looked down again, dust was rising from all over the land, and out of the dust came the great beasts, great snorting rough masses, torn from the land and given powerful legs, coming down upon those who waited, spears in hand, mouths already watering with the taste of the country's dark and thundering heart.

They waited until they could wait no more, and then they came from all sides, shouting, waving, despite their small size terrifying the great bison, forcing them across a plain filled with so much sky the bison appeared to rise, thunder making them fly, up and over the edge of the steep ravine.

Where they became part of the land again, where they entered the people's bodies, where they became stone.

Come here child, the old man said to the small boy standing in front of him. But he said this in his head, for his tongue had become stone again. And the lost child in front of him was no longer a human child, but a stone child who would never say his father's name again.

My story is out there, he said with his stone tongue to the stone boy. *Can you hear it crying?*

Mesa Verde; The Ugly Boy's Story, 1202-1248 A.D.

The village called him the ugly boy because of his head. No one knew why he had such a head—those who remembered remembered a normal head when the ugly boy was born. They wondered if something was wrong with his mother's cradleboard, if it was too hard, or if there was something bad about the wood, but it looked like all the other cradleboards in the village. Something had happened to the ugly boy's head while he slept, but since the rest of the village slept at the same time, no one knew what that thing could be.

The village did not like the ugly boy because of his head that looked like a bear's or a raccoon's head. But they went to him whenever they did not understand a thing, or worried about a thing. They thought he might know some things because of his strange head.

The ugly boy did know some things—he knew that the rain would go away, and that the crops would go away, and the animals. He knew how things looked under the ground. But he did not want to tell the village these things. They sat around and waited for him to open his mouth and tell them some stories. But the ugly boy closed his mouth and closed his eyes and told them nothing with his mouth or his eyes. Finally they went away angry, and no one asked him questions anymore.

The ugly boy sat all day in the kiva and stared at the sipapu out of which their ancestors had climbed up from the spirit world to live in this world. The ugly boy sat all night on the edge of the cliff with his eyes closed and watched the canyon inside him grow deeper and deeper.

When the ugly boy was an old man a time came when the rain did go away, and the crops, and the animals. The elders decided they would have to leave the cliffs and go where other people lived. The ugly boy was not an elder, however old—he had already lived longer than any born the same summer as he. People said it was his head that made him live longer than anyone else. But in this village he would always be the ugly boy, never a man, and never an elder.

A few at a time the people left, so quickly it might have been the wind choosing them as was its way, and leaving the rest for later, blowing the ones it chose to where no one might find them again. They left many of their things behind. They believed their things would someday make them return.

But the ugly boy kept his eyes closed, not wanting to see their faces, because he knew the villagers would never return.

"Come with us. Come with us, Ugly Boy," they would whisper into his ear, not because they liked him, but because it would be a bad thing to leave one of their people behind. But he would ignore them, not even shaking his head, until one by one they gave up in disgust.

And then they were gone, and there was only the ugly boy and the things he saw underground.

The ugly boy sat there for a long time, until the animals who had gone away before the people had gone away came out and gathered around him. Bear looked at the head that was like Bear's head and lay down beside him. Raccoon sniffed the head that was like Raccoon's head, and then put his own strange head into the ugly boy's lap. One by one the animals came, looked, sniffed, and stayed with the ugly boy.

Then the ugly boy opened his mouth wide as if to eat the animals, but stories came out instead. Stories of the villagers and their cliff dwellings, stories of how mud was carved and buildings were raised so that the people could live inside the ground once again, stories about how they all disappeared again, through that great sipapu which led them underground and into the world from which all true stories come.

The animals listened to the storyteller for years until they understood the lives of men and women. Then one day the storyteller also disappeared into the underground that was everywhere, but his stories continued, telling themselves.

Don't you know, my child, in the beginning there were no Indians, no bison, no living things. There was no earth. There were only the tall blue skies, the old man told his son of stone, even though the stone boy told no stories in return. *Manitou bored the hole in heaven so that he might find new things to see.*

Telluride; The Snow's Story. 1967 ... 1902

He'd been skiing most of the afternoon. Off-limits, where he shouldn't be, but it looked pretty safe to him. He wasn't very good, but he was becoming more fluid in his movements, more at ease with the way the fiberglass sped over the gentle curves of snow.

He disliked snow in the city—the shoveling, the slush, the general mess of it. But up here it was something else, particularly with a light breeze skimming off the thin top layer of powder and blowing it with him down the slope, so that it was like descending through clouds.

There were only the tall blue skies ...

There it was again, a voice carried by the breeze between rows of snow-crowned lodge pole pines. A deep, distant-thunder voice that made the slope under his feet vibrate ever so slightly.

Then the ground shifted, and he heard the thunder again, louder, shaking the whole mountain, and he found himself looking up into the tall sky, even though he knew that wasn't the thunder's source, and saw the hole that had been bored there, and this blinding face peering through.

He was *with* the snow now, taking the mountain with him in his descent, passing a weathered, broken sign—Liberty Bell Mine—as the air suddenly darkened and ancient shacks tumbled past him, men in old-fashioned clothing still clinging to the jagged beams, horses rolling, their saddles tearing off, their long necks bending, and then everything was white, and he could feel that brilliant face smiling at him.

Wherever he touched, trees sprang up. The sun shone through the hole he had made in heaven to warm the air and melt the snow.

Fort Collins: The Grasshoppers' Story, 1873

Abigail was sweeping the dust out of the downstairs rooms when she saw the first hopper. She was startled at first: she'd been thinking the thing was just a little clump of sage and dried mud when it grew legs and jumped at her. Maybe it wouldn't have been such a big event if she hadn't already been upset—now that the new town was going up, folks like Abigail in Old Town were feeling talked about, like they weren't good enough for the New Town folk. The land company had advertised for folks "of good moral character" to buy lots in New Town. Did they think they were all drunks, beggars, and injuns over in Old Town? She was a preacher's daughter, and owned two good church dresses. Her husband worked hard and weren't no drinker. She ought to march right into that land office and throw them dresses on the desk! Then let them tell her she weren't good enough for New Town living! Now that banker what left town with all their money—that banker was the low life. She came from *decent* folk.

This army post they put up to protect the stage line from the Utes was on its way to being a city, she reckoned, but she wasn't sure she liked it much.

The other thing peculiar about that first grasshopper was that it spoke to her. *Paradise,* it said right out. *Paradise.* It made her want to laugh. The Fort was a far piece from any Paradise; it was a hard enough trip just travelling down to Denver.

But then the grasshopper opened up like a book and got bigger. It hopped through the open door and out into the yard.

Abigail leaned on her broom. Things weren't right. They never felt too much right but they felt even worse today. It was the middle of the afternoon and here it was getting dark already. Maybe they were due for one of them awful dust storms. It took her two weeks to clean the house to Frank's satisfaction after the last big one. Weary, she dropped her broom and walked to the door.

And found a tall sky just *full* of hoppers, covering up the sun like a widow's hood and shaking the trees, the bushes falling apart and dancing away in pieces. The blankets she had out on the line were ragged strips of cloth, and little pieces of bark littered the ground. Here and there she saw chewed up tool handles from the livery stable next door: the horses were in there screaming. She put her hands over her ears and tried to go back inside, but the grasshoppers were on her dress now, and she couldn't get them off. She ran around the yard and snagged the edge of her dress on a stake and both her dress and her petticoat tore, showing her leg to above the knee. She yelped as the hoppers got inside her dress. She turned her head as best she could to see if anybody was looking at her nakedness, but all she could see were the hoppers flying at her face.

Something made her look up right then, and she saw him standing there: an old injun fellow. But he didn't look right. She kept staring at him, knocking the hoppers off her face, until she could really see him: the way the skin on his face moved like bug bellies, the way his hair fluttered up like the dark backs of bug wings, the way his fat lips opened and closed like that first hopper she'd seen on her floor, the way his body suddenly broke apart so that she could see right through him then all came back together again. That old injun man was made entirely out of wriggling, swarming grasshoppers, looking at her, looking at her naked leg, trying to tell her a story.

With the small end of his staff Manitou fashioned the fishes. In the forests he picked up great handfuls of dry leaves which he blew into the air to become the birds. From the middle of his staff he created the beasts.

Denver: The Dust's Story, 1935

Bishop Frank Rice of the Liberal Church leaned back in his sack cloth and puffed on a cigar. News reports were saying that the dust storm covering Colorado was a thousand miles in diameter and had dropped 300 pounds of dust per acre in the last thirty-six hours. The Bishop was wondering if there was any way his congregation of winos, beggars, and prostitutes might gain ownership of all that new land. Surely the Colorado constitution had never accounted for land dropped onto the state by the hand of God himself!

Downstairs his flock was having a prayer meeting, keeping out of the hellish dust outside: he could hear them singing, glasses smashing. It did his heart good. Maybe tonight he'd baptize another dog.

Downstairs the scapegoat was bellowing. He'd told his congregation time and again that they were to cast their sins onto the goat, but nothing else. He'd have to go down; he couldn't tolerate an animal being abused. Besides, if one of his flock released the goat again his Larimer Street neighbors would complain.

Tonight's sermon would be on those official saints of the Liberal Church P.T. Barnum and Tom Paine, and maybe a bit on Colorado cannibal Alferd Packer. Certainly the bible sanctified cannibalism. Leviticus 26:29, "And ye shall eat the flesh of your sons, and the flesh of your daughters shall ye eat." The bishop had a watch chain he could show the crowd Packer himself had made from his shoulder-length hair.

Of course Packer was buried now, well on his way to dust. Dust and dust and more dust filling up the tall skies. All of it waiting for his unfortunate flock to grab hold of and plant crops in, maybe build a house.

Then the Bishop Rice stared out the dust-laden pane into the fierce face of God, who said to him, "*Enough! Drop these burdens of Earth, Foolish Ones!*"

The good bishop nodded, and poured himself another drink.

But all were not foolish during that time of the great flood, I tell you my children. There was the man Tlaz, swimmer, and the woman Toluca, life. These two are the original ancestors of the Utes.

Big Thompson Canyon: The Rain's Story, 1976

She and her brother were alone in the tent when the wall of water struck. Their parents had gone for a walk up the trail somewhere, had disappeared behind trees and rock. They'd said they wanted to see what the river was doing. There had been lots of rain that weekend. *The god of the rain thought he was more important than the god of the sun,* a voice inside her head said.

She lay down in the tent, tired of the way her brother complained about everything. She wasn't sure if she fell asleep or not—that's what she kept telling her rescuers. She wasn't sure if she had fallen asleep.

She wasn't sure because she'd had this dream that was so real it had to be true. The canyon walls had suddenly gotten fuzzy, and then they became water. She and her brother had been trying to walk out of the canyon. They were holding hands they were so scared, because of these tall walls of water. Inside the walls of water they could see other people: men, women and children, even animals, trying to get out, trying to break through the walls of water but they couldn't. The walls of water bent with their fists but would not break.

And she remembered feeling bad, because she didn't want the people to break through, because if they broke through those walls then maybe the water would get out and sweep her and her brother away.

They ran as fast as they could hand in hand, afraid to let go of each other. Then an old man's voice flooded her head with a story. *They commanded the seas and rivers to release their waters upon the disappointing land and utterly destroy it!*

"No!" she screamed, but it did no good. The story swept over her and her brother and she never saw her brother again.

The days Tlaz and Toluca spent floating in their canoe were without number, with only the endless sky above them and the endless water below. But over time they discovered maize stalks rising from the waters, and on each an animal family; the house of Mouse and the house of Gopher, the houses of Prairie Doer, Cottontail, Badger, and Bear.

West Divide Creek: The Bear's Story. 1905

The old Ute was supposed to go with him, show him the way, but at the last minute said he wasn't going, something about how the bear was the master of the beasts, interpreter of the word of Manitou, which made no sense to Corrigan, so he went up the mountain by himself. Teddy Roosevelt had made the same trip earlier that year. Teddy Roosevelt had hunted the bear, so why couldn't he? "It's a democracy, ain't it?" But the old Indian probably didn't know much about politics.

Corrigan had a good horse, the best money could buy, but it still wasn't easy going. The melting snow had turned the mountain slopes to grease, and the shifting shapes and shadows on the hills made the horse jittery, bucking and shying for no good reason.

Corrigan found the grizzly late in the afternoon, or maybe it was the grizzly that found him. He came up behind it, up a narrow ravine. At first he thought the animal was a boulder, or a big shadow under the low trees, but the light wasn't right for that. His horse made a sound like he'd never heard before, reared up, and threw him off.

Then the bear turned around and showed Corrigan its eyes. Even from that distance, Corrigan thought the eyes looked human, the way they moved, the way they looked into him, and he felt a shiver he couldn't control. He wished he had brought some dogs. Everybody knew you hunted a bear with dogs; what kind of fool was he?

What do you want, in the house of Bear? Corrigan heard it plain as day. The bear stared at him. And suddenly he saw that it *was* a stone he was looking at, a stone shaped like a bear, but a stone just the same. He walked closer to examine the great stone head. The eyes blinked at him, human eyes, and then were stone again. In the tall skies above him, he could hear the chanting of the wind.

In that first time of times, there were those who drowned on the road to heaven as the waters rose and still they quarreled. What happened to those drowned ones no one knows.

Pike's Peak; The Drowned Ones' Story, 2315 A.D.

As the dropship descended into Colorado Springs the captain pointed out Pike's Peak and ran down a brief history of the area, Grant was a little surprised, or what passed for surprise in someone who had come to expect anything. He hadn't thought it to be a mountain at all. He'd been half-asleep, certainly, studying the research being transmitted to his palm screen from the office back in New York Inc., but he'd been sure the tall dark blue shape was a rain cloud, a thunder head, a storm descending out of the vast sky, just asking to be neutralized by the weather stations below. Not a mountain, and certainly not the mountain that was his final destination. Somehow he had expected it to be smaller.

The research scrolling across his screen and chattering away in his inner ear plant was hardly essential to his mission. Just a bit of colorful local history he'd requested on the Peak, something to tell Angela about when he got back.

The bits about Sergeant John O'Keefe interested him most. O'Keefe had been an enlisted man in the U.S. Signal Corp sent to the top of the Peak during the winter of 1876 to operate the weather station there (the kind of weather station that had measured, not changed, the weather, he reminded himself).

O'Keefe had been a consummate liar, convincing the townsfolk below that a colony of giant rats lived on the Peak, and moreover, had devoured the O'Keefes' infant girl Erin. This was followed by stories concerning giant herds of black-tailed deer, roving packs of ravenous mountain lions, and culminating in reports of renewed volcanic activity on the mountain. All of it false, of course.

Grant supposed that if the highly civilized and sophisticated citizens of the current city were to find out about his researches, he would be thought of as some sort of great prevaricator. He was to take over an abandoned weather station on the Peak, not the same one—O'Keefe's was long gone—but no doubt in a similar location (and again, of the predictive sort only), set up the new equipment, and scan the tall Colorado skies for spiritual manifestations. Ghosts to the layperson. The problem with those terms was that they suggested a particular sort of origin and, perhaps, intent. At least the government now had ample proof that spiritual manifestations existed—although they weren't sharing much of that information—but they had no hard data as to the dynamics or mechanics involved. Theoretical spiritual physics was still a joke, mostly.

Actually it had been the weather people who'd first put his agency onto Pike's Peak for the experiment. Their micro-detection technology had discovered a pattern of spiritual manifestations in the high air around the Peak. Grant's job was to bag and transport some specimens.

After the dropship landed, an Air Force shuttle took Grant and all his equipment directly to the top of the Peak. In a few days he had the collecting dish for the experiment in place, the dimensional coils tested and running (although he wasn't too pleased with the phase variations). It *was* beautiful up here, a sky that went on forever, with peaks and valleys opening up to show even more vistas like a promise. He'd have to include more environmental video in the next personal transmission back to New York Inc., otherwise Angela wasn't going to believe him.

The first thing caught in the collector was a tumble of thunder, and Grant found himself looking up into the sky even though he knew the thunder wasn't coming from there. The thunder turned in on itself eventually and disappeared.

An hour later the collector picked up an aged voice.

Once upon a time, farther back than you, or the oldest ... the voice said, and the voice said again. This repeated itself every five marks for most of the day before finally dissipating. Grant was a bit disappointed; he'd wanted to hear the rest of the story.

Then in the middle of the night the alarm pulsed in his inner ear and he rushed to the collector to find manifestations cascading out of the collector, slipping under the barrier and flowing lava-like down the side of the mountain. Indians and fur traders and ranchers and Doc Holiday (or so the man claimed), and a petrified figure being carried by two men in overalls, an endless parade of trains and wagons, a couple of soldiers from the African campaigns of 2105, the former (and seriously insane) leader of the United Asian States, dead bison and mules and horses and the largest rats he'd seen outside or inside a zoo (or were the animals extinct now?).

Once upon a time, farther back than you, or the oldest grandfather can remember, the ancient voice continued, the Great Spirit Manitou gave Colorado to the first people for a Paradise ... and Grant could not stop it, could not prevent the story from overflowing the Peak and descending irresistibly out of the tall skies and down the mountain to engulf the civilized people below.

Tlaz and Toluca took all the wriggling things that lay dead after the waters went away and they buried them, banishing pestilence from the land of Colorado forever.

Lake City (Cannibal Plateau): Alferd Packer and Paul Bunyan's Story. 1874

Packer knew the land well—they should have listened to him—knew it like the back of his hand even though he hadn't been through most of it. He'd seen it in a dream, the land, full of meat and silver, the San Juans bursting at the ridge-lines just waiting to give it all to them. Crazy Utes didn't know a damn thing about a white man's dreams, a white man's visions when the hunger is upon him.

But somewhere in the blinding snow Packer lost the vision, had it stolen from him by some claim-jumping half-breed, and he wandered for a time alone, with nothing to see but the white outside his head and the black inside his head. Until the giant came.

The giant stepped out of a window in the tall skies and sat down next to him and explained to him about how things were going to have to be. A great Blue Ox curled up around the giant like an old hound dog in front of the fire and the giant said, *in the beginning, in the beginning, once upon a time, once upon a time, dear friend, farther back than you, there was a story, and the story created Paradise where we all might eat and never go hungry—don't look at the ox! don't you go looking at my ox that way!—have you seen the giant rats of the Peaks? have you seen the giant jackalopes of the valleys? have you seen the sugar beets they grow out on the plains bigger than your average-sized man? Alferd, my boy, it's all there for the eating, the putting in the mouth and chomping down, with a little cornbread, a little green for color, all that bright red rock meat, and acres of timber, gold, and silver, yours for the eating! once upon a time, once upon a time, so far back even your grandfather wouldn't remember …*

And consume Packer did. He ate the snow and he ate the timber; he ate the fear right out of his companions' eyes, and when he'd eaten all he could see, he dug down through the earth to eat the massive red meat that bled there, sharing this sacrament and every story he could think of with the great Paul Bunyan, his only friend and companion.

And in memory of the maize stalk Tlaz and Toluca named their child Quetzalcohuatl, which means "Green Feather," who lived to an ancient age, and told his children and their children these stories, and many many others.

Then the old man let go of the last of his stories, and went the way of stone.

Leadville: Mrs. Guerra's Story. 1995

Now she was as old as the Indian had been the last time she'd seen him, and sitting in her back yard with her face toward the sky she could see all the old man's stories returning, and all she had to do, what she needed to do, was just pick the one story that would be hers to tell.

THE SOUND OF HAWKWINGS DISSOLVING

When my hawk discovered her, Ellen was slumped semi-conscious on the other side of the yellowed windowpane. Her arm crawled up the glass, stiff-fingered, matching my hawk's motions stroke for stroke, claw for claw. She'd always been like that on a high: playful, morbid.

I had arrived outside Ellen's third-story window only a few minutes after my hawk. I hung upside down from the awning over the window, staring past the hawk and into Ellen's face. She hadn't seen me yet; she couldn't until my familiar flew in, and I followed it. Her looks gave me second thoughts about entering at all: sallow skin, lined and ancient-looking, paper-thin flesh angling into bone. Stringy black hair. I'd almost forgotten this side of her.

She jerked the window open as I knew she would, but whether out of some sort of childish curiosity or suicidal impulse I couldn't be sure. Turning abruptly from the rush of the hawk, she began pacing the room restlessly, then sat on one section of the semicircular green sofa, rearranged items on the zebra-striped coffee table, got up, stared listlessly at Chagall's "I and the Village" on a side wall, paced, rubbed her hands together.

As I drifted through the window her gray cat began an agitated pacing by the back wall. She cursed it vehemently. I moved a phantom hand along Ellen's throat, sensed watering eyes, runny nose, and a cold burn buzzing across her body. No question—she was junk sick.

She stared out into the space where my face would be. Her

eyes seemed to have nothing to do with the rest of her features, independent, moving with their own life. Her face had been taken over by the heroin. When my face and body began to congeal into visibility for her she screamed. My hawk landed on the back of the sofa and, its wings gently fluttering, watched her cat. The room seemed to pulse. Sometimes I resent the extreme sensitivity my ghost body can have.

Oh, I'll use the word, although "ghost" is hopelessly inadequate as a label. I use it ironically, even mockingly, but words do have their limitations. What else might I call myself?

She blinked, licked her cracked lips. Her entire head quivered. She held her arms tightly in the sudden cold I knew she must be feeling, but which I would never feel again. I would have allowed her to hear strange music, rattling chains, and moans, but I was trying to be kind. I knew I would try for only a short time.

With a yellow dress hanging loosely from her shoulders, a white bag purse around her thin wrist, she walked with me into the street. An old man with dark matted hair lay on the sidewalk, clutching a stained paper bag. She didn't notice. I grabbed her face with my hand and looked into her empty eyes, seeking the beautiful green I remembered, but the irises were dull. Her eyes used to make me able to imagine myself at her birthplace, a southern farm, cutting hay, gathering walnuts.

She had adjusted to my presence. There are few surprises for the heroin addict. Perhaps she thought I was a hallucination. But at least I was a familiar hallucination, I suppose, something she could talk to.

"I want something from you, you know. That's what I'm here for," I told her, but I wasn't sure it registered at that point. We were in an all-night cafe, and I'm sure the half-dozen other patrons could hear her speaking, seemingly to herself, but she wasn't the only one talking to herself in the cafe that night. People ignored her.

Then her eyes seemed to clear; she looked at me directly. "Well I don't have anything left to give."

As yet I didn't trust her enough to tell her about the child.

I merely watched her in silence, trying to feel her out. She was actually worse than I remembered, talking aimlessly to me; I wasn't even sure she knew who I was. She talked on and on without focus, a listless monologue.

My hawk was hidden in the shadows above the dark blue cafe curtains, a still gray shadow.

"My father was kind to us girls, but he certainly made us work. He certainly did. I loved him so. We'd spend all day gathering walnuts and he'd walk us home, an arm for each of us. He called us his princesses, bought us lovely blouses and hard red candy." She smiled until the muscles tightened in her face, and leaned forward conspiratorially, "Many men loved me, so many, but he was nicer than any man I ever met. He looked good even at fifty, wore the same size clothes he did in high school."

I felt a twinge of jealousy and was surprised. She still had a piece of me. I tried to make my question less personal, anonymous: "Do you remember—any of your lovers?"

"No ... no, none of them. Lovers come and go. You only really remember your family. I remember my sister Anne. Eloise ... my mother. And my father."

We left the cafe and headed down Monument Avenue, my hawk fluttering above our heads.

Monument is lined with buildings of various styles: Spanish alongside Gothic alongside English Country Manor. Now that the rich have migrated to the suburbs, students and the welfare old rent subdivided rooms and apartments. I remembered standing in an alley after walking blocks—Ellen and I had fought. I listened to a violinist play sections from Vivaldi in a back window above. Then his wife screamed at him. I had been drinking again—it seemed as if she were shrieking the building down. The violinist screamed back; there seemed to be a violent scuffling. The violin came sailing out of the window and I ran.

"Ellen, don't you remember me?"

She turned and looked up into my dark hair line, the widow's peak. She smiled and threw back her hair, laughing. "Mark, where have you been?"

We walked out beyond the museum, to the park, where

paddleboats rocked in anchor at a pier. I felt unexpectedly affectionate at that moment, and held her tightly,not sure what she would feel of my ghost form—I'd never done this before. I wondered cynically if she could even tell the difference between me and a living body. Everyone's a specter when you're up on junk. But although it was cold she wasn't noticing it, and her junk shivers seemed to have stopped. My hawk looped around us; I needed its proximity to hold her this way. Once again I was amazed by the hawk's intuitiveness. I hadn't even had to signal it.

Although ghosts don't really breathe, we do have a sensation as of inhalation/exhalation. Memories of our past lives make themselves known this way. That is... the closest thing I can think of is colors. Our memories manifest themselves as colors.

I breathed in this manner the yellow of my past life with her, the silver of the days after I left her, back into imaginary lungs, and let the months since my death drift out from my phantom tongue, drape the maples, enter ghostly reflections far out on the lake. Ghosts travel widely—I breathed out the chinook I rode that first time I was in phantom, then burning in Mexican desert, then cold under city asphalt, imagined heat, imagined cold, then with lovers in a park far away but similar to this one. Breathing them in and out, inhalation and exhalation, the colors lingering in the park about treetops and hedgerows before finally fading. A passerby would have considered them mirages, an effect brought on by some chance arrangement of streetlights and fog.

Birds fluttered in the maple tops, no doubt disturbed by the presence of my hawk.

A young man loitered on a park bench in front of us. In the moonlight a hairless face, plucked eyebrows, almond skin. Ellen walked over and sat beside him. I felt very much the voyeur. They exchanged words, money, and an envelope.

She was quiet as we returned to her apartment. I wanted to hold her, cover her face with spectral kisses, but my hawk held back. I knew he wouldn't consent to those special maneuvers a familiar must perform before I could make love to Ellen. His intent was obvious from the way he held back, just out of the range of the streetlights. I felt myself dimming; was he going to make me disappear? I followed Ellen back to her apartment, a few steps behind, like a pale shadow. She spoke with her head up, out into the darkness—a monologue again, although I knew it was vaguely addressed to me. I answered her, in the same way, a distant echo.

"You were always right, Ellen. I couldn't last. Two months after I Left here."

"I'd have loved several if I could. I'd have loved you, Mark. But deep down, I knew you weren't what I wanted."

"She wasn't anything special, no more than you. But it was the accumulation of hurts and humiliations, you know? You never quite loved me. I don't think you could ever decide."

"Father always made us girls feel good, protected, you know? He was always thinking up new things for us to do; we were never at a loss for entertainment. All my lovers have been so boring, in a way. I couldn't find anyone I really wanted, who was really entertaining to me. But they couldn't understand that."

"I'd grown up thinking no one could love me, so maybe I was hard for you or anyone to convince. It happened again—another woman walked out on me. That's all I could think about."

"I tried to get interested, I really did, but things would all go wrong, so I'd stop being interested, and then I'd be bored. There was never anything to do or say. When I'd say something everything would go all wrong and I'd just have to shut up. I'd just have to sit in my room, there was never anything to do or say."

She couldn't talk. Seems she felt guilty she didn't love me. I pressed her, and she left. The waiter came and I didn't know what to say.

"I was kind to them all but they still couldn't understand."

"I started off slow with the sleeping pills..."

"They would get mad and say I didn't feel anything for them."

"I just wanted to scare myself this time I think ..."

"But I was always kind."

" ... but, Ellen, I went too far."

"I let them take me to bed; what else did they want?"

"I couldn't come back...

"I was always kind."

"I couldn't wake up, Ellen."

"I stayed quiet for them."

"Ellen, it was too easy to sleep."

In the alley three men in dark coats were rolling a drunk, "working the hole," as I remembered the slang. The lush came up slowly, and the biggest man kicked him in the mouth. Ellen passed the coughing and spitting at a fast trot.

I lay with her that night on her balcony; she never could sleep indoors during the summer. Red glow over the rooftops. Sweet flowers in the air. My hawk stayed distant, perched on the back of the sofa. Ellen breathed into me with jackal's breath.

She ate an early breakfast in a cafe on Grace Street. Or rather, she ordered it. We had been talking about large meals we remembered with our families, which made her think of late breakfasts with young boys she was dating, who presented these meals as if they had invented this romantic new idea. She was getting jittery. Looking over her shoulder, picking up and replacing the fork and spoon, rearranging her napkin. She left early, and I followed her at a distance. I really believe she had forgotten I was there.

I was feeling playful, hiding in alleys and dark entrance foyers, knowing all the time that no one could see me anyway. I draped myself over a tavern sign, hung strings of myself down, breathing memory in and out so that I must have resembled a multicolored negligee. A drunk stumbled into me and thought he was choking to death, swinging his arms, fighting imagined cobwebs, and my hawk circling him. The moon seemed pierced by a steeple. I imagined a score of pale bodies spilling from its ruptured center, end over end. Landing in the street, they became pigeons.

A man accosted Ellen in front of her building: "Are you anywhere?" Obviously a friend, I thought.

She shook her head, "I'm good for a couple of days." He lurched past me and my hawk sideswiped his head. He ducked, clutched the back of his head, looked around confused.

My hawk reentered her apartment through the window, but I chose to float in through a rent in the wallpaper, between two virgins and a goat.

I watched her shoot up.

I drifted over and leaned against the nape of her neck, clutching her shoulder muscles with imagined claws. The hawk alighted on her shoulder and dug his claws in. I wrapped myself around her, bleeding her pain and relief up into me, my arms, the dust blowing behind my phantom eyes, the great emptiness swelling inside me. I really wanted to know what she was feeling, this once. I brought up the memories of my human limbs and body, turning my form a hazy blue. I sensed the morphine claw, digging into the backs of my remembered legs, climbing up and flowering in the neck, muscle and tissues floating up from bone. And a remembered self-condemnation coming up in a red wave:

"Always the victim, Mark?"

Ellen seemed to be feeling very little. After so many times it's like eating breakfast.

She moaned, easing back against the wall. Her eyelids closed in slow motion. Soon she was asleep. I asked my hawk to perch near her, to protect her, while I dissolved myself into pure strands of silver ectoplasm. Even ghosts need to recharge at times.

But the colors of memory would allow me no rest. Silver: nights with Vivaldi on the player, when Ellen would leap from her chair and drag me, dancing across the old violet rug, her hair swinging side to side, eyes flirtatious. This would pass in minutes; she'd fall back lazily into her chair. The dancing had been planned, a deliberate attempt to stir herself up. Orange: her days waiting for the next fix, three times a day like meals, everything else an excuse, a pretense, until she got her fix. White: nights reduced down to Vivaldi, and Dylan, and watching over her body slumped on the couch, lying on the rug. My arms too tired to hold her. Green: days shrunk down to Dylan, and Vivaldi, and so much booze my throat was coming up bile; fantasies of the welfare apartments across the street exploding, the tenants hanging inside, naked and eyes vacant. Gray: a few bouts with uremic poisoning, feeling swollen, the room smelling like a toilet. Brown: days she spent searching out a meet, working her outfit, dropper and needle, wrapping a collar; her nights sleeping, an occasional job.

I hoped to be gone before I discovered how she was supporting herself these days. She couldn't be hitting up her dad anymore, and I was out of the picture. I remembered her a year before, talking about white slavery as if it were a game.

"Ellen, you've got my baby in you. That's why I came back."

She looked awful—her face dark and insect-like, eyes too far gone for tears. "I don't want a baby now, Mark. Maybe later. Why don't we wait awhile, let me get over this little habit of mine."

"Ellen... Ellen, listen to me. It's too late; you've got the baby now, and it's well along. Listen to me."

"I'll kick it soon; I know I will. We can get married, Mark. Buy us a little farm. The baby can grow up right."

I sensed my hawk ruffle his back feathers, turning his head anxiously back and forth. "Ellen, no. It's too late. You've got to do something now. You're carrying my son, and he's..."

"We'll have a big wedding. My father might come to give me away.

The hawk beat a frantic tattoo with its wings.

"Ellen, my son's an addict!"

We took a bus into the country, just like old times. I thought maybe it would make a difference. She'd be relaxed; I could get to her then. I'd talk her into seeing a doctor.

We kept the hawk hidden in her picnic basket. She thought it a fine game, and giggled constantly, poking it lightly with her fingers through the cloth. My hawk remained still.

"Mark, I'm cold." People were watching her suspiciously.

I put an intangible arm around her, wondering what manner of comfort it might provide. The bus eased out to the interstate.

An old man sat in front of us, his smile taking up the slack in his cheeks. He nodded when we first sat down, tilted his head in a mechanical way. A brief reach to his shoulder told me he

was going to die in a few months, much pain erupting through
the joints and chest muscles. The bus let us off at a side road,
then we walked about a mile.

Ellen's body was like a white frond submerged in the creek.
Fluffed out, and buoyant, but with occasional dark streaks. I sat
on the bank, the hawk at my feet studying the opposite bank
for signs of small game. Abruptly it took off and began circling
the water.

Ellen looked good in the water. I wanted to hold her, but
I suspected that if I got closer my desire would vanish. Better
to watch her. I had loved her, perhaps I still did. But she had
always demanded I be someone else, that I be strict with her,
then that I give her warmth even as she clawed my face, that
I keep her in line, that I hold her when she was sick. I always
became the wrong thing with her; it was always something else
I needed to be. My love began to drain away; but not completely,
never completely. There was always a strand that held me.

When I'd killed myself I was angry with her, lying there,
pain like tiny bombs exploding behind my eyeballs, down the
optic nerve and into my gut. I kept seeing her face.

"I got tired of waiting, Ellen. You were never going to get
yourself clean."

I drifted over to an outcropping of rock and sat there. I could
see the top of Ellen's head, the occasional stroke of a pale arm.
She wouldn't be able to see me; my hawk was too far away.

I remembered an old man I had watched die a few months
before, in Colorado. He had bent over, hacked, coughed blood.
No one else around, but me, the specter, the phantom, the
ghostly observer. A three year old girl was beaten in Chicago
by her drunken father; I hung against the door and watched. A
West Virginia miner died in a cave-in beside me.

They had all died on the same note, the same vibration,
something only a ghost might sense. I could remember my
hawk trilling with that same terror as the deaths occurred, that
fear of ending.

My son.

I had always wished for him, but was too embarrassed to
admit it. The women I knew had always made fun of the idea.

Ellen said it was male pride. Having a child. Strange as it seemed at the time, I would have liked to have given birth myself. But now… ghosts aren't easily embarrassed.

A whiteness of protoplasm, squirming under the sun and sucking air.

My son wrapped his arms around my phantom legs, buried a dark head against me, beckoning my hawk with his free hand. I manufactured new memories, and made colorful shimmers around him. I remembered picking him up and burying my face in his soft belly, kissing him wetly until he giggled. His face was large, seeming to cover the sun. Soft green eyes and a widow's peak. I put him on my shoulder and carried him up the hill to watch the sunset. We sat in the dirt and played marbles: catseyes, steelies, rolling off under the grass, frantically searching for them. We played hide and seek behind the white house and hid in terror from my father. But we held each other and there was no pain. We built a fortress out of sticks at the creek mouth. He broke the skin on his knee and I held him, applied iodine, told jokes and tickled him so he wouldn't cry anymore. I gave him a bath in the kitchen sink; he giggled and kicked violently, throwing soapy water into my face, burning my eyes. But I laughed too. He fell asleep on my bare chest wearing just his diaper. I fell asleep too and Ellen had to put us both to bed. These new memories I had made spun lazily around us, their colors gradually fading until they had disappeared.

We rode the bus into Richmond with the spirit of my son between us, although Ellen couldn't see him. He fell asleep against me.

Back in her apartment Ellen sucked air, hard, and main-lined one into her leg before I could stop her. My son awoke, startled and crying, and began to fade.

Minutes later I could sense his pain inside Ellen's womb. My hawk was soaring through the apartment, circling, screeching.

I extended an appendage and touched Ellen's face: her eyes wide, cheeks swelling, fingers enlarged, an unpleasant burning.

I sensed that odd vibration in my hawk's wings, the trilling, the high-pitched shriek as it crashed into the living room wall, crushing its head. Frightened, I reached back into Ellen.

My son had died in her womb. There seemed to be a howl turning in every corner of the room.

I was only dimly aware of my hawk—his head, body, wings disintegrating, himself drawn instantly into spirit. I wrapped Ellen's body in my shadowy self; she was dying.

Some of the old tales about ghosts have a grain of truth to them. Not everyone makes it; some need help. Neither Ellen nor my son was strong enough to manage the transition without help. But I only had energy enough to bring one of them across. Ellen's life was real, ongoing, the baby's life was an imagined thing.

I had to choose; it was going to end for either Ellen or my long awaited son. Only one would have a second chance, as a phantom.

I reached out for what remained of Ellen.

The hawk's spirit was too swift even for me to follow, a roaring through the room that took my son on into ghost before I could reach Ellen. The hawk made the choice for me. Ellen spilled out onto the floor like an emptied bag.

Ghosts travel widely. And all time is the same for us. I can see dawn rising out beyond the James River, and my hawk and son circling the Carillon Tower in their play. I cannot reach them; they soar too swiftly for me. But I still follow. My son pursues the onrushing hawkspirit as it heads out to sea, and I follow. It's a game to him, a race, and he giggles among the clouds. I try not to envy him. Our appendages seem wing-like to us in our current form, dissolving in the dim light, becoming yellow, white, then transparent. Our imagined hawk claws trail into tendrils of silver rain cloud. My son dissolves so quickly out over the ocean, expanding into the morning at an ever-widening angle, so quickly I find him hard to pursue. But I manage to dissolve almost as quickly, mix into his thoughts my lost memories of bone and muscle. We enter the James one after the other and seem to set it afire; red and orange trails glow on the surface awhile before fading. In every flash of water, there's a fish. I can almost touch them. In every space of sky, a fish. Hanging there, luminous.

With large, pained eyes. Mouths howling love.

RIVERBANKS

He had been standing for some time.

Realizing that, in itself, led him to the conclusion that something was off, distorted, wrong. He felt himself misplaced, put away in someone's pocket so hastily that memory failed to keep pace with the quickness of hand.

So now he was lost.

Where he was now standing—in order to have a better perspective for gazing, for spying—he knew he should have been sitting, resting. For he had been in this place, standing, for a very long time now. For years, it seemed.

It should have been impossible to stand for such a long time. But he had always been patient, had always known that what he wanted lay there in the distance, just beyond the thin gray line of the horizon.

Where top half met bottom half, like overlapping sheets of fine, white writing paper.

The gray horizon line shimmered in the distance, and that's what got him walking. His need to touch it, fall into it, and pass beyond.

After only a few steps, the line appeared to widen. By the time he was only minutes away from its edge, he could smell the pungent saltiness of the water.

The river extended as far as he could see to the left and to the right. The banks seemed oddly independent of the water, swollen here and there like tissue around a wound increasing in infection, pulled back from the shimmering gray in some areas and drawn tightly to it in others.

In fact, as he gazed off to left and right, vast areas of the river were hidden by the riverbank, as if the riverbank extended much farther into the horizons than the water did.

But that was illusion. All he could count on was the endlessness of the wound of river.

And as he stepped closer it widened, the waters spreading until once he arrived at the very edge of the riverbank the river seemed improbably broad.

And swift. The narrow ripples in the gray surface, almost parallel, raced snake-like from east to west.

Too swift to swim it. He could only watch.

The riverbank beneath his feet dropped off sharply into the gray water, although this close to the bank the water appeared bluer, deeper, making him wonder if the river bottom might be convex, a condition he had never thought possible before.

The edge of the bank seemed pinkish—a clay mixture. He turned slowly, hesitantly, to look back in the direction from which he had come, and gazed for a long time at the unbroken stretch of sand. He had no idea where the riverbank might end.

If there had been a road, he might have said the riverbank ended there, but there were no roads. At some point, perhaps, there was another river, or this same river come round again. With accompanying riverbank. At which point this particular riverbank might end.

He wanted to cross the river but even thinking about it frightened him.

He missed having someone near him, an imaginary someone since, no matter how hard he tried, he could not recall one personality he had ever met.

He missed, although he had never met. He missed their conversations. He missed doing things.

The gray stretched out and out side to side like arms stretching, inviting his embrace. He yearned for other arms.

The emptiness here invited heat. But the only heat was caused by the energy of his thoughts.

He gazed across the river and felt like a fool. The opposite riverbank, the one forming the other side of the wound, appeared to be exactly the same terrain, so there was no point in crossing anyway.

He tried not to think, for to think when there was nothing to do, to think by himself, was to think like a fool. A romantic. There was no one else. There was only the wound and the edges of the wound.

The emptiness above the river appeared to fill with a reflection. He stared at himself, seemingly across the river, for days, if days were possible.

Into an image of himself that seemed somehow softer than himself.

He felt a cool, removed laughter he could not bring himself to release. All this romanticism. Creeping in because he was so tired, because he had been doing the same things over and over for such a long time. As if weariness were expressing itself in the illusions of romance. He could almost make himself embarrassed.

He allowed his emotions to cool. He filled himself with riverbanks.

The almost-image of himself became a physics problem, a curiosity.

He stepped closer to the edge of the bank, studying the distant image for any abrupt change. He nodded and looked for a mirror reaction, but the figure was too far away for him to make such a close distinction.

He jumped up and down. The distant image appeared to waver.

He began to walk the riverbank east to west. And this time he was sure of it: the distant image followed.

At some point between waking and half-sleep—for even though he was always on the riverbank, standing, gazing at the unfocused image on the opposite riverbank, he had a sense of small spells of half-sleep or remembered sleep or a nostalgia for true sleep even though they differed only slightly from spells of wakefulness—he decided he had been vaguely aware of that image's presence his entire lifetime. He was, in a sense, an expert on the subject, even though he knew almost nothing about it.

It made him curious.

He wasn't sure if he had ever tried to speak to the image before, call to it. So now he did. He opened his mouth carefully, as if the words were sharp edged and a bit dangerous, and tried to push them over the river.

"Is that *you?*" he cried.

Saying the words agitated him. The river appeared to change color ever so slightly, as did the image with which he was attempting conversation. It wavered. He thought it bowed a bit.

"You?" the image seemed to echo. But he didn't think it was an echo at all. The image was speaking to him.

The image stretched an arm out toward the river, gestured with a hand.

He leaned so far forward he thought he might tumble down the steep bank and into the river, but fear did not deter him from leaning.

You ... But he wasn't sure if it was himself or the image speaking.

The river was a wound running swiftly, the riverbank the edges of flesh puffed or drawn with infection. He wanted badly to sleep, knew he had not truly slept for a very long time, and yet also knew he had slept far too much.

The blood was washing up over the edges of the riverbank, now covering his feet and staining him, now receding into the wound.

But that was only a dream, a dream he'd had while standing, gazing at the distant image that might or might not be the mirror of himself.

After all, something *had* to happen.

He tried to think of a time when he'd been asleep, not pacing the riverbank, not gazing across at the other image. It was difficult to be aware of sleep, and he couldn't find a memory of rising up out of sleep.

But there had been a time he hadn't felt such a *wrongness*, a *misplacement.* There had been a contented time, he knew, when the riverbanks could have wounded the landscape endlessly and it wouldn't have bothered him. There had been a time when he wouldn't have even noticed another image; it would have been so much a part of him. Like the riverbank and the gray water.

He wouldn't even have noticed himself pacing.

He thought about having been asleep for a very long time then, and about how dreaming was simply a way to recall those glorious eons when he had *always* been asleep.

And then had awakened, had found himself on the riverbank which seemed to stretch forever, bordering an equally endless wound of shining gray waters, where he felt compelled to gaze and pace constantly, for he was so profoundly misplaced, seemingly no longer a part of anything.

He couldn't stand still.

For he realized that once he had awakened he had fallen immediately and completely in love with some image he had never even seen, some *other*. It really didn't matter which image, as long as it was *other*, facing him from another shore, another endless stretch of riverbanks.

And that was a knowledge he could not absorb without running, running hopelessly left and right along the riverbank. It didn't matter in which direction, as all directions were the same, and endless.

He looked across the river as he ran, and saw that the other image ran as well, with a similar kind of desperation. Which lifted his spirits, to find this sudden and unexpected communion.

They ran together, parallel to wounds and infected riverbanks, and mutually aware, he thought, of each other's desperation. But the river grew no narrower—he hadn't expected it to.

If anything it expanded, until he could barely see the other, frantic image on the opposite bank.

He should have stopped; it was foolish to continue his running.

But he didn't. For he now knew that love was created upon his awakening and once you knew that the only thing you

could do was run. And run. And run until you were completely exhausted and fell asleep again.

For that all-encompassing sleep—where the river is a wound drifting through your head and the riverbanks your own flesh parting to let the waters through—that was the final goal of love. To return to where you had been before, such a long time ago.

To sleep.

Before love had been invented, before it was necessary.

He ran a good race, as did the other image on that other riverbank. He thought they acknowledged the mutual admiration of their own courage as they ran into exhaustion. But he could never know for sure.

He could never know for sure what the other thought in any given situation.

Darkness overtook him.

He had been standing for some time.

Something was wrong. He had been misplaced.

He was lost.

TEDDY BEAR WINTER

It was the boy's seventh winter, but the first he thought he might be able to enjoy. Always before when cold weather came it was a time of great busyness, of hard work, of gathering food, firewood, carrying it back to the ancient ruins for storage within the nest-like jumble of concrete and metal and wood that was their home.

The animals came out in the winter, the fur-bearers, and ventured closer to the ruins than at any other time during the year, for they had even less food than did the people. So in winter the boy's father and mother told him to stay away from the edges of their tumbled city, else he'd be dinner for some sharp-toothed beast. Stay inside. Don't go out after dark. Play the old games with his sisters. Listen to the stories of how-it-had-once-been, before the bright light came and the city did somersaults, before the sky turned inside-out.

Back in how-it-had-once-been the animals were smaller, tamer. Some might even have eaten from your hand. Now the beasts were angry and fierce, and of darker variety, just like the world itself.

Life had slowed down this winter. He did not know why. Less food had been gathered. Less wood. The adults seemed more relaxed, without their customary winter frenzy. There appeared to be no desperation this season. The adults sat, and talked. Some meditated. But ail made their bears, sometimes working late into the night fashioning faces, bellies, and limbs, painting eyes like no other's.

The snows had come early this year. The people wrapped their bodies in whatever old furs they could find, but for the first winter the boy could remember they did not send hunters out for replacement pelts.

Still, there were enough old furs to cover them. So many looked like the animals they feared. The boy sometimes thought each adult chose to wear the fur of the very animal he or she feared most.

In the early mornings ice hung in ribbons from frosted, twisted metal. Ice sheeted the few intact stretches of concrete. The ancient ruins glistened in the morning light and cold as if brand new. As if the old disaster had not happened, and they were living in a fairy city.

His grandmother was helping him to make a bear of his own. She said that once upon a time they manufactured such things for children to play with. Now everyone had a bear, and they all made their own.

When the bear was still just an anonymous shape-arms, legs, large belly and a wide expanse of faceless head-it began to sleep with the boy, keeping him company through the long winter nights. Watching over him through nonexistent eyes during the long winter afternoons when he was warned not to venture outside because he still might sicken and die, or be torn apart by sharp animal ways.

The boy didn't really believe them, but knew there must be some reason the others remained inside.

Sometimes he talked to the bear, when he had nothing to say to the people. And he would feel his own echo turn into a small growl within his throat.

All would gather around the fire each night to tell of the times before, times before even the cities rose up out of the land, and all had roamed the earth together, of one mind and of one voice and of one dream concerning the world.

But then one morning they had awakened from the one dream, and each was alone, strangers to each other.

They talked of these things, isolated eyes reflecting the orange fire. Their bears' broken glass eyes glistened in much the same way.

He himself would dream of these before times, when no one thing could be feared more than any other thing, since all were part of every other.

The bear's face was a long time coming, because it had to

be exactly right. Eyes wide-set like his own, the same color. The mouth line with the exact same curve.

He'd awaken from the dream with the bear beside him, glass eyes alive in the morning light. He'd hold it close and smell the old fur from some dead animal, and look for images of other lives in the glass. He'd clothe it in the scraps from his own winter coat.

One morning his grandmother awakened him early. The night had barely begun to break apart outside. She told him to bring his bear and join the rest. Outside. He climbed the ladder to the outside, the bear wrapped tight against him.

They were all there at the edge of the ruins, each holding a particular bear. They began walking toward the tangle of woods.

One by one they set the boars into the deep snow, facing the woods. The boy was reluctant to leave his there. He wanted to run. After all, this bear looked like him. The boy wondered if they were leaving their bears for the animals to rip and devour. It felt like a sacrifice.

Come along, she said, taking his hand. Come along, it's time. He started to twist in her arms. He started to cry out. But her arms were too strong for him, her presence too commanding. Here, she said, pulling on his hand.

He stepped back to observe the line of bears, all facing the woods, all with their rumps pushed into the snow. Each bear's face reflecting the owner's.

Sometimes he heard a soft murmur, sometimes a snatch of near-forgotten song.

Then his grandmother took him by the hand and led him home with the rest of the people. They all lay down and slept together.

And they slept for a very long time.

When they finally awakened they had no more bears, but the boy no longer felt the need for one.

He growled and spat. He ripped his bedding apart with his claws. He always felt like playing among the dangerous shadows in the woods.

But most of all he no longer felt alone. And when he dreamed the dream of everything, he too was part of the one voice, the one mind. He was part of the dream.

TIME AND THE EXILE

David hadn't thought about the war in years, but then the car reached the top of the hill, a bruised gray sky filling the windshield so that he was thinking he'd better be ready for the worst kind of storm, and then suddenly he was dropping down the other side as if he were descending out of that strange sky, and there was the apple orchard down below, spread out along both sides of *Autoroute des Cantons-de-l'Est*, Highway 10. And he was thinking of the war, and wondering how he had ever managed to keep it out of his mind all these years.

"Parlez-vous anglais? Do you speak English?" he asked the old man walking along the side of the road. After all these years in Canada, and a number of sales trips through Quebec, David still knew only a few useful French phrases.

But the man paid him no attention, even when David stopped the car and shook his map out the window at him. The map unraveled, its colorful veins reaching for that awful sky, and tore in a sudden gust of wind, pieces of it flapping away. David figured he should have stayed on the *Autoroute Transcanadienne* along the St. Lawrence. But he'd never been good with maps or directions, despite the travel his job required and his almost twenty years here.

"Bonjour!" he called out. A broad piece of his map flew down again and adhered, fluttering, to the back of the old man's leg, but the fellow walked on, taking no notice. David tried to stifle a laugh. *"Je desire le carte routier!"* he cried with strained cheerfulness. "I want the road map."

The old man turned and looked at David, and the sun,

momentarily breaking out of blue gray, created a yellow sheen on his skin, so that David was sure the man was Vietnamese. The man seemed to be wearing black pajamas, as if he'd just gotten out of bed and walked away, perhaps from some nursing home somewhere. Traumatized by the war? David immediately wanted to assure the old man that he'd never been there. He'd come here, to Canada, to become a salesman of farm chemicals rather than be a killer in Southeast Asia.

But then the approaching storm swallowed up the yellow light, and it was an elderly pale Quebecer in a dark wool suit he was looking at, and not some other exile from the war.

The old man stared at him with a look of apprehension. He said something in French David couldn't quite understand. Then he said, *"Je ne comprends pas."*

I don't understand. *"Je ne comprends pas,"* David replied.

The old man's face twisted in pain. He reached up with a trembling hand and rubbed the side of his neck. Another momentary glimmer of yellow light illuminated a raw, angry wound there, some sort of skin cancer crusted with dry, dark blood. David looked away from the man, then, toward the apple orchard. Everywhere he looked the trees hung heavy with perfect spheres of bright red blood. Some dropped with the wind into piles of bloody meat beneath the trees.

"Je desire consulter un medicin!" the old man cried out. David stared at the man as he cried and gestured toward his wound. *"Je desire consulter un medicin!"* he said again, sobbing, a look of torment in his eyes.

"You want a doctor?" David asked.

The man nodded, his eyes glazed, stuporous. He pulled out a long machete from behind his black pajamas and advanced on the car, his mouth a bleeding rictus.

"Je regrette! Au revoir!" David shouted, and drove away. In his rear-view mirror he saw the man staring after him, looking puzzled.

The apple orchards stretched on for several kilometers. Then there were dairy farms. A sign for the Chateauguay River. Route *barree*. Road closed. *Entree interdite.* Access prohibited. He was diverted through a series of detours, and it seemed he passed through the same intersections a number of times.

Once again he found himself thinking of the war. It made no sense, really. He'd put all that behind him a long time ago. When he'd first come to Canada he'd already determined he would never be going back, whatever happened politically in the States. He'd avoided the various Canadian committees set up to aid the resisters, because these were programs for Americans, and he had decided he was *Canadian* from his very first day. He paid no attention when the Americans announced their Amnesty program. It had nothing to do with him—by that time he'd felt as if he'd always been Canadian. David had no friends among the resisters—from the beginning he made sure all his friends were Canadian.

The first place he'd lived in Canada had been Toronto, which had seemed remarkably clean compared to American cities, with relatively low crime, a well-run community, friendly, beautiful. What American cities should have been, what they had always promised but never delivered.

In those early years he had read newspaper pieces about the new exiles, read them as if they were dispatches about some strange new breed of person he could never understand, a people very different from himself. He remembered reading that many young radicals left the U.S. because they were convinced they would have become violent revolutionaries if they'd stayed. Did they really want young men capable of such violence in their beloved Canada?

After a few years in the country David was telling people at the office that he'd been born in Manitoba, his wife's native province. Their daughter Amy—one hundred percent Canadian—celebrated her twelfth birthday just this past week. That's where he belonged now, with them. He had no business in sales. He'd never been that good at it. But at the time he left the States he'd been a chemistry major. So he'd fallen into a series of chemical and agricultural-related sales jobs in Canada—whatever he could find—all inevitably leading to his current position.

The road twisted through a heavily-wooded area. He couldn't quite identify the colors and smells; they reminded him of his childhood, and he knew he'd never associated them with Canada. Then he saw the first small frame houses, so much like his native Massachusetts. This back road quiet as a New England lane.

Pont, the sign said. Bridge. But it was a covered bridge, just like one of those which had led into his own home town so long ago, in that other lifetime, with that other David.

Arret. Stop. Across the intersection was a country inn. He recognized it. Simpson's Inn. He just couldn't make out the sign. It seemed to be in some sort of foreign language. *Libre* service, the sign at the small gas station said, the station his cousin Billy had owned. *Huile*, above a picture of a can of oil. *Vide. Plein. Sans plomb. Essence.* Somehow he knew he could not park in front of his small hometown courthouse, where the sign said *Zone de remorguage.*

Then the familiar village green and the white church steeple. It was the town he had left twenty-five years ago. The place he had once called home.

No one was out on the streets or sidewalks. He climbed out of his car to confront a blue-gray storm filling the sky, isolating him, making him feel he was the only one alive.

He walked across the street and stepped up onto a startlingly clean sidewalk fronting a small store. He could not read the signs. He knew they weren't in English. But he didn't think they were in French either.

A man stepped out of the shadows at the back of the store and approached the large front window from the other side. He had a yellowish face like the old man David had encountered out by the apple orchard. But as the man neared the glass he came into sharper focus, and David knew then this man was his father. Older, but very much recognizable.

David pressed his own face against the glass, so firmly he was aware of his features distorting. He didn't much mind the sensation—perhaps if his face changed enough he would feel right at home. On the other side of the window his father was talking to him. *Why'd you kill the dog, Davy? Especially that way? What's wrong with you, Davy?*

His father's face grew older, paler, until it wasn't his father's face at all anymore. "What is this place, father?" David asked the face.

"*L'Estrie*," the face replied, but in David's head it sounded strange. It sounded like "home."

His father had wanted him to go to war just as he had gone, just as his uncles and grandfather had gone. But David knew that would have been the wrong thing. His family had been poor, however, just a bunch of small-time apple and dairy farmers. And back then they didn't give out CO status to poor boys. Poor boys were supposed to go over and fight, kill or die.

David backed out into the street. Suddenly there were people all around. Farmer types. Salt of the earth. New Englanders. Suddenly he was thinking of his wife, of his daughter Amy, wishing he were at home with them, hoping there was a wife, a daughter, that other home.

"Why'd you torture that little cat, Davy?" an elderly woman asked him. She looked like Miss Mays, the woman who lived across the street when he was a little boy. He looked away when she started wrinkling up, shrinking, becoming Asian.

"What did you do to your cousin, Davy?" Officer Parks asked him. The town policeman had pulled him out of class to ask him this and now everybody knew, and all David could think about was how he could get even. "We can't find her, and we've looked everywhere!" But Officer Parks was wearing black pajamas instead of his uniform, and David would have laughed in his face if the man hadn't been carrying that machine gun.

"Why, Davy, why?" his little cousin said, her dress torn, her bare shoulders covered with dozens of light brown freckles.

"Don't go, Davy," his father said, raising the machete with his thin yellow arm. "You'll go bad there, Davy," he said, as he lurched toward him, swinging it at his face.

"Already bad," Miss Mays said, grinning with no teeth in her small, mama-san face.

David turned, wanting to get back to the car, to get away from this town where everybody knew him. Where everybody knew he hadn't gone to Canada because of some noble principle, or because of fear of what might happen to him.

He had gone to Canada because of fear of what he might do, because of what he knew he had the power to become.

But the diminutive people with their black pajamas and their weapons had completely surrounded him, and looking around he could see the huts and the fields and could smell the burning petroleum smell that was nothing like autumn in New England, and nothing like Canada at all. For this was the true landscape of his childhood, the land he had dreamed of long before he'd even heard the name Viet Nam.

"Y atil quelqu'un qui parle anglais?" he asked the crowd, giggling. "Can anyone here speak English?"

And they all laughed in return, their ancient, foreign laugh. And handed their fellow exile the guns and knives so that he might change their flesh in his secret frenzy.

David accepted these gifts gladly, and, weeping, went to work.

UMBRELLAS

"I don't want you to go," my lover said behind me. But I was too busy looking out the window and watching the city streets to reply. We had made love all that day with the shades pulled, moving together even as we were half asleep, and now I wondered if our dreaming had changed the world outside. Normally, of course, the notion would have seemed silly to me. I pressed close to the window as if it were an aquarium. The skyline obscured the umber waters of early evening.

The unlit street below our window had filled with elderly women, all in dark dresses and hair coverings, carrying their unopened umbrellas.

"Who are they?" she asked over my shoulder.

"Old women," I said, as up and down the street one after another of the umbrellas bloomed into perfect, round, dark flowers beneath the near-invisible rain.

"Widows," she insisted. "They're widows, aren't they?"

"Yes," I said. But you could not see them for their umbrellas. As the rain grew hard, and silver, the surfaces of the dark blooms began to shine, until they seemed like the ghosts of so many dead jellyfish floating down the channel of the street. On either side the tall buildings were so black as to be featureless, sheer cliffs to wall in the rising tide of umbrellas. And widows.

"*I* don't want you to go," she said again softly, distractedly. "They seem aimless. Where are they going?"

"They're blind," I said. "They're old and they've worn out their eyes looking for so long." The somber shades of the umbrella flowers soothed my eyes. "The army requires men like me," I said. "Men who will go without much thought about it. Just go, whatever anyone says."

"I suppose I'll grow old and blind as well," she said. "From waiting. Looking."

She said more, but I had stopped listening. The shadow flowers drifted by my eyes, each with a blind widow clinging to its stem.

And like my father and grandfather before me, I had been in love with them all my life.

MORNING TALK

"I tell you, there's something *wrong* with the boy!"

Once again the noise from the kitchen had awakened Michael, who now had his small body stretched out from the bed, leaning precariously over his toy chest in order to put his ear against the door.

Again he heard the raised voice of his father, and in the background, silence. His mother never said anything during these early-morning conversations. Michael imagined tears, protestations, trembling entreaties for his father to be more reasonable, to be more loving, but he never heard them.

"I can't put up with it, Clara! And I'm *not* going to put up with his craziness anymore!"

It was generally the same conversation every morning, the same lecture, the same little talk. There were only slight variations in the wording, and the event that set off his father's anger was a little different each time.

This time Michael had built a fort out of old bricks in the driveway. He had forgotten to tear it down before his father got home from work the previous night. His father had run into it, and the new Cadillac had a small scratch.

But his parents had these conversations every morning. Michael had gotten used to it. The puzzling thing, however, the really disturbing thing, was that the kitchen was right off Michael's bedroom. His parents *had* to know that he could hear them when his father talked so loudly. Michael was only ten, but he knew everything that was going on in the house that way. He had come to believe that this was the way his parents let him know things they wanted him to know.

Again, his father: "I don't care! He's bleeding me, Clara!"

Again, his father: "He's killing me, Clara!"

Again, his father: "Things could be a lot easier around here if ... ."

Sometimes his father's voice trailed off at just the right moment, before Michael could find out what he had planned for him. But his parents only let Michael know what they wanted him to know.

Early morning, every morning, it was the same. Michael had several questions he wanted answered, suspicions he had; and every morning he tried to listen as closely as possible to discover those answers.

But he never could listen quite carefully enough. Always his father's voice would trail off, and Michael could not catch it.

"I don't know why we ever ... ."

Michael listened carefully each morning to see whether he was really adopted, to see whether they were planning to get rid of him, to see whether his mother too hated him.

But his father's voice always trailed off, and his mother never spoke.

"You're too *easy* on him, Clara. You coddle the boy. I don't know why I put up with *either* one of you! I'm just going to have to ... ."

He heard noises out near his door; he sneaked back under the covers, as he had many times before, and pretended to fall asleep.

He'd die ...

Michael woke up confused and disturbed. It had never happened that way before. He'd pretended to be asleep when he heard his father approaching his room, and he'd actually fallen asleep.

He wondered what time it was. It was still dark outside, or dark *again* outside. Had he slept through until night?

He'll be dead ...

But there they were in the kitchen, talking, no, whispering this time. And that couldn't be right, what he'd thought they'd said; they were whispering purposely so that he might misunderstand, so that it might worry him.

We kill …

He crept out of his bed and put his ear against the door.

Better off dead …

He shivered in his pajamas. But it was summer, and they couldn't be saying this.

Go to the door and …

Of course, he must be dreaming, and he must be about to wake up now. He *must*.

Go to his door now …

He began to cry, bringing his feet up and down in time to his small wails; in horror, he saw that he had wet himself, that the pool of urine was spreading around his feet. They'd *kill* him for this.

Now, do it, now …

He must be imagining it He must be dreaming.

Open the door…

He burst through the door screaming, running through the kitchen, crying out in terror as the hands clutched at him. If he could only make it to the back door, if he could only run fast enough!

Michael … Michael … Michael …

The two shadowy forms had trapped him; there was no more room to run. His father stepped out of the darkness, his face pale, lips white, blue-tinted, reaching out to Michael

He handed him the knife, the hammer, this man who was going to kill him, and pointed at the corner where they had their kitchen table.

His mother sat in a chair, her face drawn and her eyes wary. She seemed to have been crying; her eyes were deeply etched in red. She wore her prettiest pink nightgown.

His father gestured again and pushed Michael toward her with a sour-smelling hand.

It was then that Michael noticed his own hand: the exposed blue veins, the white skin, the tattered pajama sleeve. And then his feet, the broken toenails, the raw red places. Just like his father.

Michael …

His mother began to weep again, her voice a high keening

wail, as he first looked back at his father and then approached her slowly with the knife pushed forward in his frayed-looking, little-boy hand.

RE: VISION

When new writers asked Wilson for bits of seasoned editorial advice he only had two: "Don't include a cover letter—there may be five writers in the free world who can write a decent one." And "Don't send me anything on funny paper." This particular author had violated both of Wilson's major tenets. The note scrawled at the top of the first page—not even on a separate sheet of paper, mind you—stated I DESPERATELY NEED AN EDITOR! in bold black letters. Indeed! He should have stuffed the manuscript into its crinkled return envelope right then and there. But the author's second major violation stopped him; the paper was rubbing off onto his fingers, disintegrating like a mummy on its first exposure to modern air. Wilson made himself handle the pages with some delicacy— already parts of words had vanished, syllables and stray punctuation rubbed off into the ether. The paper itself felt granular, powdered. Examining the rubbed off bits under a magnifying glass, he found them to be triangular in shape, hundreds of them, of near microscopic size.

Cautiously he carried the manuscript over to the copier. By the time he had the thing duplicated there was nothing left but a scattering of abrasive ash. After such an event he could not help but read the manuscript copy he had made.

In fact the tale indicated quite a bit of talent. It was a sword and sorcery sort of thing, but the author had avoided the usual mock medieval background and used a contemporary setting instead. Chicago, if he wasn't mistaken. Wilson thought he recognized the John Hancock Building, although it wasn't mentioned by name. Certainly the street names were Chicago street names.

The hero (same name as the author; that made Wilson smile but it would have to go) was being stalked by a creature of "night and fog," occasionally tentacled, now and then possessed of an ear-shattering screech, as the hero made his way to work each day. The hero, it seemed, was a young broker. The ending was inconclusive, and ultimately unsatisfying. More of a problem, however, was the author's occasional lapses in everyday logic. Wilson slipped a sheet of stationary into his Olympia (no word processor for him), and banged out his response to the story. After the obligatory chastisement concerning submission form and mechanics (and he had to understate himself here—if he said what he really felt the young author might never submit again), he got into the question of logic: "Despite the rather weak ending and somewhat predictable appendages of your 'monster' (tentacles, indeed), I think your story is close to being publishable. But you really must do something about the errors in background and logic here. For example, I spend a great deal of time in Chicago and know that both Washington and Randolph are one-way streets. You've also placed the Shedd Aquarium too far north and the Buckingham Fountain too far South. The Art Institute is on Michigan Avenue, by the way. If I'm not mistaken you'd have it in the middle of Grant Park! It's also quite evident that your monster moves far too slowly to be any real threat to your hero. Why doesn't he simply buy a gun and shoot the thing? But for all these difficulties I found your writing to be remarkably vivid and unusually convincing. Therefore I'm eager to 'hold your hand,' as it were, through a number of revisions. I'm sure that, together, we can develop a publishable tale out of this!"

Wilson was surprised, and pleased, to receive a revision of "The Dark, Following" two weeks later. A neatly typed note, like the manuscript itself on good quality white bond, was attached to the first page:

Mr. Wilson:

Thank you so much for your editorial comments. You have saved my life.

Sincerely, Abram James

Funny how the name felt unfamiliar, although Wilson knew

that must have been the author's name in the first place. But 'Abram'? He would have thought such an unusual name would have lodged itself in his memory.

Wilson smiled at the exaggerated gratitude of the note—new authors being prone to such outbursts. Then he read the revised story with rising anticipation. He was pleased to see that James had corrected all the Chicago references. The prose was clean, logical, direct. It maintained the remarkable vividness he remembered from the earlier version. The story was highly realistic and ultimately convincing. It was the narrative of a young stockbroker by the name of Abram James and his trip into work one morning, a trip during which nothing unusual occurs.

Wilson sat back in his chair. No monster, no anxiety. No suspense or fantasy element in the piece at all. Well, it wouldn't be the first time a young author had missed the point. Wilson attached a form rejection and slipped the manuscript into its crisp, clean return envelope.

And it actually wasn't all that surprising to him when two weeks later Wilson received another manuscript of the odd, crumbly sort, the words on this one seeming to disappear even as he breathed on it. He struggled with it over to the copier, the triangular bits massing at the edges of the paper where they delivered a series of nasty cuts. As he watched the last page dissolving atop the copier's glass window (scarring it permanently in the process), these words in huge florid black script, vaguely reminiscent of a nervous child's handwriting, bled through to the back of the page before just as quickly bleeding into the air:

FIXX THIS ONE, EDITOR MANNN ...

The story, "Eaten by the Dark," followed a vintage New York editor, in a New York distorted past all recognition, as he attempted to make his way home one evening, forced to run screaming through traffic, down dark alleys, desperately diving into abandoned subway stations, his only weapon his pen which he wielded with grim satisfaction.

WANDERLUST

After that many centuries, he had learned many things. He had been an expert at many things; sometimes to be an expert in one field meant he had to empty himself of his knowledge of another. At one time or another he had been a doctor, a lawyer, an engineer, an architect, a teacher, a laborer, a craftsman, a police officer, and, several times, an author of books.

Occasionally he attempted to re-read those books written out of his various lifetimes (he had never been particularly famous, so the necessary searches had been extensive and expensive), but found little that was recognizable in them, or much to his taste, for that matter.

Actually, he didn't like thinking about his life in terms of centuries. Such a measurement seemed to minimize it, by making conceivable the enormity his life had become. He preferred thinking of his life in the measure of lifetimes, for there were often several lives to be had in a single hundred years, and someone from the beginning of a century would find very little to recognize in his own life at the end of it. Sometimes he had lives, and families, which lasted him only a few years, until some bond developed which he knew might break his heart, and he felt compelled to travel on. And even so he sometimes stayed too long.

"Daddy? Why so sad, Daddy?"

Some of his children were special to him, out of all the hundreds who'd passed through his lifetimes. There was one in particular, a daughter. He would never forget her face, although he would try. Sometimes it was difficult to place a face with a name. Many times he'd been forced to use the same name a dozen times or more. But not in her case. But now he made himself not say her name. He made himself not think of it.

"Daddy? I *love* you, Daddy!" Sometimes, hard as he tried, there were those whose voices he simply could not tune out.

What he had never been, he finally decided after the consideration of a multitude of such lifetimes, was a great father. He had concluded, reluctantly, that great fathers could not, would not outlive their own children. Perhaps once or twice, by accident. But not so consistently, so stubbornly.

"Daddy, I painted you a flower!" It required a moment to regain his bearings. This voice, he realized, was close at hand. But she looked so much like the other one. Black hair, blue eyes. He reached over and took the picture from... he fumbled for a name ... Denise. He smiled and gave her a hug. After hundreds of children, the gesture was all too familiar. How many hugs had he given over the centuries? How many had he received? Sometimes late at night he tried to count them, as if he were counting sheep. Much to his surprise, they continued to comfort him and lull him to sleep. A million nights of sleep, a billion hugs recalled and clung to. How could he continue to provide such hugs? And yet each time he attempted to feel something, and tried desperately to remember which child he was embracing.

After Denise left his study he examined the flower for a long time. Children's drawings, like those of all primitive peoples, had changed very little over the centuries. Their flowers looked like people. As did their houses. Everything they drew looked like people. All things had heads to live inside and mouths to speak with.

And yet people had been vastly overrated. He had discovered early on that they simply did not last.

Denise was a perishable flower, however beautiful, however much he might love her in his way.

She would grow older than he and forget what he had been. She would die before him and he could not forgive her that betrayal. So at some point he would have to leave her, escape this family, and begin a new lifetime.

They would search for him, he knew. Denise especially, he could see that special, stubborn yearning in her face even now when she perceived the distance in his face. The distance made her want to cling. He had seen it before. He had seen it hundreds of times before. But not one of his children or ex-wives had yet been able to find him once he'd gone. He was the professional traveler, after all, the ultimate escape artist. He had been doing this too long to make mistakes. Unless he wanted to.

This last thought alarmed him, and stirred a vague memory of a little girl clinging to his arm, proclaiming her love, as he tried to make his escape.

Daddy, I need you! Then there were the screams of ultimate betrayal, as he tore yet another child away from him.

But Denise's screams now were those of feigned, playful alarm. Outside his window she made her noises with his other children: Robert aged five, Cheryl aged four. Together they sounded like the static from distant radios. In another time there might not be any radios, and he wondered, briefly, what his children would sound like then.

Denise was seven, and too wise for comfort. There had been other such children; he tried not thinking of their names.

Sometimes gazing into her pale blue eyes he thought she actually might know. But he saw no resentment there. If she actually knew, there would be resentment.

He turned back to his computer and continued work on his essay. During this lifetime he considered himself a philosopher. He wrote numerous unpublished, unpublishable essays on a wide range of topics. He had the luxury to do this because of a variety of investments made under hundreds of names. He doubted seriously he would ever turn to fiction again. Having lived so many fictional lives, he found the idea of fiction often banal, and sometimes even painful to contemplate. At least philosophy dealt with questions which could not be answered.

His current obsession was reincarnation. He typed the word over and over again in a number of different languages, until it filled the screen, remaking itself, reincarnating itself, again and again until the word was almost unrecognizable. He made up spellings in languages which did not exist. He invented spellings in anticipation of shifts in the language to come.

The idea of reincarnation had always troubled him deeply.

If reincarnation was a reality then his immortality had denied him a considerable number of different lives. Not that he needed any more lives per se, but in his present condition, because of the curse of memory, all his lives were the same life, despite their differences. There was no individuality of moment for him - any particular moment was instantly associated in his mind with hundreds of thousands of similar such moments spread out over his lifetimes. Deja vu had become something commonplace, and ultimately, depressing.

Even his own good luck had become depressing. He *could* die, he believed, from an accident, from some mishap, from being in the wrong place at the wrong time. He seemed to be immune from disease, and early on he had discovered that attempts to take his own life were doomed to failure.

He lost control over his body. He suddenly became unable to pull the trigger. Such attempts were apparently against the religion of the man who had condemned him. Only bad luck might kill him.

Outside his office window he could hear the guests arriving. Four and five-year-old guests, for the most part, because they were here for Cheryl's birthday party. He would need to leave his desk at any moment to take up his role as the doting father. Such activities provided him the little real pleasure he ever had with his children. Small children, being only half-formed, being actually very little more than a dream and a collection of hopes, were at times remarkably easy to please. Unlike adults. There were so many things you could *do* for them. The older they got the less you could, in fact, do. They became adult-like, and alone in their heads. They died before you, although they desperately did not want to die. They knew what dying meant. And older children had independent thought and memory, all of it designed to slip inside you and fill you up with their lives, the long gray march of the past. The very idea made him feel ill, made him feel like screaming.

Daddy, I really need you now ...

Instead he gazed at the enigmatic phosphors on the computer screen. If reincarnation was truth and he had been exempted from it, then perhaps he had been exempted from the possession of a soul as well.

Ironically, the possibility that he lacked a soul did not trouble him in the least, not simply because he was not likely to die, but more that he had long ago stopped believing in the tangle of Christian myths. Supposedly that was why he was here today - those myths - but after such a long time he had quite forgotten what the Christ had even looked like, his likeness long since supplanted by the bad paintings hanging in churches around the world. He could not even remember the exact words of the insult he had supposedly said to the man. It may well have been impolite; he remembered himself back then as having been rather impolite. But he didn't believe he could have said anything so terrible to have deserved such punishment. Particularly in the light of his current beliefs.

It was a darkly funny thing, to have been so terribly punished by the curse of a powerful figure, and later to become convinced that that power had been a fraud,

Daddy, you believed in me …

He could easily imagine the Christ reincarnated as some sort of petty politician or pop star.

"John?" The knock at the door was remarkably soft. During his more recent lifetimes he had taken to choosing women who largely left him alone.

"Come in, Mary."

The woman's face was pale, her hair short and brown. She could have been anyone of a hundred wives. He had learned a long time ago not to marry for love. But he was always very kind; he owed them that much. "John. I'm sorry to disturb you at your work,"

"That's fine. Don't worry about it." He smiled. It never ceased to amaze him that his facial muscles could still construct a smile. "I suppose the party is about to start? Is that why you've come for me?" He smiled again, wondering if he could still hold a smile long enough for the purpose it was intended. The purpose was to relax the other person, to make them feel better about themselves. There was nothing worth worrying about. Nothing mattered that much in the end. Relax.

But apparently he had not held the smile long enough; Mary looked awkward, confused. "No … it's an old woman. She says she has to see you."

He considered having Mary tell the person to go away, but he thought it might be too stressful for her. She wanted so badly to please. He decided to release her. "Show her the way in. Go back to the party."

The old woman who came to his door was sixty or seventy; he had never been very good at guessing ages. White hair with streaks of its original black. Fading blue eyes like his own. Like hundreds of others. Some man's ancient fantasy, some boy's grandmother, a man's never forgotten daughter. Like thousands of others.

He held his smile as long as he could. "Daddy?" she said.

He held on to his smile but the muscles had weakened. His smile no longer helped. "You found me," he finally said, calmly, or perhaps it was simply that he lacked energy, "You were one of the smartest, the most clever. And you cared for me in ways I'd never seen before. I really should have expected it."

"It has been quite difficult. But you left clues. Did you know you left clues?"

"You were always special. I stayed as long as I could." He started to say her name, but stopped. He had probably loved her more than any of them, and yet he knew he might still say her name incorrectly. "Even after I knew you probably suspected what your father was I stayed … "

"It was terrible after you left," she said.

"I knew it would be. It is always terrible. I love all of you as long as I can, I try to be a good father … "

"You're not my father! My father wouldn't have left me!"

He threw away his smile, "Don't say that."

"Momma was *devastated!* What did you think was going to happen to her?"

"I know what it must have done to your mother, and I am sorry for it. I have done this to more mothers and children than you can possibly imagine and each time I am painfully aware of the terrible thing I have done. But don't ever tell me I'm not your father. I rocked you in my arms when you were no bigger than a kitten. I carried you up to bed at night. I kept watch at that same bed all night if you were sick and couldn't sleep. I held you and sang to you and anguished *over* every cough and sneeze. No other man will do the things I did for you."

"And then you *left* me!" she screamed.

"And then I left you," he agreed quietly, watching as she pulled the handgun from her ancient, tattered purse.

"Why, Daddy?" She smiled his smile, and held it as long as he had ever been able, "Why?"

He spoke easily, the thoughts readily accessible even though he had never attempted to access them before. "Because you were no longer a child. I no longer knew what I should say to you. You were more than a dream. You became another living soul who will eventually die and the memory of your living will enter me and remain there an eternity and don't you see that is *too* much, too many lost children inside me already, wandering lost and unable to die?"

"You've already forgotten me! You don't even remember my name!" The gun shook with her sobbing, so that he had the sudden fantasy that it was the gun itself talking, the gun barrel her wide, explosive mouth.

"I could never forget you. Don't you know? I run from all of you because I cannot forget you. But particularly *you*. You were the special one, the one who always knew. Somehow, you recognized it. Just like now. Now you know how to help me. Now you know what you have to do."

"Then tell me my name, Father! What is my name?" the gun shouted, wavering.

He smiled, and held the smile. He knew his children well. But especially he knew her.

"Daddy, tell me!" the gun cried, and descended into an inarticulate wail. He held onto his smile. His smile had worked. He fell to the floor.

"Jane," he said, proud to have remembered, to have known all along. "Jane," he said again, but thought the names of all the others, all the others who at last had a father worthy of the name, who at last had a father who could die before them. "Your name has always been Jane," he said, at last closing his eyes.

WAR ON THE DOWNSIDE

Corporal Benning is complaining about the snakes again. I suppose I should be spending more time with him. I have a duty. The heavy responsibility of command. But increasingly I find myself avoiding the troops. In their own little worlds now— probably not a great deal I could do for them anyway.

When I do go to him this time—a shabby form curled up among the shadows and hillocks of this odd, solidified "mist"— I'm actually a bit startled. I crouch beside the man, holding his hand and gripping his shoulder, telling him everything is all right, that the snakes are only shadows, shadows with a life of their own, certainly, but physically harmless shadows just the same.

I try to avoid Benning's wild-eyed stares, his nervous whimpering. I'm not even sure he's hearing anything I'm saying. I'm not sure I believe anything I'm saying myself. The snakes, the long sinuous lines of black undulating over Benning's body, writhing and probing, are not just vaguely-formed shadows anymore. I'm beginning to see a pattern of scales in the translucent gray. And I remember Sergeant Marx, screaming.

It never changes. Not really.

The deaths are not as final, but perhaps it would be just as well if they were. Something is always destroyed; some part dies which does not come back. And after a soldier has undergone a number of these "small deaths" there is little point having him or her under your command. That soldier is no longer any good to you or himself.

Command also changes little. A computer is inadequate to the *real* decisions. And one of the problems of command is what to do with those soldiers. Might as well let them die out here in the spaces between the stars, I believe, than have them die at home, as they surely will, destroying the rest of their family in the process.

Most of my squad was brand new with me at the beginning, four Downside forays ago. Nothing left for us but to stay out here. I'm not sure I could allow any of us to return home even if we had the choice. This is our place now, Downside.

Reynolds is arguing with his father again. I think Reynolds told me the old man died...when? Twenty years ago? A short time ago I saw Reynolds take a swing and the punch passed through the bellowing, red-faced man. Of course. But I wonder how long before one of Reynolds's punches lands on solid flesh?

This was only my first command, so perhaps I have no justification for making philosophical statements about war. But there have been few in these wars to acquire a second command, so my own experience would actually be above average,

"You turn upside down." That's the way the soldiers on the line describe travel out to the Downside. And I suppose for a succinct, one-line description of the feeling one has when a transport goes "under" and comes back out again into a space which is not like space at all, I could do no better. One moment you and your buddies are sitting in chairs or lying in comfortable bunks waiting for the thing to happen, and the next you're having your intestines wrung out, and your head is somewhere beneath your bunk screaming with dreams and remembered scenes and voices from the walls. They now have pills which help a little, but they can't seem to prevent the hallucinations, just decrease their intensity a bit. Downside is shaped differently from other kinds of space, and the human mind turns itself inside out like an old purse, shaking out any loose change before righting again.

No one but soldiers ever goes to Downside. There's nothing there. There are places a ship can come to rest, and the soldiers can get out and walk around. Have to really, since it's still quite difficult maneuvering a ship once it's *inside* Downside. What you have to walk on is a little like solid cloud, or mist, as best I can describe it. There are a few other features: solid mist shaped into rocks, boulders, hills, wall-like cliffs. But that's about all.

The only reason for going to Downside is that the enemy lives there.

Sometimes you feel like some sort of advance "demonstration." A sampling. Command Central seems an impossible distance away. It is easy to think they might have forgotten you. Time itself seems different on the Downside, and you worry sometimes that perhaps the war has been over for years, but no one ever sent for you. You wonder if maybe in the excitement of victory or the despair of an almost total annihilation they have completely forgotten you. They would not want to return to Downside if they could avoid it.

I decide to muster the troops. Perhaps not a very rational decision under the circumstances, but some order is necessary if we are to survive the Downside for any length of time. Besides, I have not lost hope completely that we will be able to overcome these visitations, that the soldiers will bolster themselves, and perhaps even retaliate in some way. The original strategy called for us to keep the enemy occupied with us, making inroads into its mental defenses by means of our own strength of will. Although that strategy has proved too difficult for our powers of concentration up until now, I have great hopes that we will come around and give the enemy a "run for his money," as it were.

"Hold onto yourself, man!" I tell Benning, who has somehow managed to crawl out of his shadowed hiding place and join the rest of us. He dances a strange, wild-eyed dance, his body writhing and jumping nervously, the dark snake-shadows rippling up and down his tall frame. I suppress a small cry when one of the snake-heads turns to me displaying its bright, perfectly-formed fangs.

I keep seeing Sergeant Marx, his fear finally made real, destroying him …

"I know this is difficult, but they're counting on us!" Sergeant Baker enters the circle warily, an enormous dark figure

- its features indistinguishable, its fur coat but partially formed
- slobbering and chewing at her heels.

Reynolds is screaming at his father, periodically stopping to hear what I have to say, and then continuing to scream at his father again. He seems to be following my little talk pretty well, so I suppose I have no reason to complain. I can see his father's eyes, now, and part of the nose has congealed out of the dark oval of his face. The eyes are red, fierce; so far he looks every bit the madman Reynolds has always said he was.

"Our Command has not forgotten us," I tell them, trying to put conviction into my words. "We are an important outpost. If we fall the others surely will fall! Command will give us all the support it can!" Reynolds screams and claws at the gray area of his father's face; a thin, liquid-like shadow seems to be trickling down. "We must follow our orders without regard to the dangers involved. Ours is an invisible enemy, but we must do our best." Baker screams and breaks the circle, the shambling form chasing her.

Her foot is bleeding. The rest of the squad sees this and bolts, taking their phantoms with them.

The lives of so many soldiers, under my guidance and will... and I am beginning to feel that I have failed them.

It is no longer a necessary feature of modern warfare that a soldier understand who or why he or she is fighting. That is the essence of what the "professional soldier" has become, particularly since the advent of the Downside Wars. Jobs are a scarce commodity and you only have a limited number of types to choose from. Usually if you are not in some form of communications you are a soldier. Professional soldiers are paid just a bit better than communications workers. Sometimes that small variance is essential; most of my command have large families, brothers and sisters and all, that they're supporting. The family's account back on earth accumulates credit each minute a soldier is out here.

I've heard that Command Central has some sort of bug planted on each soldier, so that when death inevitably comes a signal is beamed to the bank back home, a final death benefit is automatically paid, and all further payments are halted. I've no proof of that, but I do know communications in regard to such matters are amazingly, unexpectedly fast.

"What are we, our lives, in comparison to the lives of all those we protect? We are the advance guard!" I scream at Reynolds, and he in turn is screaming at his ever-more-detailed father. I shouldn't be doing this. But my frustration is great. These soldiers, and countless soldiers and civilians beyond them, depend on my actions, my decisions.

Certainly, I wanted this responsibility. After all my years of study I thought I might be passed over for command. I worked for the position I now have and I won it cleanly. I too have a large family at home; they depend upon my salary to maintain a good life in the midst of spiraling inflation, and food and housing shortages. What would they do if I were to fail? None of my brothers or sisters is yet old enough to take on such a position, nor would I want them to. One of us on the Downside is quite enough.

I might have resented this, but I don't. This is my profession. I follow orders; I do not question.

I refuse to listen to the voices inside.

I refuse to listen to the screams of Sergeant Marx.

The other thing, of course, is that you never really see the enemy. Not in the way we usually mean seeing. It is actually difficult to piece together a complete explanation for that, at least one free of folklore and paranoia. I do not believe that I personally know anyone who has a complete explanation to relate. So I make do with published "fact," speculation, innuendo, rumor.

Once upon a time (as all good fairy tales begin) there was a starship (actually a freelance freighter) in the midst of undisclosed interplanetary explorations (its last contract had been canceled and the captain/owner was hellbent to find a base with a waiting commission) when something strange happened to the crew.

One of the cooks complained of headaches and unusually bad nightmares continuously for two days before attacking an assistant with a laser knife. A cargo mate thought he was being devoured by a giant, spider-like creature before he cut his own throat in desperation. Two of the navigators left an airlock without pressurized suits. They thought their families were waiting for them beneath the trees outside.

There had been space-related psychological distress before, of course. A number of kinds, not easily classifiable but reasonably treatable. The medic on board had never seen anything of this character, however, and in panic linked up with a Majormed computer on board the carrier Bahama. The captain was incensed—Majormed links costing a small fortune in fees—but before he was able to sever the link the Bahama's Surgeon-general was on the line, wondering what the hell was going on. The Majormed had signaled his office that it had nothing in its record to compare with the combination of symptoms and tests the medic had reported. The captain and the Surgeon-general then proceeded to abuse the sound levels on the line until the Surgeon-general agreed that his office would pick up the costs on the computer link.

Before long a medical taskforce had been dispatched to the freighter (any new space-related maladies were taken quite seriously in those days), and many of that crew also exhibited similar symptoms. The surgeon in charge was himself attacked by an instrument-wielding nurse.

Although they were rarely able to contribute anything to such investigations, a group of theoretical physicists were brought to the freighter as per standard procedure in space medical matters. They were as surprised as anyone there to find a problem suited to their specialty.

Something was odd about the space around that freighter. I've heard a number of theoretical descriptions of that anomaly, contradictory gobbleygook for the most part. A general I know, however, summed all the theories up rather nicely: "The freighter was trapped in what looked to be a giant hemorrhoid."

I am surprised to see Sergeant Marx back with us again. "I'm glad you decided to honor us with your presence!" I say loudly, sarcastically. Sergeant Marx does not reply. Instead he screams, hoarsely, his throat raw and sore from all the hours he has spent screaming before.

"We will not disobey orders," I tell them, attempting to look each of my soldiers in the eyes in turn as I speak to them on this serious matter. This proves to be a difficult undertaking, as their eyes have that curious fixed and blank stare so characteristic of soldiers too long in the field under stress. I know from my studies that this is a look common to all wars, all time periods. But particularly hideous during the Downside Wars, when the stare is often accompanied by a madman's scream.

"We will persevere," I tell them again. "Although we are almost out of supplies we shall not rebel! We will remain loyal to command. We will remember!"

It is then, staring at Sergeant Marx, listening to his screams, that I remember that Sergeant Marx has been dead for some time now.

Several of the physicists involved in the investigations believed the spatial anomaly to have been created by artificial means. Although theirs was the minority opinion, it won favor among the military and several key politicians. A military strategist quickly theorized that this would make an incredibly effective weapon, and in no time at all it was generally accepted at Command that, indeed, this had been a weapon, an attack on us by some alien race. Several advance ships were sent, with the predictable results of crews going quite out of their minds.

Several strategies were soon devised involving intense concentration, meditation, and crash training in more esoteric mental abilities.

And so the Downside Wars had begun.

Of course, we have never seen the enemy, except in the form of our little obsessions and fears. This has naturally proven to be a serious obstacle to the furtherance of the campaign as our soldiers often lapse into periods in which they do not believe that the enemy even exists, and that they are laying down their lives for no good purpose. We attempt to counter such doubts as quickly as possible through group discussion and other methods, but this has not always been effective since some of those at Command seem to have similar doubts.

Fighting the enemy has depended on some rather nebulous weaponry at best, but Command seems to feel that just our presence in the Downside will prevent the enemy from spreading any further. We still do not know, however, if Downside is itself the home of our invisible enemy or merely a staging ground for their military assault.

The enemy has yet to fire upon us with conventional weaponry. I suppose that is a definite sign of their alieness.

Fortunately, I don't seem to be affected quite as severely as the others. A few minor illusions, certainly, but I'm sure they are more from the intense stresses which go with command than anything else. At least I'm still able to perform my duties; I'm sure I'm still able to lead. I do not know if this is because of some small physical or mental difference, or because of some whim on the part of the enemy. I sometimes amuse myself by conjecturing that perhaps the enemy has spared me in deference to my rank.

Sergeant Marx agrees with me I see. Between each burst of screaming I see him nodding his head.

There are those scientists who have conjectured that perhaps Downside, and the entire matrix of "enemy" phenomena which goes with it, have something a bit more intimate to do with the human mind and its accompanying fears and obsessions. They wonder if the anomaly which is Downside is a breakthrough into some part of human subconsciousness itself, a hole broken into the deepest layers of the human psyche, allowing the monsters and demons there to escape.

Naturally as a practical soldier I find these speculations to be a bit difficult to swallow. But nevertheless the scientists' further warnings invariably produce a shudder. Some of these theorists also believe that by disturbing this area, by encroaching on the "space" formed by Downside, we are risking a worldwide mental catastrophe. Perhaps Downside is a part of every human being's mind and we risk seriously unbalancing that part.

I do not question orders from Command. I do not disobey.

And yet I have some concern that there are elements here we know nothing about. I don't believe we should be tampering with matters we don't completely understand.

What is it that we are fighting?

I see it again. It is happening right now.

Sergeant Marx is being torn apart by the giant spider. It has been his biggest fear. It is sawing through his neck and he is screaming. He has been the first to show the symptoms, the first to have fears congeal into shadows. It is tearing at his eyeballs. The shadows have solidified rapidly for him. It is plunging its mandibles into his mouth, probing. Soon we all know the spider has become physically real, that the damage being done to Sergeant Marx's body is real. It is stripping the bloody skin from his skull. We know what is in store for all of us.

And still Sergeant Marx is screaming inside my head.

One of our orders was to capture one of the enemy as quickly as possible, interrogate it, then describe it as accurately as possible. Catalog it, as it were. That order gave me many sleepless nights, trying to come up with some sort of plan for capturing the enemy, trying to develop a system for cataloging all the various aspects of said enemy, et cetera. I lectured the troops many times on that same subject: the need to describe the enemy in intimate detail even though they might be terrified. I suggested that perhaps they might even feel *compelled* to describe the enemy in great deal, in order to "capture" it and make it safe, as it were.

But secretly I thought that even I would be literally petrified by the first glimpse of the enemy. How could I describe it then?

The enemy has escalated the conflict. Sergeant Marx comes to me, fully restored, but with the giant spider clamped to his arm with bloody mandibles. Reynold's father is screaming at me.

"I'm sorry!" I begin to weep in front of Sergeant Marx, touching him, seeing that he is indeed solid flesh. "Perhaps I wasn't suited to command, but I did my best. I would not have sent anyone to their deaths if I could have helped it!" Sergeant

Marx stares at me with ill-disguised disgust. He is unforgiving; he intends to make me suffer. "I did my best! I could not do more!" I scream at him.

My family is standing behind Sergeant Marx. Their mouths gape, mocking me. Father accuses me with his eyes—I did not advance far enough. Mother sneers—I should have stayed home with her, while my brothers laugh mirthlessly. How dare they, when I have sacrificed so much for them!

The remainder of my troops gather with these. Reynolds and his father stand side by side, staring at me with obvious menace. Sergeant Baker leads the hairy creature away from her half-gnawn foot, so that it too faces me. Corporal Benning's snakes form a writhing line in front of him.

All of them … seem so real.

The staff at Command, the clerks, strategists, theorists, the commanding generals line up in rows beyond these. All turned my way.

They begin to advance, their arms waving listlessly in the air.

They are hundreds of giant spiders now, their dark legs waving listlessly as they raise them towards me.

Me. The enemy.

WELCOME TO RODEOMART

"Ten minutes until product release ..." The loudspeaker began the countdown. Keith continued to flex his fingers, practicing the snatch, the grab. He was limber, he was strong, he was the perfect consumer. It was a shame, he supposed, but live shopping was no longer an activity for arthritics, the frail, or the reflex-impaired. Let them order their goods out of catalogs. But for a real bargain, and a chance at the latest technology, there was simply no beating the monthly product release at Rodeomart.

"Nine minutes, thirty seconds until product release ..."

Up and down the line the customers edged forward eagerly. The man standing next to Keith had enormous shadows under his eyes, and his fingers jerked electrically as he nervously opened and closed his hands. Earlier he'd told Keith he'd been in line all night. It had been a bad idea–Keith knew from experience that early arrival gave you little advantage in a game requiring alertness and quick reflexes.

"It isn't very fair," his grandmother said behind him. "This heat. Us old folks can't handle this kind of shopping. We should just make do with the old models."

He hated repeating himself, but conversations with his grandmother were, by necessity, a few basic ideas endlessly repeated. "That's why people your age get a surrogate. Remember? I'm your surrogate."

"I *know* that. I'm not senile, you know? But that doesn't make it fair. What about folks who can't get a surrogate?"

"If they don't have a willing family member or can't afford to hire a surrogate they probably can't afford the new models anyway."

"Maybe the old models are good enough. I *like* my old models."

Well I don't, he thought, but he said, "Studies show that having to learn new technology keeps old minds sharp."

"Sounds like store propaganda to me."

"That doesn't make it any less true, Grandma."

"Seven minutes until product release ..."

The crowd breathed as one creature, releasing a long ragged sigh. He looked up and down the line, now fanned out along this end of the store. Here and there he found somebody dressed for work, and one lady foolishly sporting high heel shoes, but for the most part people were dressed in exercise clothing, sweat pants, track shorts. Some had knee pads. A couple of jokers wore full cowboy regalia. The competition for this release looked weak.

Apparently his grandmother didn't speak for her generation because there were quite a few older women this time. So much for the old cliché that updated product releases were all about men and their toys.

Everyone carried his or her new lariat awkwardly. Despite the lessons the store provided–for a fee, of course–the room was just too crowded, and a few lessons hardly made the average consumer skilled with a rope. Keith practiced all year for these new product releases, but finesse was impossible under these circumstances. Most people tried to get too fancy anyway. A quick lasso and drag was really all that was needed.

"Five minutes until product release ..."

He felt a tickle of anxiety which he did not attempt to suppress, but prepared to re-channel it into a reserve of quick, explosive energy for the task to come. He had spent much of the previous day studying the glossy brochures and magazine articles on the new products, locking the slender lines, the curves and recesses, into accessible memory, a template he could focus and fantasize on. Even knowing that the companies paid their graphic designers fortunes to make these images of steel and plastic look like flesh and silk, more seductive than anything which might be experienced firsthand, he could not resist their appeal. He didn't care that he was being manipulated. He had given himself over completely to the lure of the latest and greatest.

Someone at the back of the line had been saying he'd heard there would be shortages, that many of the branches wouldn't be getting their full allotment. That stirred things up a bit. Someone else started arguing with the man. His grandmother started to fret about it. Impatiently he reached back and tried to pat her hand. There were always these little anxious discussions before a new product release. They didn't bother him—he just saw them as more distraction for his competition, which could only be a good thing.

"Two minutes …"

He crouched, leaned forward. Up and down the line the more inexperienced consumers moved about, not sure which foot to lead with, or where to hold their lariats so that they wouldn't get them tangled up with the people next to them. Good—more distraction in the line. He scanned the lengths of the display aisles, focusing on the double doors at the end of each. The products would be released there, in no particular order, and having no relation to the products already shelved along that particular aisle. A lot of new consumers didn't understand that, and made too many assumptions. You couldn't assume anything if you were going to be a good consumer—even the advance product literature had to be read with a grain of salt. You had to keep your mind clear and eyes open.

Approximately half-way along each aisle a red line had been painted on the floor. Customers weren't allowed to move forward until the new products reached this line. Clerks stationed along the sides of the store would pull you out and to the back of the line, invalidating your selections, if you violated that rule. People should know better, but there were always a few false starts.

The alarm squealed like an electrocuted pig. Off to his left one woman fainted, taking down several others with her in a tangle of rope and struggling limbs. A collage of brightly-colored plastic and shiny metal exploded through the double doors. "Get me something good!" his grandmother screamed behind him.

A runaway toaster was the first to make it to the red line in the aisle directly in front of him. He ignored it, of course, but at least half-a-dozen customers raced forward, spinning their ropes, knocking each other into the shelves on either side. Each year it seemed the management augmented some minor appliance with a great deal of unnecessary power in order to make an early splash, and people always fell for it, eager to grab the first shiny thing racing by. The government really ought to regulate that sort of thing.

Rumbling up behind the toasters were a few bulky consoles, TVs and stereo systems, some sort of innovative sewing machine, a large automatic cooking pot or two. Behind those wheezed the fastest vacuum cleaners with a few slower models right behind. Then a smallish refrigerator, and hiding here and there among that bunch, the small electronics. He raced forward then, arm stretched high to keep his lariat out of reach.

Almost immediately he had to leap over a steam iron with a teenage boy in hot pursuit. But then he stepped on the hand of a young woman lying in the aisle attempting to strangle a hand mixer into submission. She screamed and grabbed the bottom of his track pants, yanking them part way down. Not to be distracted, he reached down with his left hand and forced his pants back into place, kicked a tumbling microwave out of his way, dodged a pair of coffee makers in the process of being roped together by a bald man in a pinstriped suit, and spying a small personal digital assistant flying through the air, snagged it with his now-free left hand and tossed it into the bag hanging around his neck.

A woman behind him screamed in either glee or terror. She may or may not have been his grandmother.

Two women argued over a washing machine, both of their ropes cinched tight about its middle. They were advised via the speakers to drag the washer over to the sidelines for adjudication, which they did with no pause in the argument.

Several customers lassoed each other. One or two managed to laugh it off, but more than a few fists were thrown. One of the cowboys roped product after product with genuine skill, dragging them to the sidelines where helpers loosened the lassoes and organized the items into piles. This was usually considered suspicious, and no doubt the cowboy would be reminded of the No-resell agreement he had signed. Supposedly the store had a reputation for aggressive follow up investigations and prosecutions.

When the second wave of products and shoppers was released he was still out on the floor with a handful of other holdouts. Holdouts were usually those shoppers who hadn't found everything they'd wanted yet, and were stubborn enough to continue shopping even through injury and fatigue. The second wave of consumers was normally more aggressive, having lost patience while watching the first wave grab the best bargains. Keith sustained several surreptitious punches during the rush, but still managed to snag the latest in compact music systems, a small flat-screen television, and a do-it-yourself home surveillance system.

The yellow light was rotating overhead, so the shoppers rested as helpful clerks came into the aisles and assisted the injured to the medical stations, tallied initial purchases, and swept up broken product from the floor. He handed the PDA to a young female clerk and signaled his grandmother to confer with her at the checkout stand. His grandmother appeared flushed with excitement.

Around him his fellow shoppers sat on the floor or leaned against the shelves. They avoided eye contact. He was pretty sure the man sitting on the floor nearby had a broken arm, but when the clerks had come around offering medical aid he had denied it. The young woman lying next to him obviously had a broken leg, judging by the strange turn it took somewhere between knee and ankle. It was wrapped in a fishnet stocking with a thick, obvious seam up the back, and Keith was fascinated by the way the seam twisted in the area of the leg's distortion, as if attempting to create some new mark of punctuation. He felt himself somewhat aroused, and embarrassed, looked away. Another woman standing a few feet away was crying quietly, the hand holding the rope shaking. Her once-stylish outfit was smudged and torn. She stared at the yellow light, apparently waiting for the exact instant it changed color and she could complete her purchases.

A man in running shorts squatted over some unidentifiable, broken appliance at the side of the aisle. He muttered something repetitive and angry as he attempted to free the destroyed object from his lasso.

There were still a few shoppers waiting their turn at one end of the store, but most had left. By the checkout stand his grandmother was pointing at her watch and motioning him over. He ignored her and looked down at his bloody hand on the lariat, trying to calm himself.

He'd gotten everything he'd set out to get, but he still wasn't ready to go. He really didn't know what else he wanted, but knew he would recognize it when he saw it.

At the end of the aisle the release doors drifted open a few inches, pushing discarded bits of packaging and lost parts aside, a fine mist billowing below the edge of the doors. Keith looked around to see if anyone else had noticed. There had been no announcement, so no one had paid attention. He gathered more of the rope into his hands and crept forward slowly, expecting at any moment to be stopped by some clerk or other low-paid employee, but he was not.

With one shoulder he nudged the doors back the other way. They were hollow, aluminum, and seemed to weigh nothing at all. When he first entered the cavernous warehouse area he thought it empty, the heavy-duty shelves devoid of both new releases and replacement backstock. He remembered the rumors of shortages. Just the other day a neighbor had dared suggest that the current economic climate could no longer support huge super stores like Rodeomart. Keith had just laughed. People looked for any excuse not to try out new things. But that was what living was, wasn't it? Trying out new things? If there was a shortage of new ideas, new products, didn't that really mean a shortage of life itself?

But here were all these empty shelves, these empty boxes, trash littering the floor. No more products, no employees, no goods, no services. He started to leave. He'd find somebody he could talk to. Not some clerk. Somebody in management.

Something clanked off to his left. A rattle of small parts spilling. A whirr and sigh of motor. He clutched the stiff loop of rope to his chest and ran to the end of the aisle, then one aisle over, then another.

The appliance was tall and thin, gleaming, bent over with its back turned. It rotated its head, the rest of the chassis following, small chewed metal bits dropping from the slot in front. It raised one tube and attachment, wiped at the slot with an almost human-like gesture, plastic shielding sliding back inside the steel shoulder blades to uncover its electric sensors. Servos purred, hydraulics coming to life with a wet, metallic groan. The long limbs began to propel it towards him, an artistic warp of metal, the delicate bends in the self-balancing structure making him hold his breath.

He had no idea what it could do. He had no idea if it was even for sale. But he brought the rope up aggressively, making a small, involuntary cry as he desperately cast his loop, because this was something he just had to have.

But it was *so* quick, a marvel of cutting edge hydraulics and digital gyros. It had his rope, running it rapidly over hooks and levers, wrapping him tightly with it, so efficiently, he felt one rib crack agonizingly, followed by another so painful he couldn't even scream.

Its breath was oil and silicon, overheated circuits and sour exhaust, and its kiss answered all his needs, as he'd always known it would.

THE WORLD THROUGH THE TREE

Once again Ain had returned to the tree of his parents, the great willow at the edge of the marshland, but with little of the peace he had brought to his journey in former times. For Ain knew this would be his last time, and he was not sure whether he was saddened or relieved.

From the opposite edge of the marsh the willow looked much like a fountain of green, shimmering light, the spray spreading fan-like before falling to the wet ground. The sun had just risen, adding an orange halo to the tree's silhouette. Ain knew as he drew closer the tree would lose this impression, for the early morning breeze would bring the rustle of the many leaves, and he would be thinking then of grass skirts and straw shades.

The tree was quieter than usual as he approached it, but he tried to believe he was merely anticipating the worst. After all, he was still some distance away: although as small as most of the older elven-folk, he was heavier and sank a bit into the marsh with each step.

But he knew, too, that most of his elders were dying or changing. How could he be sure his parents, or any of the others, were still left?

He was changing, too, he considered grimly, but onto a different path.

Once beneath the old willow he heard a scurrying in the upper branches. He looked up anxiously. A small head with bright eyes peered down at him.

"Ain?" the head said, then purred brokenly. Ain was troubled by the purr.

"Mother?"

The head disappeared. He could hear a series of whistles, grunts, and purrs in the upper branches hidden from him.

Ain began to climb and was pleased to see that he still retained at least some skill at it. When he reached the branch where the head had appeared he stopped and looked about him. "Mother? Father? Lael?"

The purrs and grunts picked up again, this time from a shadowed area closer to the main trunk of the old willow.

Ain crouched low and closed his eyes, then moved forward into that darkness. He tried to let the willow take him within, but did not know if the connection would still be strong enough. After a few moments, the familiar yet vaguely uncomfortable sensation of webs passing over flesh came to his body, and he felt himself moving into the shadowed part near the trunk. His body protested a moment, feeling heavy and awkward as it attempted the transformation, so he concentrated further, picturing a bridge in his mind, a passageway, and finally slipped through.

They were there, his family, mother and father and his sister Lael. His father approached him, his eyes wide and bright so that Ain had a small moment of hope that he might not have lost everything, that there might still be home here.

But his father's eyes suddenly grew dull. When he opened his mouth to speak only grunts and purrs came out.

Ain stared at his father. The hair had grown over his cheeks and forehead. The teeth were sharper than before, the posture of the body more crouched. When his mother and Lael moved up to join his father, Ain saw they looked much the same,

No longer elven-folk as he was no longer elven-folk. But in different ways. He had always been closer to the human side of elven nature than the animal side. Another side of the bridge. He found it difficult to even look at his family now. The bridge which had been the elven race was disappearing from their faces.

Lael moved closer, "Ain?"

Ain stirred anxiously, then moved to her, but suddenly her eyes went dull. She tried to bite him.

Ain stepped back as Lael retreated into the shadows, grunting.

He moved away from his family to another branch. There

he curled up and closed his eyes. He felt sure that even in their present state they would not disturb him. Somehow they would recognize what he was doing and respect it.

He pushed his thoughts out into the tree. He let his mind drift, following his thoughts, pulling apart and drawing out like a thin cloud. Then his nerves, his blood, the strong pulse of his heart, the long sigh of his escaping breath ... awkwardly, roughly, so that he knew indeed this would be his last time. He would be too different before long. The world would be too different.

Ain saw the world through the tree. He drew moisture in through his skin, tasted earth on his feet, and sun-filled morning air in his fingertips. He felt marshland spreading out around him, distant hills within his scope. And all glowing, all filled with white, green, yellow, and brown.

He felt the ghosts of elven-folk within his hair and ears, all those who'd been born and died within the scope of the old willow. He looked deeply into the barrows, wells, and standing stones where they once dwelt and found that they were few, and wondered when they would be none.

He sensed the richness, the many-sided manifestations of life in the wood, now only half-recalled, shadowed parts of his mind. Those who were once numerous, who were powerful: he knew this might be his last time for recreating them. The green folk, the hags, bodiless powers and children of the serpent, the wandering dead, demons, dark elves like caterpillars grubbing the dirt, all the elder races dwindling away within him.

Ain was overcome with sadness, a sadness which expanded even as these last visions through the tree were leaving him, and he knew he would never see such things again. The elven-folk were now so small inside himself he knew he would never be able to find his way back. The threads of their being grew dim as the knowledge inside him grew more ponderous—the knowledge that at last he had grown to be completely alone. He would hear no more voices in his head.

When Ain awoke his family was still there with him, almost unrecognizable to his changed senses. He could not even feel sad over their loss. They were no longer elven-folk, but animals much like squirrels or moles. Their eyes showed no recognition of him.

There were many legends among the elven-folk of how occasionally a couple from the elder races would give birth to a mortal child. But none, Ain realized, had considered what eventually happened to all such parents and their children.

The world constantly changes. Ain's family became Animal, even as Ain became Man. And the bridge the elven-folk made between the two would soon be no longer.

Ain began to descend the old willow for the final time.

TEN THINGS I KNOW
ABOUT THE WIZARD

One: That He Has a Beautiful Daughter

Clarence first met Amanda in the market place when she stole several fruits from his vending cart. He'd been completely entranced by her: her long silky black hair falling loosely to her shoulders, her narrow face and full lips. And her eyes, like emeralds on snow. He was watching those eyes when he should have been watching her hands. It was only as she started to turn away that he saw her slipping the fruit into the front pockets of her dress.

He stood in complete bewilderment a moment—by her clothes she'd seemed well-off—before jumping over the side of his cart and bounding after her, heedless to the fruit being spilled and retrieved by eager passersby behind him.

The girl was fast, and Clarence had a difficult time of it just keeping her fleeting form in sight. She seemed to know well the lanes and back alleys—surprising for someone of her bearing—and it took all of Clarence's experience not to become lost himself.

But finally she made a wrong turn, and Clarence found himself face-to-face with the beautiful maiden, her back to a dead-end. He had her! But she smiled much too engagingly, he thought, for a thief caught in the act.

He stared at her for some time; she examined him with those emerald eyes just as intently. Clarence knew how to handle the ordinary thief; he had a great deal of experience in the marketplace. But he had no idea how he should speak to a lady, even if she were a thief.

"You took my fruit!" he finally blurted out.

She merely smiled and nodded.

"You didn't pay!"

She laughed out loud.

"But why?" he asked.

"Why ... I was hungry," she replied in a soft and musical voice.

Two: That He Has a Very Unusual Daughter

Clarence spent the following weeks with the maiden, whose name was Amanda, in considerable mental and emotional confusion. He was never quite sure what she was thinking, or what she meant by some of her bizarre statements.

"Where do you come from?" he'd ask her.

"Past the moon and beneath the tavern floor," she'd answer.

Such nonsense...but he found her utterly fascinating. He couldn't control himself. He couldn't stay away from her.

More than once he had to stop her from stealing something from a local shop. She didn't really need to do such things; she simply enjoyed the challenge, she had told him. But still she persisted, and more than once they had had some close calls together. Many of the local merchants were quite capable of handling their affairs without benefit of law. Clarence found himself constantly afflicted with aches and pains acquired during Amanda's escapades.

She was prone to marked swings in mood. One moment she might be laughing with him and the next screaming. He could never predict how she was going to react to anything he said. So any indication of a mood shift made him anxious.

It soon became obvious to him, however, that Amanda had grown fond of him as well. Even though she complained about his inability to talk back to her, to be more forceful, she wanted to spend most of her time with him, she said. And despite her strange ways he felt the same. "But my father is a wizard," she told him. "And you must meet him first, and impress him if we are to marry. That may prove difficult, Clarence my love. He is a strange man, but he's of course responsible for my existence." She laughed.

Clarence didn't know quite what to say.

Three: That He Lives In a Dark, Secluded House by the Sea

Clarence could not fathom the materials the wizard used to build his house; they appeared to be an amalgam of contradictory substances. The house was part of a granite cliff, with trees and other *vegetation* so mixed in that they appeared to be part of the structure itself. A large cypress melded into the roof line. A boulder formed the central portion of one of the countless chimneys. Clay and steel and cement supported one of the outside walls. There were circular doors, rectangular doors, and triangular doors. Vines covered some oddly-shaped windows and uncovered others. Strange animals nested in the weirdly-angled nooks and crannies. The lines of perspective appeared contradictory.

And one section of the house seemed impossibly dark, even in the morning light, as if that section of the house had been fashioned of night itself.

It had taken them two days' journey to get there, and Clarence had wondered the entire time if it was worth the effort. Amanda complained about her father constantly: how he attempted to control her life, how he had adamant opinions about almost any subject, how he inflicted "silent rages" upon anyone who dared disagree with him.

But when Clarence had questioned their going Amanda had lashed out at him with an unexpected viciousness. "Because he's my *father*!" she cried. "It's for me to decide whether to visit him or not!"

So they'd made the trip, through wastelands and mysterious dream-like landscapes Clarence had never known existed. The wizard was indeed isolated; there seemed to be no other dwellings as far as the eye could see. Clarence couldn't understand why anyone would even want to live out there.

"You grew up in this place?" Clarence asked as they stood below the wizard's cliff-dwelling.

"I did…" Amanda whispered.

"I don't understand. Who were your friends? Who did you play with as a child?"

She turned to him with a slight frown. "I didn't have any friends," she said flatly. "Any companions I had my father made for me out of dust and swamp water."

With that she turned and guided him to the steep staircase climbing the cliffside to the wizard's house.

Four: That He Is Very Old

The wizard sat behind an immense table piled high with books. He was difficult to see behind the dusty volumes: only a purple-sleeved arm at the side now and then, white and fish-like hands, or the top of his head, nearly bald and intricately veined.

"Father..." Amanda said with a nervous edge to her voice.

There was no answer.

"Father, I've come home to visit. I've brought a friend."

Clarence heard a chair scrape, a dry cough, and a small, wizened figure crept around from behind the table. Clarence relaxed a bit at the wizard's appearance: he seemed to be only five feet tall or so, and quite frail. Who could fear a man like that?

But the wizard suddenly straightened up, his back unbending, shoulders broadening, head pulling erect so that he was quickly over six feet in height and fixing Clarence with large bloodshot eyes.

Clarence stepped back and allowed Amanda to approach her father.

"This is Clarence, Father. My friend."

The wizard stepped forward out of the dim light so that Clarence was able to see his features more clearly. His skin was so white it appeared to be luminous, his bald head like an oval of light. What little hair he had was white and cropped closely, making a band above his ears. He also had a short white beard which covered his chin. His eyes seemed terribly mobile in contrast to the rest of his features. His mouth was a rigid line. Although his features did not in and of themselves seem ancient, his entire aspect was one of incredible age. Clarence sensed that the wizard was the oldest creature he had ever met.

The wizard did not speak to Clarence.

"It has been a long time between visits, Amanda," the wizard said to his daughter.

"I...I've been away." For the first time Clarence saw Amanda avert her eyes in embarrassment. He had never thought before that she could feel such a thing.

There was an awkward silence during which Amanda seemed to be struggling to find something to say. Her father waited impatiently.

"How has your health been?" she finally asked.

"Well enough," he said, then. "You may spend a few days here, Amanda. But I have my work, and will need solitude thereafter." He turned and left.

Amanda stood there quietly, and Clarence could not approach her.

Five: That He Is a Shape-shifter

That first day in the wizard's house proved to be a long one for Clarence. Amanda was sullen and irritable with him much of the time, and the wizard seemed to be virtually ignoring them.

But when he questioned Amanda about her father's absence she lashed out at him. "Open your eyes, can't you! He's watching us both constantly! He doesn't even make an effort to hide it!"

Clarence looked around uneasily. "I ... don't see ..."

"Look! There he is now!" she cried, and pointed at a corner of the room.

Clarence looked where she pointed, but saw nothing but an untidy pile of clutter. "Where? I don't see him!"

"The mouse! The mouse you fool!"

Clarence stared. There was a mouse there, a small gray one. It wrinkled its nose at the two of them and then scurried into a small hole in the debris.

"Your father?"

"Of course..."

Six: That He Is Not Really Bad, Just Arrogant

Clarence saw many other animals, and one time a small dwarf with an immense red nose, all of whom seemed to observe him with a bit too much intensity, a bit too much interest for normal creatures of that type. He began to feel watched, constantly. Amanda told him there were no pests or animals of any type in residence at the house, normally; the wizard used a charm to keep them away. So any other creatures or personages found there were the wizard himself. Clarence encountered a cat, a dog, a small wren, a caterpillar, a spider, a cricket, and a moose (which he was startled to discover in his bedroom one evening) in just his first two days in the wizard's home. He became particularly careful of his actions when he was around Amanda.

This angered Amanda greatly and twice she pulled Clarence close for an embrace when one of these creatures was in the room. Clarence sputtered and tried to pull away, a nervous eye on the creature.

"Coward!" Amanda screamed, and began hitting Clarence across the chest. "Spineless idiot!"

But the rest of the time she was distant, preoccupied. She seemed to want to have little to do with Clarence.

The wizard did not do anything which might be called bad; even Amanda's many complaints about her father did not seem to add up to the evil man Clarence had first visualized.

The wizard was merely head-strong and arrogant; he was daily exposed to the temptation of great power, and obviously the wizard often gave in to this temptation. He enjoyed using power, and used it extensively. Who could really blame him for that?

"So many…like my father…they start thinking they're gods in their old age." Amanda said to him. But as far as he could tell, the wizard had not gone that far.

One of the wizard's most disturbing amusements was his habit of producing ghosts from the past, either replicas of Amanda's childhood companions he'd manufactured previously or figures from Clarence's own childhood. Clarence felt as if he were constantly dreaming, confronted daily by his long-dead parents, the pet lizards he once owned, his long-dead sister's three-year-old self, and assorted young friends, most of them long-forgotten.

Amanda's "ghosts" were a bit more exotic. A giant spider with bright red eyes and eighteen legs. A large fat, jelly-like creature with one thick leg. Two sets of Siamese twins. A large bird with a bell around its neck. And a few a bit more disturbing: a hideous deformed head that talked, a small subhuman which bled from its ears constantly and impossibly, and a furry creature which screamed piteously in constant pain.

Amanda was on edge, her eyes darting, her hands dry and raw from rubbing them together. Clarence could not understand why the wizard, whom neither had seen for more than a few minutes in his true appearance, would do this to his own daughter. What was he thinking of?

Seven: That He Has a Separable Soul

Clarence discovered that after several days he was growing increasingly angry with both Amanda and her father. The wizard was needling him almost constantly, sending all manner of apparitions into his room to disturb him. And the wizard's presence was almost a constant. Many times Clarence did not know whether a particular presence was the wizard in disguise or one of his manufactures.

So surprisingly he found himself talking back to Amanda with more fervor, not letting any of her small jibes past him.

He had actually expected she would like him better that way, of course. But that wasn't her reaction.

"You're getting to be just like him!" she screamed at Clarence. "You have an opinion about everything, and you think you're the only one who knows the truth!"

One day Clarence and Amanda sneaked into the wizard's study when they knew he was out in the woods. It was unusual for him to be away. He spent hours here, working long into the night with little or no sleep. The study was an immense, drafty chamber, filled with books, manuscripts, odd statues and carvings, jars full of substances, preserved animals, and all sorts of mechanical instruments. Clarence did not like the place and wanted to leave, but Amanda wouldn't permit it.

"I think he's keeping some important secrets from us; I want to find them."

She began to rummage through all the strange articles. Clarence stood watching nervously. Then he heard a bird cackle, and jumped. He sought the source of the sound in the darkness.

"It's only Janalai," she said chuckling. When Clarence still looked puzzled Amanda grabbed him by the hand and pulled him into one of the corners. She lit a small candle and a yellow glow illuminated the objects there.

A bird sat in its nest atop several old barrels and large books. The column looked unstable but the bird seemed content enough. It had a long neck and a bright green head. Ragged purple feathers protruded from its sides helter-skelter, looking as if the bird had been in a serious accident.

Amanda walked over to the bird, clutched its neck, and pulled it roughly out of its nest. A silver egg lay within.

"See," Amanda gestured with her other hand. "Janalai guards my father's soul."

"His soul?"

"Many wizards are able to remove their souls," Amanda said. "They hide it somewhere, as in this egg. You can't destroy a wizard until you first find the hiding place of his soul, actually. It makes them almost indestructible."

"But why does he leave it in such an open area? Someone could come in here and steal it!"

"He moves it to another hiding place periodically. Although there has been no need of late to do so. No one comes here anymore. My father is not an active enough opponent for anyone to want to kill."

Clarence looked again at the egg, and shuddered, imagining it falling to the hard rock floor.

Eight: That He Is In Complete Control

On the fifth day Clarence discovered he could not leave the wizard's house. He simply wanted some fresh air, then found there were no more doors to the outside and all the windows were bolted. When he went to Amanda to tell her about this she shrugged. "So, what did you expect?"

As a child, Amanda once told him, she'd thought her father could do anything. He always seemed to know what she was thinking. And when she'd misbehaved she believed he had paralyzed her because she'd been unable to move with the consequent fear. He knew what was right and wrong and had the power of life and death over her. He was in complete control.

There was no escaping him.

Nine: That He Has a Test for Me

On his last day at the wizard's house Clarence woke up on the floor of a great dark hallway, a place he had never been before. He stood up and began to walk down the length of this hall when the walls started to shift, sending him scrambling madly to avoid being crushed by the moving stone.

He found himself in a small room with the walls slowly closing in on him. He had to move the heavy table around quickly so as to wedge the walls apart.

Suddenly the floor dropped out from under him and he found himself on the table and sliding down an immense stone ramp. He had to leap off before the table smashed into a wall at the bottom of the ramp.

Then all the creatures he'd met from Amanda's past began chasing him, and no matter how fast he ran he seemed to get no farther away from them.

Suddenly he was in the same long corridor he began but the walls were lined with pictures now, and as a floating ball of light descended by each one he was able to examine them. They seemed to be several pictures of Amanda, a picture of the wizard, and of another woman who Clarence had never seen before.

Ten: That a Wizard's Daughter Is Hard To Love

The wizard was suddenly at his side, seeming impossibly tall. "My wife..." the wizard said, gesturing toward the picture of the unknown woman.

"My mother..." he said, and pointed toward one of the pictures of what Clarence had thought to be Amanda. Clarence started to protest involuntarily, but was able to control himself.

"Amanda ..." the wizard said, pointing to the next picture, " ... and her sisters ..." He swept his arm across the length of the hall, and the descending lights illuminated countless other portraits, all looking exactly like Amanda's.

The wizard turned to him. "I never knew my mother; my father was a great magician who took her away from me. But still she did not have to go; she did not have to leave me. Each time I have lost Amanda one such as you has brought her back to me. I keep remaking her, her companions, and yet still she is ungrateful ... still she leaves me..."

Clarence ran through the hallway, through the doors, up winding staircases. The wizard seemed to put nothing more in his way. Clarence did not slow down until he reached Amanda's door.

He heard her crying within. He opened the door slowly.

Amanda was playing with her companions: the small subhuman bleeding, the little furry thing crying, the deformed bodiless head talking with maddening animation.

Amanda was beginning to fade, as her companions were beginning to fade. Somehow she looked older even as she began to disappear, but Clarence could not be sure. He remembered what she'd said so long ago: He is of course responsible for my existence ..."

And then she was gone completely. A gray mouse scurried out from under the bed, staring at Clarence as it wiggled its nose. Then it became a ferocious-looking silver cat that ran out the door screeching.

Clarence knew that Amanda would soon be appearing in the room again, a new and different Amanda for the wizard to love.

But he did not wait.

PUNISHMENT

Jennifer was driving me crazy. She had been hanging around the house all day, pacing, restless. Picking up a book or a magazine, glancing at it a few minutes, then dropping it again. Nibbling at television segments, switching channels every few minutes. Not bothering to check the paper to see what was on, or forthcoming, content to indulge in this frenetic inventory of random images. I'd warned her about the TV before, about how she'd wear out the tuner. I'd been lecturing her for years about how a television set was not a toy, and that she'd have to use it correctly or she wouldn't be permitted to use it at all. But I couldn't correct her now. I found it difficult to say anything to her. When she looked at me, she looked past me. She was distracted, thinking about something, and it made me very nervous because I could never figure what she really thought about anything. Everything she did was unpredictable. Things would break or become rearranged, strange bills would come to the house or strange people would show up on the front steps, and there seemed no other explanation except that Jennifer had had her hand in it. Although I can't say that we ever caught her at anything she couldn't explain her way out of. That made it all the worse, however—we knew she had been doing things and yet we couldn't confront her directly about them.

"I'm going out now, to Marcie's."

I was relieved. She made me uncomfortable hanging around like that. And, unaccountably, afraid. But I couldn't forget that I was still her father. I had responsibilities. A duty to my daughter.

"You'll be back by bedtime, Jennifer. Am I right?"

Again, she stared past me. When she looked like that I

would have sworn that, deep down, she hated me. But who could know? I had no idea what she felt about anything; I didn't even know if Marcie was her best friend, or just a casual friend. "Of course," she said. "I always am."

The uneasiness she'd caused me made me angry. "I don't like that tone. You're my daughter; I have a right to expect you home on time."

She stared past me.

"Do you hear me, Jennifer?"

"Of course, Father." She looked bored; I felt silly. "I promise I'll be home at the correct time."

Five minutes later she left.

She didn't come home until late the next afternoon. We'd been frantic. And she'd sneaked into her upstairs bedroom and gone to sleep. We didn't even know until my wife opened her door to put some of her laundry on the bed. My wife came running down the stairs, insisting that I go wake her, have a talk with her, "throw the book at her." She was afraid to do it herself. But then so was I. I was afraid of what might happen, and yet I couldn't even imagine what that might be.

I thought my daughter might try something awful, and yet I had no idea why I would think such a thing. So I convinced my wife we needed to give her some space, some time to work out her own problems. And I used that as my excuse for not going upstairs and talking, confronting my Jennifer.

The baby watches you, and yet you don't have the language with which to admonish her. You shout at her; she can't look at you this way. But she maintains her cool control. Everything you can do will not change her.

My wife and I have always put great stock in being good parents. We decided early on that we would bend over backwards to be fair to our daughter. We would always listen to her, we would not unfairly accuse her, and we would give her plenty of chances to do the right thing.

Punishment, if it had to come to that, would be logical, suited to the infraction. If she stole something, she had to give it back and apologize. If she broke something, she had to replace it. If she violated the rules while playing outside, the following day she would not be allowed to play outside. If she was careless with the TV, she could not watch the TV for a logically-arrived-at period of time. If she wasted someone's time and energy, she owed that person an equal amount of time and energy. We didn't want to be too harsh, or too easy.

"You are not allowed in our bedroom when we're not here, Jennifer! You've no business here! We don't go into your bedroom, ever. That's how much we bend over backwards to respect your privacy. Most parents don't do that; they go into their kids' rooms."

"I know." She was so calm it infuriated me.

"As a consequence you won't be allowed downstairs for a week. Of course, that also means you won't be using the TV room, either."

"Okay. I understand." Then she turned and went back upstairs.

I couldn't believe it—no reaction at all. She spent most of her time in the TV room. My wife and I seldom used it, and perhaps it was a more neutral place than her own room for getting away from things. Although what it was she needed to get away from I had no idea. But I respected her right to have such a place, whether I completely understood it or not. After all, I was trying desperately to be a good parent.

I knew that room was terribly important to her; she shouldn't have been so calm about the punishment. What it was, I concluded, was that she was pretending that the punishment didn't matter, that we couldn't do anything to her that mattered. She was in control. That was the way she walked the line without tipping over into outward disobedience: she just made herself not care. It was maddening.

And what had she been doing in our bedroom?

Children had obviously changed since we had grown up. By the age of eight they were hardly children anymore. They didn't respect people's property, and they had lost their fear of the police. Their childhood innocence had been replaced by a tangle of resentments. My wife and I agreed on that point. It was a frightening thing, what children had become in recent years. It was difficult, trying to imagine what they might be thinking. We weren't sure how things had arrived at such a state, but all the books said it was the lack of punishment, or the lack of logic or consistency to it. So it seemed that punishment was the thing to work on with our Jennifer.

She had been a beautiful baby: silky blonde hair, great green eyes. Her lips were exquisitely sculptured, divided neatly in half by a subtle fold. I remember her beauty startling me at the time; I hadn't realized a baby's looks could affect me so.

"What do you suppose she's thinking?" I asked my wife. Our daughter Jennifer stared up at us, practically unmoving, her green eyes drinking us in.

"I don't know; do babies think, really?"

"I'm not sure. I suppose it's something like thinking ... maybe 'reacting' would be a better word, though. But somehow, from the look of her, I don't think their reactions are really all that simple."

Jennifer's eyes didn't track; I found it discomfiting to watch them. I wondered if she could possibly understand anything we were saying, or perhaps babies naturally misunderstand. They don't know the language yet, so they imagine what the adults must be trying to communicate. God knows what they must think. Jennifer seemed to be listening, but do babies listen? I think they do—I really think they do.

The baby stares at you, and it makes you so uncomfortable you want to leave the room. But you can't leave the room. After all, you're the parent. You become frightened that you might be tempted to strike such a child, if it doesn't stop. There seems to be something willful in the stare. You're not sure what you should do about that. After all, you're the parent. And it's your responsibility to civilize this child and yet encourage it, allow it to be what it really wants to be. But what if it wants to be a monster? And you start thinking of ways, of logical consequences, that will get rid of that stare that makes you so uneasy.

Deciding at what age to instigate this program of logical

punishments was our first difficult parenting decision. Many parents start shortly after birth—mistakenly, I think. They ignore the baby if it cries excessively—they don't want to spoil the child. They restrict its movements; they lecture it using their harshest tones. And some few actually spank the baby. All these punishments indicate a basic misunderstanding of this stage of life. This is the animal stage, the beast stage, I think. And if the baby isn't allowed to live its bestiality to the fullest there will be that much more difficulty when it is time to civilize the child and bring it into the human community. You wouldn't cage a squirrel, or lecture a badger. So why use punishment on a baby?

"You haven't been to school all week. Where have you been?"

"Just around."

"Around where?" I realized I'd shouted; she'd gotten to me. Bad technique. I wanted desperately to take it back; I couldn't afford any mistakes with my daughter. Everything counted.

"The park, mostly. Sitting, you know? Catnapping. Once or twice down to the drugstore. And once over at the video parlor."

"I want you to write down dates, times, places."

She just looked at me; I watched her closely for any indications of a smile. Then I'd really "throw the book at her." But she was good with that face of hers; you couldn't tell what was going on. I realized I'd just made a very parental-sounding and impossible demand. And she knew I'd realized that. Once again she retained control over the situation.

"I can't do that," she said. "I can't remember that exactly." I was trying to think of a way out of my impossible, guaranteed-to-lose demand, when she added, "No one could."

I could have hit her, and she knew it. And she knew I wouldn't let myself. "What can I do to make you stop? How bad a consequence does it have to be?" I was shaking.

"I don't know, Father." She stared right through me.

My wife and I were convinced that you should start using punishment around the age of two. This is the time when the child can truly be manipulative, can hide its true motivations from the adult.

Jennifer always made us a little uneasy with this punishment schedule, however firmly we believed in it. For even as an infant she seemed manipulative. She'd scream and we'd come running only to see her lying there peacefully. Or she'd be obviously so tired she was nodding off in your arms, but still wanted to wander off when you set her down. When she was old enough to walk she was constantly running for the road, then stopping just as suddenly before she got into any real danger.

"What is it with her? She just stares at you, like she knows she's in complete control."

"She's just a baby."

"Is she? What's a baby supposed to be like, anyway? I never knew any babies who acted like this, did you?"

Later we would both wonder if we should have been firmer when Jennifer was a baby. But how do you ever know? Adults are basically afraid of children, I concluded. I never shared the idea with my wife; it would have upset her too much. Because she was even more frightened of Jennifer than I was, I'm sure. The fear comes, in part, from the amount of responsibility a parent has. You have to civilize this creature, make it a contributing member of society. But it's alien, essentially, and doesn't share your values or goals. It's as if you're trying to take a native of some other planet and force it into a mask so that it will pass for a human being. And maybe after a few years, if you're lucky, it forgets it ever was an alien and truly believes itself to be a human being capable of programming other new arrivals on our planet into a human resemblance.

Often I tried to remember what it had been like when I was Jennifer's age. For the longest time I thought I could remember. Then I realized it was an adult myth of childhood I was recalling. I couldn't remember my own childhood accurately at all.

We wouldn't make things easier for her. She would be exposed to whatever consequences the real world had to offer. That was the way it was supposed to work. But after a time we began to wonder if our daughter was impervious to those consequences.

The baby watches you discussing her, and knows—you are convinced—what you are thinking. What you are saying.

When the baby moved away from us, crawling on the floor, she was all back and head in her roomy flannel nightgown. I'd swear she was a crawling torso, born without arms and legs. And when I finally saw those little hands and feet I'd swear they were prosthetic appendages, so unnatural they seemed.

"She's gone again." My wife poured the orange juice that morning, her hands trembling. But her voice sounded as if this were an everyday occurrence. And that was almost true.

"She's probably in the neighborhood."

"I hope the weather is okay today." My wife always said this. Practically whispered it.

"I hope so, too. But she's the one choosing to be out, just remember that. I guess I don't even worry anymore. She always comes back, so I guess I figure she must be capable of handling it out there. One thing, though."

"What's that?"

"Lock the doors, and the windows. I won't have her sneaking around, the way she's acting. It's like we're under siege here, subject to sudden assault. There's no telling what she might do, and I won't have that worry hanging over my head anymore."

"But how's she going to get in?"

"She'll come to the front door and knock like a decent human being, or she won't come in at all."

There were periods—six months in the middle of Jennifer's sixth year, three months near the beginning of her seventh— in which she was a real terror. Every few minutes she'd whine or yell or hit or disobey us concerning some minor issue. You couldn't allow her out of your sight during those periods—she might walk into someone else's house and steal food out of a refrigerator, or strike another child to take a toy, or throw rocks at a passing car. She became uncharacteristically unkempt—she always looked as if she had slept in her clothes. I would have sworn her face had grown wrinkled and brittle that year, as if whatever had caused her behavior was a disease that also aged her.

"You can't do things like that, Jennifer! You're not the only person in the world! How is anyone going to like you when you act that way?" She stared right through me. "They're just not, that's the answer! No one's going to like you, or trust you, Jennifer!"

The baby drank it all in, with no reaction. Sometimes you just wanted to beat the lesson into her. But that would be an awful thing; you couldn't think about that. You wanted to be a good parent. But the baby was in complete control.

Raising children, trying to help them become civilized human beings, was the most frightening thing in the world. It was a horror.

"She's been in the neighborhood. I think I saw her coat in the distance." My wife looked as if she hadn't slept in days.

"She'll come around eventually. I'm through chasing her."

"But it's been four days!"

"And you know she's okay. You said yourself she's been in the neighborhood. So she must be okay, right?"

"But we're her parents ..."

"I made the police report, didn't I? What more can I do? It's up to her when she comes back. She's in control of that."

My wife just shook her head and lowered her eyes. I was thinking of Jennifer's presence, wandering the outskirts of our neighborhood. I looked out the window; it was starting to snow. But Jennifer being out in that kind of weather wasn't what was chilling me so thoroughly then. It was the image of her trying to break into our house after we'd gone to sleep, our guard down, our lives so vulnerable. And her succeeding.

As Jennifer grew older she was subject to terrifying outbursts of violence with little provocation. All you had to do was tell her to do something she didn't want to do. With every action she begged us to hit her, to match her violence with some of our own. But we resisted. We shook inside, but we resisted. She seemed inhumanly stubborn.

We watched her behavior for a very long time, obsessed with it until our vision of her pressed farther and farther into the future. A criminal teenager. A criminal adult. I found myself reading about the frequency of women being executed for murder in our state.

Punishment made no difference at these times. The awful behavior persisted. Was there some mysterious factor in the way we treated her that had caused it all? It was a cliché to say the problem had originated in the family dynamics themselves, a cliché that we'd always thought terribly unfair. But we had to wonder if, in this case, there was some truth in it.

She seemed totally unaware of the feelings of others; she didn't care whom she hurt. "Sociopath" was a word we dared not use in each other's presence. Was there something hereditary in her behavior? My wife and I could not discuss this aspect, but we watched each other's behavior carefully, and wondered.

A few times while she was missing in that storm I thought I saw her in the distance, but of course I couldn't be sure. And it made me feel a little guilty, not racing across the blanket of snow to find her and drag her back home with me. The blue color of her coat, that candy-striped scarf she always wore. Her heaviest clothing—as if she had known it was going to snow.

"What if she dies?" Each night when we turned out the lights and crawled into bed my wife would start talking about her. She'd drone on about the same points night after night.

I had no reply for that one. We're all going to die, and there was no reason, in any case, to think that Jennifer was in a great deal more danger than sitting in her own home or walking to school alone. But I couldn't say any of that to my wife. It wouldn't have reassured her. It would, in fact, have made it worse. "She'll be okay," I said lamely.

"She's punishing us," my wife said, for the hundredth time. She always sounded as if she blamed me for it.

It worried me—it was well-known that the parents of demanding babies were more likely to argue, to experience various crises. Most of our arguments had been about Jennifer anyway, ever since she was born.

The baby stares at you. You will never understand why, but you are convinced the baby knows far more than you, or at least it knows a great deal about things you never even knew existed. Secret rules operating upon the world. It's a very different creature from what you've become. That's why it so often seems to stare past you, at the darkness behind you. That's why it smiles when you offer up your meager, self-serving punishment.

It snowed off and on for four days. We continued to see what we thought were glimpses of her in the distance, but nothing ever definitive. The police were becoming irritated with all my calls; they made me promise I wouldn't bother them anymore, but they promised to call me as soon as they uncovered any leads. It was clear from their tone they were pessimistic about the possibilities—they kept suggesting that Jennifer was just another runaway. But I knew better. I didn't know if I was more concerned about her safety or about her sneaking up on us unannounced. Surprising us.

I didn't tell my wife I'd been calling the police like that. I suppose I still wanted her to think I intended to follow the "logical consequences" philosophy of leveling punishment to the end. Jennifer's being out in this snowstorm was a logical consequence of her running away. The real world was therefore punishing her, not us. I thought the police half-understood that also.

But they'd asked me several times why I hadn't gone after Jennifer when we thought we caught glimpses of her in the distance, a sudden apparition in the breaks of the storm. Each time I explained to them my ideas concerning punishment and they seemed to understand, and yet they continued to ask this question again and again. I knew I was telling a different officer each time, but it still seemed to me they shouldn't be asking that same question all the time.

I asked myself repeatedly if perhaps my wife and I had overreacted to Jennifer. When I talked to the police I found it difficult to recall specific incidents to explain why we had to take the disciplinary measures we did. It all seemed a little silly and overblown now. But when they removed their pressure and weren't questioning me it was clear how extreme Jennifer's bad behavior had become. She refused to accept our authority in any form. What could we do? She was denying our role as parents and we had to get that role back. She had to learn to accept our punishment.

Sometimes you wonder if you are totally unqualified to take care of the baby. This is a frightening thing for you. But the doubts are always there, and become more prominent the more you discover how alien the baby is from you, how very different. How could you be expected to raise a creature of an entirely different species?

I knew Jennifer had been in the house for a couple of days. I could feel her presence, but although I searched everywhere I could not find her. Our things were rearranged. Some things were missing. A chill was brought into the house with her.

She was there, somewhere, in the house.

She decided I couldn't leave the bedroom at night. When I'd get up to use the bathroom in the middle of the night her cold hands would be on me, restraining me. She decided I was reading too much, or spending too much time in the TV room. When I stayed more than five minutes in that room she made it unbearably cold, or she'd shadow the TV screen, or she'd blow the pages back and forth restlessly in my hands.

At night she would whisper in my ear, and then pretend she hadn't said a word. She stared right through me; I could feel her eyes.

Occasionally I caught glimpses of her—turning a corner or rising up the shadowed staircase. I wondered if she was having boyfriends over—I could hear other teenagers in her room some evenings—but she didn't give me the opportunity to admonish her. A few times I ran into her in a darkened room, face-to-face, but she continued to stare through me, punishing me. I loved my daughter, and needed desperately to understand her. But when I tried to embrace her she was gone, and I was embracing the dark.

I began to worry about physical punishment. I could see my daughter's hands in the dark—the daughter I knew I still loved, no matter what—and I could no longer sleep the night completely through.

The baby stares past you, into the dark. You cannot know what it is thinking because its mind is very different from yours. You love it without considering and yet you have no idea what it is you love. Its mind is alien. It knows things you will never know. It cries and wets its bed, making you feel inadequate, throwing a tantrum and waits for you to react. The punishment it has devised for you is both straightforward and logical.

WRITING IN THE DARK

He'd always written in the dark, using only a small lamp with dim bulb to illuminate his keyboard. Only in the dark could he believe the events which occurred on the page. In the glare of day he could scarcely *think*, much less imagine. Eventually he became convinced that the self existed but peripherally during the daylight hours, when it was merely a prop for the live-action movie being shown for the benefit of others. The true self came out after the sun went down, where it rearranged the world in its own image.

Fiction seemed problematical at either time. Chris was convinced that during the day fiction was virtually impossible. The brightly colored, illuminated surfaces provided no room for doubt or equivocation. However shallow its surface, day life was utterly convincing, and had to be believed. Night life, on the other hand, had become the realm of the essential self, and because of that was a terrain sculpted out of hidden truths, however fanciful or impossible its dreams.

After numerous unsuccessful attempts at fiction-writing, Chris decided to write his autobiography. He didn't know whether his life was interesting enough to warrant such a project—he didn't think that was the point. Writing in the dark seemed ideal for an autobiography—he thought it made it far less likely that he would lie. And he desperately needed to finish something. Besides, everyone had always said he told great stories about himself.

He jotted down notes nightly. Some of the most important of these notes were executed in complete darkness, and sometimes were quite unreadable when he switched on the light. But in these instances he simply made up a new realization and jotted it down, and often these made-up realizations became the most accurate and telling. The notes—concerning likes and dislikes, scattered opinions and memories, snatches of description and color, births and deaths and ambiguous transitions, moments and hours and weeks and adventures—became a pile, and the pile became an accumulation and the accumulation became a large box in the center of his desk filled with his life. Finally one evening he began taking the slips of paper out of the box one at a time, entering them into his computer, and creating the necessary missing connections. These connections, he quickly realized, were the most important part of the entire project. Connections were what he had been missing in his life all along. Connections occurred everywhere in the darkness, but seldom were seen beneath the sun.

He was born in chapter one. A good place to start. He grew and developed, made first friends and first words all the way down the first page and over to the top of the second. He'd never remembered much about his early years, but he supposed a liberal application of imagination bred in darkness was necessary, even when writing one's own biography.

He had to imagine how his parents had been; he remembered so little about them from those first few years. He imagined they had been a little like TV parents, although he suspected that was probably wish-fulfillment on his part. Their language and manners would have been coarser, of course, their lives a bit less interesting. He could rightly assume that they had loved him and wished the best for him, although they hadn't had the benefit of meaningful, well-scripted dialog to express such sentiments.

In these early chapters all the observations seemed fresh and new. But after a time, the themes and characters blurred, became difficult to distinguish. Each night was like every other night, dark and cold and seemingly endless. One friend became confused with another; he supposed that could indicate a certain degree of self-absorption on his part, but too many names began with the same letter and had a similar sound.

Here he attended his first school, There was his first kiss. On page forty-eight he broke his leg and spiraled down into his first adolescent depression. Early loves lasted barely a paragraph. Dreams of the future went on for pages. Entire chapters were devoted to acne, sexual fantasies, and fears of death. He tried several times to characterize his young self in a sentence, but crossed out all such attempts.

Character creation proved to be more difficult than he'd anticipated. Childhood friends seemed to make a little more sense now than they had then, but he had continuous doubts about the accuracy of his memories of them. The characters of his childhood refused the reins he offered them, and chewed up the typographic landscape like madmen or saints.

After a time it occurred to him that his parents made a little more sense once put down on paper. Decisions and actions which had appeared to be arbitrary now seemed inevitable in the stark reason of darkness, given their character and the tenor of the times. Interestingly enough, this perception did not lead to additional empathy for his parents. Long ago he had concluded that we all fail each other, but that didn't make the failures any more palatable.

Again and again in his nightly recollections he was struck by how different he had been than he had remembered. Sometimes he didn't recognize himself at all. Now he seemed to have so little in common with this early self. This early child was trapped forever here in the first part of the book, never provided access to Part Two.

The writing went on and on. He began to sleep through the days in order not to waste a single moment of inspiring night. The pages accumulated into a stack over a foot high. He began taking meals in his office and seldom went out of it. Occasionally his wife and four children would stay up with him, rapping lightly at the door, begging in their sleepless voices for him to come out, but he told them he had a strict, nonnegotiable deadline, and there was nothing he could do about it. Sometimes friends came by to see him and spoke through the door, but he told them he had no words to spare them until the project was done. Then, he was sure, there would be time for friends and family. If for no other reason, he would need more raw material.

Midway through the book he entered college. It struck him how closely he resembled characters he'd encountered in the books he'd been assigned to read for various literature classes. And how sometimes he seemed less a person than a landmark, a place other people passed through on the way to their own true lives. He was a person whose face was often recognized, but whose name was seldom recalled. A bad bit of characterization.

While working on the chapters concerning his early middle age years he was amazed by all the objects and people who populated his work. He wondered what could have happened to them all, how he could have lost so much. Year after year they disappeared from attics and basements, drawers and albums, vanished one by one from the yards in his neighborhood, the streets of his town. Now they were scribbles on slips of paper, a mere parenthetical comment in a volume of several thousand pages. Nights were particularly well-designed for the solitary figure, he thought. The darkness had limited room; extraneous characters were not welcome.

During the writing of those chapters elucidating his mid-life crisis he was bothered that so much was obvious and predictable in the plot. It disappointed him there hadn't been more surprises. So little suspense, so little mystery. So little of the suffering seemed to have any purpose. So much gratuitous violence and pain. Fresh evidence was hard to come by. He brooded over his failure of talent. At times the only surprise seemed to be that he had survived.

When blocked, he composed answers for the interview questions he would be asked once he'd become rich and famous. "Writing an autobiography is like making a new beginning, putting your life into rewrites." It was a wise answer, suitable for almost any question.

He finally buried his parents on page eight hundred, although they'd died many years before. Starting the next chapter was like lowering an enormous white sheet over their graves.

Some of the worst events had never occurred, but their imagined unfolding left him shaken. The darkness facilitated the visualization of the awful. But some of the most wonderful things in retrospect seemed so insignificant he didn't bother to include them.

Later he went back and edited out his sister. They never got along anyway. He considered giving some of the minor characters in his life a larger role, but was afraid the narrative might wander out of his control. Off in the shadowy margins darker than the dark he wrote within, unwritten lives stirred impatiently. Yet so many of his people refused to speak on these pages, withholding their answers, becoming merely silhouettes in the night's dream.

As he neared the climax he worried about writing too fast, becoming a hack, afraid he'd gloss over any future successes and arrive at the end without having fully appreciated them.

He lost track of the last time anyone had knocked at his office door. He lost touch with cycles of day and night and had forgotten the heat the sun made when it touched his arm. Now and then he thought he heard someone on the outside calling his name, but there were so many disparate character voices in his head he really could not be sure. After long, wearying stints in front of the machine he wondered whether he was a kind of ghost writer, slaving over some work-for-hire.

In his book he came to resemble everyone, and no one. He required nothing to keep him satisfied. His wife had long ago divorced him and remarried. His children had left years ago to become doctors and lawyers, but seemed incapable of writing letters home. It was a cliché, he knew, but it was no less true for that.

The tenses shift, finally, toward the end. He has caught up with himself. He is in the now.

He lives, he thinks, in a kind of Minnesota. It is nighttime, and he is snowbound. The darkness threatens to fill up with the brilliant white flakes of day. The thought of seeing himself illuminated by sunlight in some way terrifies him. Outside the ancient paper trees change color, although he never sees them. Snow is a heavy brush dipped in white and pounded all over the landscape in frustration. Or so he imagines; he really doesn't care. He is too busy recording the habits of the vast army of his dead characters, whose whispers issue from dry and crumpled pages littering his floor. And certainly it is his floor; he owns it, just as he owns the computer, the table, the chair, the walls, ceiling, and the night which has completely consumed him.

Although he has kept them alive all these years, his characters still refuse to embrace him. Now that he is old he is careful not to think about the other lives he could have written, or who is writing this life down, whose byline will appear beneath the title of his final published volume.

His greatest failure as a writer, he now realizes, as the night grows darker still, is that he has never been able to imagine a happy ending.

NIGHT MARKET

CO WRITTEN WITH MELANIE TEM

Cara really had to have a good time tonight. The way that beagle at work had looked at her, obviously knowing he was about to die.

She didn't really mind assisting when animals were euthanized—in other words, killed, helped to die. The vets referred to it as "put down." People outside the profession called it "put to sleep," which made it hard to fall asleep herself when she went to bed that night. She was actually sort of drawn to that part of her job—not something she'd tell anybody, but she kept thinking she'd understand what death was if she was present often enough, touching the animal at the exact instant it passed from alive to not alive.

The vets said animals only understood they were sick, and that's why they hid sometimes—it was a self-protection instinct. But Cara loved animals more than she loved people, and she knew it was something else. People could stare death right in the face and say it wasn't there for them. But animals knew.

This morning she'd walked in, and one of the other assistants was holding the dog on the table while the vet prepared the injection, and the dog had looked right at her. When she moved, the eyes stayed on her, those brown eyes surrounded by so much white, strained into a teardrop shape. Dogs didn't cry—their tear ducts drained out to their noses, one of those vet things that were kind of fun to bring up in casual conversation and gross people out about. But dogs and other animals could still show sadness, and give their eyes that desperate shape, and stare at you, even when you moved all around the room trying to escape them, the eyes following, like a final sad dance.

Then it was done. The dog had gone limp. The owner had cried. The vet had spoken gently. Cara had stood back, waiting to clean everything up. The dog's brown eyes had stayed open.

So Cara had really wanted to forget about all that and have a good time. But this was not her idea of a good time. It was hot sitting here in the car, even though the sun had gone down behind the buildings. Her AC wasn't that great. She was tired from work. The new outfit wasn't as cool as she'd thought when she'd paid too much for it. The weed was only okay. Eli was being uncommunicative and she didn't know him well enough yet to interpret his long silences and few words; by the time she did, she wouldn't care.

Hopefully she'd at least get decent sex out of this before she lost interest. A kiss at least. So far, they'd barely held hands. What was up with that?

"Night market," he'd called it when he'd invited her to come. "A carnival for adults." That had sounded interesting. She liked carnivals and markets well enough.

And this new relationship with Eli wasn't very boring or irritating or demanding yet. Cara had always been better at getting into relationships than staying in them.

"There," Eli muttered.

"What?" But he didn't elaborate, leaving her to figure out for herself what he was talking about. An ordinary-looking box truck was pulling in off the street, then two more.

Fear prickled in her stomach and she took another ineffective toke, imagining her dorky little Subaru surrounded, trapped, crushed by the square, plain, sinister trucks, more of which were arriving. But they all kept going to the far end of the lot and lined up around the edges.

Eli hadn't mentioned the trucks. Even if he had, she probably wouldn't have thought until she was in their midst about the one that had almost killed her years ago. Now they were streaming into the gravel lot in this warehouse district Cara hadn't even known existed this close to downtown. Some of their headlights were eerily pale in the twilight; others didn't have theirs on at all, as if they were prowling and didn't want to be seen. She'd been in high school and getting out of a relationship with her usual lack of finesse when she'd encountered that truck just like these. Its brights had blinded her. She'd been drunk and stoned and seventeen and angrier than the silly argument at the party had warranted. The truck hadn't hit her. It had filled her windshield and forced her off the road, totaling her car and landing her in an ICU. She'd never seen the driver. She had seen an old woman sitting in the gravel, watching her and smiling around the shadows in her face and fingering the tear-shaped buttons down the front of her shirt that had caught Cara's lopsided headlights and the flashing lights of the emergency vehicles.

That thing about the buttons had never made any sense, of course. How could she have seen the shape of something that small? For that matter, how could she have seen any details about the woman at all? She'd been driving so fast and she'd just noticed this figure—waiting, watching, judging her. The woman could have been any age. It could even have been a man. Whatever, it was like it had been waiting for her to have an accident. Like her parents waiting for her to screw up again, both of them when she was growing up and then just her father enough for both of them, though for all she knew her mom might be watching and waiting and sending her "I told you so" messages from beyond the grave, wherever that was.

By the time Cara had been coherent enough after the accident to try to find out who that had been by the side of the road, anybody who might have also seen the person—cops, EMTs, other motorists-—had disappeared. The driver had never been found, so somebody was going on with their happy life not knowing if Cara was dead or not, maybe not even wondering.

For a while then, Cara's life had been all about recovery, physical therapy and meds and rest and exercise and her parents talking about her responsibility in the accident, by which they really meant it was all her fault. She'd just wanted to escape, to crawl off and hide like some animal waiting until death happened, or life. Only gradually had she realized just how close she'd come to dying that night.

So what was she supposed to do with that realization? It hadn't made every day more meaningful, as some people claimed a near-death experience would. It hadn't cleared her mind. If anything it had just made her more anxious about what each day might bring. Did dogs have that kind of anxiety? She didn't think so. It seemed to her they expected death eventually but they didn't know whether they'd be just sick or if they'd die at some particular moment. For sure they didn't cry over it.

Not that she'd cry over it, or tell anybody. When things got to her, she was the only one to know, so she wouldn't have to listen to how she'd brought it on herself.

She almost never drove at night anymore. Good thing Eli liked to drive. It wasn't that she trusted him-she didn't trust anybody—but so far, anyway, he was fine with driving her wherever she wanted to go. Maybe she should trust him less for that very reason. You could never tell people's real intentions. And yet you had to rely on them, you had to tangle up your life with theirs, so that if they messed up you were screwed and if you messed up they were. How many people had been killed because of violent or careless or overwhelmed or stupid other people? Probably lots.

In a way it bothered her that Eli didn't ask or even seem to notice that she didn't drive at night. Anyway, it wasn't as if she was scared of the dark—she wasn't a baby. But she also knew the world wasn't the same in the dark as it was in the daylight, no matter what her father, Mr. Rational, used to tell her. He'd say anything to calm her down, whether it was true or not, which meant she hadn't been able to trust what he said and that'd made her even more nervous.

"You just can't see all the details, so your fears fill in the blanks."

Bullshit. Cara knew that if you stared into the dark long enough you could sense the doors, giant rectangles that hadn't been there in daylight. Ever since right after Mom died, she'd tried it now and then, and she could see them. Rectangles. Doors. Big enough to let a truck through. Certainly big enough for an old lady to come in and out of. Was that what she had been—some kind of escort? She'd looked frail, but perhaps strong enough to take her father when the heart attack had silenced his constant advice.

Someday Cara herself would go through one of those doors. Maybe tonight, maybe in the next five seconds. Or maybe when she was a hundred. Maybe by herself, but maybe with an escort. But someday.

More snuffling box trucks were in the parking lot now, and more regular cars, and more people, some of whom must have walked or taken Light Rail because there weren't that many cars. And beyond that, out past the reach of the light, more rectangular patches of darker dark.

"Okay." Eli dropped his roach into an empty beer can and got out of her car.

She weighed her options: leave him here, but that would mean she'd have to drive home in the dark. Take a taxi or get somebody else to drive her home. Wait for a while and watch. Catch up with him now just to see what would happen.

Stay, she decided. Join in. Experience whatever this was. Life was too short to miss anything. And who cares if it's dangerous? You're going to die anyway. Everybody is.

As she made her way toward the line where Eli was standing at the open back of one of the trucks, odors of weed and beer and things cooking and incense washed over her even though the air was heavy and still. She really shouldn't be doing pot, with brain aneurysms running in her family; talk about tempting fate. But what difference did it make? Fate would get you when it damn well wanted to, tempted or not. She was already on borrowed time, twenty-one months more than Mom had had. And counting.

"What's going on?" she asked Eli, no doubt pointlessly. "What is this place?" That was probably the wrong word, since this "place" didn't exist without the trucks.

Eli said, "Come on," and somehow he'd already escorted her to the front of the line.

They stepped into a country diner, complete with a curved counter and high stools, Dolly Parton singing from what Cara guessed was a jukebox. The big-haired waitress plunked two bowls of mac and cheese down in front of them. Eli leaned over and whispered, "it's the only thing on the menu."

Cara didn't want to eat. Mac and cheese was fattening. And who knew what was in this stuff? Or how sanitary the kitchen was? Or who'd had their hands in it? Did the Health department even know about this "carnival for adults"?

"It's great," Eli said with his mouth full. For him, that was practically a treatise.

Cara took a tiny bite, and it actually was good, suspiciously good. She scooped up a larger spoonful and some of the fluorescent glop spilled on her sleeve, which made her think of that morning in college over breakfast with the guy she'd spent the night with and was seriously wishing she hadn't when she'd spilled hot coffee on herself and for some reason had run out of the café.

Talk about making things worse for yourself. The coffee hadn't been hot enough to burn, so the only damage would've been the stain on her jeans. But she'd forgotten about the steps and fallen all the way down and cracked her head and gotten a concussion. It would have been humiliating if she'd been conscious, but she'd just lain there like road kill.

They'd kept her in the hospital for two or three days because they hadn't liked how her eyes looked or something. One of the doctors or orderlies or whatever who'd come by in the middle of the night had had tear-shaped glittery buttons on his coat. It was an odd thing to remember, or so she had thought at the time. The seven gleams of them had caught her eye as he'd leaned over to tend to her, and she'd tried to look into his face, but because of the gloom could see only the thin curve of his mouth and the pale patches that must have been his eyes.

What if he didn't know what he was doing? There was no way she could tell. People died all the time because medical professionals were incompetent, or worse, one of those "angels of mercy" you were always hearing about. They could kill and kill and nobody knew. Cara'd tried to stay awake the rest of the time in the hospital, as though that'd keep her safe, as if anything would keep her safe, but exhaustion and the meds had made her sleep a lot so who knew what had really happened?

The waitress wore a pale pink uniform. Tear-shaped buttons

sparkled over her impressive chest every time she came back, to ask how everything was, to bring more napkins, to bring Eli a second chocolate malt, to ask again how everything was. Cara stared at the buttons, which was embarrassing—it must look like she was staring at the boobs.

When she forced herself to look up into the waitress's face, there was something weird about the smile. And the eyes—big and beautiful, but fixed, too perfect. Were they glass?

Cara looked down at her plate. No cheese could be that orange. And if you were a waitress, you could poison so many people. Cara was sure she'd read about cases like that. She bit her lip, and her mouth tasted like blood and fake cheese and something bitter hiding underneath like some terrible secret. She got up, excused herself, and hurried out of the truck, leaving Eli to finish his mac and cheese and hers, too, she didn't care. Leaving him to wonder what was wrong with her, except he probably wouldn't. She slipped on the ramp but managed not to fall.

The parking lot was now full of people, climbing into these dark boxes, climbing out again. In and out of these shadowed doors. People had even brought their kids. Little kids. It wasn't safe.

Eli caught up with her. "Okay, let's go."

Cara didn't know him well enough to read his expression. Pitying? Repulsed? High? "No, no, I don't want to leave," she said, even though maybe she did.

"You sick? You look pale."

"Sorry, sorry. I don't know—something about the atmosphere in there—so close. Or the food. Let's try some more—it'll be fun."

"Fun" was not exactly the word for it. The next truck had been converted into a strip club, every bit as tacky as a real one. It was packed. Once again, somebody shut the door behind them. Cara told Eli she didn't like it when the door was shut. "Effect," he explained, not explaining a thing. "But we can leave." She shook her head.

On the tiny elevated stage, a teenaged boy slowly took off his clothes to the accompaniment of canned drums and horns.

He was pretty cute, in an unfinished sort of way. Then a girl wearing nothing but a bowler hat and fishnet stockings with sparkles sang a bawdy song and swung around a pole. Not wanting to draw attention to herself, Cara finally sang along with the crowd. She didn't especially want to be staring at the girl's open crotch, but Eli was probably enjoying the show, in his so-low-key-you-wondered-if-he-was-breathing way. What she could see of his face looked relaxed and expressionless.

The girl came over, swinging her hips and lowering her head. Past the sparkles that were now inches away from her face so she couldn't miss their tiny tear shapes, Cara saw eyes, but there weren't any eyes, really, just two empty holes. In the dancing girl's hand was something shiny. A knife. To cut out Cara's eyes and make her into something like the girl. What was this, some sort of especially bizarre S&M place?

But it was just a piece of jewelry. A sparkly pin. A necklace. It was just a tear-shaped necklace made of layers of tear-shaped stones, or tears turned to stone, or maybe even actual tears—the necklace appeared to fade, to dry up into wisps of hair and light as Cara reached for it. Why would she have accepted a thing like that from a girl like this anyway?

Experimentally she put her hand on Eli's thigh. When he didn't respond, she took her hand away and pretended she hadn't done that. Why had she? She was anything but turned on.

Two women were now having oral sex onstage. Then a young girl came out twirling tassels from her nipples. Something for everyone. Huge silver tears were painted on the child's dimpled cheeks. She turned her head, disgusted. Surely this was an illusion—the girl must have been a midget, or some sort of lewd puppet. There were laws.

She wanted to leave, yet couldn't make herself leave. They stayed for the whole show, which by the end involved a German shepherd and pee and a gun shooting, hopefully, blanks.

The dog had stared at her, as if asking her what can I do about it? There's nothing I can do.

The rowdy energy in the club—really just the back of an ordinary box truck—made the crowd seem bigger than it could possibly be in this confined space. The performers, still in their costumes or lack thereof, came around holding out containers for tips. It really looked as if none of them had eyes. Dropping a five into the pseudo-child's plastic Halloween pumpkin didn't make Cara feel any better.

Without saying anything, Eli got up and left. Maybe he'd spotted somebody he knew—it wouldn't have hurt him to introduce her. Maybe he was stealing her car. Or he was just using the restroom, most likely a porta-potty in the parking lot or some twenty-four-hour fast-food place nearby; she ought to figure out where it was before she actually needed it herself.

The crowd she was part of was moving out of the strip-club truck. Without exactly deciding to, Cara went, too. Another crowd was waiting to come in for the next show. Outside like this, uncontained by the box of the truck, it didn't look like as many people, probably no more than twenty.

Not seeing Eli or a porta-potty, she decided, since she was here and probably never would be again, why not try more of the fantasy night-market trucks, other people's special places where they shut the door and trapped you inside and made you see what they wanted you to see and share their secrets and dreams. Why not?

Maybe she'd make her own fantasy world and bring it here to the night market. That'd be cool.

There were all kinds of reasons why she wouldn't, of course—she'd have to buy or rent one of those creepy trucks, she'd have to drive it at night, and she'd have to actually come up with her own fantasy world which she had no clue about. Did she have any secrets or dreams? Not really. But it was cool to think about. Maybe she and Eli could do it together, if she could ever find him. If they kept seeing each other. She saw her car where he'd left it, so at least he hadn't stolen it and left her to figure out how to get home.

There was a "dream library" where you wrote a dream on a scroll of paper and the "librarian" rolled up your dream and slid it into one of the many pretty jars and bottles on the many shelves. The lower part of his face was blanked out and he just had tear-shaped empty holes for eyes; what a creepy, real-looking mask. people around her scribbled down their dreams enthusiastically, furiously, some of them even pulling on her arm to get her to write hers but she couldn't—she didn't have any dreams anymore. Could a person die of dreamlessness? She made up something about eyeless faces and broken glass, and the librarian nodded and hid it; she didn't even see what jar he'd put it in.

When she left she and everybody else crunched over stuff that she hadn't noticed coming in. Down on the dark floor she caught glimpses of droplets of glass like frozen tears.

For a while then, Cara went randomly from one truck to another, wherever she could get through the throng. There was a spaceship with aliens inside anxious to pull her apart and see what made her tick, see if they could make her cry. There was a funhouse with distorted mirrors and when she looked at herself in one she couldn't see her eyes and the smile on her face was someone else's—a waitress's or a librarian's or that of an old woman wanting nothing more than to die.

Did Cara want to die?

No, she was scared of dying.

But did she want to be dead?

Thinking about that made her stop still. People bumped into her and went around her, some of them saying sorry and some telling her to move it or worse and some not seeming to notice her at all.

She couldn't come up with the answer, so she just walked on to the next truck. Now that she'd been inside some of them, they didn't necessarily seem like threatening places anymore. She wondered whether the first one, the one that had run her off the road and almost killed her, had had somebody's fantasy world inside it, too.

The next truck she went into was a church with a stained glass window and incense and organ music and a bloody cross. Other than the performers, if that's what they were, she was alone. They told her there was nothing to fear, death was just another door and once you opened it you'd be inside God's own special dream. Cara did not find this especially reassuring.

Now the priest was tossing holy water on her, drops like

God's own tears that flew and burned and would have dissolved her flesh if she hadn't shaken them off. They made a loud clatter when they hit the floor in this echoey place.

"Why don't you just take me and be done with it?" She didn't think she really meant that, but that's what came out of her mouth almost automatically, as if she'd been rehearsing the line for years. The priest just smiled, his eye holes widening and his teeth falling out, skin so thin his head was like a grinning skull. Cara left and no one tried to stop her.

The crowd had begun to thin out, and it seemed to her there weren't as many trucks now. She was surprised to realize she didn't want the Night Market to end before she'd experienced every one of these boxed fantasy worlds. She didn't see Eli. Her car was still there. The stench of weed was faint, and the aroma of beer was faded and stale in her mouth. From habit she wished for a joint or a brownie, but in a way she was glad to be doing this on her own and not high.

The disco dance truck, where the ball spun multicolored flecks of light that might look like tears if you really worked at it, didn't do much for her. The post office truck was just plain boring. A post office? Really? Somebody fantasized about a post office?

Then, somewhere between the slaughterhouse truck and the Inquisition torture chamber, the conviction came to her that if she didn't get out of the Night Market right away she would die. Now. Tonight. And if she didn't stay until it was over, she would die then, too. Maybe not right now, but she would. No matter what she did, she would die.

Well, of course. Everyone could say that. If they just would.

Her brand-new shirt and pants were ruined, spattered by drops of blood from the slaughtered animals and the tortured people. Surely the human victims, at least, had been actors, and the blood had been fake. But with her luck it would stain anyway.

A vague despair over her ruined clothes and not particularly wanting to see Eli again and the general weirdness of the evening made her burst into tears. It had been such a long time since she'd cried it felt as if the tears were etching her skin, dissolving her eyes. Her vision became distorted. Her eyes ached. She didn't even try to stifle her sobs, didn't care much that it would ruin her make-up or what people would think if they saw her this way.

She realized she was leaning against one of the box trucks, one she thought she hadn't been in but they all looked alike from the outside and it could have moved from one parking space to another. Where were the drivers? Had they just mingled in with the crowd? Were they napping in the cabs? Did they know what they were hauling? Was there a big market for this sort of thing?

Tears were running down her face and wetting her collar. The force of her sorrow or fear or release or whatever it was bent her over, and her tears fell onto the pavement, tinkling like broken glass when they hit. Her mother used to call this, what? "Crying your eyes out." Could you really cry your eyes out? Had Mom cried like this when she'd realized she was going to die? *Had* she known? Did Dad have a premonition that his heart would break at just that instant?

"Cara."

From that blurry border between the night market's bright lights and what passed in the city for total darkness, Eli was coming toward her. She thought this might be the first time he'd actually said her name. He had a dog on a leash.

Cara crouched and held out her arms to the dog, crooning, weeping. She couldn't tell its breed or its color—mixed breed, probably; dark-colored. She couldn't tell if it was male or female, and she didn't want to think of it as "it."

He was old and sick. His slack, toothless mouth hung almost to the pavement. Both his eyes were capped by milky cataracts. He snuffled loudly, turning in her direction, her smell in his nose.

Crying now for the dog in addition to everything else, Cara murmured "come here, pretty boy" and "poor baby," and the dog followed her smell and the sound of her voice and made his painful way toward her, pulling Eli with surprising strength so that the leash was taut between them. Cara didn't especially want Eli to come to her, just the old dog, which paused to lick at the pavement. There was a brittle clatter as hard things struck together. *My tears*, she thought, *all my tears from my whole life*, and squinted to see the glistening glass piled like jewels in the lights of the parking lot. Eli bent and scooped them up.

The dog was determined to get to her. Some animals could sense when a person was sick. She'd seen dogs at work who could sense a seizure before it happened, and she'd read about some who could smell or in some other way detect cancer earlier than doctors could. This dog's big runny nostrils were flaring as he made his way toward her, tugging Eli along.

Eli slung the tears at her. Her own tears, sharp and hard. Cara twisted her head but they struck her on her back, arms, chest, belly, and everywhere they hit they drew blood.

"Stop it!" She stood up, swaying, and tried to move out of range, but he was rapidly closing the gap between them, or maybe she was inadvertently gliding closer—she wasn't sure which direction she was moving. Her intentions kept leading her the wrong way.

The three of them stepped around the parking lot, circling, dancing, a clumsy ballet. Blood and tears made her eyes sting. The dog moaned and squealed, almost a song, then in slow motion jumped up against her softly and slid down her body to collapse at her feet.

Just before Eli's arms closed around her and their open mouths joined in their first kiss, she saw the tear-shaped buttons on his shirt flowing in an endless stream.

THE FINAL APPRENTICE

The tiny creature struggled mightily between the narrow arms of Andrew's forceps. With a slight tremble in his pudgy hand Andrew held the magnifying glass for his apprentice to see (again his final apprentice was reminded of the great age of this, the last wizard of the world, semi-retired), "There boy—identify that one for me."

Apprentice (still wearing "the horns of befuddlement" Andrew had awarded him the week before) sidled slowly over and bobbed his head dumbly like a reluctant steer at a Texas barbecue. He draped one bloodshot eye over the glass. "Ummm … ummm."

"I'm waiting, Apprentice."

"Well … he's approximately two inches high, I'd say. His coat is covered with several dozen patches of bright colors. His face is withered, wrinkled, a lost, panicked look to the eyes…" He straightened suddenly. "I swear, Master Andrew, Lord of the Pierced Earrings, Enchanter of the Fifteen Speedy Launderettes, Vizier to the Sweaty But …"

"Apprentice, *please* …"

"Oh … well, he appears to resemble the former president."

Andrew shook his head. "All presidents look like that once they're out of office. It's all the acrobatics, I hear. But his identity, Apprentice? Of what species is this particular elf?"

Again Apprentice leaned over the glass. By now his breath had quite fogged it, but he did not dare tell Andrew this. He absently stroked his horns. "Massariol?"

"Apprentice! Massariol come a foot high with red knee socks!"

"Ummm … ummm. Salvanel? Bwbach?"

"Apprentice!" Andrew's great beard unfurled in anger. He took a sudden step toward him in his baggy green overalls.

"Barabao? Giane? Follet?"

"Apprentice!" Andrew's beard curled and uncurled like a party horn.

"Kobolde? Pixie? Rutabaga? Republican?" Andrew started swinging his arms in rage, the magnifying glass in one hand, and the elf-between-forceps in the other. "Castanet? Calliope? Kristofferson?" Andrew started chasing Apprentice around the room, the horns of befuddlement catching on beaker stands and distillation tubes and pulling it all crashing down. "Diehard? Veg-o-Matic? Energizer?" Andrew threw up his arms and the magnifying glass wedged into one eye socket like a monocle. "Brassier? Brisket? Bluebird? Brownie?" The elf-between-forceps flew end over end and landed with a tiny but fruitful thud. "Magpie? Mistress? Misogyny?" Apprentice had no opportunity to avoid it, "Diaphra …" *SPLAGG!* And suddenly Apprentice's feet had left him and were flying south for the winter.

Andrew attempted to follow them but couldn't quite attain departure speed, his own feet snared by the horns of befuddlement which, for the first time, he regretted having given his apprentice. Suddenly he was draping Apprentice like a rug woven by Persian opium addicts.

Avoiding eye contact with his all-powerful mentor, Apprentice poked a finger into the sticky mess in his right palm and stirred it. "Of course!" he cried. "It's a Fortune! And here I thought they were extinct!"

Apprentice mopped the specimen room wearing the long, tattered "ears of the hopeless" (the horns of befuddlement were currently keeping his boss the last wizard Andrew entertained— even now he could hear from down the corridor the hatchet ringing off those noble branches of bone, punctuated by his master's shouts of glee). An open copy of *The Field Guide to Elves, Dwarves, and Others of Abbreviated Stature* hung suspended from a stiff wire that curved over his head and attached to the

back of his collar. He had to turn the pages with his tongue.
He observed that the colored illustrations tasted not unlike his
mother's home-baked matzo. So Apprentice mopped and read
and toiled with tears in his eyes, now and again pausing to wipe
his nose with one ragged, hopeless ear.

"Hey, burro-head, got a match?"

Apprentice looked warily at the row of cages lining the far
wall. Leprechauns, Goat People, Fountain Women ... all the
bigger types were quartered there. Then he noticed the one who
had spoken to him: fiery red eyes and eagle-taloned fingers,
protruding teeth and that unmistakable red cap. Like one of
Santa's elves the day after the Christmas Eve keg party.

He wasn't supposed to speak to the Red Caps. Ever. "Fairy-
punks," Andrew called them. They lived only in places with a
history of violence, like fortified castles or discount stores. They
dropped great stones on the salesmen who came to their doors
and dyed their caps with the blood. And on top of that they
wouldn't even return their victims' sample cases. Their filthy
chambers were littered with desk calendars and ballpoint pens.
They also could foretell disasters by making a loud noise like
three cats Scotch-taped to the vanes of a ceiling fan (as part of
his home-study course in wizardry Apprentice had tried this
out just so that he might recognize the sound—now and then his
pets still thanked him for this experience with small aromatic
gifts left in his sock drawer).

The Red Caps were a sturdy, gray, and exceedingly cranky
breed of elf.

"Come on, kid. Bloody hell. I'm dyin' in here."

Apprentice could see that the nasty-looking creature had
at least seven or eight cigarettes shoved into his wide, tooth-
studded maw. "Don't you know that besides being bad for you,
smoking is terribly out of fashion now?"

"Bloody hell. We Red Caps are from the British Isles.
Scottish, mostly." The Red Cap wiggled his heavy eyebrows.
The cigarettes bobbed up and down like albino porcupine quills
piercing his lips.

"Oh ..." Comprehension dawned so unfamiliarly across
Apprentice's face he had an urge to run and wash it off. Then

he frowned. "No. I'm not supposed to talk to you. I'm in enough trouble already."

"Is this the way you treat a guest? No towels, no little soaps, no mints on the pillow?"

Apprentice patted his pockets. "I've got a little piece of Baby Ruth here somewhere ... it's a little linty ... er ... the lint is probably green ..." He wrestled not to look confused and lost the match. "But you're a prisoner."

"Iron bars do not a prison ... oh, forget it. What's your name, kid?"

"Apprentice."

"I didn't ask you what you did for a living."

"No ... Apprentice."

"Funny name to give a kid, even one with long ears."

"My mother had very definite vocational plans for me."

"Mothers are like that. Unrealistic. It can be pretty traumatic for a kid. Mine wanted me to be a Boston Celtic."

"Is that like a Druid?"

"Forget it, kid. Don't strain your ears. What's that book you got?"

"An identification manual, for you little people."

"That's very politically correct of you. I bet in private you refer to us as *shrimpy bastards* or *elven scum*, right?" Apprentice did his best to look indignant. "What's the matter? Stomachache?" Apprentice buried his face in his guidebook, stroking the pages with his tongue (and wincing at another paper cut), pretending to read. "You should try that with some ketchup."

"We're collecting you. I suppose you know that." Apprentice peered around the edge of the book, looking for the Red Cap's reaction.

"Yeah, I figured. I used to collect you big guys, but I had a problem finding large enough jars."

Apprentice leaned forward on his mop, and then struggled to remove the handle from one nostril. "Thish ismot ... *ah* ... this isn't something to joke about, you know. Master Andrew, Keeper of the Jerusalem Stringball, Protector of the Westminster Pail, Litigant in the Superior Court of the State of New York, Finder of Lost Loves, er, and many other things too numerous to mention in this particular bit of dialog, is the world's last remaining wizard and I am his final apprentice and it is our task now that magic grows old-fashioned and passé to capture every last remaining sprite and elf of whatever stripe ... *er, some* of you are striped, I'm sure of it ..." He fumbled uselessly with his guidebook. "... after which time there will be no more magic or fantasy to ... well, to confuse the issue."

"He, this Andrew-of-the-tortured-explanation, *he* taught you this?"

"Er ... yes."

"And what, pray tell, is to replace magic and elves in this new world order?"

"Well, *science,* of course, and domestic services. That sort of thing. Of course, we already *have* science—rockets and electricity and gravity and all that stuff—but so many people still believe in magic and fairies and other superstitious things. Master Andrew says science doesn't work as well as it ought to and so now it's time to get rid of all that other stuff and as the world's last wizard the responsibility has fallen to him and it's a lousy job but the benefits aren't so bad."

"Bloody hell, I'm a *superstition?*"

"Well, you have to admit you *do* look like one."

The Red Cap nodded as if in grudging agreement. He wiggled his cigarettes again. Apprentice was amazed at the elf's talent. *He* could never have talked so clearly around that many cigarettes and protruding teeth. "Your Master Andrew wears green overalls."

"He's preparing for a life after magic. He's been taking a correspondence course in Electronics and Small Appliance Repair. He says green overalls are a more fitting uniform for the new age."

"His green overalls are baggy. They're not 'fitting' at all."

"Master Andrew says comfort in the seat area helps him to think."

"He *must* be in control of a powerful magic, if he hasn't broken down and turned you into a doorstop yet."

Apprentice thought this might be the famous Red Cap

sarcasm he'd heard so much about, but wanted to see the elf's face to make sure. He moved his head to the side quickly, hoping to get a better look at the Red Cap, but the book sprang immediately to partially block his view. He jerked his head back and forth several times in this manner, until finally the book shot back violently and slapped him in the face. "I'mb sborry," he mumbled through his bleeding nose. "That bwas siblly."

"Your Master Andrew doesn't look like much of a wizard to me."

Apprentice was seriously offended, a difficult feat to manage with a bloody nose. "How can you say that?"

"He's, well, a bit on the chubby side for a wizard, isn't he?"

"He likes chocolates. He says they help him focus."

"Well, Mr. Accessory ..."

"Apprentice."

"Everybody knows you should never trust a fat wizard. It shows he's been spending more time with the cakes and custards than with his studies. They say the more rib that shows, the wiser the wizard." By logical progression, of course, this meant that the wisest wizards were the dead ones, but Apprentice said nothing. After all, the Red Cap's teeth *were* sharp. "*You*, at least, study hard, I hope."

Apprentice casually reached up and rubbed from his chin the white sugar left over from his late morning snack. "Hard as a Poltersprite."

"Ah, they just like to make noise. A wizard has to be more than that. A wizard is a self-starter like, well, like a pig on hot asphalt."

Apprentice blushed. His master had told him this very thing many times. Apprentice himself was not so enterprising. Sometimes it was necessary to light a fire under his feet, and in fact oftentimes Master Andrew had cheerfully obliged. But the blisters felt much better now. "Master Andrew always says mosquitoes would make great wizards—that is, if they weren't so small and if they weren't insects and if they didn't die so quickly and all ..."

"A wizard has to be forceful, determined," the Red Cap continued, "and bondable. To the talented wizard, nothing can ever be totally unexpected, except perhaps finding a chicken with decent athletic ability."

Here, the evil imp had hit a sore point. Many had been the hours Master Andrew had laughed out loud while perusing this very same volume, and yet he selfishly refused to underline the good parts for Apprentice.

Apprentice raised his hand, dropping the mop handle. "Wizards know how to *transubstantiate!* Oh, they're *big* on that. You know, base metal into gold, water into wine, vast forests into knickknack shelves, that sort of thing ..."

The Red Cap continued. "A wizard understands everything about spirits and their doings. He knows their abilities, their tricks, and their secret savings accounts. A good wizard can play a spirit like Eric Clapton plays guitar, although perhaps with a little more bass.

"Oh, and don't forget their knack for finding magical objects: amulets, lamps, swords, crotchless panties, potions ...

"They tend to be loners. Now, occasionally they might attend an office party, but they always leave before those funny games with the photocopier begin ..." The Red Cap stopped. "You know, I *like* you, kid."

Apprentice looked down, embarrassed. Not only because unsolicited expressions of endearment made him shy, but because he had just discovered he had one foot wedged inside his mop bucket. "Well ... maybe you Red Caps aren't so bad, either." He tittered softly.

"How about that match, then? You know me ... I'm not going to *bite.*" The Red Cap laughed, too vigorously it seemed. But Apprentice made himself laugh too.

"Sh-sh-sure. Why not?" Apprentice walked over to the cage, lit a lint-encrusted match that had been resting in his pocket for years it seemed, and lit each of the Red Cap's cigarettes in turn.

"Apprentice?"

"Yes, Mr. Red Cap, sir?"

"You just lit three of my teeth."

"Oh, sorry ..."

The Red Cap leaned back against his cell wall, sighing, blowing smoke, and wincing from the pain, although not necessarily in that order. "By the way … did your Master Andrew explain to you how, after he collects us all, he's going to get rid of the various members of fairydom?"

"Well, not exactly."

"Guns or poison, probably."

"Oh! Of course not!"

"Bloody hell. Sounds like a little fairycide to me, leprechaun-lynching, dwarf-butchery, coup de gnome. Many names, but the results are always the same."

"Never! Never!"

"Well, enough of *my* problems. You have your studies to complete, right? Read me a little from your guidebook. After all, I *can't* know *everybody*."

Apprentice ventured to formulate a studious expression, but as in most of his attempts to strike a particular pose, he looked to be in the throes of indigestion. "Well, let's see, there's the Giane from Sardinia. Wood spirits with long breasts who occupy themselves with spinning and memorizing soup can labels. Despite their talents they have difficulty finding dates on the weekends."

"Maybe if they memorized the sports page …"

"It says here they sing sweet lullabies in their caves to men who fall in love with legumes and are brokenhearted when these haughty legumes refuse to wear the lingerie the men have ordered specially for them from mail-order houses in California."

The Red Cap nodded sagely. "The Giane have lost all interest in normal sexual relations, I hear, nine of ten greatly preferring animal husbandry."

"Then you know them?"

"Not intimately. I assume you've captured these creatures?"

"They're in the back playing poker with the goat people."

"Then I hope it isn't too friendly a game. What's in it for you, anyway, 'Prentice?"

"I get to become the next wizard, after."

"After what?"

"After all the magic is gone."

"Isn't that a little like being made captain of the ship after it's been left permanently in dry dock?"

"It's not all magic, being a wizard, you know."

"Enlighten me."

"Wizards get to know things. I like knowing things. Master Andrew, Grand Dragon of Small Appliance Maintenance and Repair, is learning all about televisions, radios, microwaves, that sort of thing. I'd like to know things like that. I'd like to know anything,

Mr. Red Cap."

The elf looked at the guidebook in Apprentice's hand. "You know your elf and fairy families, or at least you're *working* on it."

"But what good is that going to do?" Apprentice blushed. "I'm sorry, Mr. Red Cap, but all you folks are going to be gone soon. Remember science? Maintenance and repair?"

The Red Cap smiled, his countless huge teeth practically exploding up out of his gums. "Bloody hell, Apprentice. I have an idea."

"Apprentice! Apprentice, where are you?" Master Andrew splashed across the wet floor. He had been unable to find his assistant anywhere. And worse, all their specimens were gone, every last variety of dwarf, fairy, elf had vanished. "Oh, damn!"

He didn't really care all that much, actually. It was a new world out there. There was no place for a fairy kingdom anymore. They had lost their ecological niche. He and Apprentice had been feeding and sheltering most of them for years. They wouldn't be able to last more than a few days on their own.

He stopped and stared at the counter that ran across the back of the room. All the cages for the smaller sprites had been removed and the space had been filled with a variety of electronic gear instead. Upon closer examination he discovered they were some of the televisions, stereos, home computers, CD players, and VCRs from his shop upstairs, the ones he hadn't yet been able to figure out how to repair. They were all plugged in to the strip of outlets above the counter.

He walked up to a stereo and turned it on. Beautiful, almost unearthly music flooded the chamber.

He flipped on a TV. Cowboys rode across an endless range of variegated browns, a sunset of reds, blues, and greens sweeping the background.

He pushed a button and the computer beeped into life. He poked and stroked VCR and CD player controls. Lights blinked. Motors whirred smoothly.

"They're all in perfect working order, sir!" Apprentice said behind him.

Master Andrew turned to his apprentice, who wore identical green overalls to his own. "Very impressive, Apprentice," he said. "I didn't even know you were studying such things."

"I ... I seem to have a natural affinity for the work."

"Yes ..." Master Andrew gazed about at the happily humming machinery, filling the air with the warm aroma of electrified chips, diodes, and resistors. "Very impressive. There are more upstairs ... I'll bring them down to you straightaway." He started toward the staircase, and then turned. "The fairies, Apprentice? The elves? What did you do with them all?"

Apprentice smiled and laughed softly. "Never-never land, boss; Never-never land." Then he winked.

Master Andrew laughed with him. "Ah, yes, never-never land. I didn't think you had it in you, Apprentice." Then he climbed the stairs.

Apprentice went over to the stereo and peered closely at the speaker cloth. The voice inside was unearthly. With his eye up to the loose weave he could just barely make out the tiny siren within, its head thrown back, mouth open to expose a throat that plunged deep into the heart of fairyland.

He moved to the television and lowered his head as close as he dared to the screen (he knew he would never be able to quite trust the radiation given off by such things). The tiny cowboys inside turned on their horses and waved to him, the artificial sun in the distance reflecting off their elven smiles.

Finally he stood by the desktop computer. A toothy grin filled the screen. "What did I tell you?" The Red Cap's voice was static-filled, but recognizable just the same on the cheap speaker. Tiny puffs of cigarette smoke exploded rhythmically from the disk drive door. "A little cramped, but still ... I don't mind calling it home. Certainly better than the alternative."

"There's some dirt on your little window thingie," Apprentice said with concern. He raised the mop that had been leaning against the wall. "Let me get it for you."

"Apprentice ..."

Too late the mop slopped over the screen, water sloshing into the ventilation grille. The screen made a popping noise, and there was a soft scraping from somewhere deep inside the computer and the straining sound of something winding down.

"Bloody hell," the speaker murmured. "Bloody hell."

DYING ON THE ELEPHANT ROAD

Sometimes a moment's mistake tells the whole story. In Abraham's case, it was love for a woman which sent him foolishly leaping in front of a panicked herd of elephants, waving his hands, shouting, trying to divert them from trampling his beloved, who'd already had the good sense to get herself to safety.

Abraham's own good sense, unfortunately, had always arrived late. His last thought, before the herd pounded him into gooey mortar for the stony trail, was simply, *oh Lord, what have I done?*

His next few thoughts were less focused, hampered by the fact that bits of his brain were widely scattered and confused by a vision of the tattered little man hovering over him with a small jar, one bent twig of a finger dripping ointment.

"Try not to wince overly much, would you?" the fellow admonished. "It makes it difficult to put things back together straight."

Abe recognized him—a ragged beggar who squatted beside the elephant road all day. Not a very successful beggar, since he never asked for anything, simply stared at the merchants and other travelers with large, red-haloed eyes. Never said thank you, either, when anyone threw him a coin. Was he taking advantage of Abe's unfortunate accident by robbing him? Abe tried to squirm away but felt, oddly, as if he had nothing to squirm. He felt his facial muscles shudder.

"No twitching, either, if you don't mind," the beggar said. "Or is having your chin under one ear a look that appeals to you?"

Abe had no idea what he was talking about, but tried to remain still. The ointment *was* soothing, with a bit of tingle. Between applications the beggar picked things up off the road. Abe couldn't quite see. His head was tilted back as if he were looking out of a hole in the pavement. But somehow the ointment seemed to be lifting his body a little higher each time. Then he noticed that the beggar's fingers, both of his hands, his wrists, parts of the arms were stained. Disgusting. But beggars were occupationally filthy. He couldn't stand to see the beggar putting those stained hands into the ointment and then touching his body.

Abe tried to speak but could not. It wasn't that he was hoarse, or momentarily inarticulate. He didn't seem to have the necessary mechanism.

His eyes must have betrayed his distress, because the beggar said, "Wait a moment. We are not quite there yet." And then the beggar reached forth those blood- and gore-encrusted appendages and put them all over the lower half of Abe's face. Abe discovered that he could now turn his head, and when he did he was assaulted by the sight of his ruined left arm, no hand visible, and as he looked down he realized his head was attached to nothing more than a mat of blood, torn tissue, and bone fragments.

"Oh my Lord!" he cried. "My hateful, miserable Lord!"

"Please don't do that," the beggar said, pursing his lips.

"This is rather delicate repair work, as you might appreciate."

"Ointment! You're going to fix me with makeup!"

"Well, that is hardly accurate. Besides, far more than your face is in need of restoration."

Abe might have argued the point, but he lost consciousness instead.

Abe awakened under a tree off the side of the elephant road. He seemed to be sitting, his back supported by the trunk. He looked down, and that appeared to be his torso and legs beneath him—at least they were of the proper size and proportion, but wrapped in clothing not his own. He raised his hands and examined them. They looked like broken pottery clumsily glued back together.

"The lines will fade over time, although there may be some residual scarring. No doubt you yourself will always see the scars, even after they've disappeared." The old twist of a man busied himself as he talked, putting things in glass jars, stoppering and labeling them. The contents were red, pink, white, yellow, unidentifiable yet vaguely familiar.

"Please don't tell me that that's me in those jars," Abe said hoarsely.

"Well, obviously not all of you. A little bone, a little blood, inconsequential bits of organ, a finger-sized strip of brain. Nothing essential, I assure you." He paused, apparently puzzling over how to word a particular label, then looked directly at Abe. "I might have asked your permission, perhaps, but people in your condition are seldom able to give the question due deliberation."

"You aren't a beggar, are you?"

The not-a-beggar laughed. "Philoneous, a wizard. Last name missing, or stolen—I'm still trying to work that little conundrum out. Pardon these poor threads, but they make one anonymous, a good thing, I think, even in the best of times."

"And yet I've seen you accept coins, scraps of food from the passersby."

"I never return gifts of money, do you? And I don't always eat the food. In any case, these pieces of you are payment for services rendered. There are always bits left over when you put something together, have you noticed? And I assure you, I know what to do with those bits. I will get far more out of them than you ever could."

"I think I'd like to go home now," Abe said weakly.

"I am sure you would. But first I need you to perform a small task for me. A minor favor, but it is the final payment I require for this major miracle I have performed for you." The wizard's smile wasn't very wizardly. To Abe it looked like the lopsided grin of a fool.

"I'm afraid I'm not at my best," Abe replied.

"Of course not—not everyone made pavement is able to talk

about it afterward. Here, come walk with me. The exercise will help you feel better, and I can inform you of your task."

Abe did not want a task to do. In fact, Abe wanted nothing. A thorough trampling had relieved him of all desire—he wondered if Philoneous might have collected his desire into one of those jars. But he had no will, either, and so followed, content to have someone tell him what to do.

But he couldn't quite bring himself to set foot on the elephant road. What if Philoneous hadn't found all of him, and he trod on his own remains? The wizard gently coaxed but finally gave in and walked with Abe a pace off the roadbed. Abe lagged behind him a step, watching the way the old man moved. He walked with a certain regalness, despite the shabby robes. Satchels and bags and jars hung all over him, swaying and clinking and giving the illusion of some sort of mobile shop. And he diverted his path for no one, whatever their station. They all stepped out of his way.

The road was full of merchants and shoppers, students and priests, the periodic strolling musician or jester. And true beggars, their hands thrusting like the beaks of eager geese. The occasional cart. And of course the occasional elephant, revered and untouchable as they had always been. He felt the various puzzle-pieces of his flesh shrink away independently, making him burn and itch all over, but he dared not scratch for fear of de-quilting himself. At least these specific elephants were calm and walked among the people as if they owned this road, which—of course—they did.

Suddenly the short wizard was right under his shoulder, peering up with that loopy grin. "The problem, you see, is my hat, or lack thereof." Naturally Abe's eyes were drawn to the wizard's scalp, bald and raw as a plucked chicken's, as bumpy as a bowl full of beans. Unhealthy, split beans.

Abe averted his eyes, mumbling "I see your need."

"The merchant Vangelin has it, claims to have won it in a dice game. I have no memory of such a game, but that's never been proof of anything. Suffice to say he has my hat, and he keeps it well-guarded. He collects them, you know. Hats."

"People collect hats?" Abe didn't want to appear

unsophisticated, but he was genuinely surprised by the idea.

A large woman pushed between them. She had six or more small children strapped around her waist. She told the children a story as she darted forward.

"He's quite fashion-conscious when it comes to hats," Philoneous continued. "I collect, other things, so it wouldn't be proper for me to make fun of another man's collections. Why, what do you collect? And don't tell me 'failures.'"

Abe stared at his feet, wishing the wizard had spent more time with them—he appeared to be missing some toes.

"Cheer up, lad. Get my hat back for me and you'll have a wizard's gratitude, and that's no small thing."

They were entering the restaurant district. Large balconies full of diners hung from the buildings like nests against cliffs. But he had no desire for food—in fact, the idea made him feel ill. Had the wizard put his stomach back in? "Why can't you 'magic' the hat away from him?"

"We don't call what we do 'magic.' We are not magicians. We have definite limitations. Surely you know that much?" Abe didn't, but wasn't about to admit it. "We are scholar-technicians, at least that's how I look at it. I require ingredients, tools. I know how to use those ingredients and tools to a very high level. That is the wizardry occupation in a nutshell. And the merchant Vangelin is a very powerful man. His guards would know not to let me that close."

"Then why not simply buy another hat? Why all this bother?"

"A wizard's tools are not replaceable. They are uniquely individual."

"Your hat is a tool?"

"Oh, of great importance! It is both gateway and reservoir, shield and chalice. It is a focal point for transformations and communications. It holds everything I can put into it, and gives up only what I tell it to. Its delicate lining is stained with my dreams. It also hides those ugly scalp bumps you've been trying so hard to ignore."

"Then why choose me? I'm hardly anyone's idea of a champion."

If the wizard answered him Abe did not hear, for at that moment he was sure he saw his beloved, the woman he had given up his life for, sitting in a nearby balcony dining with another man. He would know that profile anywhere, the long regal nose, the eyelashes as full and luxurious as butterfly wings, the lips pouting just as likely with amusement as with disdain. And her hair a waterfall of chestnut.

She glanced his way and his heart stopped. She leaned forward, pulling her hair aside with tiny fingers, apparently to get a better view. Then she shook her head and returned her attention to her dining companion.

"I recognize her from the road," the wizard said beside him, "before your unfortunate mishap. Did you know she was well out of the road before you threw yourself in front of the herd? No, of course you didn't. You also didn't know she didn't stick around afterward to see if she could help, because—of course—you were dead then. She could hardly control her impatience—she didn't even look back."

"She must have been too upset."

"Hmmm, perhaps. But she appears to have recovered well. What's her name, anyway?"

"I have no idea."

"Of course you don't. You've never even spoken to her."

Abe gazed down at the wizard. "How could you know such a thing?"

"Such a commonplace deduction requires no wizardry, I assure you. Don't you think, after all you've been through, that you should introduce yourself?"

"She is so beautiful. I don't know. I don't want to interrupt her evening."

"You have interrupted *your life.* Have some perspective. She may be beautiful to look at, but from what I've seen of her, and I've spent some time up and down the elephant road, she is beautiful the way a garment is beautiful. That gentleman up there is eyeing her as if he were buying a new coat. In any case, what if we waited until she finished eating, accost her in the street?"

"I just don't know if I should do something like that."

"You're the one who interrupted a highly annoyed collection of elephants! If only you had hesitated *then!*"

"I just don't want to make a mistake."

"Oh, bother! I need a champion who'll make a decision, who isn't afraid to throw himself at elephants, if I'm ever to get my hat back!"

Philoneous fumbled with the numerous pouches tied around his belt, finally choosing one and drawing from it a diaphanous cloth that fluttered out into a large flag. He held it high in one hand, apparently so as not to drag it in the street. He looked at Abe and grinned, responded "Cape lining" to the unasked question, and ran for a nearby staircase.

Abe stood at the side of the road, not sure what he was supposed to do. The crowds pushed around him, everyone else apparently well-versed in what was expected of them. They were an exotic mixture of colors and perfumes, but he saw none with his sort of variegated, patchwork flesh. He wondered if he smelled peculiarly, given his recent history. He tried an armpit, the webbing between fingers. He could smell nothing out of the ordinary, but he thought it a difficult thing, trying to smell your own stink.

A commotion on the balcony distracted him from his self-examination. There stood his beloved and her lucky dining partner. Then something fluttered up above her head, and she was running, her companion shouting. There was Philoneous, at least as much as one might see of him above the balcony wall—his wizened head, his arms up waving—apparently running in circles, being chased, or chasing, Abe's beloved, her entire head now enveloped by the fluttering cloth, her companion struggling to pry it off her.

A few minutes later Philoneous ran back into the street carrying aloft a beautiful reddish-brown cape with cowl. He passed Abe with no acknowledgment. After a small hesitation Abe chased after him. They passed through a series of jagged lanes and less-than-lanes, careful to avoid the occasional slow- moving elephant left to wander unhindered into the farthest reaches of the city. Eventually the wizard pulled him into the shadows of a stable.

Philoneous held up the cape. "Slip it on. It is yours, for now."

Abe never would have thought to wear such a thing, but it was so beautiful he could not resist. Immediately the neck clasp joined beneath his throat like the interleaving fingers of two delicate hands. The luscious perfume of the cape nearly made him swoon.

"How does it feel?"

"Marvelous," Abe admitted.

"Good. Leave the cowl down, else you might find it a tad crowded."

Abe puzzled over this instruction until warm breath softly caressed the back of his ear. *What is the meaning of this? Who is this person?*

Abe jumped. He tried to pull the cape off but the clasp held fast. The clasp tingled and burned to the touch. "Philoneous?"

Is that the name of this twisted little dwarf? Tell him to stop this, whatever it is, right now. And you let go of my hands, if you don't mind.

Abe squealed and dropped both hands, falling backwards into the wall behind him. *Aagh! You fool! You are crushing me!*

"Philoneous!" he shouted. "What have you done?!"

"No need to panic. You were the one torn apart by elephants, remember? Here." He plunged his hand into his shirt and pulled out a square of shiny, stiff material, which he quickly unfolded into a mirror. "Use this to look more closely at the cowl. Focus particularly on that gap visible slightly right of the base of your neck."

Abe did as he was told. In the dark hollow inside the cowl he made out a long, delicate, flesh-colored shape, and above to each side the beautiful eyes, the butterfly lashes, and below the pouty lips baring his beloved's teeth.

Has no one told you it is impolite to stare at a lady above your station?

"Allow me to introduce the Madame…," Philoneous began. "Oh, what was your name again?"

Oljon, you diminutive cretin.

"Hmmm. Yes. Well, this is the reckless young man who

saved you, or tried to save you, as it were, if you in fact had needed saving."

I know of no such person.

"Come now. You knew exactly what happened to this unfortunate lad. I saw everything. Certainly he was a fool, but he *thought* he was protecting you. That should count for something."

The cowl did not reply.

Philoneous looked up at Abe with a sad smile. "I am sorry if this embarrasses you. It has become obvious you would not have completed your mission under the previous circumstances. I need someone both reckless *and* motivated, and with the ability to make a decision. I think that perhaps the two of you together, well, do you understand? Once you have gotten me my hat, I will turn her back into a lady, or whatever she was, again."

And if we fail?

"Then young Abe will have you, but you will remain a garment. But surely that condition is not an unfamiliar one?"

You are an evil man!

"Well, hardly. I am not always a nice man, but your standards of evil are unrealistic, I think."

"I have to wear her—*this* cape, until the task is complete? I cannot ever remove her—*it*?"

Philoneous scratched at his thinning beard. "It *is* customary to attach some highly impractical, completely useless loophole in such situations, or so I have observed in the stories told by others far older than myself. Quite frustrating for all concerned. So then, suppose you can remove her, once only, and only for the purpose of transferring her to another? And even then, only for a count of thirty. She will always come back, one way or other."

Abe closed his eyes. "Perhaps you should have left—" he mumbled, and stalled, unable to offer more.

The only portion of the merchant's sprawling compound not under heavy guard was a narrow section of wall at the back, cast in shadow by nearby buildings and planted thickly around its base in thorn bushes. The only opening in the otherwise sheer wall was a small window at least the height of twenty men above the ground. Philoneous had supplied a pair of "cat's claws" to meet the challenge of the wall—a kind of glove with metal tubes that went over the fingers, ending in extraordinarily sharp "claws" that went easily into the brick, the whole contraption braced over the arm with an arrangement of lacings and metal rods.

Abe supposed Philoneous had counted on his reckless nature where women were concerned to get him past the thorn bushes. The wizard had no doubt assumed Abe would just foolishly throw himself into those bushes and climb from there onto the wall despite a fire of pain in back, legs, and groin. The wizard, unfortunately, had been correct.

Actually, the most difficult part of the mission so far had been the company.

There are thorns in my beautiful hair! Thorns! And you stink! You are sweating and you stink!

"Madame." Abe took a breath and prayed for patience. "Properly speaking, that is not your hair anymore—it is a cape. But still, I apologize if I have damaged you in any way. Are you aware that I have thorn problems of my own? Twenty or thirty, I would say. In my feet, my lower legs, my belly, my thighs, and a nasty one in the groin area."

I know. It is quite disgusting.

Abe ignored this. "I smell because I am exerting myself. Despite the help of the wizard's claw-things, and they are quite helpful things, certainly, this is very difficult work. Hard. Labor. This labor naturally makes one perspire. If you were not a cape resting comfortably on my back, but someone having to *labor* up this wall, why, you too, Madame, I assure you, would stink."

She said nothing then, a blessing he'd felt too confused to wish for. Wasn't this the thing he'd always wanted, to have intimate talks with her in the closest proximity, her arms thrown about his neck?

And despite his annoyance, he recognized that his major fear of falling was what his weight might do to her upon landing.

There was a vague satisfaction now in the rhythmic, ever-so-soft pocking sound the claws made as they sank into brick, too soft for any guards to hear but loud enough to count off his vertical progress. He'd never imagined himself capable of such a physical feat and assumed that, besides the engineering miracle of these cats' claws, some rearrangement resulting in better efficiency had occurred when the wizard had reassembled him. Certainly this didn't feel like any magic he'd been told of when he was small. This felt more like old- fashioned ingenuity at work.

Which might all come to naught without perfect execution of a brilliant plan. And he had no real plan, much less a brilliant one.

Your skin is patterned with all these lines, hundreds of them, as if it were a map that had been creased and creased again, then perhaps crumpled into a ball before being smoothed out again and stretched across a frame.

Abe attempted not to sigh. "The lines are seams, from when he reassembled me. I told you about the reassemblage, how I had awakened mostly head and barely that."

But surely a wizard could have solved such a drawback. Perhaps you moved, or otherwise followed his instructions poorly.

"I really don't think he considered it a problem. He is not much into appearances—haven't you noticed?"

I realize this has caused you discomfort. I am truly sorry for that, but I did not know you before, so I tried not to think about what had happened to you. I've never liked thinking about sad things—there seems no point. Why would anyone want to think about sad things?

"I don't think I even know how to answer that."

I cannot as well. See? We are understanding each other.

"I'm fast approaching the window—any ideas about that?"

We should climb inside, if at all possible. It is getting quite cold out here.

"And then?"

And then we must find this hat.

"That is simply amazing. If you should have further ideas, please do not hesitate to share."

The interior of the merchant's dwelling was quite noisy. Abe had expected some sort of tranquil mausoleum, lit by a few well-placed lanterns whose light was only now and then shadowed by the gentle glide from room to room of barefoot servants. It was the kind of peace only the rich could afford, and which he—the youngest of sixteen growing up on a poor farm—had always dreamed of for himself. The master of such a house might spend his time reading and listening to soft music, not hanging onto a sheer wall for dear life while being harangued by a talkative cloak.

But clearly some sort of celebration was taking place. Waves of sound climbed the stairs and rushed down the halls, rattling anything not spiked or tied to the richly-decorated walls. There was indeed music, but it was a raucous sort as if the instruments were thrown at each other by impatient apes. Abe heard footsteps, and fearing that his patchwork face would betray him, he pulled the hood up over his head.

WHAT are you doing?! He was not sure where her lips were currently located, but they had definitely brushed his face. It did not matter that it had been accidental, or that they had been flapping in anger. They smelled faintly of cinnamon and fish.

"Shhh. They'll hear."

She said nothing more but made subtle nudgings with jaw and cheekbones as if to create more room inside the improbable geometry of the cowl. It was not as if two heads were occupying the cowl—more like a head and a third, or a head and a half. Either way, he hoped the drunken guests now passing noticed nothing unusual. As they strode by he raised his chin slightly for a peek—they each wore several elaborate hats jammed one atop the other pushed down almost over their eyes. Perhaps they weren't drunk so much as visually impaired?

But they were laughing, pointing at the hats and howling. Once they'd gone Abe made his way toward the stairs from which they'd come. He descended rapidly and, despite his beloved's protests, kept the cowl firmly in place.

The great room of the house of the merchant Vangelin looked more like a busy outdoor market than the dwelling of a man with taste and refinement. As he made the last few steps off the stairs a large black bird perched on a towering hat (complete with colorful windows and tiny pennants flying) soared his way, wingtip leaning into the cowl and touching his nose. His companion squealed, pulling away hard enough he had to grab the cowl on both sides of his head, gripping it desperately to keep his face covered.

Abe staggered to the floor and almost ran into a tall man with an even taller hat encircled with multiple spiraling rims. "Careful," the tall man admonished, then leaned over and tapped the top of Abe's head with one ridiculously long finger. "Not much of a hat," he said, frowning. "I don't know why you bother to protect it." He strolled away.

Could you please be more careful? she whispered urgently, spraying his forehead with spit.

"Then calm down," he murmured back, looking for her eyes and finding one in a far off corner of the cowl. It was bright blue, intelligent, a star.

Abe stepped more carefully then, keeping his breathing as steady as possible, thinking that if he kept things calm, he might pass that calmness along to her. But this did not prevent him from feeling considerable surprise at what he saw in the house: heads held rigidly to balance towering collections of hats, hats molded of paper and cloth and foil and fur and—apparently—garbage, hats looking like shoes and books and animals and cages and even—disturbingly—like human heads, including human heads exactly like the human heads wearing the human heads. Hats with wings and legs and tails and fields of glittering, startled eyes. And wandering through the crowd were dogs, cats, pigs, some with fancy hats of their own, others bareheaded, the shreds of their hats hanging from their mouths.

"What is wrong with these people? How much did they spend on all this distraction?"

Really? I find some of these quite—well, I would certainly wear some, perhaps not all—

"Madame, have you lost—?"

Wait! I believe that is Vangelin!

Abe experienced the odd sensation of Madame Oljon aligning her face with his, pushing eyes and lips forward past his own as they both stared at the small figure near the center of the room, sitting cross-legged on a high cushion, naked save for a loincloth, smiling idiotically (not unlike, Abe thought, the wizard Philoneous's own idiotic smile). In all aspects of his person unremarkable.

But what *was* remarkable was the large hat of gently shifting colors, tip softly collapsed, rim fluttery with light, floating and turning a head's height above the near-naked man's hairless, mottled pate.

"Isn't that a rather large hat for Philoneous's tiny little head?"

Focus, please. I tire of this position.

"Certainly. But how do we retrieve the hat with all these people here?"

See the staircase behind him? You could reach out and snatch it away! Nothing could be easier! Quickly, we need a distraction!

"What kind of distraction? If I do anything these people will be watching me, and then how will I grab the hat?"

Think of one! If we do not retrieve that hat I will remain in this state forever! Damn that wizard for attaching me to such an imbecile!

"I will count to thirty. Be ready." Abe snatched off the cape and planted it roughly on the back of a large passing dog. The animal reared up on its hind legs, howling, and raced around the room, the frantically flapping cape fastened securely around its neck with the pale, clasped hands. Abe imagined the Madame's fury and could not resist a smile.

As Abe bounded up the staircase hanging over Vangelin, the caped animal continued to wreak havoc in the room. Towering hat collections toppled into one another as guests lost their balance and fell. Delicately-placed hat superstructures and accessories snapped, crumpled, and littered the floor as debris to be tripped, slipped, and stumbled upon. The other animals, now agitated beyond endurance, shook off their ridiculous headgear and attacked their masters and each other.

By the time Abe reached the correct landing and leaned over to grab the wizard's hat, the room was in full, running disaster. Vangelin looked helpless, throwing up his arms as his guards rushed in and began wrestling with his guests. "No, no!" he cried, but without further elaboration the guards clearly did not know what to do.

Abe did not have to grab the hat so much as receive it. Once he touched it, it leapt into his arms, quivering like some frightened animal. Since the hat had had no actual physical contact with Vangelin, the merchant had no idea it was gone.

Abe tucked the hat under his arm and raced back down the stairs. He could feel the hat folding, shrinking with each step. As the caped dog passed nearby Abe reached out and grabbed the cowl, pulling it from the dog and snapping it around his own neck in one movement.

Not so rough! You will rip me!

Abe felt the wizard's hat folding itself smaller and smaller and then sliding into his hand. He pocketed it.

I was afraid you might not retrieve me in time! I tried, but I lost count after ten—I was so frightened!

Abe did not tell her he'd completely forgotten to count at all. The grand front doors yawned open before them.

Why are you slowing down? We must leave!

"There are guards around the door! They're watching every guest that passes through. If we attempt to approach without some sort of hat on my head we will draw too much attention to ourselves."

Then get a hat somewhere!

"Do *you* see an available hat? Every hat I see is either on someone's head, clutched desperately so as not to be lost, or lying in shreds on the floor." He felt the cape suddenly writhing about in a frenzy, twisting and rising off his back. "Don't panic now! Be still or they will notice us!" Then he felt the cape cowering on top of his head.

Keep moving, and glance to your right.

Abe saw the mirror, and as he passed, a reflection of a grand chestnut-hued turban wrapped expertly about his head. The guards barely spared them a glance as they passed.

When they were out of view of the compound Abe ran to put some distance between them and whoever might follow. But even at this pace he experienced considerable pain—obviously he hadn't healed completely. He could feel various organs struggling against each other as he pushed his body on.

You are slowing down again.

"I am."

I have really had enough of this 'style' of existence. The sooner we reach that foul master of yours, the sooner I will be my old self again.

"I am breathless in anticipation. Or is that fatigue? By the way, he is *not* my master, any more than you are."

Move along faster! I insist!

"I really can't right now. There's an elephant ahead and I can't get around it. They move quite slowly, you know, when they're not trampling someone to pieces."

I will not forget such a, such an experience!

"Nor will I, hopefully. Right at this moment it feels like the most real experience I have ever had."

Abe walked slowly, but still was soon alongside the elephant. He was surprised that he was not frightened—perhaps he was simply too tired. He gazed into the elephant's eye, then rested his hand on the rough flank. Then, with little consideration of the consequences, he leapt up and clambered onto the elephant's back.

What are you doing? This is forbidden!

"It's dark, no one will see. Besides, this elephant, I think he owes me at least a ride."

You are impossibly reckless!

Abe sighed. "And thanks to the wizard I now know that recklessness is both my talent and my one true calling." He rocked his body forward, nudging the elephant behind the ears with his knees. "Go, please," he said less-than-firmly.

The elephant remained statue-still.

I do not believe that is the proper command.

"Have you a better suggestion?"

Since climbing onto these creatures is forbidden and riding them out of the question, might it be possible there is no command that will work?

A few minutes later having completely exhausted his working vocabulary, a dejected Abraham slid down from the elephant's back. He trudged down the lane, the folded wizard's hat secure under his belt. The cowl and cape fell into a sullen silence, interrupted now and then by a furious repositioning on Abe's head and shoulders.

Hours later dawn peeked over the tops of buildings and light began to fill the lanes. Hours after that Abe slumped to the pavement beside one of the public wells, filled both hands with water, and poured them over his face.

You've wet me!

"Aren't you as hot as I am?"

Of course, I am! Much hotter in fact—remember I am doomed to shelter you, and what, exactly, is to shelter me in return? Nothing! But that doesn't mean I want to be wet.

"Sorry, but the heat makes my seams itch."

Ugh. Please don't talk to me of seams. You are lost, I assume. You kept saying the way to the wizard's abode is complicated and that was why our journey was taking a lifetime, but that is simply because you are lost.

"It *is* complicated because he never told me where he lives. I think he forgot to."

And why did you not mention this before?

"He just showed up last time. I assumed he would do so again."

How are we ever to get the wizard his hat back? How am I to return to my normal self?

"Funny, I was wondering how I was ever going to get you off my back."

Idiot! In this heat I will surely catch on fire before the day is done!

"Wear this. It might help."

What are you doing?

Abe unfolded the wizard's hat. It expanded immediately, the tip rising into the air like a tent top, unfurling the sides and blowing out the glistening rim. He slipped it over the cloak on top of his head. He leaned over to admire his reflection on the surface of the water. It looked grand.

This looks ridiculous!

"It'll keep the sun off until we find the wizard's house."

Some hovel, no doubt. I—

The wizard's hat suddenly leaned over as if imbalanced but still firmly attached to Abe's head. His neck strained under the pressure as he stared at the filthy cobblestones. He could see the shadow of the hat and the bent tip suddenly spinning like a weathervane.

The hat rose, dragging his head and his unfortunate neck with it. It tilted slightly, giving his head a somewhat quizzical orientation, and then he was moving, stumbling sideways in an attempt to keep up with his headstrong headgear.

Where are we going?

"Ask the hat—I'm just trying to keep my neck from breaking!"

The hat dragged them around the corner and down a succession of narrow alleys. Abe was able to rotate himself somewhat until his body was properly aligned with the hat's forward movement, and eventually discovered he could sense when the hat needed to change direction and adjust his position accordingly.

Still, the journey was no easy endeavor. Several times he had to leap over animals and prostrate beggars, mount staircases with no regard to the people already using them, plow through busy market stalls and slip through horrid pools of stagnant waste.

Finally they were headed toward a door of dubious vertical clearance, and only as he readied himself to knock did he realize the hat had no intention of stopping. At the last moment he thought to lower his head, and they rammed hat-first through a shower of splintering wood.

A few moments later Abe was looking up from the floor in a daze as the hat sprang into the air and, spinning, lowered itself onto the bumpy bald head of the beaming Philoneous. The tip bowed, the hat bulged about its base as if containing an explosion, and then it settled, content.

Philoneous looked down at Abe, shaking his head. "Well, I *suppose* I could find a few jobs around here for you to do in order to pay for the broken door."

Abe staggered to his feet. Philoneous's quarters were a riot of vase and jar, feather and hide, eye and claw, filth and gleam, contraption and destruction, mounted head and preserved foot, collected and dispersed and dissected and generally rank. He also had a very nice display of framed doilies along one wall.

Get me off get me off get me off!

"Excuse me, Mr. Philoneous, sir, my—erm—beloved has a request?"

"Ah, yes, the delightful Madame Oljon!" Philoneous grabbed the cloak at the back of Abe's neck, ripped it off (the hand clasps raking at Abe's throat as they attempted to hold on), and began twirling it rapidly in the air while mumbling indecipherably fast.

The cloak suddenly whistled, jerked, and ballooned with a rude bladder sound. Madame Oljon tumbled out, all legs and arms, and the cloak disappeared. She struggled to her feet, stunned, her beautiful chestnut hair now a pile of brownish mulched rubbish. Abe tittered despite a desperate attempt to suppress it.

"Why is he laughing?" she demanded.

Philoneous considered her. "Well, it's—fashion was never— I'm sure eventually—" He stopped. "Frankly, Madame, you have a rather serious case of hat hair."

Madame Oljon screamed something inarticulate and stalked toward the doorless opening.

"Erm—Madame?" Abe called out. She spun on him. "What is it, idiot?"

"I thought maybe—you might have a nicer sister at home?"

She turned back around and walked out, her hair snagging on a sharp piece of broken door frame. She tugged, a patch of hair ripped out of her scalp, she staggered, and continued on her way.

"Didn't even say goodbye," Philoneous mumbled. "Ah, yes, well I have some reading to catch up on. You can start your servitude—erm—work as my assistant—now by, yes, organizing this room a bit. I'm quite sure it will be obvious where everything goes. And don't throw anything out, not even those bits of wood. Everything's useful, I always say. My, I'd forgotten what it's like having an assistant, it's been so long."

Abe studied the catastrophe awaiting him. "So what

happened to the last one?"

"Oh, you'll find him there on the shelf somewhere." The wizard smiled, and gently stroked his hat.

ABOUT THE AUTHOR

Steve Rasnic Tem was born in Lee County Virginia in the heart of Appalachia. He is the author of over 400 published short stories and is a past winner of the Bram Stoker, International Horror Guild, British Fantasy, and World Fantasy Awards. His story collections include *City Fishing, The Far Side of the Lake, In Concert* (with wife Melanie Tem), *Ugly Behavior* (crime), *Celestial Inventories* (contemporary fantasy), and *Figures Unseen,* his Selected Stories. His novels include *Excavation, The Book of Days, Daughters, The Man in the Ceiling* (with Melanie Tem), *Deadfall Hotel, Blood Kin,* and the recent *Ubo.*

Steve Rasnic Tem's short fiction has been compared to the work of Franz Kafka, Dino Buzzati, Ray Bradbury, and Raymond Carver, but to quote Joe R. Lansdale: "Steve Rasnic Tem is a school of writing unto himself." His 400-plus published pieces have garnered him a British Fantasy Award, World Fantasy and several Bram Stoker Awards.

Curious about other Crossroad Press books?
Stop by our site:
http://store.crossroadpress.com
We offer quality writing
in digital, audio, and print formats.

Enter the code FIRSTBOOK
to get 20% off your first order from our store!
Stop by today!

www.ingramcontent.com/pod-product-compliance
Lightning Source LLC
Chambersburg PA
CBHW072112250626
47159CB00007B/2415